THE
JERUSALEM
SECRET

DESTINY IMAGE BOOKS BY RON CANTOR

Identity Theft

Leave Me Alone: I'm Jewish

THE JERUSALEM SECRET

RON CANTOR

DESTINY IMAGE® PUBLISHERS, INC.
P.O. Box 310, Shippensburg, PA 17257-0310
"Promoting Inspired Lives."

This book and all other Destiny Image and Destiny Image Fiction books are available at Christian bookstores and distributors worldwide.

For more information on foreign distributors, call 717-532-3040.
Reach us on the Internet: www.destinyimage.com.

ISBN 13 TP: 978-0-7684-0926-0
ISBN 13 eBook: 978-0-7684-0927-7

For Worldwide Distribution, Printed in the U.S.A.

1 2 3 4 5 6 7 8 / 20 19 18 17 16

DEDICATION

To Elana, the love of my life, my partner in crime...

ACKNOWLEDGMENTS

After I wrote *Identity Theft*, I knew I would have to write the sequel. No problem, I had plenty of free time. However in January 2013, I was asked to become a full-time pastor in Tel Aviv, and it turned my life upside down! "Upside down" in a good way—as I have loved serving with our amazing pastors and staff—but I could not find time to write. I would go away for short writing trips, but it was tough. Finally on April 2015, I went north to a kibbutz overlooking the Sea of Galilee. After five days I was nearly finished. But it wasn't until I got home that the baby was finally birthed.

I was riding my bike on the boardwalk at Tel Aviv the day after returning when it came to me like a flood. Tears streamed down my face as I saw the ending. I raced home to my computer, and shortly thereafter it was finished.

Writing a book is never a one man show, and there are several people I would like to thank.

First, I would like to thank everyone who bought *Identity Theft*. When I changed it from a teaching book to a novel, I knew it was either going to be silly or really good. Your feedback has been amazing. Reading the almost all five-star reviews on Amazon is humbling. And the constant *nagging* emails and Facebook posts urging me to finish the second book were always received with joy. Finally you get to find out what happened in David's world as his wife, Lisa, comes crying out of the house—just moments after his salvation.

I want to thank the amazing team at Destiny Image, Ronda Ranalli, my former publisher and Larry Sparks, the present publisher. Working with you has been a delight. I never forget the day I met you at Messiah 2012, and to my shock, you offered me a book deal. You sought me out!

I had little hope that *Identity Theft* would be published by a traditional publisher. This was one of the greater blessings in my life.

Hope Flinchbaugh took my first draft and added story and flair to the book. She is an amazing fiction editor and writer in her own right. Thank you Hope!

I want to thank Sar El Tours who hosts our twice-a-year Israel tours (www.LivingStonesIsrael.com!!!) for putting me up in that Kibbutz hotel for five days. One of the amazing things about it was that a good part of the story takes place right on those very shores of the Sea of Galilee that I could see out my window.

I cannot forget the Maoz Israel office in Dallas, who fulfill orders and serve me tirelessly. They understand it has nothing to do with me, but the *WHY* we do what we do. They understand the vision. Thank you to Betty, Michelle, Jeannie and especially Christy. And to Ari and Shira Sorko-Ram, Maoz Israel founders, who gave me a platform to expose the great Identity Theft.

I want to thank my wife for allowing me to take the time to devote to writing and my three amazing daughters, especially Danielle, who has always been my biggest cheerleader for writing.

Special thanks to some superb theologians who allowed me to email them questions and helped me find quotes: Michael Brown, Daniel Juster and Asher Intrater. I mean who emails Michael Brown and gets a response within minutes? Thank you!

And I must mention, against his wishes, L.P. in the mailroom, who packages and ships your books. He is overdue for a raise!

And of course, let me offer thanks to the victim of the greatest act of *Identity Theft*—Yeshua, the Jewish Messiah. I wrote these books so folks could meet the Jewish Jesus—the historically accurate Jewish.

PROLOGUE

Rabbi Goodman agreed to meet with me, but our meeting location made me a little nervous. I'd hoped for a more casual setting like Starbucks—neutral territory where my questions would not be considered blasphemous or even challenging. In the end, I agreed to meet in his office at the synagogue—our congregational building.

It was unusual to see the synagogue so empty and dark, save the dim lighting from the windows. I paused before the holiest place of the synagogue, the Aron Kodesh—the Holy Ark. It was here that the Torah scrolls were kept and opened only for special prayers or for reading the Torah during Shabbat services and the holy days. The Aron Kodesh was intentionally placed on the eastern wall of our synagogue so that every time we prayed we faced the holy city of Jerusalem. I paused and briefly prayed that I would find what I was searching for during my talk with Rabbi Goodman.

Prayer had become increasingly important to me lately. I remembered as a boy my grandmother, Bubbie Gershom, took me to her synagogue prayer services. All of the people in Grandma's synagogue swayed back and forth, a new phenomenon for me. When I asked her why they did that, she said, "Why, David, think of yourself as the flame of a candle, flickering back and forth as your soul reaches upward to reach God with your prayers."

It was a nice picture. But we didn't sway back and forth at my parents' synagogue. For some reason, I never really thought about that until now. Was our candle extinguished? Of course we were Conservative, not Orthodox. There are three main types of Judaism. We have Orthodox, which is very religious, where your entire day, week, month, and year revolves around Jewish tradition. Conservative respects the traditions, but expresses itself primarily inside the synagogue, not at work or in the supermarket. And there is the Reform, where Jewish tradition is interpreted in the most liberal, progressive ways—even to the inclusion of gay and lesbian rabbis and cantors. From a religious or traditional point of view, I was very content as a Conservative Jew. However, from a God point of view—I was lost.

I made my way around the bimah, the podium in the center of the sanctuary, through the side door to the rabbi's office and knocked.

Rabbi Goodman extended his hand and greeted me warmly. "Please, David, take a seat."

I recalled the softball games when Rabbi Goodman showed up in his jeans and sneakers to cheer for me and my Little League team. He was tall and thin, with dark hair and beard, and he wasn't shy on the sidelines!

Unlike many Orthodox Jews, his beard was groomed, but I could see it had grayed some in the last few years and he sported a pair of wire rimmed glasses that sometimes slid down his nose as he read the Torah or read his sermons. Today, as men, we greeted one another in dress shirts and ties. As a journalist, I rarely wear a tie, but I had an event later that day. The rabbi was an old family friend, a good man. That is why it took some time for me to work up the nerve to request this meeting.

He motioned to a black wingback leather chair and pulled up a matching chair and sat across from me.

Nervous, I cleared my throat a little. "Rabbi, thanks for meeting with me. I was hoping you could shed some light on a few questions that I have. I've been doing a lot of thinking lately about religion. Well, about God."

"I have noticed that you started attending the Ma'ariv prayer services. That was unexpected, but certainly welcomed," Rabbi Goodman responded. He crossed his long legs, folded his hands, and smiled warmly.

I didn't mention it, but I chose the third prayer service at dusk simply because it worked well with my schedule. I was able to leave work and come to prayer before heading home to see Lisa and the girls. But it was a new effort, because something inside me somehow needed to connect further with God.

"For some time now I have been seeking to find deeper meaning in life. Yes, I have a great life. I love my family, my career is moving in the right direction. But a nagging thought has persisted for many months now—is there is more?"

"Okay..." The rabbi was listening.

"I have always believed in God—or at least that there is a God, but I never felt the need to go any deeper. But what if He has put us here for a purpose? What if I have some responsibility toward Him that I am not aware of? How can I just go on living life without seeking that out?"

"That is some seriously deep thinking, David. And good thinking!" responded the rabbi.

I relaxed a little and stretched my legs out in front of me. "Well, of course I began my search or investigation in the synagogue—in Judaism. Like you said, you have seen me at the evening prayer services. And sometimes I even come to the Shachrit services—but with two kids I don't like to leave the house that early. I have to be honest here. I haven't just been looking in Judaism."

I paused to see his reaction.

"O...kay," he said, eliciting emotions of curiosity, concern, and maybe a little confusion. "So, where have you been searching?"

"I started investigating some of the Eastern religions. I read a few books, but they all seem a bit too mystical. To be honest, I began to read the New Covenant."

Rabbi Goodman sat straight up. His hands gripped the arm rests. "Why would you do that? That is a dangerous book, David."

"Well, that is what I thought, but—"

"There is no *but* David. The people who follow that book are the same people who have persecuted us for two thousand years. They have killed us in their Crusades and threw us out of Spain during the Inquisitions."

Well, this is not going according to plan.

"Are you willing to throw your life away—your heritage—your family? And to join the people who hate us? My God, David, your grandfather and his sisters survived the Holocaust. And you would consider joining his oppressors? Your grandfather would turn over in his grave."

I looked down at my shoes. I never saw my rabbi so upset. Deep inside, I knew I couldn't press the rabbi further.

"David I can appreciate your desire to find a deeper meaning in life, but you won't find a deeper meaning by becoming a traitor to your heritage, your religion, your family, and the memory of your grandfather and the six million that died before him!"

A traitor?

"Well, I was just investigating, but now that you put it that way—"

"David, your parents would be humiliated," he interrupted. "Are you willing to put them through that?"

"Well no, of course not. I guess I didn't think it through."

Rabbi Goodman stood to his feet. "I'd say not. Why don't you come to the Shabbat services next week? You know that it is said that when the congregation takes out the Scroll of the Torah to read it—"

"—Heaven's Gates of mercy are opened," I finished for him. Obviously, the rabbi thought I needed God's mercy after this line of questioning.

As I drove home, I couldn't get one word out of my mind. *Traitor.* I shuddered. The last thing I wanted to do was betray my family heritage. Hopefully the rabbi wouldn't mention our conversation to my dad.

If you are still reading this testimony, then clearly you know where this search led me. An angel. An explanation. An experience. Only to lead to a terrifying accident, when my father suffered a stroke while driving to work the very morning of my visitation. The entire Jewish community was grieving over what appeared to be the end of Harvey Lebowitz. However, my journey had only just begun. Can I continue?

CHAPTER I

I hate hospitals. The smell of death just hangs in the air.

I touched my father's hand—the one without IVs plugged into it—and pictures flashed before me. The day he took the training wheels off my bicycle; his strong arms wrapped around me as he taught me to swing a bat; the manly slap on my shoulder after my bar mitzvah.

"Dad?"

Instinctively, I checked the screen again, my only assurance that life remained. It was already day five and hope was fading—I was fading.

A few days earlier, on what had been the most amazing day of my life, I came home to find out that my father had just had a terrible car accident. In a bizarre turn of events, hospital tests later proved that he had actually suffered a massive stroke while he was driving. He survived the crash, but now his brain function was affected by the stroke.

I rehearsed the doctor's words again in my mind, and tried to force the information into my frontal lobe. "Simply put, a stroke is the loss of blood supply to the brain resulting in a lack of brain function. The longer the loss of blood supply, the more damage there is. Without flowing blood, the brain will cease to function."

My skin crawled. I sat beside the man I loved most in the world in a sterilized house of death. Come to think of it, that wasn't a bad title for an editorial piece—"Sterilized House of Death." On a better day, I'd have tapped that title into my cell phone to use later on. But really, how could a place so clean feel so dirty? Maybe I felt so strongly because this wasn't my first scary experience at St. Luke's Hospital.

St. Luke's...now that is funny. I wonder how they would react if I told them that on Sunday, just five days ago, I actually had an extensive conversation with the hospital's namesake—Luke! I am sure they would lock me up on that special floor for people who see angels, demons, and dead prophets.

At least they'd renovated the place. It was a far cry from the place where Bubbie Gershom, my mother's grandmother, had breathed her last breath twenty-five years ago. That place was cold and gray and felt like *medicine* to a four-year-old. The rooms were far more inviting now. Bright colors and murals graced the walls along with black-and-white framed pictures of very happy people from every background. But as they say, *you can put lipstick on a pig, but it is still a pig!* No matter how friendly they were, no matter how much money they spent to make the place more comfortable—someone was still dying here, *all the time.* I could feel it in the air.

I prayed to God that the next victim would not be Harvey Lebowitz. And yet, outside of a miracle the doctors were not hopeful.

And to think, I was terrified to tell him the news...that his son was now a follower of Yeshua, the Jewish Messiah. Looking at the comatose, eerily still man beneath the white sheets, the man I respected most in this world, I realized that fearing his reaction to my new faith was the least of my concerns now. In all likelihood, I had lost my father, my mentor, and my best friend. I would never be able to share my story with him—or anything else for that matter.

I smelled the coffee across the hall. *Time to stretch my legs.*

I held the foam cup under the dispenser, suddenly agitated. "The whole world is going through a coffee revolution and the best this hospital can provide is that stupid machine spitting out colored water," I barked to no one in particular.

"Well, it's a good thing I am here then," said my wife Lisa. She breezed through the doorway, bringing her customary warmth into this cold establishment. Relief washed over me. What would I do without her? I kissed her lightly on the lips and led her back across the hall to my father's room, the coffee forgotten.

I couldn't have endured this without her. There was no doubt that this was as hard on her as it was on all of us. Her own father and mother split up when she was just fourteen. Her father moved to Colorado a few years later, and while they have stayed in touch, it is hardly a warm and fuzzy father/daughter relationship. From the time we were engaged, she adopted my father as her own. He really had no say in the matter. By the time we said our nuptials at Temple Beth Israel he wasn't sure on which side of the *chupah* he should stand—the father of the groom or the father of the bride. She had a way of bringing out a side of him that neither I nor my sister was able to, or had ever even thought about. We would often joke at family dinners that he loved her more than his actual children.

Despite their close relationship, Lisa instinctively knew the role she should play in this present situation. There would be time later for processing all this. Her job now was cheerleader, coffee girl, carpooler, and listener. She was really good at the listening part. She did whatever was needed so that we wouldn't have to think about it.

She put her large purse on the windowsill and held up a paper bag. "I brought you a latte from Starbucks," she announced. "Three shots for my man."

"How do you do that?"

She looked at me quizzically.

"You know, read my mind?"

She smiled and pulled the coffee from the bag. Normally I prefer straight espresso. But stuck in that hospital room, I needed something that would last longer.

"Here," she said, and offered the latte. I reached for the coffee but found myself embracing her instead.

"I'm not ready to lose him," I whispered into her hair. I choked back a sob and, once again, burst into tears. I couldn't lose my father. Not now—not after everything I had just been through. I so badly needed at least one more face-to-face communication. *How could it be God's plan to reveal the truth to me, only to take my father the very same day?* In some ways that gave me hope. God must have a plan—the timing couldn't be coincidental.

My display of emotion appeared to everyone as the emotional reaction of a loving son grieving over the potential loss of his father. But it was more than that. I had found the truth. I had met God and I wanted my dad to know it!

"Are you okay?" Lisa asked. "I know this is difficult—you and your dad are so close. But it just seems like there is more going on. Is there something you want to tell me?"

Is there something I want to tell you!? Sure, last week, I was transported, translated, teleported, or something akin to "Scotty, beam me up" or "back" to the first century where a guy—no, an angel—introduced me to Peter, Paul, and Mary—no, not the band—along with John the Baptist, all of whom, it turns out, are Jews named Simon, Jacob, Miriam, and Yochanan. The latter is apparently a Jewish prophet, and not a member of First Baptist. Oh, and then I actually witnessed the death of Jesus, whose real name is Yeshua, before becoming a participant in a cosmic battle between angels and demons over my soul. How's that for having more going on? Then, I found myself being sucked back and forth between heaven and earth until I awoke from what seemed to have been one crazy dream—that is, until the angel sent me an email confirming everything that had happened. Yep, that's right, the angel sent me an email.

Then, when I pulled up to the house—a totally different person, a "new" man filled with peace and destiny—you come screaming out of the house telling me that my father is being rushed to the hospital..."Ah, no, everything is okay—I mean, given the circumstances. This has just been really hard on me."

There was no way I was ready to confide in her or anyone else for that matter—at least not yet. We were already in a hospital. How long would it take before they locked me up in a padded room and fitted me with a straight jacket?

"Okay. I'm just worried about you."

"I'll be fine. Just please take care of Mom and my sister. They need you right now. It is too much for me to process all this and provide the support they need as well. They need someone strong and optimistic and I'm feeling neither at the moment."

"I am heading to your parents' house now. I'm sure your mother's up already and will want to come in to the hospital. I just wanted to check in on you first. It's on the way."

My mother was always the strong one in the family. It came naturally to the daughter of a successful lawyer and one who was active in the Philadelphia Jewish community. She was the past president of the Jewish Federation in Philadelphia. Both of my mother's parents were first-generation Americans. My dad's father came over from Poland after the Holocaust where he met his wife. Her parents came over from Eastern Europe just before the turn of the century. Mom's grandparents on her dad's side worked tirelessly in the New York garment business, literally making and selling their own line of clothes, saving every penny so their sons could go to school. By the time my grandfather, her father, graduated, his father was the owner of a thriving factory with one hundred and fifty employees and no longer needed to save every penny.

His brother, her uncle, took over the business and turned it into a booming retail success called Goldberg's, even though that wasn't their last name. At the time, Jewish-owned department stores like Altmans, Gimbels, Kaufmann's, Lazarus, and Strauss' were doing exceptionally well. And "Smith," the name my great-grandfather Poldansky had taken upon entering these United States, just didn't sound very Jewish. *Who needs to know we're Jewish?* he'd thought at the time. Years later, however, they realized that having a Jewish name in retail—not to mention law and medicine—was actually helpful and "Goldberg" was chosen.

With her uncle as CEO and her father handling the legal side of things, Goldberg's kept the Smiths quite comfortable for many years. Eventually they sold the store for a ton of money and watched the new owners run it into the ground. My great uncle Morton retired young and wealthy, while my grandfather moved his family to Philadelphia to join with some friends in starting up Schwartz, Steinberg, and Smith Law Offices. When his daughter brought home Harvey Lebowitz, a first-year law student at NYU, he couldn't have been more pleased. Twenty-something years later, Schwartz, Steinberg, Smith, Walberg, and Lebowitz was well known to anyone in Philadelphia—particularly to those who watch *Jeopardy* at 7:00 p.m. on WPVI.

As a teenager, I loved *and* hated it, depending on where I was and who was watching when people would walk up to my dad and say, "Hey, aren't you that guy from those lawyer commercials?" And then they would always add, *"Your case is only as good as your lawyer."* Dad was hard to miss, really. In his late fifties, he was still quite good-looking and he always carried himself as if he owned Wall Street. His short, curly hair had only grayed at the temples and he still had a full head of hair. After shooting another commercial the cameraman always told him, "The camera loves you, Harvey." Of course, Dad always passed off those comments with a laugh and a joke about his growing midsection, blaming Mom's good cooking.

Despite Mom's inherent strength, Dad's presence boosted her confidence even more. I don't think even she understood how dependent upon on him she was—not until now anyway. From the outside she was loud, he was quiet. She was opinionated, he went with the flow. She was the life of the party, he preferred not to be at the party. But in truth, he was her strength and I could see in her demeanor that losing him would take its toll. Before, nothing would shake her—but that was because nothing shook him. Without him there, she was already shaken. Her short plump frame looked stooped and tired these days. The dark circles under her eyes were telltale signs of her personal anguish.

Despite his quiet exterior, Harvey Lebowitz had a keen sense of humor, which evidenced itself in three areas of his life. When he was making those embarrassing commercials, when he was trying a case—he had the ability to use humor and wit to make the opposing counsel or a clearly lying witness look foolish—and when he was in small gatherings like watching a football game or around a family dinner.

And every now and then, the introvert would surprise us all. Once while walking down the streets of Manhattan after dinner, an annoying Times Square street preacher kept yelling, *"The King is alive! The King is alive!"* Without batting an eye, my father ran up to him in front of several dozen onlookers yelling, "I knew it, I knew it, Elvis is alive!" The very recollection of it still brings a smile to my face, even though I now know that *the King is indeed alive—and He's not from Memphis.*

Later that afternoon, I sat with Lisa at a restaurant that had clearly been built to cater to those who couldn't stomach eating inside the hospital cafeteria. While picking through a grilled chicken salad, I asked, "How are you holding up?"

"Reasonably well under the circumstances." Then she looked up as if there was a "to do" list hovering above her. "Your mom and sister are inside. I will need to pick up your sister's kids from school in about an hour and get them situated. And then I need to figure how everyone is going to get fed tonight."

"Who's watching the girls?"

"Mindy will take them home from school. They can stay with her girls until this evening."

Mindy was Lisa's best friend. She was the first to greet us when we moved into Stonycreek. From the beginning, the two of them hit it off. Fortunately, I also get along well with her husband, Michael. In most of our other friendships it has been rare that both of us have "connected" with both members of another couple. Usually one of us would have to tolerate the spouse while the other two hit it off. One couple, in particular, I now simply refuse to spend time with. Lisa and I went out with Jill and Frank only once. Lisa met Jill at the gym and the two of them just assumed their husbands would hit it off just as well as they did. Not so. By the end of that first evening, I swore I would never go out with them again. For three hours Frank talked on and on to me about his work and how interesting it was. At the end of the three hours, I still couldn't have told you what in the world he did for a living!

Michael, however, is different. We both work in journalism—he's a producer for Channel 12 News, while I am a columnist for the *Philadelphia Inquirer.* We are also both avid Eagles fans and take turns regarding whose house we would watch the game at during football season. He is even someone I can talk to about personal problems—marriage, work, etc. After my father was rushed to the hospital they made it clear they were there for us. Anything we needed, they said, just call. Of course others said that as well, but with Mindy and Michael, I wouldn't feel guilty taking them up on the offer. They meant it.

"When will you be back?" I asked Lisa.

"Hmmm...'bout seven-thirty."

"How are *you* doing with all this? Are you exhausted?"

"The truth is," she admitted, "I would probably be a complete mess if not for staying busy, so this really is the best thing for me. I don't know how I would react if I stopped running. Don't worry about me. Let's take care of your family. That's what's most important right now."

"I should probably go back over there—check in on everyone."

"Ask them to give you a doggy bag. You are going to want to finish that salad in about ninety minutes, if I know you."

And she did. That's how my metabolism works—fast. I tend to need *regular* sustenance.

"Fine. You go on. I'll get this wrapped up and then head back to the room."

A short kiss, embrace, and two-second gaze into one another's eyes, as if to say, "Let's get through this together," and she was off.

CHAPTER II

I walked across the street, doggy bag in hand, feeling a little guilty. I had to tell her. We had worked hard on our marriage. We read books, attended one or two seminars, and even met with a counselor for ten weeks before getting married. We didn't know any other couples who tried harder to stay together, but after watching not only her own parents' divorce but close to half of the parents of our childhood friends, not to mention more than a few young couples we knew, Lisa was determined to do it right. And we had no clue what *right* was. Before we got married she would say, "Please promise me you won't do to our children what my father did to me."

Because my parents are together, I really couldn't relate to her concern. Of course I would be there. *"Till death do us part,"* right? Well, that was *before* we got married. We were in love! However, *after* we married and she moved into my downtown loft, it was amazing to discover how many little things would annoy each of us. The toilet seat was left up...the toothpaste cap wasn't put back...*Why do you always...*and *Can't you ever....* And without getting too descriptive, guys are simply not used to the complexities of waxing, plucking, and shaving. I had no idea how much was involved in getting the female of the species ready for public presentation. For me, getting ready for bed meant brushing my teeth and putting on pajamas. For Lisa, it is a twenty-minute ritual of applying creams and cleansers. "Living together" was clearly different from "dating."

Fortunately, those ten weeks of premarital classes had prepared us for many of these adjustments. Sometimes we would just laugh as if to say, "Yep, they told us this would happen."

Over the years our relationship had grown from a euphoric puppy love into a romantic friendship. Once our girls came, Emma and Sofia, it evolved even further into a romantic partnership. Carpools, soccer games, piano lessons—it felt like we were in a never-ending relay race. There was nothing I enjoyed more than Saturday at the park with Emma and Sofia. After a round on the tire swing, we'd toss a Frisbee or shoot hoops.

And that's what we signed up for. We're a happy little family, and Lisa and have I always maintained strict transparency with one another, even in the little things. When an old fling contacted her on Facebook announcing his divorce, she didn't hesitate to show me. We unfriended and blocked him together. And now, here I was not being open with Lisa about the most amazing thing in my life.

For good reason, mind you. She is not going to believe me—at least not at first.

As I entered Dad's hospital room, I was surprised to see Rabbi Good-man there with my mom and sister. This is the same rabbi who had only weeks before verbally assaulted me when I merely asked a few questions about the possibility of Yeshua being the Messiah. In fact, I recall him actually saying my grandfather would roll over in his grave to hear me speak *that name* and that such disloyalty would rip my family apart. I had left his office feeling like I'd just confessed to him that I looked at child pornography. The shame was tangible. It wasn't based on theology or a study of Scriptures, but on the actions of Christians against Jews. His hypothesis was simple: Jesus could not be the Messiah because of how those who claimed to follow Him treated the Jewish people. At the time, the rabbi made sense. But that was before the angel.

That had been a few weeks ago, and this was the first time I had seen him in a social setting since. Strangely, while I was struggling to tell Lisa about my time-traveling adventure, I couldn't wait to tell the rabbi of my angelic journey. However, given the circumstances, it wouldn't be today.

"Daaa-vid!" he such with hushed emotion, "How are you, son?" He put both of his hands on my biceps and looked at me with genuine empathy. I had to let go of my little grudge. If not for Ariel, my eyes would not have been opened. Rabbi Goodman had not had that benefit. Who was I to judge? Plus, Rabbi Goodman was a good friend of my father. Dad's firm handled all the legal work for the synagogue, from real estate to lawsuits. He genuinely cared for Dad.

"I'm hanging in there, like all of us—hoping for the best."

"I was just on my way out. David, I just told your mother if you need anything, *anything,* don't hesitate to call. Okay?"

"Thanks, Rabbi."

He turned to my mother and gave her hug reiterating the same sentiments to her and then to my sister. One last reassuring glance at me and he was on his way.

"Any news?" I asked.

"The doctors plan to run some tests on him this afternoon," my sister Hope responded. "They want to check his brain function." Hope is two years my junior and we are close. She is brilliant; a graduate of Brown University whose motto, interestingly enough, is *In Deo Speramos*—"In God we trust." If that was ever true in my life, it was now. It was becoming clearer with each passing day that our only *hope* was *God*. I was always Hope's protector growing up, and she adored me for that. That is why I'd assured her that Dad's brain activity would be fine, despite knowing you don't suffer a stroke like this and come out fine, at least not without a miracle. I couldn't bring myself to verbalize the truth we all knew.

At the very least, Dad will spend the rest of his years not in a courtroom, but in a wheelchair. If he is able to speak at all, it will be barely intelligible due to the paralysis in his face or the lack of oxygen to his brain during the stroke—or both. Or worse still, he'll be stuck in this coma until we pull the plug.

That was the truth, and two Ivy League educated adults knew it. But we would not talk about it. No, not yet, maybe in a week, maybe in a month, but not now. Now, we would talk about Harvey Lebowitz return-ing to his old self, and quickly.

"If I know Dad, he'll be complaining about the food here and crack-ing jokes with the nurses any day now," I tried to sound sincere and amusing at the same time.

"I hope so." Hope smiled weakly at me, tears in her eyes.

CHAPTER III

Lisa returned around 7:30 that evening, just as she'd said. Mom and Hope thanked her. It seemed that tears, once again, were inevitable. My active, defense lawyer dad lay still. Eyes closed, hands folded, and most of all, speechless. Harvey Lebowitz was never speechless! Lisa and I stood back and looked on, our arms around each other. It was surreal to make conversations around him, but not with him. He was in the room but not really with us. Just before she left, Mom held Dad's hand, tears dripping off her nose until Hope handed her a tissue. I wiped back my own tears.

Hope finally convinced Mom to go home with her, where they would both spend the night. Her husband Mark was at her home with their children. Lisa would most likely stay with them as well, finding a friend to stay with the girls.

I cleared my throat. I had to get out of this monsoon of sadness.

"Let's get some food," I said to Lisa. As Lisa grabbed her purse, I tapped Dad's foot, covered by a white hospital blanket. "Harvey, don't leave before we get back—you hear me?" Sometimes a little humor about your comatose dad is just what you need to lift your spirits. Heck, if he could hear, I know he would laugh, even if annoyed that I called him by his first name. I would do that sometimes to irk him. Hand in hand, we walked back to the café. The staff knew us by now. One of Lisa's great qualities is that she will tell her life story to anyone willing to listen.

Managing this restaurant was different. Their steady clientele were the friends and family of children with cancer, brothers with brain tumors, and fathers suffering strokes. You had to be both tough *and* warm to work here. Max, the manager, certainly fit the tough image. He was built like a fullback, short and stocky. His biceps stretched out the sleeves of his red polo shirt, but his heart was bigger than his body.

"Hey David, how is your dad doing?" asked Max.

"No real change, Max, but thanks for asking." *Please stop asking,* I thought.

We sat down at a booth. A teenager washed the tabletop with a wipey, leaving it clean but wet. "When did they start using wipeys to clean tables? It makes me feel that I am eating off a baby's *tukhus.*"

"Yes, but a clean *tukhus,*" Lisa responded. She quickly used her napkin to dry the table, so I grabbed her a new napkin off the table behind me.

Lisa has a great wit. It's one of things that I find so endearing about her, and one of the things that caused me to fall in love with her. When I met her in college she was cute, funny, and could handle pressure. And it was at that moment, in the café next to the hospital, looking at the beautiful mother of my children, that I decided I had to tell her. We were one—a team. I couldn't hide this from her anymore. Of course it was going to sound crazy—but if I couldn't tell *her,* I would never tell anybody.

Here goes nothing.

"You asked me earlier if there was something bothering me."

"Yeah, you said it was just the issue with your dad."

"I *did* say that, didn't I? Well, I kind of lied. There is, actually, something that I very much want to tell you—in fact, I couldn't wait to tell you and was on my way home to tell you, and then this happened...with my dad."

"So tell me! What is so exciting—if it is good news, why are you so nervous?"

No going back now. "Well, there's another reason I didn't tell you. It's, ah, kind of hard to believe. Almost impossible."

"Are you pregnant?"

There's that wit.

"Very funny." She had the most adorable smile on her face.

"Seriously, what in the world are you talking about—*impossible?*"

"Remember five days ago when you came running out of the house hysterical, in tears?"

"Of course, your father had suffered a stroke and you weren't answering your phone."

"Right. Did you notice something different about me?"

"What are you talking about, David?"

"Just think for a minute. Close your eyes and think back—was there something strange?"

Lisa closed her eyes in mock concentration. Suddenly, she opened her eyes. "Yes! You had been crying!"

"Other than during a movie, when have you ever known me to cry?"

"Well, you and your father are close..."

"But I hadn't found out about Dad, yet—I hadn't answered my phone, remember?"

"You are starting to sound like a lawyer!"

"Well, why shouldn't the son of Harvey Lebowitz sound like a skilled lawyer?"

"I didn't say *skilled*," Lisa smirked. "Okay, *Denny Crane*, why were you crying?" Denny Crane was one of my favorite television characters—a lawyer from the formerly popular show, *Boston Legal*.

"That morning I went to Starbucks to work on my column. You know that for the past several months I have been seeking to find out if there is more to life than meets the eye. Is there a God? And if so, what does He want from me?"

"I know, we've talked about this. I've seen the books even if I haven't read them."

"Well, I had a something of a breakthrough that morning."

"I'm listening."

"Okay, but before I tell you what happened, let me say something." She nodded. "Every Passover we read through the *Haggadah* and recite the Passover story. We talk about the ten plagues, sticking our finger in our wine glass, making a drop of wine on our plate for each plague. We revisit how Moses led the children of Israel through the Red Sea as God parted the waters. We go through this story every year as if we believe it. But do we? Do *you*?"

"I don't know. I haven't really given it much thought. The history confirms we existed and were enslaved in Egypt. Were there plagues and miracles? I don't know. Maybe."

"Okay, but if it did happen, then the God of the Bible is real; and all the other stories are real too—Adam and Eve, David and Goliath, the three Hebrew kids walking in fire, Noah and the flood. And if all that really happened, then supernatural things could still happen, right?"

"I suppose." She looked really puzzled now.

"What if I told you an angel appeared to me."

"Did an angel appear to you?"

"Yes."

"You're crazy."

"No, I am not." Suddenly, I felt an energy I had not known before, an authority—an intensity. "I really did see an angel. And not only that, he took me back in time two thousand years. I talked to characters from the Bible. I—"

"David!" she interrupted. "Stop. You're scaring me."

Okay, calm down David. Too much too soon. "Listen," I said, more gently. "I was sitting in the Starbucks reading the newspaper when suddenly everything became white—bright, crazy white. The whitest white I had ever seen."

Lisa was looking at me now as if she was looking at someone she didn't know, but I was in too deep. There was no going back. And this energy I was feeling was amazing!

"Then an angel named Ariel appeared."

"He had a name?" Lisa questioned, as she looked at me incredulously.

"Yes, he did—you have a name, I have a name; why can't *he* have a name?

"Fine, he has name. Continue. Please."

"He told me that God Himself had been aware of my search and that God had a mission for me. He took my hand, and next thing I knew we were flying."

Maybe I should've left that out for now.

"Before I knew it, we were in the Old City of Jerusalem, two thousand years ago."

"David, you sound like a religious freak!"

"Well, that's just it. He spent the next—actually, I have no idea how long it was. In earthly time it was only a half hour—"

"Earthly time?"

"I know it sounds crazy, but hear me out. He taught me about Yeshua—Jesus. He really *is* the Messiah."

"David, *we're Jews.* We don't believe in Jesus! What in the world has happened to you?"

"I have found the truth; I'm a new man."

"Well *new* man, you are going to have to find a *new* wife and *new* home if you don't stop talking like a crazy man!"

I knew she didn't mean that. I also knew she was scared, and I couldn't blame her. I could've told her Scrooge's story and it would have been easier to believe. And then it hit me. I had proof.

"I can prove it!"

"You can prove that you went back in time, flying with an angel—I'm sorry, with *Ariel*—who told you to leave your people and your heritage and believe in Jesus."

"How much do we know about what *Zayde*[1] Tuvia, or his sisters, suffered in the Holocaust?"

"What are you talking about David?"

"Just answer the question. Please?"

"The lawyer is back," she quipped. "Very little. He never talked about it."

"And neither did my great aunts. Even Dad doesn't know to what extent they suffered."

"Okay, so, what does that prove?"

"What if I told you that they had a brother named Chaim. A Nazi guard shot him when they arrived at a concentration camp. His sisters were used as sex slaves by the Nazis. Both of his parents died in the camp, while Zayde was transferred to Auschwitz. They had come from Poland, from Warsaw. His father, my great-grandfather, was a university professor before the war. They were forced into the ghetto and then transported to the concentration camps. When the war was over he had no idea if his sisters were even alive.

"I don't know how or when they were reunited, but you know there is no way I could know any of this."

I remember how angry I was that the angel forced me to watch the story of my grandfather. It was gut wrenching. But now, I was so grateful for this information; I could prove my experience was real.

"Your angel told you all this?"

"No, Zayde told me. Well, a teenage version of him did, right after his liberation. It was a movie—I mean—"

"You talked to your dead grandfather when he was a teen?"

"No, he talked to me," I answered, sounding less and less convincing by the second. "Um, Ariel—the angel—showed me a movie where my grandfather told his story."

So much for *proof.* I was sounding more and more like a nutcase by the minute.

"David, let's suppose all this is true. Who is going to corroborate it? Your grandfather is dead! His oldest sister is dead! His younger sister is eighty-five in a nursing home and isn't very talkative."

"I hadn't thought of that. Maybe I can talk to her."

"David, she is an old lady, not well, not all there, and you are going to dredge up memories of the most horrific period of her life—of being a sex slave for the Nazis?! Stories of rape and abuse, memories she hasn't been willing to share for nearly seventy years! Really? Do you want to kill her?"

This was not going well.

"Listen, David, I'm exhausted; you're exhausted. We can talk about this later. To tell you the truth, I am so tired I don't know what to think. I love you, but you're sounding really crazy. At least for now, please let's keep this just between us?"

"Fine. Let's talk tomorrow. I was going to wear a sandwich board that says *The End is Near* and go down to Independence Hall, but I think I can keep this to myself until tomorrow," I joked. Not a good time.

And then, the love of my life got up and walked out of the restaurant without a word—no good-bye, no kiss, no hug, nothing. Strangely, I wasn't worried. I figured if God could send an angel to visit me and show me things I never imagined possible, then He could certainly work on my wife. I would have to be patient and think of a way to prove my grandfather's story. Maybe he did tell someone or maybe I could find a survivor who knew him during the war. There had to be way.

I looked up and said under my breath, "Or, you could just send an angel to her on her way home. That would save me a lot of time and *tsurus*."[2]

CHAPTER IV

The electric feeling I'd had when talking to Lisa began to dissipate and I felt drained. My thoughts returned to my father. *How would this end?* I looked for the waitress to get her attention. "Can you bring me an espresso, please?"

As I sat there sipping my espresso I took a moment and surveyed the room. A family was sitting at a table in the middle of the restaurant. In a booth, there were three young adults and a fellow the same age—too young to be as bald as he was—in his pajamas with a tube running from his wrist to an IV drip hanging on its stand. In just about any other restaurant this would have been a very unusual sight. But here, next to St. Luke's, it was normal.

In another booth across the room, Max was sitting with a customer. The gentleman appeared to be in great distress. No doubt his wife, child, or one of his parents was in dire straits. And yet, just a few booths over, a man and woman were sitting with a young girl, who was about nine with a cast on her arm. She was smiling and had chocolate fudge and ice cream all around her mouth. The sundae was surely a reward for whatever she had been through that day.

The family reminded me of Sofia at her fourth birthday party just a few months ago. We were celebrating at Jungle Jim's when she came down the slide headfirst. Her chin hit the slide hard. Next thing I remember, we were on our way to this very same hospital. She had a laceration that needed stitches. Lisa couldn't watch when the doctor gave her a shot of Novocain right in the cut. Even I cringed. But Sofia, she was resolute. She just *took it.* I know it hurt, but she refused to cry. Then they stitched her up and that was that.

The manager of Jungle Jim's wasn't very apologetic. "We can't be responsible for every—*blah, blah, blah.*" After we left, one of the other parents told him that my father was Harvey Lebowitz. Turns out, the manager watched *Jeopardy* and so immediately got a hold of his boss. In the morning, the owner of Jungle Jim's called me to share his deep concern. Harvey Lebowitz's grandkids would enjoy free birthdays at Jungle Jim's until they were eighteen. *Would you please sign this waiver if you agree?*

The guy had nothing to fear. I had no plans of suing him. Sofia and Emma were ecstatic. *But why only till we're eighteen?* I explained that long before they turned eighteen they probably wouldn't want to celebrate their birthdays at Jungle Jim's anymore. They looked at me like confused puppies—turned their heads to one side as if to say, "Whatchu talkin' about?" Not wanting to celebrate at Jungle Jim's simply didn't compute in Emma and Sofia's world.

I took another look at the families around me. Did any of them know the truth? Did they even care? Or were they like me not too long ago—coasting in life without even thinking, *why am I here?*

"Hey, David, can I getcha another espresso?" Max had left the man he was consoling and now had me in his sights. Don't get me wrong. Max is amazing. I hope his bosses understand the service he provides. He is far more than a manager. I just wasn't in the mood to talk to anyone right then.

"I'm good, Max. Could you have them bring me the check?"

"It's on the way, buddy."

The short walk back to the hospital helped me clear my mind. Dad was still in his room and the hospital had quieted down considerably.

"Hey sweetheart, are you planning on staying the night?" Theresa was a plump African American nurse whom I had gotten to know over the past few nights. She was my favorite of all of them. Most of the nurses did a good job, but there was something special about her—something "motherly."

"Yeah, I think so. I may need to get used to sleeping on couches and armchairs at home."

Did I just say that out loud? Apparently so, as Theresa was looking at me with her hand on her hip as if to say, *Is there something you want tell me?*

"I'm just kidding. I had a rather intense conversation with my wife over dinner."

"Don't you give that girl no trouble, you hear me. She's as sweet as they come, honey."

"Yes ma'am. I'll behave." She replied with a big smile and I scooted my chair closer to Dad's bed. Theresa checked the IV bag and then moved the nurse call button closer to Dad's hand, as if she really expected him to call her if he needed her tonight. "You never know, David—don't lose hope."

I looked up at Theresa. "Thanks." That small action of faith touched me deeply.

Theresa smiled and patted my arm. "This show ain't over yet, honey. No time to give up now."

I nodded, grateful for her presence, her words.

As soon as she left the room, I reached for my father's hand. It seemed like I should pray. Then it dawned on me that I didn't know how to pray. This was all very new to me. I wanted to pray to Ariel—but that didn't feel right. He was just a messenger. I lifted my head a little confused. Then, I remembered that there should be a Bible in the nightstand. I opened the drawer, and sure enough there was a green Gideon's Bible. I randomly flipped it open and my eyes fell upon this verse.

> *And I will do whatever you ask in my name, so that the Father may be glorified in the Son* (John 14:13).

Okay! That helps. I closed the Bible and grabbed my father's hand again. "In the name of Yeshua—"

Before I could even complete the first sentence, my father squeezed my hand with a vice-like grip! The room shook violently. Everything blurred, like when you shake a pencil in front of your face, but this was the whole room. I could feel myself being shot out of one realm and into another. It was not painful, but there was this intense pressure and I was moving quickly—and then peace as I began to float upward. Far below I could see the roof of the hospital, yet also see myself slumped over my dad, who now appeared to be sound asleep. I was traveling again. *How many times can this happen?*

Then everything went white. It was so white that it might just as well have been pitch black. I could not see a thing, like snow blindness in sunshine. I began to slow down and then, as if someone gave me sunglasses to withstand the brightness, my visibility returned. My feet touched the floor and, although I seemed light as air, I was standing in a large room. I couldn't even see my feet very well in the light. The walls were white, yet not white. They tingled with color and energy, like prisms of living diamonds each twinkling in its place. There were two ornate marble desks with chairs that were padded blue and comfortable looking. In front of the two desks was a long rectangular wooden table with beautiful carvings. An old scroll rested there. I was about to pick it up, but something moved and I turned.

"Ariel!" I started toward him, but stopped short. Standing next to Ariel, as if he was on his way to play golf, with a big knowing smile on his face, was a very alert *and alive* Harvey Lebowitz! Or was it?

CHAPTER V

I rubbed my eyes. "Dad?"

I shook myself a little and squinted. "Dad? Is that you? Really you?" There was something surreal about leaving Dad in a comatose horizontal position in a hospital gown and suddenly seeing him vertical and practically glowing in a white golf polo and matching white pants. My mind argued with my eyes.

Dad's arms went up and a smile spread across his face. "It's really me, David!"

"Dad, you're alive!" I shouted. I embraced him. It felt so good to feel those arms around me again, my cheek against his curly hair. He even smelled the same—Hugo Boss. I stepped back and looked at him at arm's length.

"There's something different. Something—no gray hair! No receding hairline! Wow, you look great!"

Dad gave me one of those cockeyed grins and shrugged. "Guess we're in heaven."

"I guess we are," I answered softly. Dad had dropped the extra twenty-five pounds he'd put on the last five years and he was definitely in his "happy suit," which is what I used to call his golf clothes when I was a kid because of his obvious elation over going golfing.

"Wow, you look great!" I repeated. I didn't know what to say. I didn't want to ask the obvious. Was Dad dead? Or was he here in heaven for a visit like me?

Dad grabbed me again and gave me one of his bear hugs—the kind I used to get when he coached me through Little League. "I love you, Son," he whispered.

"I love you, Dad. I'm so—" I choked back a sob that wanted to escape, even in the pristine room of light with diamond walls. My grief was not immediately gone. In fact, it was more intense than ever. "Dad?" I quickly wiped back a tear.

I felt like I had been the subject of an elaborate prank, only this wasn't *Candid Camera*. My dad's body was on earth *nearly dead* and now here we were in—where were we exactly? I guess heaven or part of it.

I looked at Ariel. "What's going on here?"

Ariel looked at me, still grinning, "Well, you didn't think we went to all that trouble to show you the truth, only to take away your father, did you?"

Remembering the darkness of the past few days, I confessed, "It did cross my mind."

"David, I am sure this is all very confusing, but trust me, Father has a plan."

Really? I looked at my dad.

"No David, not *your* father, *the Father*—as in 'which art in heaven.' And believe it or not, it includes ole Harvey here. We have been getting to know each other for a little while."

Relief swept through me. I looked at my dad. "Have you been here since the stroke?"

"Stroke! What stroke?!" He put his hand on his head as he said this with feigned shock.

Well, he still has his sense of humor.

"To tell you the truth," he said as he shot a questioning glance at Ariel, "I have no idea how long I've been here."

"David, time on earth is very different from time in eternity—in fact, in eternity there is no time or distance. Those are earthly concepts. Here a day is like a thousand years and a thousand years is like a day.[1] But yes, your father has been with me since his stroke, though for him it probably doesn't feel that long—quite the opposite of your experience!"

"Does he know?" I asked Ariel, referring to my embracing of Yeshua.

Dad put his hand on my shoulder. "Yes, David, I know."

It seemed impossible. I'd thought of a million ways that I would try to convince my father that Yeshua is the Messiah, but I never dreamed it would be this easy. "How do you know about Yeshua? What happened?"

Dad shrugged and looked at Ariel.

I turned to the angel. "Did he go through everything I went through—did he see everything I saw?"

"Well, actually, he saw a few things that pertained to his life. You tell him, Harvey."

Dad pointed to the comfortable blue chairs at the desks and we sat down, facing one another. Ariel sat on the corner of my desk, arms crossed, and listened.

I ran my hand across the smooth marble desk—the same one I used before. It was like a modern-day tablet—a stone tablet, with an iPad! The room was a little different, but the most special aspect of this visit was that this time my father was here with me. *I can't remember ever being so happy.*

Dad leaned toward me, interrupting my thoughts. "David, many years ago I represented a fellow by the name of Jackie Horowitz. He was a Jewish fellow who was being sued by his family. He came from a strict Orthodox background—Lubavitch[2] in fact. The father had recently died, leaving the children his full inheritance, as their mother had died many years earlier—in fact, giving birth to Jackie. Jackie was the youngest of nine brothers and sisters.

"Ya'akov, now 'Jackie,' had left the Lubavitch lifestyle many years ago, long before his father's death. That was back in the early seventies. Without going into his whole story, he met some Jewish hippies in Philly. These hippies were believers in Jesus. They intrigued him because these young people exuded a joy and a faith that was undeniably genuine. Something that had escaped him in all his years of religious duty, something he had never seen in any of the learned Orthodox Jews that he'd encountered at Chabad."[3] "Well, that was before my time," I put in.

Dad nodded. "Right. But Jackie had this way about him."

As much as I tried to concentrate on Dad's story, I really wanted to know two things. One, was Dad going to be healed? Two, did he believe in Yeshua? But I'd have to save my questions for later. Dad was a man with a story and he wasn't going to stop now, especially when he started up with what my mother called his "courtroom voice." Dad leaned closer to my chair. "Jackie longed to experience this type of relationship with God. He would stay up late into the night debating the Scriptures with these uneducated hippies. They showed him the prophecies of the Messiah. And he was stunned to discover that, while they didn't know the Talmud, they knew the Hebrew Scriptures far better than he did. In the end, he had no arguments left. The prophecies were so clear. And he wanted what he saw in the lives of these young people. And yet, the guilt and pressure of leaving his strict Orthodox family and community was too much. He could not bring himself to do it."

I glanced up at Ariel who was still listening, arms crossed, on the edge of my large desk. "I know how he feels," I put in.

"Can we show him, Ariel?" Dad asked. "You know, like you showed me the other events from years ago?"

Ariel nodded. "All right." Ariel slid his hand to the side of the table and buttons appeared on our desks. "Harvey, you can hit that pause button at the top of your desk at any time and explain what's going on."

Dad grinned. I shook my head. He was really into this!

The room darkened. The floor beneath our feet moved and turned our chairs toward the big screen, which was above the long table with the scroll. Within seconds, a movie played.

The scene opened with a snowy winter night and a young Jewish man driving in the dark on icy roads. It was easy to tell he was Jewish from the *peyote*—the side curls falling from his ears—that proudly announced his Orthodox beliefs to all who knew him. A black book lay in the passenger seat beside him.

Dad leaned over toward me in the dark. "That's Jackie," he whispered.

The car suddenly hit a patch of ice and swerved out of control. The tires squealed and the car jumped the curve into another lane where the high bright lights of a semitrailer headed straight for him. I felt myself tense.

Suddenly, Jackie let go of the wheel. "Jesus! Help me!" he cried.

Dad paused the film.

"According to Jackie, at the moment of impact, instead of feeling his body get demolished, he entered into what he called, 'a wall of peace.' Instantly, in that moment, he saw the Hebrew words written in light above him, 'Yeshua is your Yeshu-a.'"

"Jesus is your salvation," I said slowly, softly.

"Yes! How did you know that? That is exactly what Jackie told me it meant."

"One of the many things I learned last week," I said as I glanced at my angelic instructor. "But finish—please."

"Okay." Harvey clicked the pause button and the movie was on again.

Jackie was inside his car on the shoulder of the road, snow falling all around him. The car wasn't crushed and neither was he. Jackie blinked, and looked around him. He was on the wrong side of the road facing oncoming traffic, but no truck and no accident. He looked over on the passenger's side seat and his New Covenant that he had been studying earlier that day. Jackie stared into the book and the movie focused intensely on the page and then a line on the page. Matthew 1:21 appeared before us in flames of fire, bigger than the movie screen, just like last time.

"Whoa!" cried out Dad. For me, of course, this was already familiar territory. I'd seen far more than this on my first adventure. Since Dad's jaw was hanging open, I read the verse.

> *She will give birth to a son, and you are to give him the name*
> *Yeshua, because he will save his people from their sins.*

"It's a word play, Dad. *Yeshua* means salvation. The angel is telling Joseph to give Him the name Salvation because He will *be* salvation to the Jewish people." I looked to Ariel for affirmation and felt a sense of excitement—like I was *called* to teach these things.

"Look at you David—the Bible scholar," said the lawyer.

"You joke," said the angel, "but your son is being prepared to plead the case of the Messiah before the Jewish people. It is why he is here. We are to prepare him to make his case, and you should know better than anyone, 'your case is only as good...'"

"—as your lawyer,'" we finished his sentence in unison and laughed that the angel was obviously a *Jeopardy* fan.

"Okay, come on Dad, finish the story. What happened to Jackie?"

"So after this incredible experience, Jackie could no longer deny the truth. Despite the knowledge that he would be ostracized by his family and most likely lose everything, he became a believer in Yeshua and joined with them." Dad looked at Ariel. "May I?"

Ariel nodded.

Dad clicked the pause button and the movie appeared again.

Jackie was dressed in a long winter coat and hat as he opened a yard gate beside a mailbox with "Horowitz" written on the outside. The yard was white, covered in snow, except for the walkway and porch. He closed the gate and walked down the sidewalk to a home. Jackie stood before the door and hesitated. A dog barked from inside. He stuffed his hands in his pockets. That's when I noticed—Jackie was dressed in converse shoes and jeans, and he'd cut off his *peyote*! I gulped. This scene could be me in a few weeks. Even though we were Conservative Jews, not the strict Orthodox who wore the *peyote* and dressed in black, heads would roll when the rabbi and family discovered my faith. I looked over at my father, caught his eye. He understood. The ramifications of such a decision were enormous, whether Orthodox or not.

Dad paused the movie.

"Now you get the picture, eh, son? When Jackie showed up at his home dressed in regular clothes and with his *peyote* cut off, *he* was cut off, both from his family and from his inheritance. They even had a funeral for him and thereafter considered him dead to the family for his betrayal."

I let out a low whistle and stretched my legs in front of me. "I don't think I want to see the next part. Not exactly faith-building stuff."

"No, it isn't," my dad agreed. "They even made the cruel claim that it was the latent evil in him that had killed their mother when he was born."

"Ouch. Talk about being the outcast."

Dad nodded. "Jackie was crushed, but moved on with his life. Over time he became a successful businessman, developing properties all around Philadelphia and taking every opportunity to speak to groups of people in his spare time. Back then Messianic Jews were a rarity, so Jackie became well known for his testimony and eventually traveled all over the U.S. telling his story and explaining from the Hebrew Scriptures that Yeshua is the long-awaited Jewish Messiah.

"In 1983 when his father died, Jackie was not even permitted to go to the funeral. He was heartbroken over the fact that he wasn't able to say farewell to his father. You can imagine then how stunned he was when a lawyer contacted him about a week later to tell him that he would be receiving an inheritance. Apparently, his father had had a change of heart and, without the knowledge of Jackie's siblings, had put him back in the will."

I smiled at that. Perhaps there was hope after all. How could a father disown his own son?

"His brothers and sisters were outraged. They decided to contest the will claiming their father was too senile at the time to have known what he was doing. In which case, the earlier will should be the one enforced.

"The upshot was that Jackie called our office and I took the case. I wasn't too thrilled about defending a *Jew for Jesus,* but I had defended worse. Plus, I hated bullies and didn't like the fact that the siblings weren't prepared to honor their father's wishes.

"When I met Jackie I was fully prepared not to like him. I didn't really know what to expect, but I'd assumed he would be a religious nutcase. To the contrary, the man I met was a real *mensch*, warm and friendly, and the fact that he was successful in business impressed me as well. No matter how hard I tried not to, I found I couldn't help but like Jackie. In the weeks leading up to the trial we shared many deep, personal conversations together. Talking to Jackie about Jesus made me feel like something of a traitor to all I'd believed in. But much like Jackie with those hippies, I couldn't restrain myself. Besides—he was so Jewish. It wasn't like I was talking to a priest. Ready to see the trial?"

I grinned. "I'd love to."

Dad hit the pause button again and the movie skipped right to the courtroom scene. The camera panned across the judge, the people in the courtroom, the prosecutor, and finally rested on Jackie and his defense attorney, Harvey Lebowitz. Dad was in his finest dark suit and tie; his old black briefcase, looking much newer, rested by his chair.

The prosecutor called Jackie to the stand.

Jackie had let his beard grow out, probably out of respect for his father on this occasion, and he was dressed impeccably in an expensive business suit with a pale blue shirt and dark blue striped tie. He walked slowly, confidently, to the stand, and then turned to the judge. "Your Honor, I would like permission to make a statement that will settle this case in the favor of my brothers and sisters who brought me here to accuse me today."

The judge looked at the prosecutor, who shrugged his shoulders.

The judge nodded. "Go ahead." While this was highly unconventional, judges, as we all know, love a quick resolution to a case and the opposing counsel wasn't about to object to something that would place a nice fat check in his pocket without any effort on his part.

The camera caught the expression on my father's face and I chuckled. "You look like a deer in the headlights there, Dad!"

Dad reached up and paused the movie. "Hey, I was in shock. *I only got paid if Jackie won.* I couldn't understand what he was doing. But I was soon to find out—" *Click.*

Jackie cleared his throat. "My name is Ya'akov Mendelsohn Horowitz," he began. "I have not talked to my father in ten years—not from a lack of desire on my part, but because my family disowned me after I became a Messianic Jew." The faces of the members of his extended family hardened. I was sure that the only thing that kept them from walking out was Jackie's claim that if he could just speak, they would win the lawsuit. And I must confess I, too, was curious.

Jackie looked at the judge. "I have done very well for myself as a businessman, *b'azrat Hashem*.[4] And I want to let it be known that I did not come here today to lay claim to the $120,000 that my father left me."

Click. Dad paused the movie again.

"Dad! Don't turn it off again!"

Dad ignored me. "I was livid!" he put in. "He just threw away my fee!" *Click*.

Ariel grinned, seemingly amused at our human interactions on his turf.

Jackie turned and scanned the courtroom. "I came here today because I wanted to see my brothers and sisters, as I am not invited to any weddings, bar mitzvahs or other family events—not even my father's funeral. It is gratifying to note that the prospect of hurting me and gaining a share of a further $120,000 has not only brought each of them out today, but other family members as well.

"You will each, I'm sure, be happy to learn that I have no intention of accepting the inheritance. Instead, with your permission, I would like one hundred percent of those monies to go to the Jewish National Fund in our father's name, to be used to build a children's playground in an Orthodox neighborhood of your choice in Israel."

A murmur of surprise rippled through the room.

"I believe this to be a fair compromise. Since my father left me an inheritance, despite ten years of rejection, I don't feel it would be right for me to simply give you the funds. On the other hand, you see me as a *copher*—" Jackie looked at the judge. "In Jewish terms, that means a heretic, an outcast."

The judge tapped his pencil absentmindedly and scanned the audience to see reactions from the family. A sea of hard faces.

Jackie continued. "And you don't want me to have the money. By donating the money to a Jewish charity in our father's name, everyone wins."

The family whispered among themselves and the buzz intensified until the judge banged the gavel to restore order. "Mr. Horowitz? Continue?"

"Lastly, I want to say that I have missed you all dearly. Your decision to cut me off, to keep my wife and children from knowing their extended family, has wounded me deeply. Even so, I want to tell each one of you today that I love you and I forgive you, that I understand why you feel the way you do, but I assure you I would never do anything to harm the Jewish people. And I hope that someday we can enjoy each other's company again."

When Jackie proceeded to call each of his eight siblings by name, look them in the eye, smile, and say, "I love you and forgive you," I wiped back tears. I couldn't help it. This man's honesty and love was completely unnatural. My heart swelled with love for Yeshua, the Son of God, who set the pace for this kind of forgiveness.

Jackie walked to his seat and sat down. The camera did a close-up of Jackie with my father. Jackie smiled and said, "Don't worry Harvey, I've got you covered. Your law firm will receive a handsome check next week."

Click.

I shook my head. "That's some story, Dad. Hard to believe it's all true, a replay of what actually happened. It is cool and unnerving that heaven has an instant replay of all that we have done on earth."

Dad's eyebrows winged upward. "I understand that heaven was doing movies long before the nineteen hundreds."

I looked over at Ariel, who had pulled up a chair beside us. His long legs were stretched out in front of us and his arms crossed. "Yep. If Ariel here has anything to do with it, I'm sure we will see a few more before we leave here."

"It is true, David. God sees everything." A passage formed again.

> *Nothing in all creation is hidden from God's sight. Everything is uncovered and laid bare before the eyes of him to whom we must give account* (Hebrews 4:13).

Those words, *to whom we must give account,* sent a shiver down my spine.

Ariel words brought me back to the present. "But that's not the end of the story. Harvey?"

"After a few hours deliberation, Jackie's siblings returned with their lawyer. It was clear from their faces that the vote was not unanimous, but they did agree to his proposal. A few of them even re-established their relationship with him."

"The power of love," I mumbled.

"Indeed," Dad agreed. "And Jackie did take care of me. I received a check for $40,000 the following week—a third of the inheritance. However, I was so moved by his actions that I asked that half the funds be donated also the JNF."

"Why only half?" I joked.

"Someone had to pay for your Ivy League education!

"Over the years we have stayed in touch. I was secretly intrigued by his story, his integrity, and his faith. In 1987 he gave me a book by a man named Josh McDowell called *Evidence that Demands a Verdict.* The title appealed to me as a lawyer. The author sought to prove from the Old Testament that Jesus is the Messiah.

"It was a powerful book. He made a compelling case. He showed how Jesus fulfilled the Messianic prophecies of the Hebrew prophets, how the prophet Daniel predicted exactly when He would come, and presented such a persuasive case for the resurrection[5] that even I as a lawyer could not refute it. But I never really considered that *I* could believe this stuff.

Intellectually, it became an object of interest, but I'm a Jew—I have a family. While we were not Orthodox, I knew what it would cost me. I am known throughout the community. I couldn't see myself in some Baptist church singing hymns. It was intriguing, but I wasn't going to destroy my life over religion. I had too much to lose."

I stood up and stretched my legs, my back. Dad stood as well, and the movie screen went up and the lights slowly came on inside the room.

Jackie's story, and Dad's part in it, was a lot to take in. I had no idea that Dad was tempted all those years ago to become Messianic—to embrace Yeshua.

"I wonder how our lives would have been different if you'd have believed in Yeshua all these years."

Dad sighed. Standing here, the decision he made back then seemed to trouble him. "I'm sure your life would have been much different, David. All of our lives would have been different."

"I can't imagine what it would have been like to be raised as Jewish believers in Jesus. I guess we would have still lived as Jews, but like Jackie, we would have been outcasts—and still may be."

Dad put his hand on my shoulder. "After I had that massive stroke a few hours ago—or what feels like a few hours ago—followed by a long conversation with this fellow," he said, referring to Ariel, "and now seeing the reality of heaven, and understanding the alternative...let's just say I have a new perspective. *Nothing* on earth seems so important anymore. Position and possessions lose their significance once you know what is at stake. From this vantage point, faith is no longer purely an intellectual issue—it's real."

"Because when you gain eternal life, you gain everything!" exclaimed Ariel. "The Master Himself said, *What will it benefit a person if he gains the whole world but loses his own soul?*" (See Luke 9:25.) I wanted to pinch myself. It seemed impossible that my dad and I were actually talking about all this—without an argument! No Jew simply embraces Yeshua without a lot of backlash. Jackie was proof of that.

I sat on the edge of my desk. "Lisa thinks I'm nuts. In fact, I just told her a few hours ago, just before I came to visit you—visit you in the hospital," I clarified. "I had no idea you were up here. Anyway, she literally thought I was crazy when I told her that I was visited by an angel. And I can't blame her. But now I have a witness!"

"Speaking of 'up here,' not everyone, you know, gets to visit," Ariel broke in to our conversation. "There is a reason you are here. There will be plenty of time to compare notes later, but now it's time to get to work."

Dad looked at me quizzically. "Work?"

CHAPTER VI

Work," Ariel answered. "Your son, David here, has been summoned by the Master for this generation of Jews and many non-Jews as well. This visit is important, Harvey, because we just saw how hard this was on Jackie."

Dad shot me a sideways glance. "Well, whatever David needs from me, I'm here."

Ariel nodded. "Good."

"Does that mean Dad's going to be okay—I mean on earth? He's going to live?" That was the question burning inside me. How could I focus on learning, not knowing whether or not Dad would be coming home with me.

Ariel sighed. "The Father hasn't revealed that to me yet, David. But as soon as He does, you'll be the first to know."

"But—"

"Now, take your seats again, gentlemen, and let me explain."

Obviously, the subject was closed. I'd have to wait to find out if my dad would remain here or finish out his life on earth. I didn't merely want Dad beside me here, in heaven. I wanted him beside me on earth, too. It was a lot to take in. And Dad really hadn't said, "Oh, yeah, David, and I believe in Yeshua, too." I didn't want to push it. I mean, of course he believes—how could he have gone through all this and not believe? But still, believing in Yeshua is more than simply *believing*. The angel told me, like Yeshua, we also need to take up our cross daily—in other words, embrace the humiliation and criticism of being Messianic. Could my father handle that? He is one of the most respected Jews in Philadelphia. He is on television every night! His father survived the Holocaust.

I was awoken from this preoccupation when the angel pulled out Dad's chair. Dad and I sat down at our "tablet" desks again. *All I need now is a Starbucks espresso—straight.*

A thick golden glass with the best smelling espresso materialized on my desk. *Whoa. I'll have to watch what I think about up here.* Ariel grinned. Dad was oblivious to the humor that just passed between us, but his eyes widened as his customary filtered coffee with cream appeared in a mug on his desk as well.

"Well, will you look at that?" he said.

I sipped my coffee. I'd never tasted anything better—including Starbucks.

Ariel walked to the long rectangular table in front of the room and picked up the scroll. "The Bible speaks about many Jewish people coming to Yeshua in the last days," he said as he lightly tapped the scroll on the table. "Hosea prophesied that after the Jewish people have gone many years without a Temple or government, they will return to the Lord."

Ariel unrolled the scroll, and instantly words of fire formed in front us. The book of Hosea materialized before our eyes, and a deep male voice read the scroll as if it was a paragraph in an audiobook.

> *For the people of Isra'el are going to be in seclusion for a long time without a king, prince, sacrifice, standing-stone, ritual vest or household gods. Afterwards, the people of Isra'el will repent and seek Adonai their God and David their king; they will come trembling to Adonai and his goodness in the acharit-hayamim* [the last days] (Hosea 3:4-5 CJB).

As the words melted away, Ariel said, "There are many other prophecies that speak of this."

"But that passage speaks of the Jews returning to *King David*," my dad, ever the lawyer, interjected.

"Indeed it does, Harvey. However, this was written hundreds of years *after* King David had already died. King David was a forerunner or a *type* of the coming Messiah. Even the most respected rabbinic voices understand references like this to be referring to the Messiah. The Messiah would come through David's line and be referred to as the *Son of David*. Through Miriam He had the bloodline of David, and through Joseph, His adopted father, He carried the authority of the throne of David.

"My point, gentlemen, is that a wave is coming! Many Jewish people are going to return to the Father through Yeshua the Messiah. And even now the Lord is preparing those who will serve His purposes for this coming harvest. David, you and many more Messianic Jews like you will help shepherd these precious sheep."

A gentle wind blew across my desk and in my face. I looked at Dad. He felt it too—the breeze ruffled his hair. I caught his eye. Something was up. Ariel walked over and put his hand on Dad's shoulder.

"Harvey, we realize that you are trained in the art of persuasion, but the Father has not yet revealed whether or not you will play a role in helping David. David must be further trained, and to that end, we must begin. David, say good-bye to your father. The next time you see him, things will be exactly as they were before you left."

"But—"

Before I could get a word out of my mouth, two angels gently picked Dad up and my father was gone, escorted like a prince into the wall of light through which I first entered. I stared. *Will he wake up when I return? Will he tell our family what we just saw?*

"...David."

Ariel's voice brought me back to reality. What could I say? Ariel couldn't tell me what he didn't know. I had no choice but to continue. "Uh, sorry. What were you saying?"

"I hope you're ready to move forward." It wasn't really a question. "I want to start where we left off."

I could feel myself involuntarily changing. I had been despondent for five days, and then confused. Even after seeing my father alive and hearing that God had a plan, the oppression hadn't completely lifted. But I sensed that in my choosing to move forward, with or without my dad, all the hurt and confusion I'd been carrying would drop off of me like lead weights.

I need to believe God has a plan like this when I'm on the earth—not just up here with Ariel.

"You're right," Ariel answered my thought. "Blessed are those who have not seen and yet believe."

"Okay, I'm ready. Let's go."

"Right, David. Let's start then by reviewing some of the things you learned here on your first visit."

I didn't have to think long. "All of Yeshua's first followers were Jewish. And John was not a Baptist, but a Jewish prophet." I had to chuckle as I remembered meeting John. "Let's see. Yeshua died on Passover, was raised from the dead on the Roshet Hakatzir, the day that the Jews would bring their First Fruits offering, and the first congregation was birthed on *Shavuot*—the Feast of Weeks."

"What many non-Jews refer to as Pentecost—Greek for fifty," added the angel.

"Yes, on that day three thousand Jewish men, plus women and children, became believers and were immersed in water in the *mikvot*—immersion tanks—surrounding the Temple."

Each time I remembered something, it appeared on the massive screen. I felt like I was on the TV show *Family Feud*. It was kind of fun to think about an event and see it—and I didn't even have to click anything like Dad did when he showed the Jackie movie.

"Go on," said Ariel.

"Okay, um, the names. James' name was actually Jacob. Paul never changed his name, he'd always had two names—his Roman name, Paul, and Hebrew name, Shaul or Saul in English, and Yeshua's mother was not Mary, but Miriam like the sister of Moses."

"Okay, what was the most significant fact you discovered?" prodded Ariel.

"That's easy. I was amazed to see how many Jews followed Yeshua. Growing up in a Jewish home, I knew He was Jewish, even that He lived in Israel, but for some reason I'd never realized that the first believers in Him were all Jews—I just naturally assumed that His followers were Christians from a Gentile background, and that He'd started a new religion. The truth is, I never gave it much thought, and I certainly never knew that Jeremiah the Jewish prophet had actually prophesied that God would make a *New* Covenant with the Jewish people. And that it would not be like the Covenant He made with Moses when He brought His people out of Egypt. This time, God would write His laws, not on tablets of stone, like this," I knocked on the stone tablet in front of me, "but upon their hearts."

Suddenly the verse, in its entirety, appeared on the tablet.

> *"The days are coming," declares the Lord,*
> *"when I will make a new covenant*
> *with the people of Israel*
> *and with the people of Judah.*
> *It will not be like the covenant*
> *I made with their ancestors*
> *when I took them by the hand*
> *to lead them out of Egypt,*
> *because they broke my covenant,*
> *though I was a husband to them,"*
> *declares the Lord.*
> *"This is the covenant I will make with the people of Israel*
> *after that time," declares the Lord.*
> *"I will put my law in their minds*
> *and write it on their hearts.*
> *I will be their God,*
> *and they will be my people* (Jeremiah 31:31-33).

"Good," encouraged the angel. He waited.

He obviously wanted me to elaborate, so I did. "I never realized that there was such a massive Jewish following of Yeshua in Jerusalem. You showed me a verse in the book of Acts where Paul came back to Jerusalem to visit Jacob and the other apostles; it stated that there were tens of thousands of Jewish followers."

Instantly the verse filled the giant screen in place of the list of things I had just recalled:

> *On hearing it, they praised God; but they also said to him, "You see, brother, how many tens of thousands of believers there are among the Judeans, and they are all zealots for the Torah"* (Acts 21:20 CJB).

"Right, not only were they large in number, they also continued to honor the Torah. There is absolutely no evidence they thought of themselves as any less Jewish or that they were, in any way, part of a new religion. Some have falsely taught that the New Covenant canceled out the Torah—"

"—yet the Jeremiah verse says," I interrupted, "that the main difference between the Mosaic covenant and the New Covenant was not that the Torah would be done away with, but that it would be written on their hearts."

"Correct, and the Jewish prophet, Ezekiel, said the same thing," declared the angel as the passage simultaneously appeared on the screen.

> *I will sprinkle clean water on you* [Israel], *and you will be clean; I will cleanse you from all your impurities and from all your idols. I will give you a new heart and put a new spirit in you; I will remove from you your heart of stone and give you a heart of flesh. And I will put my Spirit in you and move you to follow my decrees and be careful to keep my laws* (Ezekiel 36:25-27).

"So what happened?" asked Ariel.

"What do you mean 'what happened'? What happened to what?"

"Okay, it is clear to you now that the Yeshua movement of the first century, sometimes called *The Way*, was totally Jewish—at least in the beginning. Yeshua didn't travel to Turkey, Greece, or Rome, but He stayed in Israel saying, 'I was sent only to the lost sheep of the House of Israel.'"

"So, what happened?" he asked again.

"I am not following you."

"After He was crucified and rose from the dead, Jews from all over Israel followed Him—not just Jews from Jerusalem—but all over Israel, even Tel Aviv."

"But Tel Aviv is only a hundred years old," I corrected him, knowing there would be a twist.

"Yes, but Jaffa was a city, and Tel Aviv came out of Jaffa. That whole area—from the present-day Ben Gurion airport, southeast of Tel Aviv, all the way past Netanya, twenty miles north of Tel Aviv—was touched by the message of Yeshua. Look at this passage. Oh, and just a reminder, the actual name of Peter was Kefa—*rock*."

"I remember, Peter comes from the Greek word for rock, Petros, but they spoke Aramaic and *rock* is Kefa in Aramaic." I was surprised that I remembered all that. It must have been the atmosphere. I'm really not that good on earth.

The large screen once again flickered to life:

> *In Joppa* [Yafo] *there was a disciple named Tabitha (in Greek her name is Dorcas); she was always doing good...*

"Whoa, what a minute. Her name was *Dorcas?*"

"Tabitha actually, but in Greek it was Dorcas. So?"

I needed to behave, but I really couldn't resist. *There was someone in the Bible named Dorcas? That's hilarious.*

"Ah, nothing. It's just good she didn't grow up in New Jersey." The angel was genuinely confused. "It's just that Dorcas is not a pleasant word in English. No worries. Continue please. I shouldn't have interrupted you."

"Well, *Dorcas* is not an English word, but it is Greek for *gazelle*."
"Okay now," I said, "*gazelle* is way cooler than *Dorcas*!"
"You know what? I think we should start a few verses earlier."

> *As Kefa traveled around the countryside, he came down to the believers in Lud. There he found a man named Aeneas who had lain bedridden for eight years, because he was paralyzed. Kefa said to him, "Aeneas! Yeshua the Messiah is healing you! Get up, and make your bed!" Everyone living in Lud and the Sharon saw him, and they turned to the Lord. Immediately Aeneas got up* (Acts 9:32-34 CJB).

> *In Joppa [Yafo] there was a talmidah [disciple] named Tavita (Dorcas in Greek)—*

"*Which means gazelle*," Ariel emphasized with fake anger.

> *—she was always doing tzedakah and other good deeds. It happened that just at that time, she took sick and died. After washing her, they laid her in a room upstairs. Lud is near Yafo, and the talmidim [disciples] had heard that Kefa was there, so they sent two men to him and urged him, "Please come to us without delay." Kefa got up and went with them.*

> *When he arrived, they led him into the upstairs room. All the widows stood by him, sobbing and showing all the dresses and coats Tavita had made them while she was still with them. But Kefa put them all outside, kneeled down and prayed. Then, turning to the body, he said, "Tavita! Get up!" She opened her eyes; and on seeing Kefa, she sat up. He offered her his hand and helped her to her feet; then, calling the believers and the widows, he presented her to them alive. This became known all over Yafo, and many people put their trust in the Lord* (Acts 9:37-42 CJB).

"When Jacob referred to tens of thousands of *Jews* who followed Yeshua, he was actually referring to Judeans—meaning Jews who lived in Jerusalem and the surrounding areas. The word *Jew* originally derived from the tribe of Judah that mostly resided in Judea, but after the northern ten tribes were taken into exile the term became inclusive of all the Hebrews who remained in Judea and eventually all Hebrews."

This was a lot to take in, and Ariel was just beginning. Somehow, it was easy to digest in heaven's atmosphere. *I hope I'll be this cognitive on earth.*

"You will pray for the mind of Messiah," Ariel put in, again answering my thoughts before I could verbalize them.

"The mind of Messiah?" I asked. "Is that possible?"

"Yes. Paul stated in First Corinthians 2:16 that believers on earth have the mind of the Messiah."

That was a new concept—one I wanted to think about further after I returned to earth.

Ariel walked toward the table and pointed at the large screen above it. A map appeared. "Now even more Jews came to faith in Yeshua in the coastal cities. You see at the end of the first paragraph, after Aeneas was healed, it says that *all* those who lived in Lod and Sharon saw him and turned to the Lord."

As Ariel mentioned those areas, the map highlighted their location and quickly showed the central market of each city, revealing the culture and language all at the same time. This was classroom technology that far surpassed the twenty-first century.

Ariel smiled as I adjusted to the quick screen plays, then continued. "The area between Lod, Yafo—or Jaffa as they say in English—and Sharon is more than two hundred square miles! That is a lot of people and they were *all Jews*. How do we know? Simple. No one was yet preaching to the Gentiles. Only Jewish people were invited to believe. The apostles had not yet been given the revelation that non-Jews could receive Yeshua."

"So, once again, David, *what happened?*"

"What happened to who? I don't understand what you are asking me?"

"How did something that was initially so completely and utterly Jewish become considered completely and utterly non-Jewish? As I just mentioned, in those early years no one preached to Gentiles—today it is exactly the opposite, people almost exclusively reach out to Gentiles and very little emphasis is put where *all* the emphasis was placed two thousand years ago—on reaching the Jewish people. You know yourself how terrified you were to accept Yeshua—even to merely consider Him was a huge step. You thought that to do so would be to reject your people and your heritage—and to convert to a new religion."

"True, I had no idea that Yeshua's mission was foretold by the *Hebrew* prophets."

"What did your dad say, just a few minutes ago? He equated becoming a believer with joining a Baptist church and singing Christian hymns. But do we see any of the first Jewish believers acting that way? Of course, at that time there were no Baptists, much less churches. They met house to house and in the Temple courts—that would be the Jewish Temple in Jerusalem, the geographical center of *Jewish* life—a strange place for the purveyors of a new religion to meet.

"When Kefa meets Yeshua, he's not worried about doing something un-Jewish. In fact, he brings Him home with him (see Matt. 8:14). His followers called Him *Rabbi* (see John 1:38, 49), not Pastor, Father, Vicar, Reverend, or Priest. So what happened to this movement, this *Jewish* movement, to make it so utterly repulsive to the people from whom it originated?"

"Well, I do know that the Church began to persecute the Jewish people. Particularly in the Crusades and the Spanish Inquisition."

"Yes, but that was many centuries later. The Gentile believers began to turn against the Jewish people as early as the middle of the first century. And this only increased in the second century. Would you like to know what started it?"

"Of course!"

CHAPTER VII

Not long after Kefa raised Tabitha from the dead, he went to stay with a fellow believer named Simon the Tanner. While there, he had a dramatic experience—"

"There you go, Angel, trying to tell *my* stories again," barked Simon Peter, as his face filled up the large screen. I couldn't forget that bushy beard and hard but warm face. Peter was strong and big—not fat, but well-toned.

"Okay, Peter, feel free to take over. I need a break anyway," Ariel said jokingly.

"Hey there, David. Good to see you again."

"It's good to see you too, Kefa!" I replied, using his Aramaic name. How cool was this. Twice in one week, *Skyping*—well, sort of—with Yeshua's disciples.

"Please, feel free to call me Peter—if that is easier for you to say."

I nodded. "Okay then. Peter."

"David, what I am about to share with you caused a massive turning point for the body of believers in the first century. Up until this time, while we were seeing thousands of Jews coming into the kingdom, it never occurred to us to preach to the Gentiles. In our understanding, Yeshua was the Messiah of the *Jews*. Every aspect of His life and ministry was foretold by the *Jewish* prophets. He died and rose from the dead on *Jewish* holidays. He poured out His Spirit on Jerusalem—not Rome—and used me and the other disciples, all Jews, to bring thousands of our Jewish brothers and sisters into the kingdom on *Shavuot*, a Jewish feast day. He spent His entire ministry teaching and preaching to *Jewish* people. He was uniquely *from* and *for* the Jews. He was indisputably Jewish property, but all that was about to change—not His Jewishness, but the way would now be opened for the nations to receive Him.

"Of course He had told us to share His message to the whole world (see Matt. 28:18–20; Acts 1:8), but we thought that meant to Jews all over the world and converts to Judaism. It just never occurred to us that we were to preach to Gentiles.

"One day I was praying on Simon's roof—the fellow who was hosting me in Yafo—when suddenly I fell into a trance. Watch this."

Peter's face flipped over as though someone turned a page, and the screen showed a man lying on a mat with a pillow under his head, taking a nap on a flat rooftop under blue skies. As the man slept, the blue skies turned into a white sheet high in the heavens. As the white sheet descended, it became apparent that it was full of animals—mostly animals that were not kosher and forbidden to be eaten by Jews. You could never put so many reptiles, mammals, and fowl together on the earth without a big fight.

Peter was sleeping, eyes closed, so it was obvious that he was dreaming. The wind whipped the edges of the great white sheet and blew until it whistled around its edges. The wind began to sound like someone breathing, and finally, a deep voice spoke from within the wind. "Get up, Peter. Eat!"

Peter's face appeared at the bottom edge of the sheet he was dreaming about. "No, Lord!" Peter cried. "I've lived by kosher laws all my life! I can't!"

The wind whipped around the sheet and howled just a little bit until the deep voice answered, "Don't call anything unclean that God has made clean." (See Acts 10:15.)

The movie ended and the Peter's face returned to the screen. "As you saw, this happened three times, and then I came out of the trance. Many theologians have misinterpreted this to mean that God was canceling the laws pertaining to the eating of clean and unclean animals.[1] But if you read the text you will notice that this was not the interpretation that *I* received...and, hey—it was *my* vision! It's not like I came down from the roof and announced that we were going to have a crawfish festival or a pork ribs barbeque.

"When I came out of the trance I was wondering about..." he raised his voice here for emphasis, *"the meaning* of the vision." (See Acts 10:17.) "I knew God was not contradicting His Word. I recalled Yeshua having said when He was with us that He hadn't come to abolish the Torah." (See Matthew 5:17.) "I understood the vision to be metaphorical—I just didn't know what it meant. I mean, what animals did you see up there, David?"

I shifted in my seat. It wasn't a hard question. "Okay, I saw snakes, spiders, lizards, slugs, pigs, horses—even dogs and cats!" My reluctance to comply with his question wasn't merely that these animals were unclean— but the thought of eating them was disgusting. It turned my stomach.

"Right. And I was still contemplating the meaning of the vision when the Spirit of God spoke, telling me that three men were coming to ask for me and that I should go with them.

"What I didn't know at that moment was that an angel, not unlike our good messenger here," he said, glancing in Ariel's direction, "had appeared to a Gentile in Caesarea, a Roman army officer named Cornelius. Unlike most Romans, Cornelius feared the God of Israel and loved the Jewish people. The angel told him to send for me at Simon's house in Yafo. Here is the account from the book of Acts." Peter clicked the screen back on and a booming voice read the words while people in the costume of that period of time appeared on the screen.

> *There was a man in Caesarea named Cornelius, a Roman army officer in what was called the Italian Regiment. He was a devout man, a "God-fearer," as was his whole household; he gave generously to help the Jewish poor and prayed regularly to God. One afternoon around three o'clock he saw clearly in a vision an angel of God coming in and saying to him,*

"Cornelius!" Cornelius stared at the angel, terrified. "What is it, sir?" he asked. "Your prayers," replied the angel, "and your acts of charity have gone up into God's presence, so that he has you on his mind. Now send some men to Yafo to bring back a man named Shim'on, also called Kefa. He's staying with Shim'on the leather-tanner, who has a house by the sea." As the angel that had spoken to him went away, Cornelius called two of his household slaves and one of his military aides, who was a godly man; he explained everything to them and sent them to Yafo (Acts 10:1-8 CJB).*

I noticed that Peter looked a little older during this period of time than he appeared right now, in heaven. Again I marveled at the youthfulness of heaven and the glorious way God chose to keep people at their finest form, face, and age in heaven. Peter interrupted my thoughts.

"Cornelius was a very special man. God chose him to be the first non-Jew to hear the Gospel. But Cornelius did his part. God drew him in, and Cornelius prayed and believed that God would answer him. Actually, he invited no small number of people to his home to hear me share, but he was the focal point.

"The next day his men arrived at Simon's house, just as I was coming down from the roof, having had the strange vision. When I learned that they were Gentiles wanting to take me to the home of a Gentile, I naturally thought to refuse. At which instant the Lord revealed to me the meaning of the vision: *that I should never consider any man as inferior*!" (See Acts 10:28.) "You see, according to our custom—not the Torah, mind you, but the traditions of our elders—we could not fellowship with Gentiles. We did not eat with them and we certainly did not enter their homes. This had more to do with ritual purity than discrimination. However, the Lord, just as He exposed religious hypocrisy by turning over the tables in the Temple, was now overturning some of our misperceptions.

"I invited them into Simon's to eat and stay the night. Simon was speechless when I did so. He had never invited a non-Jew into his home before—much less dined with them. But he consented. *When you raise someone from the dead, it gives you a lot of street cred—people tend to assume you know what you are doing,*" Peter said teasingly.

"The next morning we set off to Caesarea. As was my custom, I commandeered several young men who were part of my group of disciples to come with me. In addition to the fact that this would be a valuable mentoring time with them, I wanted there to be witnesses to what the Lord was about to do. I sensed that He was opening up a new frontier of ministry for us and it was important that others could testify in the future regarding its authenticity."

The map appeared on the screen again.

"The journey from Yafo to Caesarea today is only a forty-five minute trip, but my car was in the shop that day," Peter winked broadly. "It took us about a day and half, and when we arrived Cornelius' house was filled with all his relatives and close friends in an atmosphere charged with anticipation. I guess I had imagined a small, private conversation. I didn't really want the news that Simon Peter was hanging out with Gentiles to travel too far. At least, not before I had a chance to present the whole story to Jacob and the other brothers in Jerusalem. But the Lord had bigger plans."

Peter's "talking head" faded from the screen and this time the screen flashed still pictures of the house, Cornelius, the Gentile travelers who came with Peter, and Peter's shining face. It was truly shining, and I tried to imagine myself being put in such a position.

Peter's voice-over explained the pictures.

"As soon as I entered I felt the power of God descend upon me to preach. Any doubts I had about being there melted away as the boldness of the Holy Spirit filled me from the inside. Thoughts of the Holy Spirit's outpouring on Shavuot nearly a decade earlier filled my mind. It was the same anointing. Something special was about to happen.

"I began to share the story of Yeshua—about His death and resurrection—when all of a sudden the Holy Spirit fell upon Cornelius and his guests. They started speaking in tongues and praising God! We were all amazed. We had never seen a non-Jew receive the Holy Spirit and hadn't thought it possible. We all rejoiced, as we knew this was no small occurrence. In fact, it was the most significant event we'd experienced since the Holy Spirit fell upon us on that aforementioned Shavuot about a decade earlier.

"Recovering somewhat from the shock of it, I asked if anyone had any objections to their being immersed in water—and since no one had any—I and some of the young men traveling with me immersed them. We then stayed on for several days instructing them on their new life in the Messiah. In your day, David, it is taboo for a Jewish person to be immersed in water as a believer in Yeshua, but in my day it was unthinkable to baptize a *Gentile* as a believer in the Jewish Messiah. Quite the opposite! But oh, what a glorious time it was..."

Peter's voice and the story pictures faded and I turned to Ariel. "The woman with the flow of blood whom Yeshua healed spoke about this when she shared her story. She related how all the believers were incredulous that Gentiles were being baptized in water."

"By the time we are through, you will understand why that was. But as you can see, in the beginning, *only* Jews went into the waters of immersion and it was not controversial at all. As you learned during your last visit, immersion in water was an inextricable part of daily Temple life."

"I can't tell you how strange it is to conceive that it was once off-limits for a Jewish believer to share Yeshua with Gentiles. I don't think one Jewish person I know has ever really considered this. I mean, in today's world one of our greatest fears is of Gentile Christians targeting Jews, whereas no such thing existed in the days of the apostles; because, until Cornelius, there were no Gentile believers in Yeshua—just Jews. Now, one virtually assumes that every Christian is a Gentile."

"Right, David, but that is about to change dramatically..."

CHAPTER VIII

Ariel enthusiastically rehearsed in elaborate detail the argument that Yeshua is the way of salvation for the Jew first and then the Gentile. I tried to listen, but I was still worried about Dad. I wondered if I wasn't allowed to know about his fate because it would upset me too much and I wouldn't be able to learn all of these deep truths that I was to adopt as my own. I raked my hand through my hair and tried to think. All of this learning intrigued me, and it obviously interested my dad as well. But Dad never really came out and said he believed for sure. And what if I had to return to "life as usual" with all this information under my belt? What if Dad never woke up from his comatose state and no one in the family believed that we really talked to one another here in heaven? Or what if we get back to earth and he is not willing to count the cost of being a Jewish follower of Jesus? Was I willing?

My shoulders slumped as I thought about Ariel's last words—at least the last ones that I heard. I knew everything was about to change. *Everything.* What would Lisa think about all these changes? While I believed in Yeshua now, something inside me was unsettled. I tried not to think about all this because I knew Ariel would hear my thoughts. It occurred to me that maybe I didn't like being forced into being a modern-day Kefa, the Rock. Maybe I didn't want to be God's new voice to convince Jews that Jesus was not the leader of the Gentile Christian movement. I couldn't think of one Jewish friend who would want to be in my position right now. I could barely breathe.

"David?"

I looked up. Ariel looked about as exasperated as a perfect angel was allowed to be.

"Sorry. You were saying something?"

"We have a lot to cover," said Ariel. "But I think you need some time."

Ariel glowed with perfection of light and life. His face was flawless, his form tall and masculine, not a wrinkle or fat roll anywhere. Ariel's life here was so perfect, so easy. He had all the answers and no opposition. He just repeated God's words and everyone nodded their heads. But I was intensely aware that this whole thing was set up so that I would embrace Yeshua as the true way and then be thrown to the wolves. There were plenty of people on earth who would disagree with this new revelation. I wasn't exactly doing jumping jacks at the thought of enduring all that, especially if I had no one else beside me. What if my family rejected me like Jackie's family rejected him? Could I handle it? I mean, what were my options at this point? I'd either handle it or maybe—maybe I would cave in to the pressure and just live as a good Conservative Jew like I'd been doing before all this started.

I stretched my legs out in front of me and sighed. Ariel said nothing. He set a plate in front of me that held a golden and cherry colored fruit about the size of a baseball. "Eat this," he said gently. "Your mind will clear."

I looked up in his face. Ariel wasn't pushing; he was offering.

"Thanks," I answered.

I rolled the fruit around in my hand and then bit into it. I never tasted anything better! It sparkled like an iridescent plum, but it was larger and juicier than any fruit I'd ever eaten. The sweet juice ran down my chin and I wiped it off with my other hand. Ariel was right. My head cleared and I could breathe again.

I looked up at my angel friend. "Sorry. I guess I got a little overwhelmed. I'm not sure what to say. What does God expect?" I asked sincerely.

"He wants one thing," he answered. Ariel pointed up at the ceiling. "Surrender."

I smiled. "Yep, that would be it. Surrender."

I sighed, then bowed my head over the shiny gold plate. "Father in heaven, I come in Yeshua's name." I paused there. The last time I prayed in Yeshua's name, I was in the hospital room and the room shook like an earthquake. I waited a bit. Nothing happened this time, so I moved on.

"I can see what You want me to do back on earth. It's not real easy down there, You know? But Ariel's right. I'm struggling with surrender." I put my hands in the air, like one of the bandits on those old western movies who was caught by the sheriff. "I surrender. Do with me what You want. I'm Yours."

I looked around. Ariel was at the long table up front reading the scroll. He was true to his word—he left me alone to give me time to think.

"Amen," I said, finishing my prayer.

Ariel stayed at the table for some time and it slowly dawned on me that it was my place to call him back. "Ariel? Are you ready to continue?"

He rolled up the scroll in his hands, then tied it with a scarlet cord.

"I'm ready. You?"

I nodded. "Let's go."

Ariel sat easily on Dad's desktop and held up the scroll in the air. "Simon Peter was right to be concerned that people would not understand all this. Despite the fact that God had promised Abraham three times that through his descendants—and more particularly his seed, meaning Yeshua—*all* the nations of the earth would be blessed." (See Genesis 18:18, 22:18, 26:4.) "And even though Israel's prophets clearly foretold that many in the nations would ultimately come to faith, these first Jewish believers were initially blinded to this reality."

The clouds formed passages before my eyes. The words themselves seemed to clear my mind, and my first instinct as a journalist was take a photo of this phenomenon, only quickly realizing that my smartphone did not make the journey.

"The prophet Isaiah, for example, had written, '*In that day the Root of Jesse will stand as a banner for the peoples; the nations will rally to Him, and His resting place will be glorious*' (Isa. 11:10), while the psalmist spoke about Israel reflecting God's light to the nations. Look at this whiteboard, David, and notice how many times the words *peoples* and *nations* are mentioned."

> *May God be gracious to us and bless us and make his face shine on us—so that your ways may be known on **earth**, your salvation among all **nations**. May the **peoples** praise you, God; may all the **peoples** praise you. May the **nations** be glad and sing for joy, for you rule the **peoples** with equity and guide the **nations** of the earth. May the **peoples** praise you, God; may all the **peoples** praise you. The land yields its harvest; God, our God, blesses us. May God bless us still, so that **all the ends of the earth** will fear Him* (Psalm 67).

"And also—"

> *Praise the Lord, **all you nations**; extoll Him **all you peoples*** (Psalm 117:1).

"And again—"

> *May his name endure forever; may it continues as long as the sun. **All nations** will be blessed through him, and they will call him blessed* (Psalm 72:17).

The words went up in smoke—a pretty cool trick if you asked me. *I wonder if this is how Moses received the Ten Commandments?*

Ariel, ever the teacher, cleared his throat and tapped his scroll for emphasis on the point he was about to make. "Could it be any clearer that it was the Lord's intention from the very beginning to reach the nations through Israel?" Ariel asked rhetorically. "That God should have told Abraham in their very first encounter that *all the nations* on earth would be blessed through him? It was always God's plan to use Israel, Abraham's physical descendants, to reach the nations with the message of redemption through the Messiah. Sadly, however, Peter's encounter with Cornelius was not viewed in the light of those passages—but rather through the lens of tradition, the idea that Gentiles must be avoided to prevent becoming ritually unclean."

I thought about that. "It is ironic that Jews were forbidden to eat with Gentiles, when one considers how, in the coming centuries, the Roman Church would forbid Christians to have table fellowship with Jews!"

"Right."

"Maybe that's where we get the expression, *the tables turned*," I added.

"I'm not sure about that," Ariel smiled, "but I can tell you that, in short order, word began to spread that Peter had entered the home of a Gentile." Once again, Ariel's account of events was confirmed by the simultaneous appearance of the biblical text:

> *The apostles and the believers throughout Judea heard that the Gentiles also had received the word of God. So when Peter went up to Jerusalem, the circumcised believers criticized him and said, "You went into the house of uncircumcised men and ate with them"* (Acts 11:1-3).

Ariel stood to his feet. "This provided Peter with an opportunity to explain. Starting with his vision about the unclean animals, he told them the whole story—how God had directed him, how the Holy Spirit had fallen upon the Gentiles in Cornelius' home, and of the believers' baptism that followed. They received Peter's report with great joy." Scripture again accompanied Ariel's commentary:

> *When they heard this, they had no further objections and praised God, saying, "So then, even to Gentiles God has granted repentance that leads to life"* (Acts 11:18).

"Over the next decade tens of thousands of Gentiles came into the kingdom. The disciples began to preach the Good News of Yeshua in the surrounding countries. However, with this inclusion of Gentiles there began to emerge two rival camps of thought within the Messianic movement.

"First, there were those, like Peter, who simply invited Gentiles to repent and receive eternal life through Yeshua.

"Second, there were others who insisted that non-Jewish believers had to be circumcised and keep all of the Law of Moses; that they would first have to convert to Judaism in order to believe in Yeshua."

"Hang on, Ariel. *Jewish* preachers were telling *Gentiles* that in order to believe in Yeshua, they had to become *Jewish*?!" I asked in amazement.

"Precisely! Many of them came from strict orthodox backgrounds and could not conceive any other way," he answered. (See Acts 15:5.) My skin tingled with the realization of how backward everything had become over the centuries. "Ariel—you are blowing my Jewish mind! The majority of Jews today are opposed to the message of Jesus on the grounds that He is the God of the Gentiles. 'It's for the *Goyim*' they say, 'we have Judaism; we have the Torah.' And yet, you're saying that at one time, Orthodox Jews were running around the world telling Gentiles that in order to believe in Jesus they needed to convert to Judaism. Today, Jews who become believers are accused of *converting* to a foreign religion, but originally, it was the Gentiles who were being told to convert. This is like a religious bizarro world!"

"Bizarro?"

"Never mind, a Superman reference."

It wasn't that I didn't believe Ariel. It was just so foreign to modern-day Judaism that it seemed bogus. *I wonder if Rabbi Goodman knows about any of this?*

"David, this issue of whether or not the Gentiles had to be circumcised and keep the Torah to become a follower of Yeshua was the biggest theological controversy among the first Jewish believers. Many taught that you could not be saved *unless* you were circumcised. And to be honest, for many of the new Jewish believers this made complete sense. Outside of a divine revelation to the contrary, this was a very simple issue for the majority of them—Yeshua was sent to Jacob; to the lost sheep of the House of Israel. The first leaders clearly saw this as something exclusively for Jews. It took a prophetic vision, remember, to get Simon Peter to consider even speaking to a Gentile, and even then he did not expect the resulted outcome. When the Spirit of God fell upon the Gentiles—to confirm to Peter and the others that '*God does not show favoritism but accepts from every nation the one who fears him and does what is right*' (Acts 10:34-35)—none were more surprised than Peter."

I was actually relieved to hear that God did not show favoritism. Although we never discussed it, it sometimes bothered me that our best friends, Michael and Mindy, were cut off from all the wonderful tenets of faith that Lisa and I treasured so deeply. Even though before recently—before this search—I never really gave that much thought to the afterlife, my defense mechanism as a Jew made me think of *us* and *them*. Thinking about Michael and Mindy made me consider the word "Gentile" or "Goy" a little differently. "Gentile" wasn't exactly a complimentary word to Jewish people. But I was seeing that from the very beginning God not only cared for the Jews, but through Abraham's seed, like Peter and Paul, He reached the Gentiles. I could not wait to share this with Michael and Mindy. I really wanted to share this new faith with them as well as with the people in my local Jewish community.

Ariel smiled. "Actually, we are counting on you sharing your faith with more than just the locals."

I shot him a mock disapproving look. "It's starting to feel creepy, the way you hear my thoughts."

Ariel laughed outright. "Okay, I'll behave. But bear in mind that all of this was still several years before the New Covenant books were written. Shaul—the apostle Paul—addresses this issue head on in his letters to the Galatians and to the Romans, but both had yet to be written. And since it was to the Jews that God had entrusted the Scriptures and through Israel that God had brought the Messiah, it seemed only natural that in order to have a relationship with Him, one would need to convert to Judaism. All this came to a climax in the year 49 CE. Want to take a peek?"

I grinned. "Sure."

Ariel grabbed me by the shoulder, and within seconds we were airborne. This, I would never tire of. Every kid's dream is to fly, and despite being well into adulthood, this manner of time travel, I decided, would never get old. As we drew closer to our destination I realized we were returning to Jerusalem—where my first journey began. This time we hovered over a large meeting room. In it were dozens of men gathered in small groups, mingling as though they were waiting for a meeting to take place. Fresh fruit, such as grapes and dried dates, as well as flat round bread lay on low tables and a boy in the corner was ladling out water from a wooden barrel.

Ariel, ever the tutor, launched into an explanation.

"First, let me give you some background to what is happening down there. There are now hundreds of congregations outside of Israel with many Gentile members. Paul and Barnabas were responsible for the many Gentile believers in Antioch. However, inside Israel, the congregations remained almost exclusively Jewish. They would attend the synagogue in the morning to hear the *Parshat Hashavuah*—"

"The weekly Torah reading," I contributed.

"Yes, that was the only place the Scriptures were read. Then, in the evening, at the closing of Shabbat and the beginning of the new week, they would meet in home fellowships. However, elsewhere, outside of Israel, the Gentile believers were quickly starting to outnumber the Jewish believers."

I felt the alarm in my soul. My father and mother taught me to guard the truths entrusted to us and hold fast to the traditions of faith that were passed down to us through the centuries. Despite not being a very religious home, having seen firsthand how Hitler nearly wiped out the Jews of Europe in just a few years, living as Jews and keeping the traditions alive was everything to my father.

Dad would often warn us, "If just one generation stops keeping the traditions, it's likely that future generations will as well." And it wasn't going to start with his family.

Ariel continued. "In the beginning, these congregations honored the Jewish roots of their faith; Passover was the accepted time for Jewish and non-Jewish believers to celebrate the resurrection. The Jews were the only ones possessing the scrolls that contained the Holy Scriptures and almost all of the leaders of these congregations were Jews—at least up to this point in time. They were the evangelists who introduced the Gentiles to salvation through Yeshua.

"However, some Jewish believers were part of what was called 'The Circumcision Faction.' They came to Antioch from Jerusalem and began to teach the Gentiles that they could only be saved if they were circumcised. As I said before, outside of a divine revelation, such as Simon Peter had, this was not an unreasonable assumption. But God was not seeking to turn Gentiles into Jews. On the contrary, He was doing the previously unthinkable—He was creating, as Paul describes it in Ephesians, 'one new man' out of the two!

"Quite a number among these Jewish believers were Pharisees—the forerunners to modern-day Orthodox Judaism. Many Jews and Christians would be surprised to learn that these Orthodox Jews, after becoming believers, continued to live as Pharisees. People today routinely equate the word *Pharisee* with the word *hypocrite*, as if that is the meaning of the word. In fact, your English dictionary defines a Pharisee as someone self-righteous or a hypocrite. And it's true that many of the Pharisees whom Yeshua encountered were indeed hypocrites, preaching one thing and living another. However, there were many Pharisees who genuinely loved God and came to faith in the years following the resurrection. For example, Nicodemus, who visited Yeshua secretly by night, became an ardent believer." (See John 3:1–21.)

"Gamaliel, one of the most respected rabbis of his day, was another who displayed great wisdom and restraint when he warned the Sanhedrin, the highest court of justice and the supreme council in ancient Jerusalem, against persecuting the Messianic Jews.

"'If their message is from God,' he said, 'you will not be able to stop these men; you will only find yourselves fighting against God.'" (See Acts 5:39.) "Remember, David? We spoke about him."

I nodded.

"Paul, himself a disciple of the same Gamaliel, makes the declaration many years after coming to faith, '*I am*'—not was—'*a Pharisee, descended from Pharisees*' (Acts 23:6), and no, he was not confessing to being a hypocrite," the angel smiled wryly.

"There is a debate going on down there; one question is stirring the hearts of everyone—but I'll tell you that in a minute. First, understand that there were many who saw no contradiction in loving Yeshua, their Messiah, and continuing to be Orthodox Jews. While it is true that during the centuries in Babylon the Pharisees had substituted many scriptural injunctions with man-made rules, something the Messiah called 'the traditions of men,' they too were seeking to be faithful Jews, waiting for the Messiah. Sadly, a good number of them were blinded to the coming of the Messiah by jealousy, their love of position, and their fear of political reprisals. And it is for this reason that Yeshua leveled His harshest criticism at them. But people fail to realize that many Pharisees responded to His message and did follow Him.

"In Antioch, Paul and Barnabas came into sharp dispute with some of these Jews who were pressuring the Gentiles to be circumcised."

A passage formed before me, even as we floated over the gathering.

Certain people came down from Judea to Antioch and were teaching the believers: "Unless you are circumcised, according to the custom taught by Moses, you cannot be saved." This brought Paul and Barnabas into sharp dispute and debate with them. So Paul and Barnabas were appointed, along with some other believers, to go up to Jerusalem to see the apostles and elders about this question (Acts 15:1-2).

"The matter became so hotly contested that they decided they would take this disagreement to the apostles in Jerusalem and let them settle the issue. This proved to be the first binding theological council, and it was called and convened to answer a question that would seem silly to Jewish people today—*Do Gentiles have to become Jewish to believe in Jesus?* And that's the debate. Let's watch."

I looked down, expecting to see the entire scene move up onto a movie screen that I could watch. Instead, I suddenly found myself sitting at a low table in the very midst of this group of men! Ariel was nowhere to be found. I looked around the room and spotted Simon Peter among the men. He looked right at me but clearly did not recognize me as the American Jew he had been speaking to just a few minutes before. This was hardly surprising—gone were my jeans and dress shirt that I had been wearing; instead, I was once again dressed in first-century garb much like I'd worn while witnessing the crucifixion. My beard was grown out. *I am one of them.* When this happened before, I nearly panicked, but this time I calmed myself. *Ariel's done this before. I won't be stuck here forever.*

In fact, I decided to enjoy it this time. I stroked my long beard, rather enamored with its feel on my face. But the robe was itchy and I pulled my sleeves up to my elbows. Someone gave me a sideways glance of disapproval. I looked around. No one else had their sleeves pulled up. *Talk about peer pressure!* No need to ruin my reputation before it started. I rolled down my sleeves as a man stood up to speak. His beard was graying and he carried himself as an elder or teacher who owned much wisdom. The room quieted.

"If we are to receive Gentiles as true brothers, then the men must be circumcised and be required to keep the Law of Moses," he said. Several men nodded their agreement. "How can they expect to worship our Messiah without first becoming one of us and keeping our traditions and customs?"

Our Messiah. Amazing. These were clearly the believing Pharisees of whom Ariel had spoken—men who put forth the argument that Yeshua was the *Jewish* Messiah, so the Gentiles who want to enjoy the salvation He offers must become Jewish to do so.

Jacob (James) and the other apostles and elders took up this man's concern. There was no contention, but great discussion as, one by one, each man presented his thoughts on the matter, some with conviction and others with questions. I found myself included in their number. I just listened and hoped no one would ask me anything. After much dialogue, Peter took the floor. With confidence he recounted for them his vision and experience with Cornelius.

> *Brothers, you know that some time ago God made a choice among you that the Gentiles might hear from my lips the message of the gospel and believe. God, who knows the heart, showed that He accepted them by giving the Holy Spirit to them, just as He did to us. He did not discriminate between us and them, for He purified their hearts by faith. Now then, why do you try to test God by putting on the necks of Gentiles a yoke that neither we nor our ancestors have been able to bear? No! We believe it is through the grace of our Lord Yeshua that we are saved, just as they are (Acts 15:7-11).*

He was very persuasive. Even many of the circumcision faction seemed convinced. Next Paul and Barnabas related how God had used them with signs and wonders in preaching to the Gentiles. Everyone was silent as they shared story after story. Finally Jacob, the brother of Yeshua, spoke up. It was clear that he was the senior voice in the room.

> *It is my judgment, therefore, that we should not make it difficult for the Gentiles who are turning to God. Instead we should write to them, telling them to abstain from food polluted by idols, from sexual immorality, from the meat of strangled animals and from blood. For the Law of Moses*

has been preached in every city from the earliest times and is read in the synagogues on every Sabbath (Acts 15:19-21).

Then suddenly Jacob turned to me. He looked at me as if he knew me. I was terrified. "Levi, I want you to write this down. We will send it with Paul and Barnabas to the congregations. He added, looking at two other men, "Silas and Yehuda, you can accompany them so they will know that it is coming from the apostolic leadership here in Jerusalem."

Apparently I was Levi! I sat down and picked up the quill that served as a pen. There was an inkpot and a piece of papyrus on the table. *So far so good,* I thought, until I realized that they had been speaking in Hebrew. Just as I'd previously experienced, I had the supernatural ability to understand the languages that were being spoken, but I couldn't write in them! Or could I?

My hand trembling, I dipped the quill in the ink and simply wrote in English, as Jacob dictated. Amazingly, the letters appeared on the paper in shapes I could not understand. The papyrus was thick compared to modern-day paper, and the texture was rough and difficult to write on. I ran my fingers across it, just underneath the letters that I "painted" with the quill. Instantly I thought of the newspapers in Philadelphia and how I was paid to write something in those columns that would capture Philly's community and culture! I was thrilled to write such ancient script. What would the editor say about this? I smiled. *Imagine that!*

While Jacob dictated the letter in Hebrew, the letters that formed were definitely Greek! I quickly realized that while we were in Jerusalem, he was writing to believers in many other countries, so Greek would be the *lingua franca*—the common language of them all. As a writer, it was incredible to be given this opportunity. I managed to control my excitement so as not to arouse suspicion and continued to write:

The apostles and elders, your brothers,

To the Gentile believers in Antioch, Syria and Cilicia:

Greetings.

We have heard that some went out from us without our authorization and disturbed you, troubling your minds by what they said. So, we all agreed to choose some men and send them to you with our dear friends Barnabas and Paul—men who have risked their lives for the name of our Lord Jesus Christ [Yeshua the Messiah]. *Therefore we are sending and Silas to confirm by word of mouth what we are writing. It seemed good to the Holy Spirit and to us not to burden you with anything beyond the following requirements: You are to abstain from food sacrificed to idols, from blood, from the meat of strangled animals and from sexual immorality. You will do well to avoid these things. Farewell* (Acts 15:23-29).

I laid down the quill and looked at the beautiful Greek writing. I understood it! I was quite pleased with myself. The leaders interrupted my thoughts just then. As the ink dried, they called everyone to gather together in a circle around the four men who were designated to carry the letter around the world, as God led them. We all laid our hands on the four men and prayed for them. This was not the short Jewish blessing pronounced by Rabbi Goodman at the end of our Shabbat meeting in the synagogue. These men prayed with fervor and intensity, sometimes one at a time and other times all at once in many languages. By the time the prayer was finished, I had a quivery feeling inside, like someone turned on an electric heater inside a previously cold room in my heart. These men were my brothers—my ancestors.

"*Shey Elohim yivarech otchem,*" I said softly as I watched them roll up the letter that had been dictated to me, and somehow I knew that I said, "May the Lord bless you." They walked out together. The meeting was adjourned and *bam.* I was back in the heavenly classroom. Ariel had his back turned to me. He was at the whiteboard writing something—I think in English. I wasn't really sure anymore what language I was hearing or writing up here. I just knew that I understood it all.

He didn't seem to know I was there, so I decided to tease him a bit.

"Hey! Big guy!"

Ariel whirled around, pen in hand, quite startled. It was nice to get one over on the angel for a change.

"Maybe you could warn me the next time, before you just drop me into a meeting that took place two thousand years ago and is being conducted in a foreign language!" I feigned annoyance.

Ariel recovered quickly, of course. "Oh, come on David—what fun would that be? Besides, we're just getting started. Before the day is out, you're going to witness far more dramatic situations than that. But in all seriousness, the Master has arranged all of this so that you can experience these truths firsthand. He wants you to remember your experiences, and this is the best way. He could just give you facts and dates, but when you experience something it sears the memory. Sometimes in traumatic ways, but also for good. It will help you later. While all of this really happened, you are simply reliving a scene at a time as a means of study. There is nothing to be afraid of."

I'd always been a "hands on" kinesthetic kind of learner. God knew me well enough to present history to me in a way that was even better than a visual movie. The fact that God went to all this trouble so that I would "get it" truly touched my heart. I understood. He really cares. *God cares. God knows me. He even tapped into that fascination I've always had to record events, inform people of important things. He let me step into the shoes of a writer, a scribe from the first century.*

Ariel interrupted my thoughts. "Just remember, the scene is being replayed purely for your benefit, for your instruction."

I grinned at Ariel. "Got it." And I did get it—more than he knew. This wasn't about God just using me as a means to an end He desired. He really "got me." He understood what made me tick, and He knew better than anyone how to deliver His intentions to me in a way that I could comprehend it—even permanently imbed it—into my heart. He *chose* me to write or speak and deliver His message to the twenty-first century Jews.

I looked up. *Got it. And thanks.*

CHAPTER IX

It fascinated me that I easily slid into the scribe role in two different centuries. Still, it was a lot to take in.

Ariel sat beside me in the same chair Dad occupied earlier. "So, would you like to summarize what you know so far?"

I turned sideways to face him, leaning my side on the back of the chair. Instinctively, I stroked my long "beard." *Gone.*

"Well, I kind of miss my beard," I teased. "They are finally back in style. Although I'm all about our twenty-first century clothes. How did people walk around in that stuff all day?"

Ariel grinned back at me. "Okay, David, summarize for me. A little less fluff and a little more *stuff.*"

I knew what he wanted. *He* knew that I knew what he wanted. "Okay, it seems pretty simple. The Jewish apostles in Jerusalem decided that, according to the vision of Kefa—Simon Peter—Gentiles did not have to become Jews or be circumcised to receive salvation. Jacob gave them several prohibitions, something about not eating blood or food sacrificed to idols."

"Right."

I felt like I ought to be tapping notes into my cell phone or something, which I naturally do when covering a story for the paper, but my cell phone didn't make it here. I reasoned that if God went through all the trouble of bringing me here to see all of this, He would ensure that I retained it later on earth. So, I relaxed and sipped my coffee, still hot after what seemed like a long absence.

Ariel continued. "Also not to eat the meat of strangled animals, because that would be eating blood, and then the prohibition against sexual immorality."

"What a minute—surely God intended that the Gentiles embrace the Ten Commandments and to live moral lives? Could they lie? Or steal?" After an entire lifetime of trying to honor the Ten Commandments, I secretly hoped that they would still somehow be a part of the New Covenant.

"David, that is the exact question I hoped that you would ask. You see, the context of Acts 15 is not *moral living,* but *how do the Gentiles worship Yeshua?* The argument was not over stealing or lying, but over ceremonial identity markers—symbols of Hebrew worship. Circumcision for Israel was not a moral command, but an 'identity marker' command that branded the Jewish people as God's chosen nation."

Personally, I was glad that circumcision was a normal event for most baby boys today. I certainly didn't remember my circumcision, and I'm sure at the time I was grateful for whatever numbing meds the doctor provided. There were some perks to being born in our modern era. "So, there is nothing inherently good or noble about circumcising. And we don't bear the weight of sin against God if we choose not to circumcise our sons."

"Right. But for Hebrews, it was the mark in the flesh of identification. However, moral issues such as lying and stealing are universally wrong. Think about it. The Ten Commandments are the backbone of virtually every nation. How many nations encourage stealing or murder? And virtually every society has a weekly day off—even if not on the seventh day. But that had nothing to do with the dispute in Acts 15—the Jerusalem Council. They sought to determine how the Gentiles should worship. In pagan worship, eating and drinking blood or eating meat sacrificed to an idol were central. Jacob was telling the former pagans that, while they did not need to become Jews—embrace all the Jewish identity markers, such as keeping kosher or circumcision, in order to be part of God's household as Paul calls it in Ephesians 2:19—there were certain aspects of their former pagan form of worship that were inheritably evil. And these would not be accepted in the New Testament congregation."

"But he warns them against sexual immorality? That certainly was not a part of pagan liturgy," I countered.

"In fact it was. Temple prostitution, lying with a prostitute as part of idol worship, was quite prevalent in pagan worship. In fact, in some cases rape was allowed in pagan worship. Jacob made it clear that such practices would not be welcomed as legitimate New Testament worship. While that might be obvious to you in the twenty-first century, these former pagans had never read the Bible. All they knew was what they knew. Jacob encouraged them in verse twenty-one to continue to go the synagogue as they would see that Jacob's admonitions against certain forms of worship were upheld in Scripture."

For the law of Moses has been preached in every city from the earliest times and is read in the synagogues on every Sabbath (Acts 15:21).

"As I have shared with you before, the synagogue was the only place to hear God's Word. And it was read every Shabbat.

"Let's continue. The nature of the body of believers is now vastly different. More and more Gentiles came into the kingdom of God. While they were encouraged to honor the Jewish roots of the faith, they were not compelled to live as Jews or Hebrews, more accurately. And sadly, this is where things began to change for the worst. Remember I asked you, 'What happened?' Well, now you are going to find out. While the history is really sad, the one the Master has chosen to share it with you is someone very special.

"In your last journey, you met Peter for the first time. You also met John the Baptist—who is really John the Prophet—Thomas, John the disciple, Jacob, and others. But there is one whom you did not meet. God choose him to be the greatest theologian ever. He wrote half the New Testament and most of the doctrine that is laid within it."

I knew he was speaking about Paul, or Shaul as he was called in Hebrew.

"This rabbi persecuted the Messianic believers until he had his own dramatic encounter with the Messiah. Grab my arm; we are going to him."

We launched from a sitting position, as if the desks weren't even there. I really didn't need to hang on to Ariel's arm that hard. It was as though there was a magnet holding my hand around his wrist. We soared high through the white, then the galaxy of stars and planets, then a loud *pop* introduced us to an earthly scene below, but this time I did not see Jerusalem or any place close to Israel.

As our flight descended, closer and closer to land, it appeared to me that we were in ancient Rome. I was a little confused. Ariel had spent so much time convincing me that Rome hijacked the Messianic faith and that Paul was a rabbi, not a Catholic priest. Why Rome?

We landed on the left side of a road paved with smooth rectangular stones. Most of the vendors and pedestrians were on this side as well. Little wonder. A large public latrine took up most of the space on the right side. I'd heard about the public bathhouses and latrines in Rome. Part of me wanted to go inside and look around. The other part was glad to avoid the stench that likely accompanies such places.

Rome was known for its extensive water supply via aqueducts from the high mountains into the city. Before we left this place, I wanted to taste the spring water from one of the better aqueducts.

Men and women dressed in traditional Roman outfits walked by us—ignoring us, as if we belonged. I looked down. Yep, Roman sandals. Two metal clasps dug into my shoulders a little. They seemed to hold up an inner tunic, so I adjusted them until they stopped hurting. The tunic was soft—probably made of linen. At least that's what the tour guides told Lisa and me when we visited Rome on our honeymoon.

Our tour guide told us that all the men wore togas when on official business, but he warned us that the Roman toga was pretty difficult to wrap. Lisa tried to dress me in the twenty-foot-long material, but even with the tour guide's instructions I ended up looking ridiculous. Now, I paused to inspect the toga I wore, just so I could tell Lisa later on.

Ariel walked ahead and then stopped and looked back at me. "Coming?"

"Yeah. This is just so cool. Itchy, but cool."

I jogged up to Ariel, paying more attention to our surroundings now that I had the clothes figured out.

An open stand of hot baked bread dominated the air. Large, crusty brown loaves were stacked neatly on a long table. Passersby were counting Roman coins as they neared the stand. It was clear who was going to make the lion's share of the money today on this street.

Young children in off-white tunics played around the feet of their mothers, who were dressed in layers of colorful—well, large scarves? Material anyway. I was surprised to see so much purple and red.

Two stray dogs zipped through the legs of pedestrians, barking loudly as one chased the other around the bread table. The bread vendor grabbed a large broom and chased them off. One left, tail between his legs. The other barked harder and ran ahead, probably to get into more mischief.

Ariel kept walking and I kept up the pace beside him. A two-wheeled oxcart laden with sacks of grain crunched over the right side of the cobblestone street. The poor man tending the cart was dressed in a dirty, worn tunic and trousers, and he led the ox with a long stick, tapped his back end at intervals, and shouted at him to move.

Nearly every door to the houses hung wide open. Tables and blankets lined the roadway in front of those doors, each filled with wares of various shapes and sizes. There were clay colored pots, vegetables and fruit, a display of candles, and long folds of material. It was clear that the Roman women liked color.

A young boy with a small herd of sheep pushed his way through our little group. I couldn't resist. I put my hand down and felt the wooly head of one of the larger sheep as he passed. Suddenly, the man with the oxcart appeared out of nowhere and chased the boy with his stick and yelled obscenities at him for his clumsy shepherding. I could understand everything that the people were saying, and marveled at the opportunity to experience Roman culture. I smiled to myself. *Our tour guide would be so envious.*

We passed two women who were walking slowly, talking together as they shouldered large clay jars.

We passed a small stand of honeycomb, which added to the pleasant aroma of bread. My stomach rumbled.

Just then, two men brushed by us, carrying an upside-down dead boar on a pole between them. I looked away. *Who walks around with a dead boar on a pole? And where are all the Roman statues and busts of Caesar Augustus and Julius Caesar?*

For some reason, Ariel was not inclined to track my thoughts in Rome. Instead, we walked together and he gave me time to take in all the sights, sounds, and smells.

"You might be wondering why we are in Rome," he smiled.

"Come on, you know I am wondering why we are in Rome—although I'm not complaining. I guess you know Lisa and I took our honeymoon in Rome?"

Ariel nodded. "I do. Just one more proof that Jehovah God has ordained your days and your calendar to prepare you for all He wants to show you now."

A man of small stature walked up to us. He was nearly bald on top with a strong Jewish nose and long white beard, clearly up there in years. "Shalom, David, as you may have guessed, I am Shaul, or Paul as I was known here in Rome. You are in Rome because this is where *the great divide* begins."

"It is an honor to meet you." I felt really small in his presence, despite his short stature. I'd really not had time yet to read everything he'd written, but I knew that he penned more than half of the New Testament.

"No David, it is I who am honored. I fought the good fight, I have finished my race, but you are at the starting line of yours."

I was nearly thirty years old. I hardly felt like I was just beginning, but who could argue with Rabbi Paul, apostle of Yeshua?

"Paul is here to shed some insight on his book to the believers in Rome. There is much in there that can only be correctly understood in light of the history leading up to its writing—and sadly, only a small percentage of believers know this history. Paul?"

"David, when reading the Scriptures, it is important to take in the historical context. The Bible was not written in a vacuum, but often in response to events on the ground. In the case of the book of Romans, which I wrote in the late fifties of the first century, many factors influenced me as I wrote it.

"Let's walk this way, gentlemen?" suggested Ariel. "We have some other friends to meet."

I wondered who they could be—my knowledge was still quite limited in regard to the New Covenant. If I couldn't feel my legs moving under me, I'd have thought I was in a dream. People passed and seemed none the wiser that I was from the future, Ariel was an angel, and Paul—Rabbi Shaul—would become the most significant figure in New Covenant history, save the Messiah Himself.

My Roman sandal kicked against something that looked a bit like a penny lying on the ground. I bent down and picked it up. "Caesar Claudius," I read easily the name encircling his likeness on the bronze coin.

Across the street from us I saw a triad of statues. I immediately recognized the statue on the right as Minerva, the Roman goddess of wisdom, medicine, poetry, and the arts. Stone likenesses of Jupiter and Juno were to her right, supposedly her parents. The statues looked old, even in 45 CE.

Lisa and I had studied this in some measure before taking our honeymoon tour of Rome, but these original statues were so different from the replicas shown by our tour guide.

I nodded toward the statue. "The goddess Minerva, right?"

Ariel nodded. "Rome was full of mythological gods and goddesses long before the Messiah was born."

"As you can see, Rome was filled with idols—gods and goddesses that the Romans believed could provide rain for harvest, fertility to wedded couples, and victory in war. This was not an easy city to evangelize, to say the least. Who wanted to trade in their millions of gods for One?"

"Will we see the great Colosseum?" *How cool would that be?* I had visited Rome and seen the impressive ruins, but to see it when it was new...

"Well, only if we stay here a few decades," joked the angel. "Construction began in 70 CE, and it was finished in the 80s. But honestly, that place has no great distinction in heaven. Tens of thousands of those who loved the Messiah were killed in that despicable edifice of death."

I guess I should get rid of all the tourist pictures of me and Lisa standing in front of it, I thought.

"Actually, you will see the Colosseum later as it has some valued history—although quite infamous. Paul? Please continue," requested Ariel.

"Some young men and their families were sent to Rome in the year 44 CE. These men were Jewish disciples who had been leaders in different congregations that we planted in Asia. They went to Rome with a deep burden for the capital city, as emissaries of Yeshua, and planted many house fellowships within the city. When they arrived they encountered a small group of Jews who had come to faith during that first Shavuot, when the Holy Spirit fell upon Jerusalem. These men were on pilgrimage when my dear brother Simon Peter preached his very first message. However, with little teaching, they had not grown much. Once these trained disciples and their families arrived, they began to bear fruit. By the year 49 CE there were around five or six congregations around Rome.[1]

"However, in that same year, 49 CE,[2] not long after our historic gathering in Jerusalem regarding the Gentiles and circumcision, Claudius, the Roman the emperor, decided to expel all the Jews from Rome."[3]

I held up my bronze coin. "While he made sure his face remained engraved on the Roman currency."

Paul smiled. "Right. Claudius was not exactly a friend of Jews or Christians, and little wonder. The Jewish believers had come into sharp dispute with the Jews who did not believe that Yeshua was the Messiah. At that time Messianic Jews were still welcomed into the traditional synagogue. Some were even leaders in different synagogues. Many non-Jewish Romans also would attend the synagogue. They were intrigued by the Jewish religion. But the success of the Jewish believers in preaching the Gospel of Yeshua to the Romans brought them into deep conflict with other Jewish leaders, who were not believers—and jealous of their success amongst the Gentiles."

"I had no idea," I put in. "I've certainly never felt any jealousy over Jewish believers, only disdain for them. Of course, that was before last week. And the idea of Jewish synagogues actively seeking Gentile converts is not consistent with today's Judaism, which is quite insular."

"As you will see," said Ariel, "a lot things changed in Judaism after the success of the message of Yeshua."

CHAPTER X

I truly did want to fully understand the "Jewishness" of Yeshua, His disciples, and the first-century believers in the Messiah. Admittedly, I also hoped that I would not forget the look and feel of Rome. I tried to memorize the architecture of the bathhouses, the deep fresh smell of the bread, the feel of the heat from the flat, worn cobblestone through my sandals, the sun warming my skin until I really wanted to run around like one of the Roman children, in only my "tunic." I smiled, imagining what Lisa would say about that. A merchant passed us, walking the opposite direction, leading a donkey laden with pottery wares. He was probably a supplier for that pottery stand we saw earlier. Far ahead I could still see the oxcart and the boy with the sheep not far behind.

Paul, ever the teacher, interrupted my thoughts. "To your last comment, David—a little-known fact today is that Temple Judaism was very evangelistic. Jews sought to attract the Gentiles to the God of Israel. Hence, we see in many places in the New Covenant that Gentiles were present at the synagogues, and this added strife."[1]

"Apparently, Claudius wasn't very amused by the conflict between the Messianic Jews and traditional ones," I added.

"Exactly," Paul agreed. "So he expelled all Jews from Rome—a community of about forty to fifty thousand people.[2] He made no distinction between Messianic Jews and Jews who did not believe in Yeshua when he forced them to leave. He really didn't care what they did, only that he was rid of them."

"What about the Gentile believers in Rome? Did they leave with the Jewish believers?"

"A few," Paul answered. "But most Gentiles stayed in Rome because their families and jobs were here. So Claudius's expulsion of Jews left the new Gentile believers in charge of the congregations. They had no formal theological training, and with the Jews gone, no Bible to read as, naturally, the Jews took their scrolls with them.

"Unlike in your day, David, where people have the entire Bible on their phones—oy, just to have a phone in my day—the Bible was written on scrolls. And there was no such thing as a *pocket scroll*," he smiled. "It would take an entire room to store all the scrolls! And keep in mind, the books of the New Testament were not yet written, so we relied completely on the Hebrew Scriptures."

"What's that?" I asked, pointing to a large bridge-like structure that was at least four stories high.

"Ah, that is one of nine aqueducts that brings millions of gallons of water into Rome each day."

"Seriously? In the middle of the first century?"

Paul smiled. "Really. Let's head that way."

Paul led us to a fountain of sorts, a square pool of water that gurgled in the center, the water obviously coming up from underneath.

"Supplied by one of the aqueducts?" I asked.

Paul nodded. "This one is from a spring. The water is clear and much colder than some of the others."

I cupped the water in my hands and lifted it to my mouth. Wow! I'd never tasted water so icy cold and sweet.

"What's the secret?" I asked. "This is the best water I ever tasted!"

"The spring," Paul repeated. "Rivers and streams from the high mountain fill several of our aqueducts, but the best drinking water comes from the underground springs. Those waters are not dirtied by rain storms or people."

"No wonder people regarded Rome as the heart of civilization," I said. I turned to Ariel. "And the Jews were kicked out?"

Ariel nodded. "The exodus of Jews from Rome was recorded by the Roman historian Suetonius and can be verified.."[3]

"Yes, and that was how I came into contact with our dear friends from Rome." Paul added.

A middle-aged couple approached us, and I stood as Paul embraced them both. Then Paul turned to me. "Right on time," Paul smiled and continued, "My friends, this is David, the young Jewish man Ariel told you about—from the twenty-first century."

The couple looked as though they were carved out of statues—absolutely beautiful, both of them. In the twenty-first century they could easily be models on the front page of *Time Life* magazine. The joy on their faces made me miss Lisa, and again I wondered what she would think of all this.

"Good afternoon, David. My name is Aquila, and this is my dear wife Pricilla. We met Paul at Corinth, in Greece. Shall we sit over there, under the shade of that tree?"

Everyone looked at Ariel, who nodded and led the little group to the shade. Having no seats, we all sat in the grass in a circle.

"David, Ariel asked us to tell you our story." Aquila looked at his wife. "Of course, we were only two of many thousands of Jews who were exiled from Rome in 49 CE."

"An event which is also recorded in history and can be found in Acts 18," said the meticulous angel. And a passage appeared with flaming words encased in clouds right before our eyes.

> *After this, Paul left Athens and went to Corinth. There he met a Jew named Aquila, a native of Pontus, who had recently come from Italy with his wife Priscilla, because Claudius had ordered all Jews to leave Rome* (Acts 18:1-2).

"So you are them? In the passage?"

Aquila continued, "Yes, young man. We were already settled in Corinth when Paul came from Athens. We were coworkers together for several years, not only in Corinth, but also at Ephesus in Turkey. We saw many Jews and Gentiles come to faith in Yeshua as we planted congregations. Paul would tirelessly reason with both Jews and Gentiles in the synagogue. Finally, because the infighting became abusive, we advised Paul to leave and focus on reaching the Gentiles.

"Back in Rome, we hosted a congregation in our home and had a similar experience in the synagogue. The Jewish leaders—who did not join our ranks—began to persecute us as many Jews and Romans were coming to faith."

"Yes, but even after we left the synagogue, many Jews followed," said Paul. "In Corinth, the synagogue leader and his whole family followed Yeshua! We immersed them in water and enjoyed a wonderful season of bearing fruit for the kingdom in that Greek city."

"Sadly," Pricilla added, "after the exile, the young Gentile believers in Rome—without a Bible to guide them—created a belief over the next several years that God had rejected the Jews. In their minds, they replaced the Jews as God's chosen people. With no one to correct them, they developed strong attitudes against the Jewish people—believers and unbelievers. Of course, had they had the *Tanakh—the Torah, the Prophets, and the Writings*[4]—they could have referred to the many promises of restoration that God made to the people of Israel."

One of those promises appeared in the clouds of smoke before us. I read them aloud.

> *This is what the Lord says,*
> *he who appoints the sun*
> *to shine by day,*
> *who decrees the moon and stars*
> *to shine by night,*
> *who stirs up the sea*
> *so that its waves roar—*
> *the Lord Almighty is his name:*
> *"Only if these decrees vanish from my sight,"*
> *declares the Lord,*

"will Israel ever cease
being a nation before me."
This is what the Lord says:
"Only if the heavens above can be measured
and the foundations of the earth below be searched out
will I reject all the descendants of Israel
because of all they have done,"
declares the Lord (Jeremiah 31:35-37).

"You see, David," she continued, "the Lord could not reject Israel, even if He desired to do so. He is bound by His own Word. As Paul wrote," she glanced in his direction, "to young Titus, God cannot lie." (See Titus 1:2.) "But again, the Roman believers had no Scriptures to guide them those several years."

Aquila jumped back in. "They became convinced that God was judging the Jews and that was why we were kicked out of the capital city. Let me note, David, after the exile, the congregations in Rome became the first congregations without Jewish believers. Until this time, even in predominantly Gentile congregations, there were many Jews—and the Jews were often in leadership as they were often the founding evangelists of the congregation. The Gentiles were very dependent upon their Jewish teachers. I am by no means implying that the Jews were better or more important than the Gentiles, but merely that their knowledge of the *Tanakh* was far more extensive than that of the Gentile converts. This lack of scriptural knowledge led to *feelings* dictating theology, as opposed to the Scriptures—and this led to deception."

"To be clear," Pricilla shared, "initially they were brokenhearted that the Jews were forced to leave. We were the mothers and fathers of their congregations. After the Jews left, however, the congregations continued to grow under their leadership. Only then did this sentiment—*that the Jews were no longer needed* or, even worse, *under judgment*—began to foment.

"In the later part of 54 CE, Claudius died and Nero, his great-nephew, became the new Caesar. Claudius had adopted his great-nephew when he married his niece, Agrippina. This ensured that he would have an heir to his throne. One of the first things Nero did was allow us to return."

"That was about the only decent thing Nero did," added Ariel.

Paul leaned forward, toward me, the excitement obvious on his face. "Thrilled to hear the news that they could return to their precious congregation in Rome, my dear coworkers Priscilla and Aquila journeyed back to Rome, along with many other Jewish believers. I had left them in Ephesus some time before, in order to return to Jerusalem to greet the believers there and to celebrate Sukkot—the Feast of Tabernacles. From there I journeyed back to visit and strengthen all the congregations we had planted. It was after I had returned to Ephesus that news reached me that Priscilla and Aquila could return home."

"Yes, we could not wait to be reunited with our sons and daughters in the faith," shared Aquila. "However, after five years of believing this lie about the Jewish people—we returned to a different Rome. The congregations had grown under the non-Jewish leadership and outnumbered the Jews—which was a joy to see! That was the goal—to make disciples in all nations. However, the Messianic Jews were treated poorly upon our return, like second-class believers. Many of them had never even met us. This was devastating for us. We sent word to Paul."

"When I received the report from Pricilla and Aquilla of this discrimination—and keep in mind, word traveled very *slowly* in those days. We didn't even have texting!" cried Paul as he feigned shock. In a more serious tone he shared, "I was deeply grieved. For days I wept in intercessory prayer over this situation. This was the opposite of what the Lord expected from the Gentiles who had been adopted into the household of God—grafted into the Olive Tree."

"Olive Tree?" I wondered aloud.

Ariel gave me a look that reassured me that all would be explained soon.

"Imagine a situation where adopted kids began to judge and mistreat the natural-born children. What if the adopted children told the natural ones, 'Our parents don't love you anymore. We are now their favorites!' How would the generous parents react to such ingratitude? The Roman Gentile believers, instead of being grateful they were adopted into God's household, actually persecuted God's chosen nation. And yet, the Father had compassion on them, as He knew without the Scriptures they were ignorant of His plan.

"The Holy Spirit urged me to bring some correction to this damaging doctrine. I planned to visit Rome and deal with this in person. But first, I had to return to Jerusalem. For some time I had been collecting an offering for the poor in Jerusalem and it was urgent that I deliver it. They were in the midst of a terrible famine and suffering persecution from the religious leaders. As one who used to lead this persecution, it was important for me to be a vessel of comfort to my Messianic brethren there. Furthermore, the offering was an opportunity for the new Gentile congregations to honor the roots of their faith by supporting the Jewish believers in Jerusalem. As I would eventually write to the Romans..."

> Now, however, I am on my way to Jerusalem in the service
> of the Lord's people there. For Macedonia and Achaia were
> pleased to make a contribution for the poor among the Lord's
> people in Jerusalem. They were pleased to do it, and indeed
> they owe it to them. For if the Gentiles have shared in the
> Jews' spiritual blessings, they owe it to the Jews to share with
> them their material blessings (Romans 15:25-27).

"Even though my primary task was to spread the Good News of Yeshua to the nations, my heart was always broken for my own people. Wherever I went I encouraged the Gentiles to give back materially to Israel for what they received spiritually. This was universally accepted until my dear brothers in Rome allowed the enemy to poison their hearts against their Jewish brothers. I had to reach out to them not only for the sake of the Jewish believers, but also for their own sake. Turning against Israel after freely receiving the grace of God, was a grievous transgression that the Father would not—could not—ignore."

It was little wonder that God chose Paul to begin so many churches and to write much of the New Testament. I found myself hanging on his every word, and his body language was so animated that I could almost see him speaking at our synagogue next to Rabbi Goodman—almost.

Paul continued. "However, I was delayed in my journey and spent three months in Corinth. It was at this time, seeing that a visit to Rome in the near future may not be feasible, that I decided to write the Roman believers. Truthfully, I was unsure if I would even survive a trip to Jerusalem in order to go to Rome, as the persecution had grown fierce in the holy city. In fact, I would receive several prophecies on the way to Jerusalem that persecution awaited me." (See Acts 21:4, 10-11.) "But I would not be dissuaded. I was willing to die for the name of Adonai Yeshua."

A passage appeared in clouds of smoke that I assume those passing by could not see.

> *And now, compelled by the Spirit, I am going to Jerusalem, not knowing what will happen to me there. I only know that in every city the Holy Spirit warns me that prison and hardships are facing me. However, I consider my life worth nothing to me; my only aim is to finish the race and complete the task the Lord Yeshua has given me—the task of testifying to the good news of God's grace* (Acts 20:22-24).

"Yes, those were my words to the elders at Ephesus. I was weeping as I spoke them..."

Paul seemed to lose his composure or get lost in thought.

The angel gently brought him back, "You were explaining about writing Romans?"

"Yes, I am sorry. Eh...as I was saying, with Rome being the most influential city in the empire, I took this opportunity to lay out some of the most basic and yet significant truths regarding the message of the New Covenant—and when I say *New Covenant*, I don't mean the books of the New Testament, but the actual *Covenant* that Yeshua cut when He gave His life as a ransom—the covenant to which Jeremiah referred when he prophesied, 'I will make a *New Covenant* with the house of Israel and the house of Judah.'" (See Jeremiah 31:31.) "In Romans I made the case clearly, simply, and succinctly that there is nothing anyone can do to save themselves. There is no work or actions that can earn eternal life.

"I shared with them that when Adam sinned, we all became sinners through him—through Yeshua's righteous and sinless death, we can be made righteous. His resurrection was the evidence that death no longer has dominion."

It was getting dark, and the words now appeared in fire before me:

> *Consequently, just as one trespass resulted in condemnation for all people, so also one righteous act resulted in justification and life for all people. For just as through the disobedience of the one man the many were made sinners, so also through the obedience of the one man the many will be made righteous* (Romans 5:18-19).

"David, we have all sinned and fallen short of the glory of God." (See Romans 3:23.) "And there is a consequence: the wages of sin is death—eternal death, and there is no getting around that—but, praise God, the gift of God is enteral life through Messiah Yeshua, our Lord!" (See Romans 6:23.)

"The congregation in Rome was the only congregation I wrote to that I had not previously visited. It was the only congregation to whom I wrote where I was not the spiritual father. However, the situation was grave and they needed an accurate theology regarding Gentile believers and the Jewish people.

"Ninety-nine percent of people who read the book of Romans completely overlook the *reasons* why I wrote it. Some are offended by the fact that I speak in such absolute terms of God's faithfulness to Israel, while others actually believe that when I wrote—well, dictated to my dear son Tertius—the word *Israel*, I was referring to the Church!"

"So, what we have here is four stages of the Roman congregation in a short period of time:

1. Just Jews in the beginning.

2. Jews and Gentile converts.

3. Then after Jews are exiled, one hundred percent Gentile.

4. And finally, after the Jews return, Gentile dominated and treating the Jewish returnees poorly."

The sun was setting now and Ariel had one more destination he wanted me to see.

CHAPTER XI

The group stopped walking as we approached an ancient Roman building. It wasn't very big, but displayed a large Menorah, a seven branch candelabra, over its entrance. I recognized the Hebrew written above the door. *Shema Yisrael Adonai Elohehu Adonai Echad—Hear O Israel, the Lord your God, the Lord is One.* While I was far from fluent in Hebrew, most of the Jewish kids in my Bar Mitzvah class would be able to read the most famous creed in Judaism—*the Shema.*

"David, it was a delight to be with you," said Aquila. I extended my hand and he shook it with a smile.

"I'm so pleased to meet you—both of you," I answered.

"We can't wait to see how God uses you in the future," added Pricilla. "Good-bye, David," and she kissed me on both cheeks and they turned and walked away into the crowd. Within seconds they were gone.

Ariel directed our attention back to the large ancient building with the Menorah. "David, this is the oldest synagogue in Europe. In fact, the oldest Jewish community in Europe was established here in Rome. It dates all the way back to the Hanukah story, when Judah Maccabee and his small army defeated the Greek Syrian King, Antiochus Epiphanies. In 161 BCE, Jason ben Eleazar and Eupolemus ben Johanan came as envoys from Judea. Over the next century and half the Jewish community grew and synagogues were built.

"Most Jewish people are not aware of it, but synagogues were not part of Judaism until after Israel was conquered by the Babylonians in 586 BCE. The Temple was destroyed. Without a Temple, sacrifices ceased and the focus moved from the Temple to the local synagogue, to the weekly meeting where the Torah would be read."

"This synagogue dates back to the first Jews who came, but was empty for those five years after the Jews were forced out of the city," Paul added.

"That began the shift toward Gentile-dominated Christianity," said Ariel, "and the beginning of replacement theology."

"What exactly is replacement theology?" I asked.

"We will have plenty of time to discuss that in detail later, but suffice it to say that it is the belief that the Church is the *new* Israel, and the Jewish people are no longer the chosen people of the Lord and the Church has replaced her. But first, we need to finish with Romans.

"Paul will be staying with us a bit longer. You have no idea how privileged we are to study the book of Romans with the author!" he said with genuine excitement.

But he was right—I did have *no idea*. A week ago I couldn't have told you very much about the apostle Paul or Rabbi Saul, as some call him, other than that he wrote some of the New Testament. I had no clue that he was a famous rabbi who persecuted Messianic Jews. But seeing how seriously Ariel took this, I understood that it was quite unique. I was pretty sure that most people didn't get to fly with angels and go back in time either. I think I was sufficiently in awe of the entire situation, even if I could not fully appreciate it.

We entered the synagogue, which was in need of some repairs. Weeds grew between the rocks in the courtyard. And inside it wasn't any better. No one had been here in some time.

"What year is it?" I asked.

"David, it is the beginning of 54 CE, just before the Jews would be allowed to return," answered Ariel. "Let's have a seat."

As the three of us sat down the entire room began to change. Our three chairs moved to a round table that came forth out of the earth. The drab atmosphere turned to a heavenly presence. The empty ark, where the Torah scrolls would have been stored, turned to beautiful marble as it increased in size. A curtain formed to cover it and then slowly opened, revealing not only a Torah scroll but more than a dozen smaller scrolls. A golden light shone from within, but there was no source—or at least none that I could see.

Our table was made of marble, but in front each of our seats built into the face of the table were computer screens. When the table was off or in sleep mode, you would not even know it was a computer. But as soon as the angel touched it, it lit up.

I looked at Ariel as if to say, *What is this?*

"Well, that old synagogue needed an upgrade for our purposes. Paul, would you like to begin?"

CHAPTER XII

Our seats at the round table were more comfortable than sitting on the ground under the tree, and the Torah scroll accompanied by a dozen smaller scrolls intrigued me. They actually appeared to be breathing, like a chest going up and down with the inhaling and exhaling of air.

"David we could study the entire book of Romans, verse by verse, but that is not our purpose," said Paul. "You will have time in the future to do your own study. For now, I want you to see the connection between the Roman believers and seedlings of replacement theology—the belief that because of Israel's rejection of the Messiah, God has eternally rejected the Jewish people, taking her calling away and giving it to another—the Church.

"Now that you understand the history—Claudius exiling the Jews of Rome and the Roman believers turning against their Jewish brothers—you can understand why I wrote the things I did. Others who don't know the context assume that I was favoring Israel above the Gentiles. But in truth I was combating the beginning of a deadly theology that would not only cause the deaths of many Jews but take the Church in an ungodly, even racist, apostate direction.

"Some think that chapters 1 through 8 are the most important, and then I just ramble on about Israel from 9 to 11. However, the issue of Israel's continued election and the responsibility of the Gentiles to reach them—not reject them—was the primary reason I wrote Romans. Notice I did not write much about this in my other letters, as this was the only congregation at the time that had embraced a form of replacement theology. In the other congregations, from Ephesus to Philippi, there was a healthy love and respect towards Israel—recognizing that, as Yeshua said, *"salvation is from the Jews"* (John 4:22).

"Let's start right in chapter 1." The table lit up and each of our screens read:

> For I am not ashamed of the gospel, because it is the power of God that brings salvation to everyone who believes: first to the Jew, then to the Gentile (Romans 1:16).

"I was not saying that Jews are better than non-Jews, but warning the Romans to not lose sight of their roots. God has an order. He chose to bring forth Messiah through Israel. Without the Jews, the Romans never would have heard of Yeshua—about salvation. It was the Jews who spread the Good News to Rome.

"Furthermore, as I share later in the book, Israel, despite her unbelief, is beloved on account of Abraham, Isaac, and Jacob—the patriarchs.

"I find it very interesting that those who are offended at God's favor on Israel seem to miss my words in chapter 2."

> There will be trouble and distress for every human being who does evil: first for the Jew, then for the Gentile; but glory, honor and peace for everyone who does good: first for the Jew, then for the Gentile. For God does not show favoritism (Romans 2:9-11).

"As the Master said—to whom much is given, much is required. Even as salvation is first for the Jews, because of the special role in history that they play, so is judgment for our disobedience. It cuts both ways."

Something didn't make sense to me. "If they claim that *all* the promises of God are now to them, why do they not claim this verse as well? If the Church has replaced Israel, then that verse that speaks of judgment being first for the Jew should really mean the Church?"

Paul laughed but added, "Amazingly, according to a very convenient theology, the curses remain with Israel. And that is not the only place where folks seem to read a few verses and then ignore the rest. In chapter 2, toward the end I speak of circumcision and the fact that circumcision is of no eternal value. I was seeking to help them see that God was not calling Gentile believers to become Jewish—that what is far more important to God is the heart, not a cut in the flesh.

"However, many use those verses to say God no longer expects Jews to fulfill the eternal covenant He made with Abraham in Genesis 17. Let's take a look:

> *Circumcision has value if you observe the law, but if you break the law, you have become as though you had not been circumcised. So then, if those who are not circumcised keep the law's requirements, will they not be regarded as though they were circumcised? The one who is not circumcised physically and yet obeys the law will condemn you who, even though you have the written code and circumcision, are a lawbreaker.*

> *A person is not a Jew who is one only outwardly, nor is circumcision merely outward and physical. No, a person is a Jew who is one inwardly; and circumcision is circumcision of the heart, by the Spirit, not by the written code. Such a person's praise is not from other people, but from God* (Romans 2:25-29).

"Well, if I may, it does *seem* like you are saying that there is no need for circumcision," I gently challenged...not because I disagreed—I was talking to Paul for goodness' sake—but to seek clarity.

"*There is no need* in regard to heaven—eternal life. I was stating, first of all, that there is no value to a non-Jew, the people to whom I was writing, in getting circumcised unless they were going to convert to Judaism and take on the whole of Torah—something Jacob made clear in Acts 15 that they did not need to do. They will obtain no special grace or favor from such an act. The covenant of circumcision had nothing to do with the Romans.

"Second, I was stating that even for a Jew, God is far more concerned with his life, his devotion, and his humility than He is with something that he encountered when he was only eight days old, something that was forced upon him. I didn't say it was worthless, but compared to what we receive through Yeshua, it pales. The cut in the flesh was an identifiable mark that revealed that someone is a member of the people of Israel. But it did not signify a heart of devotion.

"And furthermore, David, read what I wrote next!" exclaimed the apostle. "Better yet, let me read it." The apostle was full of emotion and with that emotion he read.

> *What advantage, then, is there in being a Jew, or what value is there in circumcision?* **Much in every way!** *First of all, the Jews have been entrusted with the very words of God.*
>
> *What if some were unfaithful? Will their unfaithfulness nullify God's faithfulness?* **Not at all! Let God be true, and every human being a liar** (Romans 3:1-4).

"This is why it is so important, David, never to develop a doctrine without taking the whole of Scripture into account. You cannot understand Romans 2 apart from Romans 3. I could not have been more clear.

1. To the Jew, circumcision, while not essential or even connected to salvation, was very much a part of their Hebraic calling.

2. Even in unbelief, God will honor His promise to Israel. God actually set up the covenant that way in Genesis 15. God alone made covenant with Abraham without requiring him to do the same—instead, He put him in a deep sleep. This covenant of grace enables the Master to bless Israel even if she is in unbelief.

"You see, David, unlike the New Covenant, the covenant of circumcision was not a covenant that promised eternal life. It was specifically between Abraham and his natural seed. And to this day the Master honors His promise to Israel through circumcision. The Jewish people are blessed. Despite their rejection of Yeshua from the majority—*there has always been a faithful remnant*—God continues to honor His covenant."

"You can see that evidenced everywhere," I said. "Today Israel sits on a tiny sliver of land in the Middle East. Despite being attacked by her neighbors over and over again—first by Egypt, Syria, Iraq, Jordan, and Lebanon in 1948, and then by terror organizations like the PLO, Hamas, and Hezbollah—God has honored His covenant with Israel. Outnumbered by more than hundreds of millions and surrounded by more than twenty countries who would be happy to see her driven into the sea, Israel not only has survived but thrived and is the most productive country in the Middle East in regard to science, agriculture, and medicine."

Paul smiled. "Yes, we've been keeping up with current developments in Israel.

"I'm really not so smart, but the progress of Israel since 1948 fascinates me! Think about it, David. While Jews only make up a minuscule percentage of the world's population, less than two tenths of one percent, they have won fifteen percent of all Nobel Peace Prizes. Much of the technology that the world uses today came through Jews—from voicemail to medical breakthroughs like the PillCam that is used by doctors to see inside someone's intestines. Israel has the highest ratio of university degrees to the population in the world. She has the largest number per capita of startup companies in the world. Israel's 100 billion-dollar economy is larger than all of its immediate neighbors combined. Israel is a worldwide leader in solar energy and electric cars. AOL's instant messenger, though I know it is now outdated, was developed in 1996 by four young Israelis."[1]

Very cool! Rabbi Shaul, who lived 2,000 years ago, is talking to me about AOL!

Ariel crossed his arms and lit up just a little. "Go on Paul. Don't stop now."

Paul picked up a goblet of water that had appeared on the table and took a drink. "How funny it is to listen to activists encourage people to boycott Israel, not realizing that much of the technology they use in their activism was invented by Israelis! They should get rid of their Apple computers as the flash drive was designed by an Israeli. In fact, they may need to get rid of all their computers, as many of Intel's chips, the most well-known chip producer in the world, are developed and manufactured in Israel. An Israeli created the algorithm for sending email—so they should definitely stop and go back to the oh-so-efficient postal service. And sadly, if they are willing to use a cell phone—it is very difficult to find a *juden-frei* cell phone as so much of the technology was created in Israel—they definitely should not use the newer smartphones as the chipset is Israeli."

I was smiling at this point. Paul was pretty proud of his heritage, and as he expounded on modern-day Israel, something I was abreast on, I was beginning to catch some of his fervor. He continued.

"They should delete their Facebook accounts as so many of their third-party apps were invented by Israelis. And by all means, don't use the popular WAZE GPS program—yes...Israelis. And never use Google again, as they paid one billion dollars for it!"

"Okay, I think we get the picture Paul," Ariel chimed in.

"It was even a Jew, Phillip Semmelweis," the apostle wasn't finished, "dubbed *the savior of mothers,* who discovered that if doctors simply washed their hands before delivering babies, the infant mortality rate could be reduced to one percent, saving millions of children over the past century and a half. This is simply the blessing and favor of God."

"Why then do Jews even need Yeshua if they can be so blessed simply through circumcision?" I asked.

The theologian answered, "Because while obedience to the covenant of circumcision—the purpose of which was to keep Israel as an identifiable, covenant people on earth—can bring blessing, *it cannot get rid of sin.* And sin must be punished.

"This is where many get hung up. They don't understand that God can honor two covenants at one time. The New Covenant surpasses the covenant of circumcision in every way, but that doesn't mean that it cancels it out. And part of the covenant of circumcision was God giving the land of Israel to the Jewish people as an everlasting possession."

The screen lit up and a passage appeared. Paul read again. I was sure he wanted to emphasize certain parts, so I listened carefully.

> *I will establish my covenant as an everlasting covenant between me and you and your descendants after you for the generations to come, to be your God and the God of your descendants after you. The whole land of Canaan, where you now reside as a foreigner, I will give as an everlasting possession to you and your descendants after you; and I will be their God* (Genesis 17:7-8).

"So you see, David, God who cannot lie gave what was then called Canaan to Abraham and his seed after him. And what did we need to do to inherit this land?" He read again.

> *Then God said to Abraham, "As for you, you must keep my covenant, you and your descendants after you for the generations to come. This is my covenant with you and your descendants after you, the covenant you are to keep: Every male among you shall be circumcised. You are to undergo circumcision, and it will be the sign of the covenant between me and you. For the generations to come every male among you who is eight days old must be circumcised, including those born in your household or bought with money from a foreigner— those who are not your offspring"* (Genesis 17:9-12).

"Yet still, despite these verses and scores of others, there are many in the Church world who despise Israel. Despite her miraculous rebirth, survival in the worst of conditions, surrounded by nations who want her to cease to exist—despite her prosperity and generosity to the world, there are still thousands of theologians throughout the world who refuse to believe that her reemergence is a fulfillment of prophecy. *And they even quote me!* One of the main reasons I wrote Romans was to dispel such nonsense!"

I felt I needed to reiterate what Paul said, just in summary, to be sure I was truly getting this and comprehending the Roman connection to Judaism. "So, circumcision was a covenant exclusively with the Jewish people. It didn't promise eternal life, but blessing in this life—including the land of Israel. Still, only through Yeshua can a Jew, or a non-Jew for that matter, gain eternal life?"

"Oh David, if only the Romans were as quick to understand as you! However, we are just getting started! The heart of my letter—at least the part that pertains to Israel—begins in chapter 9. I deeply wanted not only the Romans, but also believers everywhere to understand God's heart for Israel—His firstborn. I truly don't know how I penned the words. All I can say is a deep burden of intercession came over me. For quite some time I could not even speak or dictate the words. I was overcome with love and compassion for my Jewish brothers. At that moment I would have done anything to see an awakening amongst my people. However, most readers miss the emotion with which I was communicating."

"In fact," interjected Ariel, "most people envision *this* when reading the Bible." He swiped the screen, and a movie played. The scene reminded me of Alistair Cooke from *Masterpiece Theatre*. A man sat in a chair, prim and proper, and with a British accent gently quoted the passage Romans nine.

"That wasn't me, David. I was fiery and passionate."

I laughed at that. "Oh, I can imagine you were, Paul! Don't let me hold you back!"

Paul smiled at that. "I had my share of confrontations over the years. While the Lord radically changed me from the man who allowed Stephen to be stoned to death, giving me far more compassion and love than I ever knew were possible, I was still as bold as a lion and willing to confront false teaching with passion.

"When I wrote those words, I was not wearing an evening jacket, getting in some light writing before an after-dinner drink and bedtime."

"Here is a more accurate picture," said Ariel. He swiped his hand across the screen and the scene changed. It was clearly an ancient edifice. I saw three people. One was a younger man, simply sitting. Another young man was sitting at a desk of some sort with a dipping ink pen in his hand and was writing on papyrus. I recognized the paper, as I had just written on papyrus in the first session. In the middle of the room, literally on his knees, was a younger version of Paul—still older than the other two.

Ariel pressed play and the younger Paul began to cry out.

> *I speak the truth in Messiah—I am not lying, my conscience*
> *confirms it through the Holy Spirit* (Romans 9:1).

Paul is breaking down, struggling to get the next words out. But before he continues, Ariel presses pause. I looked at him with a little frustration, desperately wanting to hear what came next.

"In a minute, David; but first, do you find anything interesting about this first sentence?"

I reread the verse which was displayed at the bottom of the video and then looked at the angel with what I am sure appeared to them as a blank expression.

"Read it again please," asked Ariel.

"Okay, 'I speak the truth in Messiah—I am not lying, my conscience confirms it through the Holy Spirit.'"

Still nothing.

"Don't you find it interesting that Paul the apostle, a trained and respected rabbi, the most prolific Bible writer and congregational planter, is prefacing a statement with the words, *I am not lying*?"

"Come to think of it," I reasoned, "yeah, that does seem a bit strange. That would be like the President starting off his State of the Union Address by adding, 'Oh, by the way, I plan to tell the truth tonight.' And that takes into account that politicians *do* lie—all the time!"

"How much more our dear brother Paul here, who was writing *the Bible!* In addition to being known as an honest man, he literally was writing the word of God, and God cannot lie. So why do you think he felt the need to add this preface?"

"Well…" I was searching for words. "As a journalist, when writing I have sometimes written something close to that. Of course it was always tongue in cheek, as my readers know that I am not getting paid to lie to them. But sometimes I have to report on something so outlandish that I have to add something like, 'I am telling you the truth here' or 'This really did happen!' For instance, just before Christmas there was a man in Philadelphia who dressed up like Santa and rode a motorcycle in the freezing cold, right past the Liberty Bell, intending to blow himself up and give credit to ISIS. He was actually a lone wolf. Luckily, the FBI was tipped off and they stopped the guy, but who would believe a story like that? I guess Paul was going to say something that was hard to believe."

"Exactly. Paul was about to share something the Romans deeply needed to understand—something that they needed to *feel*. And yet it was a statement, even coming from Paul, that they might find hard to believe." He pressed play.

Paul was still on his knees in the middle of the room. He was weeping, pounding the floor. In fact he was grieving as if someone had died. He gained his composure and lifted up his head and said:

> *I have great sorrow and unceasing anguish in my heart. For I could wish that I myself were cursed and cut off from Messiah for the sake of my people, those of my own race, the people of Israel* (Romans 9:2-4).

Again he began to wail before wiping the tears away and continuing.

> *Theirs is the adoption to sonship; theirs the divine glory, the covenants, the receiving of the law, the temple worship and the promises. Theirs are the patriarchs, and from them is*

traced the human ancestry of the Messiah, who is God over all, forever praised! Amen (Romans 9:4-5).

The screen faded. I didn't know what to say. Seeing that type of emotion was intense—even embarrassing in some ways. They were both looking at me for a response. I didn't know what to say. Even though it was less than a minute of video, I felt like I had just sat the through the most intense two-hour tearjerker ever. Finally I found my voice.

"Were you saying that you were willing to perish—to go to hell—if it would mean that the Jewish people would believe in Yeshua?" I asked, incredulous.

"Indeed I was. Again, that is why I began the passage with the words, 'I am not lying.' The truth is, it was the grace of God in me speaking. In and of myself, I was selfish. That type of intercession is beyond human ability. Moses also experienced such intercession for the children of Israel. The Lord was angry with Israel, but Moses said:

> *So Moses went back to the Lord and said, "Oh, what a great sin these people have committed! They have made themselves gods of gold. But now, please forgive their sin—**but if not, then blot me out of the book you have written**"* (Exodus 32:31-32).

"Earlier in the chapter the Lord offered Moses the chance to start again with just him to create a great nation. A selfish man may have been attracted to such an offer; a typical politician would have jumped at it. But Moses took on the Lord and fought for Israel. Just read."

I did.

> *"I have seen these people," the Lord said to Moses, "and they are a stiff-necked people. Now leave me alone so that my anger may burn against them and that I may destroy them. Then I will make you into a great nation."*

But Moses sought the favor of the Lord his God. "Lord," he said, "why should your anger burn against your people, whom you brought out of Egypt with great power and a mighty hand? Why should the Egyptians say, 'It was with evil intent that he brought them out, to kill them in the mountains and to wipe them off the face of the earth'? Turn from your fierce anger; relent and do not bring disaster on your people. Remember your servants Abraham, Isaac and Israel, to whom you swore by your own self: 'I will make your descendants as numerous as the stars in the sky and I will give your descendants all this land I promised them, and it will be their inheritance forever.'" Then the Lord relented and did not bring on his people the disaster he had threatened (Exodus 32:9-14).

"This is the truest form of prayer there is," the rabbi continued, "and it moves the heart of God. However, many suppose that my love for Israel was merely because I was Jewish and therefore don't take the words as seriously as they were intended. This was not a letter to my sister! I was writing the word of God!—though I did not know it at the time. Although God worked through my personality and emotions, it was His heart for Israel I was expressing."

The room fell silent as the teacher gave the pupil time to digest. Finally, I whispered, feeling awkward for even adding my thoughts to the rabbi's emotional discourse, "And indeed, Yeshua did die for Israel several years before, proving His willingness to take their place in receiving God's judgment."

"Yes, that's right," Paul answered. "But when you speak of God's heart for Israel, all that some people hear is 'God likes the Jews better!' Yet God's heart is so much bigger than that. He can love and favor Israel as His firstborn nation and still love all the other nations He created. One of the most popular misunderstandings of the Scriptures is that God's first plan was just for Israel. However, because of Israel's sin, He is now moving among the nations.

"This is completely inconsistent with the Old Covenant. To come to this conclusion one would need to ignore scores of passages where God speaks of His heart for the nations. These passages were written hundreds of years before the first coming of the Messiah."

Ariel added, "Remember, David? We looked Psalm 67 where David asked the Lord to 'be gracious to us and bless us,' meaning Israel, 'and make His face shine on us.' Why? 'So that your ways may be known on earth, your salvation among all nations.' This little passage reveals God's plan for the nations long before Miriam gave birth to the Messiah or before Peter arrived at the home of Cornelius. His eternal plan was that God's light would shine on Israel and the nations would be drawn to that light."

Paul jumped back in. "It wasn't that God loved Israel more than any other nation, but that God's plan was to use Israel *to reach* the other nations. This is what Barnabas and I said in Acts 13 when some of my Jewish brethren were resisting the message of the Gospel." The passage appeared and I read aloud.

> *Then Paul and Barnabas answered them boldly: "We had to speak the word of God to you first. Since you reject it and do not consider yourselves worthy of eternal life, we now turn to the Gentiles. For this is what the Lord has commanded us: 'I have made you a light for the Gentiles, that you may bring salvation to the ends of the earth'"* (Acts 13:46-47).

"We were quoting Isaiah 49. The calling on Israel was to be a light for the nations. For this reason, God honors and blesses Israel—and as was our practice, we always took the message to the Jew first. Whenever we went to a new city, we would go straight to the synagogue."

I suddenly remembered how Luke showed me nearly a dozen passages during my first heavenly experience from the book of Acts, all of which emphasized Paul's custom of always going to the Jewish synagogue first when entering a new city.

"Yes, I remember Luke shared that with me last week."

"Ah, that is right. This is not your first heavenly rodeo. But getting back to my plea for Israel's salvation in chapter 9 of Romans. As I said, I was expressing God's heart for Israel to the Romans. They needed to understand the human ancestry of Messiah was through Israel—they are His brothers, and as such, the firstborn among the nations. It is only natural that it breaks the Messiah's heart that His brothers in large part have rejected Him.

"What was also heartbreaking was that these young Roman believers had been deceived in judging their Messianic Jewish brothers and were in danger of bringing judgment upon themselves. One of the primary reasons I wrote Romans was to protect them from that judgment—to give them a theology that would show them their need to honor Israel, their older brother, and in doing so protect themselves.

"They developed a theology that God had rejected Israel," Ariel interjected. "So Paul wrote in Romans 11 verses to contradict this."

"Again, David, I was not just writing to protect the Jews, but to protect the Romans from coming under judgment." The screen lit up. "Go ahead, read," encouraged the rabbi.

> *I ask then: Did God reject his people? By no means! I am an Israelite myself, a descendant of Abraham, from the tribe of Benjamin. God did not reject his people, whom he foreknew* (Romans 11:1-2).

"Well—that's pretty clear," I stated the obvious.

"I used the strongest possible language in Greek. Some translations use "God forbid." That is closer to my intention. Literally I said, "May it never be!" And I repeated it.

> *Again I ask: Did they* [Israel] *stumble so as to fall beyond recovery? Not at all! Rather, because of their* [Israel's]

transgression, salvation has come to the Gentiles to make
Israel envious (Romans 11:11).

"Through Israel's rejection, salvation came to the nations? But you said earlier that God isn't finished with Israel. But this sounds like He may be and is now focused on the nations, or the Church," I questioned.

"David, you missed the second part of the verse. Salvation came to the Gentiles through Israel's rejection *so that* Israel would be provoked to jealousy and return to the Messiah. Look at the next verses."

> *But if their* [Israel's] *transgression means riches for the world,*
> *and their loss means riches for the Gentiles,* **how much**
> **greater riches will their full inclusion bring!** *I am talking*
> *to you Gentiles. Inasmuch as I am the apostle to the Gentiles,*
> *I take pride in my ministry* **in the hope that I may somehow**
> **arouse my own people to envy and save some of them.** *For*
> *if their rejection brought reconciliation to the world,* **what**
> **will their acceptance be but life from the dead?** (Romans
> 11:12-15)

"My point, David, was simply this. Israel's rejection of the Messiah does not result in God's rejection of Israel as His chosen people. And that in the end, they will return and that will result in 'greater riches' and 'life from the dead'! There is a time coming in which the Jewish people will receive their Messiah; in fact, it has already begun. You are evidence of this."

"And my father?" I asked, still wondering if Dad had actually solidified his faith or still needed more convincing.

"Yes, *and* your father," agreed Ariel with a big smile.

Tears sprang to my eyes. I needed to know that. My first question was answered. I wondered how much time had passed on earth, and if my head was still lying across Dad's chest while I visited here. My second question lingered. More than ever, I needed to speak to him again—alive and on earth. Would God allow Dad to snap out of this coma? Would we all see him alive again, on earth? *How could anyone deny Yeshua is the Messiah if both of us testify?*

If Ariel read my thoughts, he didn't show it. In fact, he seemed more eager than ever to explain the Roman connection. "This move of God upon Israel will release blessing on the Church worldwide."

A fancy type of PowerPoint presentation popped up on the screen. I had to hand it to these guys. They varied their teaching methods and held my attention. But to be truthful, at this point I was hooked. I had to know the truth about what happened in Rome and how it changed history for Jews and Gentiles alike.

"Let me make a few points," said Paul. He stood and walked around our table and touched a button near him. A subtitle appeared on the screen with a map on the side that included Israel, the Mediterranean, Rome, and all points in between.

1. Despite Israel's rejection, God has still called Israel.

> *For the gifts and the calling of God* [to Israel] *are irrevocable* (Romans 11:29 NKJV).

"Let's start here," said Paul. "The calling of God on Israel is eternal. It cannot be removed. These are not my opinions—the theology I was sharing was nothing new, but based on Old Testament promises. In fact, in many respects New Covenant theology is merely expounding on Old Covenant theology. Promises are fulfilled, not canceled...such as the one from Jeremiah that Pricilla shared earlier."

"Right," I jumped in. "Something about only if the sun and moon stop working can God reject Israel."

"Yes! And so many more."

> *I swear by myself, declares the Lord, that because you have done this and have not withheld your son, your only son, I will surely bless you and make your descendants as numerous*

as the stars in the sky and as the sand on the seashore. Your descendants will take possession of the cities of their enemies, and through your offspring all nations on earth will be blessed, because you have obeyed me (Genesis 22:16-18).

Yet the Israelites will be like the sand on the seashore, which cannot be measured or counted. In the place where it was said to them, "You are not my people," they will be called "children of the living God" (Hosea 1:10).

"The days are coming," declares the Lord, "when I will bring my people Israel and Judah back from captivity and restore them to the land I gave their ancestors to possess," says the Lord (Jeremiah 30:3).

In that day "I will restore David's fallen shelter—I will repair its broken walls and restore its ruins—and will rebuild it as it used to be, so that they may possess the remnant of Edom and all the nations that bear my name," declares the Lord, who will do these things. "The days are coming," declares the Lord, "when the reaper will be overtaken by the plowman and the planter by the one treading grapes. New wine will drip from the mountains and flow from all the hills, and I will bring my people Israel back from exile. They will rebuild the ruined cities and live in them. They will plant vineyards and drink their wine; they will make gardens and eat their fruit. I will plant Israel in their own land, never again to be uprooted from the land I have given them," says the Lord your God (Amos 9:11-15).

"You cannot read Jeremiah 30 and 31 and not believe that God has a future for the nation of Israel. Here is just a sample," declared the angel.

Sing with joy for Jacob; shout for the foremost of the nations. Make your praises heard, and say, "Lord, save your people, the remnant of Israel." See, I will bring them from the land of the north and gather them from the ends of the earth. Among them will be the blind and the lame, expectant mothers and women in labor; a great throng will return. They will come with weeping; they will pray as I bring them back. I will lead them beside streams of water on a level path where they will not stumble, because I am Israel's father, and Ephraim is my firstborn son.

Hear the word of the Lord, you nations; proclaim it in distant coastlands: "He who scattered Israel will gather them and will watch over his flock like a shepherd." For the Lord will deliver Jacob and redeem them from the hand of those stronger than they. They will come and shout for joy on the heights of Zion; they will rejoice in the bounty of the Lord— the grain, the new wine and the olive oil, the young of the flocks and herds. They will be like a well-watered garden, and they will sorrow no more (Jeremiah 31:7-12).

Paul pointed at the last verses from Jeremiah. "In this passage God confirms Israel's call as 'foremost of the nations,' and to be clear, that is referring to God's calling on Israel to reach the nations, not God loving Israel more than other nations. He also confirms that Israel will be reestablished as a nation, which happened in 1948. He speaks of bringing Jews from the 'land of the north.'"

"Referring to the Jews of the former Soviet Union!" I eagerly added, happy to contribute something and show I was not completely ignorant.

"Right, David," Paul chuckled as if to say, *yes, we know you're not stupid.* At least they didn't offer me a treat like a dolphin at SeaWorld.

"My point, David, is that one has to choose to ignore hundreds of verses in the Bible to conclude that God is finished with natural Israel."

"So why didn't they simply read the Bible?" I quizzed.

"Remember, David? They had no Bible. The Jews took the scrolls with them during those five years that they were expelled from Rome."

"Oh—right."

"Imagine their struggle. Trying to figure out their new faith without the Word of God?"

"It is no wonder they were deceived," I added.

"As you study the New Covenant, David, you will see that I had no need to address these issues with the folks in Corinth, Ephesus, or Galatia. They already understood these truths. But I had not been to Rome and was not able to instruct the believers there. And these other cities had not only Jewish leaders in addition to non-Jews in most of the congregations, but they had access to the Word of God. Let's continue."

2. Because of Israel's rejection, salvation has come to the nations.

"Now, to be clear here, it was always God's plan to use Israel to reach the nations," shared Paul.

"Yes, we just read Psalm 67."

"And so many more verses. However, in Romans I was sharing that the rejection of the Good News by the leadership of the Jewish community forced us to share with Gentiles."

"You shared earlier that you were fulfilling a scripture?"

"Yes, Isaiah 49:6 where the prophet speaks of being a light not only to Israel, but the nations. So Israel's rejection caused salvation amongst the Gentiles. However, God did not do this so that the Church could in turn judge and attack Israel, but the opposite—point three."

3. Salvation has come to the nations to provoke Israel to jealousy (Rom. 11:11).

"God created a system of mutual dependency between Israel and the nations. Without Israel, the Gospel would never have made it to Rome, and now God wanted to use the Romans, and other Gentile believers, to reach out to the Jewish people. Sadly, this did not happen for a long time.

Romans 11 was not merely a teaching to the Romans of my day, but a prophetic plea to the Church of the future to honor her elder brother in the faith. This is God's order, and He will bless this order. However, for centuries there was only a remnant who understood this."

4. Judging Israel and the Jewish people can bring one under judgment.

"If you take a look at verses seventeen through twenty-four, I explain this clearly. I use the analogy of an olive tree. The olive tree represents the household of God—all who are saved. Many people, even those who love Israel, have difficulty explaining the olive tree. However, I am going to turn to some twenty-first century help for that. My non-Jewish brother truly gets it. But first, take a read."

A passage appeared on the screen and the map morphed into a picture of two olive trees. I began to read aloud as before:

If some of the branches have been broken off, and you, though a wild olive shoot, have been grafted in among the others and now share in the nourishing sap from the olive root, do not consider yourself to be superior to those other branches. If you do, consider this: You do not support the root, but the root supports you. You will say then, "Branches were broken off so that I could be grafted in." Granted. But they were broken off because of unbelief, and you stand by faith. Do not be arrogant, but tremble. For if God did not spare the natural branches, he will not spare you either.

Consider therefore the kindness and sternness of God: sternness to those who fell, but kindness to you, provided that you continue in his kindness. Otherwise, you also will be cut off. And if they do not persist in unbelief, they will be grafted in, for God is able to graft them in again. After all, if you were cut out of an olive tree that is wild by nature, and contrary to nature were grafted into a cultivated olive tree, how much more readily will these, the natural branches, be grafted into their own olive tree! (Romans 11:17-24)

The screen changed and a man was speaking, but his words were on the screen as well and read like a blog:

1) The Olive Tree is Spiritual, Composed of Righteous, Born-Again People.

The word the Apostle uses for commonwealth is *politeiva* (politeias), akin to the English words politics, peoplehood or nationhood. Through the blood of Israel's Messiah, we Gentiles who were once aliens, have been made *nigh* (near) to the Commonwealth of Israel, *but not identical to it*. Thus we have the figure of the Olive Tree, which I suggest is the Spiritual Commonwealth of Israel. It is spiritual, because only righteous, born-again believers are in the Olive Tree, whether Jews or Gentiles.

2) The Olive Tree is a Commonwealth, with Allegiance to the King of the Jews.

Furthermore, the Olive Tree is the *Commonwealth* of Israel, because Gentiles who have been attached (grafted in) to the Olive Tree owe allegiance to Israel's Book (the Bible), Israel's God, and Israel's Messiah. It is similar to the British Commonwealth, in which the people of Canada and Australia are not actually citizens of England, but owe allegiance to the Queen, and have a special relationship with the British people. We Gentiles who have trusted in Jesus the Messiah have a special relationship with Israel, its people and Land, and have sworn allegiance to the King of the Jews.

3) Gentile Believers have a Special Relationship with Jewish Believers.

> In addition to our special relationship to Israel, we Gentiles
> who have been grafted in to the Olive Tree by faith in Messiah
> *among the natural branches,* have a special relationship to the
> Jewish believers in Messiah, who are the natural branches.[2]

"Okay, David, there is lot to unpack here. First of all, have you ever seen an olive tree?"

"Sure, in Israel. Lisa and I were part of fundraising trip from our synagogue. We raised $50,000 to purchase bulletproof school bus windows. I remember when we visited Ariel—the city for which we bought them, far deep in the Israeli heartland—we saw massive groves of olive trees. It was beautiful and reminded me what ancient Israel must have looked like." I looked at our angel. "So you are named after that city?"

Ariel nodded. "Something like that."

Paul pressed forward with his teaching. "A wild olive tree, called an *agrielaios* in Greek, was nearly useless. It would bear little to no usable fruit. A wild olive tree means that it was uncultivated—uncared for. But, because of its massive root system, it would be difficult to uproot, and it would take time for a new olive tree to mature to the point that it would produce olives. At the earliest it would take three years and could take as long as twelve.

"However, farmers discovered that if you took a branch or a shoot from a good, cultivated olive tree—known as a *kallielaios*—you could graft that shoot into the wild olive tree and it would bear fruit.

"Yet in the example the Lord gave me, He does the impossible. In reality, if you grafted a wild olive shoot into a cultivated tree, it would not make a difference—it still would be useless. However, in this case Yeshua is the root, the life-giving source, and He, through His resurrection from the dead, changes the nature of the olive branch. Not from Jew to Gentile or Gentile to Jew, but from dead and worthless to alive in the Spirit!

"Now, I explained that some of the branches were broken off. Again, this is why the tree cannot be Israel as a nation. There are many who are part of the nation of Israel who have been broken off through rejection of Yeshua. They are still Jews, still called by God, still blessed in many ways, but cut off from the household of faith—from relationship with the Father.

"Gentiles who put their faith in Yeshua are grafted into the pure olive tree. As I said, this goes against the laws of nature. In Ephesians 2, I referred to it in three different terms,

1. The commonwealth of Israel.

2. One New Man.

3. The Household of God.

"All these are referring to the olive tree made up of Jewish and Gentiles believers, but the grafted-in branches do not become Hebrews, as our brother shared in his video—else they would be subject to circumcision, kosher laws—the entire Torah! I was clear in Romans 2 that they are not.

"Sadly, many of these Gentiles who had been grafted in began to boast against the natural branches, the Jews who had been broken off, not appreciating that their participation in the tree's nourishing sap is a complete act of grace. It was the very thing I warned them not to do in Romans 11:18. The Church father Augustine went so far as to say that the only reason God left Jews on earth is so they could see that the Church had triumphed over them.

"I begin verse twenty-five with these words, *'I do not want you to be ignorant of this mystery,'* but they ignored my plea. The relationship between Israel and the Church is a mystery, but they chose ignorance.

"It would be like children who were given a beautiful playground and—well, let's look at this one in a motion picture so that you catch the full impact of what I'm saying here."

The PowerPoint disappeared and the screen grew wider. A camera shot came in from the treetops to reveal a large park below, burgeoning with children of all sizes playing on swings, a merry-go-round, a large slide and a smaller one, and a large sandbox that held a stationary fire engine for children to climb on. Squeals of delight mingled with rays of sunlight through dark green trees above. Baby carriages were parked beside benches where mothers congregated. A man was shooting hoops with a teenage boy. Half a dozen children stood in line at the water fountain.

Immediately I thought of my own daughters. Our community park has a tire swing and it is the first thing they run to whenever we stop by for them to play.

Suddenly, I saw my girls, Emma and Sofia, on the screen!

"Hey, look at that!"

But then I noticed that something was wrong. My two daughters and several of their friends from synagogue stood outside a great fence that surrounded the park. They were able to watch the children having fun, but they seemed to be locked out. My oldest, Emma, put her face into the chain link fence and yelled, "Hey, let us in! Somebody open the gate!"

A few people looked her way, then went about their own business, ignoring their plea to get inside.

One of the mothers got up and opened the gate to let in another mom with a stroller and a toddler. My daughters ran to the gate, but the mother closed it before the girls and their friends could get in. The toddler darted ahead as the mothers walked arm in arm to the park bench.

I shifted in my seat. This movie was starting to bother me.

Emma and Sofia banged on the gate, but it was as though the adults in the park could not even hear them. All the noise caught the attention of a few children on the merry-go-round.

"Hey look, the 'Crikeys' want in!" *Crikey* is a slur against Jews and is short for "Christ killer."

A few of the children laughed at that. "No Crikeys allowed," an older boy scoffed.

I jumped to my feet, appalled by the boys' accusations. "That's flat out bullying!" I yelled. "Why aren't the parents stopping that?"

The camera pulled back to show the entire playground. This time it revealed the large sign out front—Jewish Heritage Park.

The movie dimmed.

"You've got to be kidding," I mumbled as I took my seat again. I was more than riled at the way my children were treated in this movie, and then to see that park sign made my blood boil. It was actually *their* park.

Ariel spoke gently. "Using this example we can see that God desired that the children who had been freely given the playground not taunt the others, but invite them in to play. The playground was, after all, built for Jewish children. That 'park' or Church built by God was given to the Gentiles in hopes that it would make Israel envious, or provoke her to jealousy."

I looked over at Ariel and Paul, as my emotions slowly caught up to the truth presented. "But instead many in the Church attacked the natural branches of the olive tree—both the ones that had been broken off because of unbelief and those who believed and were still part of the tree."

Paul nodded. "Right. And as we will learn later, the traditional Jews were attacked at times in the most heinous ways. Under the direction of the Holy Spirit I warned the Romans that this could be disastrous."

I opened my mouth and words came out, "*Do not be arrogant, but tremble. For if God did not spare the natural branches, he will not spare you either.*" At least here, in this pristine environment, I could recall almost everything I learned so far.

"Exactly!" exclaimed Paul. "That is what I was trying to get them to see. By judging Israel, they were bringing judgment upon themselves. If God could break off the natural braches, how much easier could He remove the wild olive shoots?

"Can you quote the next verse?" asked the rabbi.

It was a gift given for this teaching session, I was sure, but I was able to quote the verse. I knew what it said—in my heart. "*Consider therefore the kindness and sternness of God: sternness to those who fell, but kindness to you, provided that you continue in his kindness. Otherwise, you also will be cut off.*"

"The Romans had received the free gift of God, but were not 'continuing in His kindness' toward Israel."[3]

"So they would be cut off?" I asked.

"Yes and no," replied Paul. "God will not take away the salvation of another, but when we enter into judgment, we limit the grace of God in our lives. In this case, the Roman Church, which began with such power, continued to move away from Scripture until the end result was almost unrecognizable from the New Testament congregation."

"So God did not leave them," I shared. "They left God."

"And the Scriptures," added Paul, "in exchange for the traditions of men. In chapter 2 I laid out the Law of Judgment."

A passage appeared and I read.

> *You, therefore, have no excuse, you who pass judgment on someone else, for at whatever point you judge another, you are condemning yourself, because you who pass judgment do the same things* (Romans 2:1).

"When you judge someone, whether it is between two people or two groups, you bring judgment on yourself."

"Sort of like that old saying, that if you're pointing at me to accuse me, remember three fingers are pointing back at yourself," I put in.

"Exactly," said Paul. "Most often we are guilty of the same things that we are judging others of doing. In this case you had an entire community pass judgment on the Jewish people. They judged Israel for being a dead religion of traditions and for seeking justification in their own deeds—a works-based righteousness. I warned them that such treatment of Israel could result in them being cut off as well. And over time, that is what happened."

"What do you mean?" I asked.

"Where did this controversy take place?" Paul asked.

"Rome?"

"Right! Not in Ephesus or Philippi, but in Rome. And where was the worldwide headquarters of the Church established?"

"Vatican City, also Rome."

"And what became of this Church?"

"I am not sure."

"Of course you are not; you are just beginning in your journey. But as you will read the New Covenant, you will not see it full of rote traditions. The focus is on intimacy with God—a personal relationship and experience. When that is lacking, we turn to religion for comfort."

"Let's take a closer look, David," said Ariel. I had almost forgotten he was there. And without notice, we were in the air.

CHAPTER XIII

As we descended, I saw the outside of a beautiful, enormous building. Steps surrounded by long monolithic columns led to a large front entrance. Tourists in blue jeans and jackets huddled around statues and busts of famous Romans. We passed a bust of a young man against the outer wall. The plate on the wall read, "Emperor Augustus."

As we descended, it was clear we were going to crash into the roof of the building. I had enough experience thus far to know that Ariel had things under control, but as we got closer I closed my eyes and braced for impact. No crash—no boom. We passed right through the roof. *Of course.*

We were transported directly into the interior of this huge church packed with tourists—obviously the twenty-first century. There were no seats. People mingled, toured, and snapped selfies. The edifice was astounding. The entire arched ceiling was painted, and each work of art was trimmed in elaborate gold framework. This was a modern-day church, but it wasn't in the U.S., that was for sure. It took me a moment to get oriented to these surroundings. When I did, I realized that I had been here before. It was the Vatican. We were inside St. Peter's Basilica, the main church structure in the Vatican and the holiest Catholic shrine.

Ancient Statue in the Vatican Museum—Emperor Augustus, Rome

It was good to be on my feet for a while. We stood beside a beam near the wall that reached high into the painted ceiling arches while Paul and Ariel were about to explain the important and noteworthy religious events in prehistoric and modern times. Quite a classroom!

"We are in Rome, but you know that," said Ariel. "Several times a day they hold *mass* here. While mass refers to the Eucharist—what I called the Lord's Supper—today it can refer to a Catholic liturgical service. In the same way that they meet in your synagogue three times a day for unspontaneous, rote prayer, reading in a language they don't understand, praying prayers that others wrote, chanting them in repetition, Catholics celebrate mass."

I'd never compared synagogue to mass, but I guess Ariel had a point.

"In Catholicism the Eucharist is thought to be the actual body and blood of the Messiah—which it isn't. This tradition has become for them the source and summit of their devotional life. Traditions are meant to be symbols representing a greater reality. When the tradition itself replaces that which it symbolizes, your devotion—if it can be called that—leads to mere superstition. Superstition is when we do something, whether celebrating the mass or wearing your lucky tie, in order to get some type of good fortune or spiritual favor—without any real relationship with the source of good fortune."

Paul's assessment on tradition made sense. "It's no different than people going to the Western Wall in Jerusalem and writing a prayer and inserting it between the cracks, right?" I asked.

"That's right," Paul answered, a big smile on his face. "Now, that Wall is amazing because of what it represents—proof of a Jewish Temple and the history of Israel. But those stones are no more anointed than any others.

"In Israel today, thousands flock to the graves of dead rabbis, seeking spiritual power. But it is mere hysteria and emotion. Heck, they built a massive church over my grave and millions come to see it every year. But my bones do not release spiritual blessings. They are just dead."

That was a creepy thought. I'm talking to a rabbi whose bones are still under the ground. Before I could ask how all that works, Ariel interrupted.

"Take a look at this scene, David." He snapped his finger and suddenly we were in another church crowded with twenty-first century tourists, many of them lighting candles while others wept over a statue. "We are in the Church of the Holy Sepulchre, where supposedly the Messiah was crucified and buried."

A huge line wrapped around something people were waiting to see. Even though this was modern times, it was all foreign to me. I'd never seen this place before. A conservative Jew doesn't exactly seek out churches when touring Israel.

"They light candles to receive blessing. It's a racket if you are in the candle business. There is even a website—for a price, they will light a candle for you at this church. Read."

While we were hovering a hologram of the website appeared in front of me.

> For the affordable price of just $14.99, we will light a candle on your behalf in the Church of the Holy Sepulchre and place your prayer on the Stone of Anointing. All candles are lit on the day following your request. To commemorate the occasion, we will send you, via email, the photos of the actual candle which was lit on your behalf and the photo of the prayer being placed on the Stone of Anointing.

"What is the Stone of Anointing?" I asked.

"It is thought to be the stone where the Messiah's body was laid after he died. The people in line there are waiting to see another stone, supposedly the one that blocked the tomb. Again, there is nothing wrong with wanting to see such things for historical value, but when you think these things can bring you power, you stray.

"In the same way that you enjoy your daughters, God our Father seeks relationship with His children," Paul said again. "Imagine if your daughters' devotion to you was expressed in repetitive tradition rather than intimate relationship. What if instead of talking to you, they lit candles for you?"

"I'd call that strange."

"Right," said Paul, "It is not a relationship."

"One question. I can't tell you who it was or when it happened, but I do remember a story from the Hebrew Scriptures about the bones of dead prophet bringing someone back to life."

"Indeed they did," said Paul. "It was the bones of Elisha the prophet. And I am glad you brought that up. We can find the story in Second Kings 13. In fact, it can be narrowed down to one verse, verse twenty-one. The Israelites were burying a man when suddenly they came under attack from raiders. They threw the dead man's body in Elisha's tomb, and when the dead body touched against Elisha's bones, the man came back to life."

Ariel broke in. "That is what we see, but do you know what we *don't* see?"

"What?"

"They didn't set up a business for the sick to come to Elisha's bones or make a doctrine that said touching the bones of dead prophets will bring the dead back to life," said Paul. "People didn't start making pilgrimages to touch Elisha's bones. In fact, Elisha was not there. His body has been decomposed. The *real* Elisha was already with the Lord. This was God's way of reassuring the people that despite Elisha's death, He was still with them. Notice that the men were not particularly brave, throwing their dead friend in a tomb, and then they sought to 'get out of Dodge' as you say in America. They knew the Lord *through* the prophet. He was their security. God was saying, 'I am what is important, and I am always here.'

"There is no example in Scripture where we are encouraged to visit graves of prophets or saints who have passed in order to get spiritual power. The Lord wants us to come to Him directly," Paul concluded.

Ariel snapped his fingers and we were in a modern-day Roman church hovering above the crowds.

A priest entered with another man. A young man dressed in white followed them with a large cross. This was jarring for me. As a Jew, the cross was never about Yeshua, but a reminder of the Crusades and the

Inquisitions. Another young boy walked with them carrying some kind of metal censer suspended from chains.

"That is a *thurible* for burning incense," whispered Ariel.

The priest made the sign of the cross, just like many baseball players do before they bat. Then the priest said, "In the name of the Father, and of the Son, and of the Holy Spirit." And the people responded, "Amen." The priest then said, "The grace of our Lord Jesus Christ, and the love of God, and the communion of the Holy Spirit be with you all."

The people responded, "And with your spirit."

"Brethren, let us acknowledge our sins, and so prepare ourselves to celebrate the sacred mysteries."

The people responded in unison: "I confess to almighty God and to you, my brothers and sisters, that I have greatly sinned, in my thoughts and in my words, in what I have done and in what I have failed to do." Then, striking their chests, they all repeated, "Through my fault, through my fault, through my most grievous fault; therefore I ask blessed Mary ever-Virgin, all the angels and saints, and you, my brothers and sisters, to pray for me to the Lord our God."

The priest then pronounced over them, "May almighty God have mercy on us, forgive us our sins, and bring us to everlasting life."

After this there were some readings and lots of repeating. Everything was scripted. It was completely foreign to me and yet in so many ways like traditional Judaism.

"You see, David," Paul shared, "the Roman church became the very thing it supposedly despised—a religion of lifeless traditions and works-based righteousness."

"What is a works-based righteousness?"

"It is believing that you can obtain God's favor based on your good deeds. Both Judaism and Catholicism teach this. *Officially* Catholicism affirms that salvation is through the sacrifice of Yeshua on the tree, but that is not how it has been practiced. The focus in a typical Catholic mass is on form, not intimacy—on performance, not personal connection. In addition, just like in traditional Judaism, much has been added."

Ariel jumped in, "For instance, David, new theologies like purgatory were invented."

"I've heard of purgatory but don't know much about it."

"Purgatory," Ariel continued, "according to Catholic Church doctrine, is an intermediate state after physical death in which those destined for heaven undergo purification to achieve the holiness necessary to enter the joy of heaven. Only those who die in the state of grace, but have not in life reached a sufficient level of holiness, can be in purgatory, and therefore no one in purgatory will remain forever in that state or go to hell."[1]

"Is this place real?"

"The better question," said the angel, "would be, 'Does the Bible speak about this place?' And the answer is *no*. There is not even a hint of this purgatory in the Tanakh or New Covenant. Its roots are in medieval Christian theology and led to many abuses in the Church."

"How could theology lead to abuse?" I quizzed.

Paul answered, "Remember that church members and even many priests were not allowed to read the Bible. This way popes and bishops could tell the people what they were supposed to believe. In fact, without purgatory, this building would not have been built. It was taught that one of the ways to escape purgatory or decrease one's time there was through something called indulgences. Indulgences are the Catholic version of the Jewish mitzvah."

"A mitzvah is a good deed," I put in. "Not a bad thing."

"Yes, but when you think about it, it is a good deed that is done in the hopes of gaining some divine favor. When in fact, all the favor we would ever possibly acquire or need was obtained when Yeshua died for us. There is nothing more we can do to please God. This is the difference between faith and religion. Religion, through guilt, imposes upon the adherent to do religious 'stuff,' if you will, in order to please God. Many do these things, both Jews and Catholics, without any real devotion to God."

"In Israel," I jumped in, "when Lisa and I were there, religious Jews went from store to store on a holiday asking people to put on *telfillin*.[2] Of course they expect a donation. They believe that by getting someone to put on *telfillin*, they will receive a blessing. The person they are urging to put them on may be an atheist, but it doesn't matter."

"Right, and in the same way Catholics observe many traditions that have nothing to do with true devotion, but are rooted in fear and guilt," shared the angel.

"So how did indulgences get St. Peter's Basilica built?" I asked.

"During the 1500s," Paul shared, "the Church sought to rebuild this structure. However, it was quite expensive. So church leaders decided to sell indulgences in order to raise money. Madison Avenue could not have come up with a better marketing plan. Playing upon the fears of those whose dead relatives were supposedly suffering in purgatory opened the floodgates. Donations poured in."

Ariel added, "During those times it was said, 'As soon as the money clinks into the money chest, the soul flies out of purgatory.' But the truth is that the Scriptures teach that it is *appointed unto men once to die, but after this the judgment*' (Heb. 9:27 KJV). And Daniel wrote *'Multitudes who sleep in the dust of the earth will awake: some to everlasting life, others to shame and everlasting contempt'* (Dan. 12:2). Yeshua paid the price for sin—to suggest that our suffering in purgatory opens the way to heaven minimizes the once-for-all-sin, for-all-time sacrifice of Yeshua."

"To be fair," Paul interrupted, "these were abuses of the doctrine of indulgences. Indulgences are actually meant to shorten the time of temporal punishment for sins that have already been forgiven. In Catholicism, while forgiveness is granted to the sinner, you still must be punished. And the Church has the authority to prescribe such punishment. Indulgences could lessen the severity of that punishment. So even if there weren't any abuses of this doctrine, in their purest form, we find nothing in the Bible about leaders in churches prescribing punishment to its members for sins that have been forgiven. Yes, sin has a price and even forgiven people may suffer for their mistakes, but not at the hands of the Church—not from the prescription of a priest.

"And despite so many unbiblical teachings, there are many in the Catholic Church who love and know the Messiah. I brought you here not to mock them, but to show you how the Roman Church became the very thing it judged."

I thought about that. "Like you said, in the same way that traditional Judaism is built upon so many extra-biblical customs—"

"The *traditions of the elders* the Master called them," Paul interrupted me, and he would know, having been raised as a Pharisee.

"Right, the *oral law*. Well, in the same way, Catholicism took the New Testament and built upon it many traditions that can't be found in the Bible."

"In fact, David," Ariel chimed in, "in the same way that Judaism believes in an oral tradition passed down from Moses, Catholicism also believes in traditions passed down from the apostles or the bishops that have the same authority as Scripture. Thus, popes and chief rabbis can manipulate the religion for their own purposes. In fact, you can find this propensity in many religions. Most people don't know it, but in addition to the Koran, Islam has an oral tradition called the *Hadith*."

"And these traditions are given the weight of Scripture?" I asked.

"Sometimes more!" Paul answered, "Even as the Talmud says that a majority of rabbis can overrule God Himself,[3] the Pope has been given authority by the Church, not God, to make binding rulings regarding doctrine, known as *Ex Cathedra*—even if it goes against Scripture. They wrongly believe that when the Pope makes a ruling on issues of doctrine, he is one hundred percent guided by the Holy Spirit—he is infallible."

All of this had a familiar ring to me. "It's just like you taught before, Ariel. When the Catholic Church changed the Sabbath from Saturday to Sunday, they taught their people that Yeshua Himself has given them authority to do so."

"Good memory, David. That is from *The Convert's Catechism for Catholic Doctrine*. And that is a good example of the Church making a ruling that is unscriptural."

"So the Roman church judged Israel, and over the centuries became the very thing she judged!"

Ariel nodded. "I'm afraid so. Walk into just about any Catholic church or Jewish synagogue and you will find a scripted service, full of tradition and lacking in power. As my dear brother here wrote about those who would have '*a form of godliness but denying its power*'" (2 Tim. 3:5).

I shook my head. This was a lot to take in, and I knew that there was no way I could comprehend and retain all of this when I returned to earth unless God gave me supernatural help. Still, it all made sense so far.

"Let's head back to the classroom," Ariel said.

I blinked and we were standing beside the desks again, the large screen before us.

CHAPTER XIV

"Sit down, David," Ariel said, pointing to his usual chair.

Paul sat beside me this time, and Ariel pulled up a chair that was shaped like an earthly school desk chair, but padded with soft gold. He turned the chair around and sat down on it backward, leaning on the back rest. "Paul, do you want to introduce this segment?"

Paul nodded. "I'd be delighted." Paul turned to me. "David, God's desire was to use the Gentile believers to reach Israel as I shared in Romans 11:11. But as we will see shortly, it didn't go that way. While we nipped the Roman problem in the bud temporarily, it came back with a vengeance. After the New Testament Scriptures were finished, some had difficulty reconciling the God of the Jews with what many called 'the Old Testament God' and Yeshua. Some even began to say they were two different Gods altogether."

Ariel gestured to the large screen and a man appeared. Underneath his picture: "Marcion of Sinope, c. 85–c. 160."

"Marcion was the son of the bishop of Sinope, a Turkish coastal city. He was not only a ship owner but a theologian. While he was excommunicated in 140 CE, his writings were well read. He claimed the Old Covenant Scriptures were not inspired—he rejected the Hebrew Bible."

I'd not heard of Marcion before, so this was all new material to me.

"Interestingly enough, Marcion embraced my epistles—one of which so clearly says, *'All Scripture is God-breathed and is useful for teaching, rebuking, correcting and training in righteousness'* (2 Tim. 3:16). Since much of the New Testament had not been written, clearly I was referring to the Torah, the Prophets, and the Writings—the Hebrew Scriptures."

Paul threw his hands in the air as if to say, *Can you believe this guy!*

"Furthermore," he said, "I use the Hebrew Scriptures in so many of my writings to confirm the New Covenant writings that it is amazing that he could have come to think that I embraced such a position. Let me say it again—just about all the theology we find in the New Testament we can find in the Old Testament. Some of it is clearer than others, but the seeds can be found in prophecy and prophetic acts.

"For instance, Yeshua's death and resurrection is foretold in Isaiah 53. The outpouring of the Spirit was foretold by the prophet Joel, and immersion in water is depicted in the crossing of the Red Sea."

"But they didn't get wet!" I blurted out without thinking, assuming, maybe, I had stumped the theologian.

Paul looked at me confused.

"I mean, in immersion you get wet because of the water, while in the Red Sea they walked through on dry ground."

Amused at my *hutzpah*, Paul shot back, "The symbolism was not the water of the Red Sea, but leaving Egypt—slavery—and going to the Promised Land. In the same way, New Testament immersion is the act of leaving the slavery of sin, the old man, for new life in Yeshua."

"Okay—that makes sense," I said with a smile, feeling a little foolish and yet bold for challenging Paul.

"And of course the doctrine of the Messiah to judge the nations and set up His kingdom in Jerusalem is well established in the *Tanakh*—just look to Daniel and Zechariah.[1] We can even see shades of the Lord's Supper in the eating of unleavened bread and the blood of the Lamb during that first Passover."

A short clip of Jews eating bread and lamb on that first Passover appeared on the screen.

"The Spring Feasts, Passover, Firstfruits,[2] and Shavuot point clearly to Yeshua's death, resurrection, and the outpouring of the Holy Spirit on the first Kehila in Jerusalem."

Pictures of each feast or holy day flashed on the screen as Paul spoke. I learned most of this as a boy when preparing for my bar mitzvah. Dad drilled these things into me. He wasn't going to let me get bar mitzvahed completely ignorant of why I was being bar mitzvahed.

Paul tapped the button on his desk each time he mentioned a new feast.

"David, you can see that the Fall Feast, the Feast of Trumpets, the Day of Atonement, and the Feast of Tabernacles all point to Lord returning at the sound of the Shofar."

A large angel with a shofar appeared and blew his horn into the heavens, a signal of Messiah's return. I was fascinated as another shofar and then another blew until many musicians in robes of white lifted a golden shofar to the sky, all echoing the mighty blast of the first. It was quite a sight!

Paul continued. "The Lord will return at the sound of the shofar, then we will enter the time of the judgment of the nations and setting up of His kingdom, whereby all nations will come to Jerusalem to worship Him." (See Zechariah 14:16.) "The great mystery of the congregation of Jews and Gentiles being formed into One New Man can be scene clearly in the Hebrew Scriptures. Isaiah speaks of the inclusion of the Gentiles."

> *I revealed myself to those who did not ask for me; I was found by those who did not seek me. To a nation that did not call on my name, I said, "Here am I, here am I"* (Isaiah 65:1).

"James quotes Amos 9:11-12 when speaking of the body of believers. In Isaiah 42 and 49 it is clear that Israel is to be a light for the nations. Through Isaiah, the Lord says that it is not enough for Israel to serve Him, but that salvation must go to the ends of the earth." (See Isaiah 49:6-7.) "And of course Abraham was called both to birth a nation and, through faith, to be the father of many nations."

The screen changed to a midnight blue sky. Abraham stood at the top of the universe and from his torso flew multitudes of stars! Some stars flew into the shape of the geographical map of Israel. Other stars flew together to form the outline of other nations of the earth, some ancient and some new. I watched, fascinated as the stars kept multiplying endlessly out of Abraham's "bosom" and flew into one another until each fit perfectly, like a large world map made of lights.

"Fascinating!"

Paul smiled. "It truly is fascinating, David. And there is a New Covenant correlation to this promise. The call to go to all nations and make disciples can be seen in these very same verses, not to mention that many of the psalms that you already read speak of God's desire that all nations worship Him."

"You see, the New Covenant is not new information but an inspired commentary of the Old Covenant—deeper and clearer revelation of that which was already revealed in a dimmer light. The New Covenant stands on the foundation of the Hebrew Scriptures. Without the Hebrew Scriptures, how would we know that the virgin birth was significant or that the Messiah would be born in Bethlehem?" (See Isaiah 7:14; Micah 5:2.)

"Marcion was labeled a heretic for rejecting the Old Covenant—and rightly so—but others who are championed today came up with theologies that equally sidelined the nation of Israel. Seeds of Marcion made their way into the theology of many early Church fathers. You can see the fruit of their labors today." He looked to the angel and said, "Ariel?"

On cue, Ariel pressed a button and a graphic of an ancient Greek manuscript appeared on the screen. It was in English, but a very flowery presentation and lots of Roman numerals.

"What it is this?"

As the angel answered, he threw me a mouse-type remote. I caught it. "David, this is the original copy of the King James Version, one of the earliest English translations and certainly the most popular of those. The translators added chapter summaries before most chapters. In modern editions they have been changed or removed. However, I want you to take a look at a few of these."

"What do I do?"

"I will give a chapter and you can look at it using your clicker and the drop-down menus above each page on the screen. You will notice that it is already on the first passage."

"Eh...Chapter XLV...I am not very good with Roman numerals, I have to confess—except when it comes to the Super Bowl!"

Paul looked perplexed at the mention of the Super Bowl—I guess some modern things they know and some they don't. The angel smiled and simply said, "Look above on the drop-down menu."

"Ah, okay, Isaiah 45."

"Now read the preface."

"God calleth Cyrus for His Church's sake."

"Do you know who Cyrus was?"

I had been given a supernatural ability to remember what I was being taught, but I didn't know *what I didn't know.* "Sorry, no. Who was he?"

"He was the King of Persia, also known as Cyrus the Great. What many people don't know is that this prophecy was given some one hundred and fifty years before Cyrus came to power or was even born. I am digressing from my point a little, because this is one of the more powerful prophecies in Israel's history. Read the last verse of chapter 44 and a couple verses of 45."

I started to read, "That saith of Cyrus, He is my shepheard, and shall performe all my pleasure, euen saying to Ierusalem...eh..."

"Sorry, David...click the menu that says *version* and chose NIV. Understand, it is the Lord who is speaking."

I continued in a more *comfortable* form of English.

> *Who says of Cyrus, "He is my shepherd and will accomplish all that I please; he will say of Jerusalem, 'Let it be rebuilt,' and of the temple, 'Let its foundations be laid'"* (Isaiah 44:28).

> *To Cyrus, whose right hand I take hold of...for the sake of Jacob my servant, of Israel my chosen...I will raise up Cyrus*

in my righteousness: I will make all his ways straight. He will rebuild my city and set my exiles free, but not for a price or reward, says the Lord Almighty" (Isaiah 45:1,4,13).

"A century and a half later, after Israel and Judah had been exiled, Cyrus the Great granted Nehemiah permission to go back to Jerusalem and rebuild the walls of the city and the city itself."

"That is amazing!" I exclaimed.

"Now read the chapter heading again, but go back to the original King James."

After few clicks, I was back. "Okay, eh, 'God calleth Cyrus for His Church's sake.'"

"Something strange about that?" quizzed Ariel.

"Well, yeah," I answered thoughtfully. "This was written long before the Church, before the New Testament. The prophet is speaking of the Jewish people—Israel. In fact, the fulfillment, like you said happened one hundred and fifty years later, was still long before the Church emerged onto the scene."

"Right, well these folks believed that the Church has always been present. And that Israel was the Church. So when they see these prophecies about Israel—to them it is the Church."

"Of course this is easily disprovable," interjected Paul. "I wrote in Ephesians that God was taking both Jews and Gentiles and making something new—the One New Man. Emphasis on the word *new*. Israel is not the Church, as many Jews are not believers, and the Church is not Israel, as the majority of believers are not of Jewish decent."

Ariel continued, "Others would agree that ancient Israel was not the Church, but still, they teach that all the promises of God that were once to Israel are now to the Church. Let's keep reading some of these headings. Go to chapter 30 and read what is says before verse eighteen."

I clicked over to 30 and read.

"God's mercies toward His Church."

"It is a wonderful promise to Israel, a promise of restoration, but mentions nothing of the Church. Now go to chapter 34 and read the heading."

"'The iudgements wherewith God reuengeth His Church.' I assume that word is *revenge*?"

"Correct, genius," the angel toyed with me, "but the passage is about God defending Zion and judging the nations. Isaiah 41 and 43 are two of the most powerful chapters in the Old Covenant regarding God's love for Israel and His promises to protect and restore her. Yet the headings read, 'God speaks of His merciful providence in regard to His *Church*,' and 'The Lord comforts the *Church* with His promises.'

"I am not done. Isaiah 52 is full of beautiful promises to Israel, yet the original King James heading is, 'The *Church* is roused with God's promise of free redemption.' Isaiah 60, which speaks of things happening today! In verses nine and ten it speaks of foreigners bringing the Jews back to Israel and even helping with her restoration. Just in the past few decades, Gentile believers have donated millions of dollars to bring the Jews from the former Soviet Union back to Israel. And millions more have been given to strengthen the Jewish nation, just as the prophecy says. Yet they wrote 'Glory of the *Church* in the abundant access of the Gentiles.'"

"This is crazy!"

"Oh, but I have saved the best for last! Go to chapter 65 and read."

"The calling of the Gentiles. The Jews, for their incredulity, idolatry and hypocrisies, are rejected."

"Ha! So suddenly Israel has reappeared. The Jews, by the mercy of these translators," Ariel was fired up, "have graciously been allowed back into their own prophecy—but only when things get dicey. So, as long as the promises were of new wine, restoration, free iPhones, it was to the Church. But the moment it turns to judgment, suddenly *Israel* no longer means the Church, but the Jews."

Paul jumped in, "In fact, some of the early proponents of replacement theology were very clear in stating that the Church gets the blessings, while Israel is strapped with the curses!"

"What's more, this passage presents a challenge to those who believe that all those promises are not to Israel but to the Church. He begins it with the verse that Paul quoted a few minutes ago that points to the fact that Gentiles will be included in the kingdom of God.

> *I revealed myself to those who did not ask for me; I was found by those who did not seek me. To a nation that did not call on my name, I said, "Here am I, here am I"* (Isaiah 65:1).

"So which is it?" The angel continued. "It can't be both. Is the Church these Gentiles who will be included or is the Church Israel?

"And to be clear, David, Israel makes it apparent that while many Jews will fall away, a remnant, even as the Church is made up of a remnant of all nations, will believe."

> *As when juice is still found in a cluster of grapes and people say, "Don't destroy it, there is still a blessing in it," so will I do in behalf of my servants; I will not destroy them all. I will bring forth descendants from Jacob, and from Judah those who will possess my mountains; my chosen people will inherit them, and there will my servants live* (Isaiah 65:8-9).

"Isaiah 49:18 is another tricky one. The heading there is "The ample restoration of the Church," but the prophecy of restoration is clearly regarding natural Israel. Click over to verse twenty-two."

I did and read aloud in the modern version:

> *This is what the Sovereign Lord says: "See, I will beckon to the nations, I will lift up my banner to the peoples; they will bring your sons in their arms and carry your daughters on their hips"* (Isaiah 49:22).

"Okay, the Church is made up of the nations, but the Lord says here that the nations 'will bring your sons in their arms and carry your daughters on their hips.' According to replacement theology, the *sons* and *daughters* are a reference to the Church's restoration. So then, who are these nations that help restore the Church? Atheists, pagans?"

"Maybe Martians!?" I joked.

We laughed, but understood his point. "It seems to me that you have to read a lot into it to conclude that the sons and daughters being restored are not Jews. If you take the passage at face value, there can be no argument. It is referring to the restoration of Israel."

"Right, David," said Ariel. "And as we shared earlier, the passages are coming to pass in your lifetime regarding Israel. You have to ignore history to have any other conclusion.

"We could go on and on. There are so many examples. But I think you understand our point. By the time the King James Version was translated, your average Christian was trained to see *Church* in place of the word *Israel* in the Old Testament."

"Unless it was a curse," I added. "It's tough being Jewish. It is one thing to steal the promises to Israel, but couldn't these kind folks take the curses too?" I said half joking. "It reminds of that scene in *Fiddler on the Roof*, where Tevye the milkman says," and I feigned a Yiddish accent, *"I know, I know—we are Your chosen people. But, once in a while, can't You choose someone else?"*

CHAPTER XV

D avid," Paul took over, "these teachings did not begin with the translators of the King James Bible, but with the replacement theology that had been the dominant view for centuries. While Marcion was a heretic, many other leaders embraced a theology that did not do away with the God of Israel or the Old Covenant, but merely taught that God had rejected Israel—cast her away—in favor of the Church.

"It was easy to assume that after the destruction of Judea. First in 70 CE, the Temple, the center of Jewish life, was destroyed by the Romans; then later, after the 135 CE revolt, all Jews were forced to leave Israel. Yeshua Himself foretold this judgment, but many Gentile believers did not see this as temporary, but permanent. One reason why there are so many promises of Israel's restoration in the Old Covenant is to reassure the Jewish people and to convince the Church that God still had a plan for Abraham's natural seed.

"As I wrote to the Romans, the natural branches of the olive tree—Israel—can be grafted back in. But these words fell on deaf ears. It didn't help that in a second revolt in 135 CE Rabbi Akiva, the most honored rabbi of his day, proclaimed Simon Bar Kokhba to be the Messiah. He was a military leader and considered Jewish believers his enemy, as they would not embrace his claim to be the Messiah."

Of course, I never heard of any of this previously. Who knew? I was horrified that even after God gave His Son, Yeshua, to save the nation of Israel, the Jews, and even the Gentiles, every attempt was made to thwart that original plan. Decade after decade some new thought or new person arose to the forefront to contradict God's original words. It seemed someone was always waiting, ready, and willing to contaminate God's intention to provide His Son's death and suffering as the atonement for our sins. And here I was, living a quiet life in the twenty-first century with my family, thinking that I had the highest and best truth. Yet we'd embraced so many lies! Something inside me quickened, a resolve mingled with fire.

I thought, *Somebody needs to do something about all this.*

Instantly I heard in my heart, *Why don't you do something, David?*

I looked up. I wondered if Ariel or even Paul heard that.

Paul was eagerly going on and on, teaching his heart out, but he paused when he noticed I was not tracking with his teaching at the moment.

"Did I lose you, David?" he asked kindly.

I shook my head. "No. Perhaps you gained me."

Paul's eyebrows winged upward. "That could only mean that the teacher of *all* teachers is speaking to you."

I nodded. "He is. Please, go on."

Paul smiled at that and clicked on a series of chronological pictures that showed the slow demise of Jewish faith. "After the crushing of the Bar Kochba rebellion in 135 CE, Christians all around the Roman empire were further convinced that God had rejected Israel forever. The Christians of his time took notice of the false claim and *the defeat confirmed it:* God was finished with Israel.

"At the time, the growing Church found itself in competition with the synagogue. In those days, Judaism was an outreach-oriented religion. Unlike today, the synagogue aggressively sought converts. The growing Church was a threat. And the synagogue was a threat to the Church. Believers could easily refute pagan religions, but it was trickier with Judaism. They shared the same Bible and the same God."

I couldn't picture my dad or even Rabbi Goodman proselytizing door to door or on radio and television shows to gain Jewish converts. "But the believers had the New Testament as well, right?"

"Yes and no. The books of the New Testament had all been written, but they were still not held in as high regard as the Old Covenant. The Hebrew Scriptures had been around for centuries, while the books of the

New Testament were still young. In fact, there were many more books and epistles written that didn't make it into the New Covenant. During the years following the Bar Kokhba defeat, the New Covenant began to grow in esteem. It was Marcion who first came with a New Covenant in 140s CE. He included most of my writings, albeit edited, and the Gospel of Luke.

"While he was excommunicated, others saw the need for an authoritative New Testament. Over the next decades, the New Covenant as we know it came into being. So at the time of the Bar Kokhba revolt, the synagogue and the Church relied on the same writings—the Hebrew Scriptures.

"In the years following the revolt, this led to error in both camps. They began to interpret the Scriptures through the eyes of their competition. For the Jews this meant taking an even stronger stance that Yeshua could not possibly be the Messiah. For the Church, instead of obeying my admonition to provoke Israel to jealousy, despite their rejection they began to despise the Jewish people." (See Romans 11:11.) "Even reading the Scriptures would prove difficult."

"Surely God's judgment made sense—they rejected the Messiah. But what's with all these promises of blessing and restoration and everlasting love?

"For them, the Temple's demise and the second crushing of Jerusalem in 135 CE was clear evidence that God had rejected the Jews. And yet, so many promises to Israel were yet to be fulfilled. And many Gentile believers felt rejected and inferior in the light of these promises, such as Amos prophesied."

> And I will bring my people Israel back from exile. They will rebuild the ruined cities and live in them. They will plant vineyards and drink their wine; they will make gardens and eat their fruit. I will plant Israel in their own land, never again to be uprooted from the land I have given them (Amos 9:14-15).

"If I had still been alive, I would have shown them how God's choosing and blessing of Israel was in order that the nations would come to God. God's purpose in choosing Israel as a priestly nation was to intercede for the Gentiles and ultimately bring them the good news of Yeshua. They were to be a priestly nation—*'a kingdom of priests,'* as God told Moses—to stand in the gap for the rest of the world." (See Exodus 19:6.)

"And indeed, every one of them can thank a Jew for their faith in Messiah. Yeshua Himself said that *'salvation is from the Jews'* (John 4:22). Second, if there were no Jews, their young theologians would have no Bible to even come up with replacement theology in the first place. But they were blinded by their own wound and the competition with the synagogue."

"How ironic," I jumped in. "Israel was blinded to the fact that Yeshua was her Messiah and the Church was blinded to the fact that God's call on Israel was...what was that word you used earlier, Ariel?"

"Irrevocable!" Paul exclaimed. "I should know; I wrote Romans 11:29. And you are right, they were both blinded to these two truths: Yeshua is the Messiah and King and the Jews have not been cast away forever.

"So, in an attempt to define themselves as the true inheritors of Israel's relationship with God, Gentile Christians eradicated the Jewish people from God's plans, substituting themselves instead. The Gentile Church claimed to displace the Jews as God's people from that time on and forevermore and blamed the Jews for rejecting Yeshua, which the Church said led to God's rejection of them.

"How could the early Christians read the promises that God had made to Israel and justify this substitution?" Paul asked rhetorically. "They found that they could do so only by spiritualizing the promises. This method of interpretation allowed them to replace Israel as the beneficiary of God's unfulfilled promises.[1]

"By spiritualizing the promises to Israel as actually belonging to the Church, they no longer felt inferior. They could now read the great promises of God through Isaiah, Amos, Ezekiel, Jeremiah, and Zechariah to

Israel without feeling any anger of jealousy toward those obstinate Jews. *Replacement theology* had healed them.

"Promises of restoration to Israel really meant the restoration of the Church. Promises of the Land of Israel to physical descendants of Abraham are canceled and now mean that believers will inherit the earth. All of God's promises to Israel are now fulfilled in believers, and the promises to physical Israel are null and void. Listen to this statement from a present-day Bible teacher."

Ariel clicked and on the screen came a man in a suit, teaching. He was thin and tall, with a short beard and a blue suit. He began to speak:

> The land inheritance, the domain of God's people if they are assumed to include Gentiles will now consist of the entire world, the Holy Land is the *world*. The Holy Land is the entire globe and is no longer the privilege of an ethnic few. In a word, the New Testament is globalizing and universalizing the blessing of Abraham. Earlier it has been tribal and local, now it is global and universal.[2]

"Here is another fellow—not quite so nice. Yet this fellow leads a church."

Another man appeared on the screen. This man was younger and much more passionate. I couldn't believe what I heard.

> The Jews are no longer God's chosen people in the New Testament. But...we as Christians are God's chosen people...the modern day nation Israel...is a complete fraud.[3]

"Wow! 'A complete fraud'!?" I said.

"All this goes back 1,900 years to second-century theologians. Because replacement theology was born out of this competition for converts between the Church and the synagogue, it was a consuming issue for many of these earlier theologians and it wasn't long before the demonic venom of hatred began to seep in. It was not enough to declare that the

Church had replaced Israel. The enemy seized this opportunity to birth a violent, bloody, anti-Semitic theology through those who claimed to love the Jewish Messiah.

"Over time this theology grew into something purely evil that not only posed a danger to the Jewish people, but the espousers of this deadly ideology. By not merely seeking to replace Israel but espousing a doctrine that *cursed* Israel, they cut themselves off from the life-giving sap. I had warned the Romans against 'boasting over the natural branches.' I told them not to be arrogant against God's firstborn, Israel, and was clear that if they persisted in judging their elder brothers, the Jews, God would cut them off too."

I thought of the movie we watched of my own daughters standing outside a playground that was designated and built to honor those with Jewish heritage. The bullying was easy to see in the Jewish Heritage Park scene. Why didn't people grasp this in our early history and stop this wretched replacement theology?

Ariel began to share. "One of the early influential leaders was a man named Justin Martyr. He invented a fictional debate opponent named Trypho. Trypho was a Jew and Justin Martyr sought to set him straight."

"I guess if you want to win argument, it helps if your opponent is fictional," I said. "You can control his responses!"

Paul nodded. "It also gives you a better chance at keeping your 'enemies at peace with you.' Let me explain how he did this. Trypho is a fictionalized Jew who is fleeing Judea because of the disturbance there. Justin has a chance meeting with him in Ephesus. Much of what he writes is brilliant, but he stumbles because he cannot see God's grace on natural Israel, even in unbelief."

A man appeared on the screen with a full beard and wearing robes. Justin Martyr began to speak.

For the true spiritual Israel, and descendants of Judah, Jacob, Isaac, and Abraham, are we who have been led to God through this crucified Christ. …Even so we, who have been quarried out from the bowels of Christ, are the true Israelite race.[4]

"Whereas I said in Ephesians that the Gentiles become co-heirs *with* Israel," Paul emphasized *with*, not *instead of*, "Justin Martyr claimed that the Church replaced the physical descendants of Abraham. We see this also in an earlier writing in the epistle of Barnabas—not my companion, but another of the same name. He wrote this before the destruction of Jerusalem in 135 CE."

Ariel clicked and a quote appeared on the screen.

> Take heed now to yourselves, and not to be like some, adding largely to your sins, and saying, "The covenant is both theirs and ours." But they thus finally lost it. —The Epistle of Barnabas

"His view was that God was no longer bound by covenant to Israel. Again, I said the opposite in Romans, *'Did God reject His people? By no means! …God did not reject His people, whom he foreknew'* (Rom. 11:1-2). And the case I make in the following verses is clear. There will always be a remnant of Jewish believers."

> *Don't you know what Scripture says in the passage about Elijah— how he appealed to God against Israel: "Lord, they have killed your prophets and torn down your altars; I am the only one left, and they are trying to kill me"? And what was God's answer to him? "I have reserved for myself seven thousand who have not bowed the knee to Baal." So too, at the present time there is a remnant chosen by grace* (Romans 11:2-5).

"In the same way that God committed to Abraham that He would not destroy Sodom if ten righteous men could be found, God is keeping His covenant with the people of Israel today based on the remnant of Jewish believers. And we do know that when I wrote that there were tens of thousands of Jewish believers."

"Where were all these Jewish believers in the second century?" I asked. "We see in the book of Acts a large and healthy Jewish congregation in Israel—heck, not only in Jerusalem, but Joppa, Lod, the Sharon, and the Galilee. Now it seems that there is no Messianic option." Listening to myself, I was starting to sound like a teacher. What was happening to me? A communicator, yes—but behind my keyboard! Now I felt this intense desire to teach—even to challenge and debate. "What happened to the descendants of the first Jewish believers?"

"David," smiled Ariel, "now that is a great question!"

I felt a tinge of pride well up within me. Yes, I could see myself addressing hundreds—maybe thousands. With the Internet I could become famous...

Interrupting my self-centered daydream, Ariel was about to bring me back to reality. "In fact, it is such an insightful query, I will let you discover the answer yourself."

"Whaaat?" Before I realized what would happen, everything was whirling around me. I was leaving the synagogue in a hurry. Sucked back into this time warp of sorts, I was spinning. When I opened my eyes, I was standing in what I was pretty sure was first-century Jerusalem. People rushed passed me, several carrying cages with doves and others shouldering lambs.

Someone far in front of me called back, "Come on Levi, Yaacov has been invited by the chief priest to speak at the Temple."

Hmmm. Levi again. Let's see where this rabbit trail leads. I followed quickly after the handsome teenager who was obviously trying to grow some facial hair. I checked my chin. *Yep, my beard is back!*

We neared the Temple courts. There had to be thousands of people packed inside the walls of Jerusalem.

"What is going on? Why are so many people here?" I asked the young man. He walked at a fast clip and I finally let him cut the path before us and followed from behind.

"Are you joking?" he called back. "It is always like this on Passover."

Ah, Passover. I then I remembered it was only a week ago that I was here in Jerusalem in another vision or visitation. I came face to face with Yeshua. I carried a massive beam to which they nailed Him. I recalled that when I caught His gaze, He looked right through me—to my soul. I saw my life of rebellion. I watched as they crucified Him—as they tore Him to pieces. That day, just a week ago for me, was seared in my soul forever.

We continued at a brisk pace, through a vast crowd of Jews teeming toward the Temple. I gasped. The Temple stood before us and a lump formed in my throat. The structure itself was magnificent, but the people—these people—were my relatives, my ancestors. I was honored to be here, to experience their worship, their interests, and their passionate observance of Passover.

When I visited Israel with Lisa, there was no Temple; only the Temple Mount remained. And the people were mostly tourists, a mixture of faiths and nationalities. And of course, instead of the Temple, Lisa and I saw a Muslim mosque on the Mount and the shrine that is in virtually every picture of Jerusalem—the Dome of the Rock.

Now I saw the temple as it really stood 2,000 years ago. There was no Dome of the Rock or Muslim mosque, only the Temple. I had glimpses of this during my first trip with Ariel, but that was before I believed. Something was different, and I was sad knowing that soon it would be destroyed. To be honest I had no idea what year it was, but I was pretty sure it was some time after Yeshua's resurrection. He said we were going to hear Yaakov. It had to be Yaakov the brother of Yeshua—James, whom I met a week ago—the one who became the leader of the Jerusalem congregation.

I followed the young man into the Temple courts and through a vast sea of people. I think if I'd stopped, I'd have been carried forward by the sheer force of the wave of humanity. Under my sandals were carefully carved stone tiles. Before us were massive pillars, one after another on each side of the courtyard. It was nearly the length of a football field in each direction. In front of me was the Temple itself. This was amazing—I was walking in front of *the* Temple! I wanted to stop and stare for a while.

"Nathan, he is speaking on the Pinnacle, we need to go," someone said to my young friend.

Okay, at least now I know his name.

"Come on Levi, let's go. We don't want to miss this. What an opportunity!" he shouted as hurried through the crowd outside.

Nathan prayed out loud as we walked. "Lord, use Your brother on this Passover—the day You gave Your life for us! Open the eyes of Your people. Show them You are the way, the truth, and the life. How fitting to use Your own brother on this Passover!"

I followed Nathan until we came to the area I knew as the quarter in front of the Western Wall. Then Nathan led us south. Nathan looked up and I followed his lead. High above us, on the southwest corner of the Temple Mount, an old man with long white hair and beard appeared high above us.

Someone shouted from below.

"Oh, Yaakov, righteous one, in whom we are able to place great confidence, the people are led astray after Yeshua, the crucified one. So declare to us, what will you say of the way of Yeshua?"[5]

Despite the large numbers, everyone waited patiently for him to answer. Judging by his age, it was at least three decades after Yeshua's resurrection. I was surprised that the whole city was hanging on his every word. I saw clearly last week that it would be false to say the Jews rejected Yeshua, as there was sizeable minority who did receive Him. Yet, I had no idea that the disciples were held in such high regard—or least Yaakov.

The old man lifted his hand to signal that he was about to speak, and just then the wind blew his long white hair and beard, and ruffled his plain robe. The audience quieted. "Why do you ask me about Yeshua, the Son of Man?" Yaakov asked, his great voice booming over the crowd below him. "Yeshua sits in heaven at the right hand of the great Power, and he will soon come on the clouds of heaven!"[6]

"He's quoting Yeshua," Nathan looked at me with excitement. "He's repeating the very words his Brother declared to the high priest. The high priest asked Him if He was indeed the Messiah and Yeshua said in response, *'I am. And you will see the Son of Man sitting at the right hand of the Mighty One and coming on the clouds of heaven.'* How cool is that!" (See Mark 14:61-63.)

I have to admit, I felt chills.

Some in the crowd became fidgety, while the majority was clearly delighted with his answer. They began to shout *"Hosanna*—salvation—to the Son of David,"[7] clearly referring to Yeshua.

Someone in the back shouted out, "Oh, no! The righteous one is also in error!"

Error? Yaakov spoke nothing but the truth—the way, the truth, and the life.

I saw movement to my right. A group of men disturbed the speech and ascended to the place where Yaakov stood—the Pinnacle.

What are they doing?

Together, the men rushed Yaakov at the pinnacle of the Temple. With angry shouts and cursing, they lifted him high and dangled him before the people.

No!

Fear rippled down my spine. The men yelled obscenities, but Yaakov did not resist them. He seemed to show no fear as the men lifted Yaakov over their heads and threw him down over the side.

The entire crowd gasped.

Thud.

His body hit the stone pavement.

I turned my head away. Who would want to watch something like that really happen? I felt sick. It was a horrible thing to do in the name of religion—any religion. What was the point? I was angry at the senseless act, yet Yaakov's courage gripped my heart.

"He's alive!" Nathan shouted.

I looked. It couldn't be!

Nathan made his way toward Yaakov and once again I let him part the sea of people in front of us and followed from behind. Could he possibly be alive after such a fall?

Nathan prayed all the way, quietly and under his breath. I wondered if Yaakov was really alive, and if he was alive what would he say?

Clearly injured and in pain, the bloodied Yaakov rose to his knees and began to pray as he held his bloody head in his hands. "I beg of you, Lord God our Father, forgive them! They do not know what they are doing."[8]

"Just like Stephen," I whispered.

"Just like his brother, Yeshua," Nathan added. We stepped toward him to help him but several religious men knocked us down and surrounded him as if possessed.

Whack! Thwack! Thud!

"*No!*" I shouted. I crawled toward Yaakov on all fours, determined to grab the legs of the man with the largest stone and bring him down. I could see Yaakov's face intermittently in between the sandals of the attackers.

Suddenly one of the Jewish priests stepped in and shouted, "Stop! What are you doing? The righteous one is praying for you!"

I relaxed. This priest looked like he was taking pretty good charge of the situation. The priest starting pulling the men back, but before he could stop them another man stepped forward, a large club in his thick hand.

Whack!

With one blow he struck Yaakov in the head and the brother of Yeshua fell slowly to the ground, his prayers ended. Blood flowed in little gushes from the gash in his head. Yaakov didn't move.

Nathan and I were speechless. Just a few minutes before he was praying that God would use Yaakov. Now he was dead. The crowd was clearly confused.

Nathan looked at me and suddenly his face became blurry. I was leaving. Jerusalem became a blur and within seconds I was standing with

Ariel. Paul was no longer with him, but another man, Yaakov, whom I just saw die, was by his side. His long white hair and beard were the same, but his white robe shone like twinkling diamonds under a stage light.

I shook myself. "Yaakov?"

"I know that must have been a shock, David. But I am okay. I was immediately received into heaven along with those who had gone before me," he reached out his arms and embraced me. "It is good to see you again."

My heart still thundered like horses after witnessing this man's death. I was utterly relieved to see him here, but I needed a moment to collect myself. *Did he just say it was good to see me again? That's right, I met the younger version of Yaakov in my earlier experience.*

Ariel handed me a piece of the fruit I'd tried earlier. They gave me time to eat a few bites. I looked from the brother of Jesus to the angel of God. I wanted to pinch myself. I mean, I knew that all the martyrs went to heaven, but this...this was...I didn't want to say it was unbelievable, but I couldn't think of a better word. My hand shook a little as I took the second bite. The fruit seemed to have a calming effect. The horses stopped galloping through my chest, and I raked my hand through my hair. "Yes, Yaakov, that was quite a shock. And it's good to see you again, too."

The fruit disappeared quickly and Ariel handed me a goblet of water. "Here, drink this."

I took a sip and the water was sweet in my mouth and went down like warm oil, healing the disturbance in my soul.

Ariel pointed to our seats. Yaakov took the seat that Paul and Dad previously occupied. Ariel straddled his chair again and leaned on the back rest. "David, it is important that we fill in the blanks here. There is much more to learn. Yaakov here was not a believer during the lifetime of Yeshua."

"Yes, I remember. He came to faith after the resurrection."

"He led *the Way* Jerusalem congregation for over thirty years."

"Eh, *the Way?* Do you mean he led the way, or there is something called *the Way?*"

A swipe of his hand and several verses appeared on the screen:

*So that if he found any there who belonged to **the Way**, whether men or women, he might take them as prisoners to Jerusalem* (Acts 9:2).

*But some of them became obstinate; they refused to believe and publicly maligned **the Way**. So Paul left them* (Acts 19:9).

*About that time there arose a great disturbance about **the Way*** (Acts 19:23).

*However, I admit that I worship the God of our ancestors as a follower of **the Way**, which they call a sect. I believe everything that is in accordance with the Law and that is written in the Prophets* (Acts 24:14).

*Then Felix, who was well acquainted with **the Way**, adjourned the proceedings. "When Lysias the commander comes," he said, "I will decide your case"* (Acts 24:22).

"Yes," began Yaakov, "We called ourselves the Way, remembering what the Master said when He was with us. *'I am the way and the truth and the life. No one comes to the Father except through me'* (John 14:6). And yes, I was the leader along with the other apostles. We were a team."

"Yaakov was respected by all the other branches of first-century Judaism including the Pharisees and the Sadducees. He was known as Yaakov the *Tsaddik*, Jacob the Righteous. Yaakov was also known as the man with camel's knees because he spent so much time in the Temple praying for the nation of Israel. Yaakov alone was allowed access into the Holy of Holies to pray once a year."[9]

"If they respected you so much, why did they kill you?" I asked.

"Well, keep in mind, David, it was a small group of people from the sect of the Pharisees who were stirred to kill me—egged on by the high priest at the time, Ananias. In fact, at that time their number in Jerusalem was much smaller than ours.[10] While it is true I enjoyed tremendous trust and relationship with the inhabitants of Jerusalem—Jewish believers and non-believers—Ananias and some others from the Pharisees were frightened at our success. Indeed, many Pharisees had already confessed faith in Yeshua as their Messiah—not the least of whom was your new friend Rabbi Shaul. It was a great embarrassment to the pharisaical establishment that one of their up-and-comers was now the most effective communicator of Yeshua's message. He was still preaching when I was killed."[11]

"That same year," Ariel put in, "Festus, the governor of Judea, died. It took some time for Nero to send a new governor. In the midst of that vacuum, Ananias devised a scheme. He gathered the Sanhedrin to get their consent. They would invite Yaakov to speak at the Temple. Their hope was that he would encourage the people not to believe in Yeshua—to deny He was the Messiah. With so many Jews from many nations in Jerusalem for Passover, they thought this would put an end to the Messianic faith. When Yaakov refused to deny Yeshua, they were not pleased. Well—you saw the outcome.

"There are some powerful similarities between the death of Yeshua and his beloved brother Yaakov," Ariel continued. "They both died on Passover. They were both killed in Jerusalem. They both responded exactly the same when asked if Yeshua was the Messiah. Yeshua said when asked if He were indeed the Messiah, *'I am, and you will see the Son of Man sitting at the right hand of the Mighty One and coming on the clouds of heaven.'"* (Mark 14:62). "In addition, what a place to speak of the return of the Messiah—from the Pinnacle of the Temple."

Yaakov explained. "You see, David, the Pinnacle of the Temple is the place where the priest sounded the shofar that announced the beginning and ending of the Sabbath. The shofar was used to call the people together, to call the elders, to announce that an army was invading, or to send the people off to war. But the greatest role that the shofar plays is to welcome a king into the city. As it is written, '*with trumpets and the blast of the ram's horn—shout for joy before the Lord, the King*'" (Ps. 98:6).

"It is true that Ananias arranged the location, but really God once again used Ananias for His own plan and purpose."

"While Yaakov did not have a shofar, he took this opportunity to testify to the coming of the Messiah," Ariel put in. "And don't take my word for it," a picture appeared on the screen on the wall of a stone. It had Hebrew letters written, but I could not read them. "David, this stone was found directly below where Yaakov was standing at the southwest corner of the Temple Mount and can be found today at the Israel Museum in Jerusalem. The inscription says, "To the place of sounding the shofar—" and then it is cut off.

"It is also interesting that his brother Yeshua was also tempted in the exact same place. After He had fasted for forty days, Satan took him also to the Pinnacle of the Temple and tempted Him to throw Himself down and prove He was the Son of God. He didn't and He rebuked Satan. Yaakov was taken here and also tempted—he was asked to deny that Yeshua was the Messiah so the people would not believe. He resisted this temptation."

Yaakov squirmed a bit in his chair, then leaned toward Ariel. "But let's be clear, angel, my death carried no special atoning qualities. I was just a sinner who was killed for my faith in the Messiah. Yeshua is the Lamb of God without blemish or defect who took on the sin of Israel and all nations so that we could be forgiven and have eternal life."

"Granted," Ariel agreed, "but He did choose you to lead the congregation of believers for its first thirty years in Jerusalem."

Not wanting to interrupt them, but yet really wanting to interrupt them, I asked, "What happened after your death? What was the reaction?"

"Well, when the new governor arrived, many of the Jews came to him to complain at the thuggish vigilantism of Ananias and he was quickly removed as high priest. Nevertheless, persecution increased against the Jewish believers. The next several years proved to be pivotal.

"After my death, my cousin and also a cousin of the Master, Simeon, was chosen to lead the Jerusalem congregation. Thebouthis, a rival of Simeon, was not happy with this and caused a split, taking many of the disciples into heresy, denying the divinity of Yeshua. Simeon too would die as a martyr many years later."[12]

"I am afraid it is time for Yaakov to go, and you still have much to witness and learn." Before the words completely left the tongue of the angel, the room was already spinning and getting blurry. I was taken up again and within a few seconds I was lifting my head up from the ground.

CHAPTER XVI

Y ochanan, he's awake," cried a young man. I tried to move, but a sharp pain pierced my temple. I touched my head—it felt like there was a bandage. I was very weak and once again dressed in the garb of a first-century Jew. Only this time my beard was sticky with dried blood.

"Levi? How are you feeling?"

Okay, I'm still the beloved "Levi."

"Weak. Where am I?"

"You're in Pella, just east of the Jordan, and we assumed you were on your way here like the others from the *kehila*.[1] What took you so long?" said the man I assumed was Yochanan. "What do you remember about yesterday?"

Hmmm, I was in a hospital, with my dying father, who, by the way, is not really dead. Just thinking about that strengthened my spirit, but surely that story wasn't going to fly here.

"I—I don't know. I can't really remember anything. In fact, you act like you know me, but I don't you. Who are you?"

I figured the best way to get information was to feign amnesia. I wasn't lying. I really didn't know them!

"Let me a take a look at your head. You passed out just after you arrived last night. Do you know how you got that nasty wound on your head?"

"Like I said, I have no recollection from yesterday."

"Thank God you made it. We were praying ceaselessly for you."

"But why are we in Pella?"

"You really *don't* remember. When the Romans began to surround the Holy City several months ago, we knew the prophecy of Yeshua was coming to pass. Our community in Jerusalem was warned by an angel[2] of the coming destruction and was told to flee. We escaped the war about two years after the revolt began" (in 66 CE). "We've been hiding here in the mountains for some time. This city had been attacked by Jewish revolutionaries earlier and was nearly desolate when we arrived, making it a perfect place to go unnoticed. You were slow to come, telling us you would make your way here later."

The young man looked at me like we were friends, and then I realized it was Nathan from the earlier vision, a few years older. He said, "Don't you remember the prophecy? The Master predicted that the Temple would be destroyed—not one stone would remain—and He told us that when the armies encircled Jerusalem we should flee to the mountains." (See Matthew 24:2; Luke 21:20-21.) "We left everything behind and headed to this place."

Yochanan appeared to go into deep thought. "It all seems like a dream now. We had glimpses of peace with our Jewish brothers, but surely that will now end. As our numbers grew into the thousands, they realized that we were not going to disappear. But in the past few years the tension increased between us. First there was the martyrdom of Yaakov, our leader. The synagogue became less and less tolerant of us Nazarenes.[3] Many of our ranks even rejected the faith out of fear, not wanting a similar fate as Yaakov. A few years ago a letter began to circulate that strengthened our resolve."

The younger man quoted from memory.

Remember those earlier days after you had received the light, when you endured in a great conflict full of suffering. Sometimes you were publicly exposed to insult and persecution; at other times you stood side by side with those who were so treated. You suffered along with those in prison and joyfully accepted the confiscation of your property, because you knew that you yourselves had better and lasting possessions. So do not throw away your confidence; it will be richly rewarded.

You need to persevere so that when you have done the will of God, you will receive what he has promised (Hebrews 10:32-36).

Therefore, since we are surrounded by such a great cloud of witnesses, let us throw off everything that hinders and the sin that so easily entangles. And let us run with perseverance the race marked out for us, fixing our eyes on Yeshua, the pioneer and perfecter of faith. For the joy set before him he endured the cross, scorning its shame, and sat down at the right hand of the throne of God. Consider him who endured such opposition from sinners, so that you will not grow weary and lose heart (Hebrews 12:1-3).

"We were reinforced by this word and endured," Yochanan continued. "Do you remember any of this Levi?"

I nodded slightly. "I'm beginning to. But please—go on. Tell the rest."

Yochanan paced to the doorway and back again. "We were determined not to lose heart, but then *this*—the revolt in Jerusalem and the Temple's devastation. I see now that the letter was also warning us that it was near. He said that the Temple was now obsolete in light of Yeshua's sacrifice and that it would soon disappear." (See Hebrews 8:13.) "We know that this is a sign of the end. Clearly the Messiah will soon return."

I didn't have the heart or the courage to explain to him that I was coming from nearly 2,000 years in the future and many are still convinced that He is coming *soon*.

"If not, I am not sure what we will do. The Jews of Jerusalem consider us traitors for fleeing. I understand them, but had they not rejected the Master this would not be happening. Somehow God will use it for good. Surely they will soon see. As our brother Paul was fond of saying, eventually *'all Israel will be saved'*" (Rom. 11:26).

If he only knew...

A woman emerged from a nearby cave that I had not noticed until now. At first she was a shadow in the glow of the fire, but as she grew close I could see an attractive middle-aged woman. Strands of brunette hair made their way from under her head covering. "I see our friend is up," she said with a smile.

"Levi, do you remember Nahama, my wife?"

"What do you mean, 'remember me'? How could he not remember me?"

"He doesn't remember anything," said Nathan.

"I brought some soup. Are you hungry?" asked Nahama.

"Yes, please."

"Nathan, will you hold this for Levi? I will go and bring some bowls for all of us."

Nahama quickly returned and a hearty bowl of soup was soon before each of us. I took a bite and my mouth began to burn. "S...p...i...c...y," I managed to say with the food in my mouth. They all began to laugh.

"Levi!" said Nathan, "You love spicy food!"

And just as quickly as I came to visit this family, armed with this new bit of information about the early Jewish believers fleeing to Pella, I was caught up again, sucked right out of that spicy reality and landed very quickly in another. I was standing outside in a courtyard, grateful that my mouth was no longer burning. I checked my beard. No sticky blood. Thankfully, no headache either.

To my right, fenced in was a massive stone, probably used as an olive press. To my left, five hundred yards away, a large lake or sea sparkled under the sunlight. In front of me was a door, as if inviting me to enter. I was much older. Physically I felt the same, but looking at my hands I was in the body of someone more than seventy years of age. I was dying for a mirror, but I didn't see one.

As soon as I entered the room, a voice called out. "Levi, is that you? Good, you're back. Come, hurry! Who knows how much time I have? We must finish."

I walked over to the voice. Clearly a man at least my age—*the new me*, as in the older me—called me from his bed. As I drew closer I recognized him. "Nathan?" Like me, Nathan was much older.

"Yes, let me continue."

Continue what? I thought. There was a desk with papyrus and a pen. I sat, understanding that he thought that I had been dictating something for him. Or had I?

"It is essential that I leave this testimony behind. Now where were we?" I looked at him with a blank stare.

He ignored my stare. "Oh yes, after the revolt and subsequent devastation of Jerusalem, in the fourth year of Emperor Vespasian" (73 CE).[4] "Well, when it became clear that the Messiah was not yet returning, our community in Pella came down from the mountains, crossed back over the Jordan, and rebuilt our lives in Jerusalem. We wept when we came into the city. Destruction was everywhere. To look at the Temple Mount and see nothing—well, it broke our hearts."

As he was talking I could see it all taking place on the wall over his head. Nathan was not aware of this. Nathan, Yochanan, Nahama, and some younger ones who I assumed were their children literally fell on the streets of Jerusalem in front of the Temple Mount and wept. I could hear the wailing of others as well. "For years we had been hiding in the mountains of Pella across the Jordan River," continued Nathan. "But this was our home. It had been destroyed. Only later did we hear the full story of Jerusalem's demise."

Somehow my hand was able to keep up with Nathan's fast pace. His telling was passionate and he looked at the wall in front of him, his mind obviously miles away from the room where he dictated his story in his old age.

"For more than seventy years before the Romans destroyed the city, the *Kana'im*—a Jewish political sect called the Zealots—sought to stir the people to revolt against Roman rule. Tensions increased between Jerusalem and Rome with Emperor Caligula, about a decade after Yeshua's resurrection, when the emperor declared himself to be a deity and ordered his statue to be set up at every temple in the Roman Empire. Of all the regions of the Empire, only the Jews rejected the decree; the Temple would cease to have any meaning at all if it were suddenly adorned with another god. The greatest creed in all of the Tanakh from Deuteronomy 6 declares, 'Hear, O Israel: The Lord our God, the Lord is one.'

"Caligula threatened to destroy the Temple. Tensions were high. A delegation of Jews was sent to pacify him, but did not succeed. Caligula raged at them, 'So you are the enemies of the gods, the only people who refuse to recognize my divinity.'[5] In his mind, they were atheists to not acknowledge that he was a god. The world still looked at the Jews as silly and narrow-minded to only believe in one God. But as fortune would have it—or *true* divine intervention—Caligula did not live long enough to carry out his wicked plan."

"Let's be thankful for that," I mumbled. "Now wait, Nathan. Give me time to catch up." My wrinkled hand flew across the papyrus and one of Nathan's children brought me a fresh inkwell. I made the final stroke and sat back. "Very well. Continue."

"Caligula's untimely death—or maybe perfectly timed—led to the salvation of Jerusalem and saved thousands of lives. However, a few decades later, after the death of Yaakov, the Zealots had had enough of Roman abuses. It wasn't just the religious mockery and the constant threat that they would attack the Temple, but also the overtaxation of the people. Even after Caligula left this earth, Jews continued to suffer humiliations at the hands of the Romans. At times soldiers exposed themselves in the Holy Temple, and it is recorded Torah scroll was burned on one occasion.[6]

"The Zealots believed that if they fought against Rome, God would fight with them. They were a brutal bunch by the end. They took over Jerusalem four years before the Romans prevailed. However, it was not the Jews who started this revolt, as many will believe, but rather Gessius Florus, the Roman procurator of Judea during that time. He was a greedy and ruthless man. He openly favored the Greek population over the Jews living in Caesarea, where he ruled.

"The local Greek population, encouraged by Florus' policies, took advantage of the circumstances to disparage the Jews. One notable instance of provocation occurred while the Jews were worshiping at their local synagogue and a Hellenist—a Jew who had assimilated into Greek culture—sacrificed several birds on top of an earthenware container at the entrance of the synagogue, an act that rendered the building ritually unclean. In response to this action, the Jews sent a group of men to petition Florus for compensation. Despite accepting a payment of eight talents to hear the case, Florus refused to listen to the complaints and instead had the petitioners imprisoned.[7]

"If this wasn't enough, Florus ordered that seventeen talents of silver be taken from the Holy Temple. He claimed it was for Emperor Nero. The locals mocked Florus by passing a bucket around the city, taking up a fake offering for the *poor* Florus. He was humiliated and sent soldiers to Jerusalem to arrest the Jewish leaders. They were not only arrested but flogged and crucified."

I groaned and laid down my pen. I felt like throwing it across the room. The news was too horrific to just document and go on. Were all nations as hard-pressed as Israel? Were all people groups as persecuted as the Jews? Not only was history overwhelmingly anti-Semitic, but what about the future? If it's true that history repeats itself, then I was about to enter the battle of the ages in bringing the acceptance of Yeshua as Messiah to my generation. *God help me.*

CHAPTER XVII

Nathan swung his feet off the bed and onto the floor. "It's terrible to recollect all of this, Levi, I know. But remember, the Jews were infuriated. They rebelled and crushed the small Roman garrison in Jerusalem. Roman troops came from nearby Syria, but the Jewish fighters repelled them. The Zealots grew in popularity as many came to believe that they too, like Judah Maccabee fighting the Greeks, could overcome the Romans with God's help. Sadly, that was the last Jewish victory in the war."

Reluctantly, I picked up my pen. It seemed Nathan was in no mood for a break.

"General Vespasian and his son Titus were sent from Rome to crush the Jewish rebellion that had spread from Jerusalem to all the land. They started in the Galilee—the Zealot stronghold. Jerusalem's leadership offered no help as they realized the hopelessness of the situation. The surviving Zealots fled to the Holy City. They confronted the moderate Jewish leaders and killed them all for not being willing to fight."

Suddenly the room darkened while a screen appeared in front of me. Nathan disappeared and I saw a website. An unseen voice began to read as I watched a movie of Roman soldiers besieging the city of Jerusalem. I ceased writing and watched.

> The scene was now set for the revolt's final catastrophe. Outside Jerusalem, Roman troops prepared to besiege the city; inside the city, the Jews were engaged in a suicidal civil war. In later generations, the rabbis hyperbolically declared that the revolt's failure, and the Temple's destruction, was due not to Roman military superiority but to causeless hatred (sinat khinam) among the Jews (Yoma 9b). While the Romans

would have won the war in any case, the Jewish civil war both hastened their victory and immensely increased the casualties. One horrendous example: In expectation of a Roman siege, Jerusalem's Jews had stockpiled a supply of dry food that could have fed the city for many years. But one of the warring Zealot factions burned the entire supply, apparently hoping that destroying this "security blanket" would compel everyone to participate in the revolt. The starvation resulting from this mad act caused suffering as great as any the Romans inflicted.[1]

I was beginning to see the angel's approach. Nathan could not tell me what he didn't know—such as the rabbinic opinion centuries later. So he would break in from time to time to fill in the gap. The room filled with light again and Nathan hadn't skipped a beat.

"One of those who opposed the Zealots was the Pharisee, Rabbi Yochanan ben Zakkai. He had pled with the Zealots to surrender. They of course refused and would have killed him, but it is said his disciples snuck him out of the city, *hidden in a coffin,* after he faked his own death. This was just after we had headed for Pella. Once out of the city he was taken, *still in the coffin,* to General Vespasian. He told the general that he had a prophecy that he would soon be emperor. Many assumed Vespasian would replace Nero, and most likely it was a politically savvy move by the rabbi, as opposed to an actual vision—but who knows?

"When it came to pass in short order, the new emperor granted ben Zakkai his request: That he could relocate to Yavne near the southern coast, above Ashdod, and start a school there to study Torah. His son Titus assumed his command.

"Titus led the Romans to break the siege" (in 70 CE). "They destroyed the city without mercy." Nathan grew silent. As a tear fell from his eye, once again the room grew dark. And again, a screen appeared and a voice narrated.

"Joseph ben Matityahu, known by most as Flavius Josephus, gives us the only firsthand account of the destruction of Jerusalem. He was once a Jewish leader who led his troops against the Romans in the Galilee. However, after their defeat in 67 CE he claimed that the Messianic prophecies that lead to the war were actually referring to Vespasian and would result in him becoming the next Caesar—the same tactic that ben Zakkai would use. General Vespasian kept him on as a slave and interpreter; however, over time he developed affection for the young man. After Vespasian became emperor in 69 CE, he granted Josephus his freedom, and Josephus took on the emperor's family name of Flavius. He was there with Titus to record the events of the fall of Jerusalem."

The rebels shortly after attacked the Romans again, and a clash followed between the guards of the sanctuary and the troops who were putting out the fire inside the inner court; the latter routed the Jews and followed in hot pursuit right up to the Temple itself. Then one of the soldiers, without awaiting any orders and with no dread of so momentous a deed, but urged on by some supernatural force, snatched a blazing piece of wood and, climbing on another soldier's back, hurled the flaming brand through a low golden window that gave access, on the north side, to the rooms that surrounded the sanctuary. As the flames shot up, the Jews let out a shout of dismay that matched the tragedy; they flocked to the rescue, with no thought of sparing their lives or husbanding their strength; for the sacred structure that they had constantly guarded with such devotion was vanishing before their very eyes.

No exhortation or threat could now restrain the impetuosity of the legions; for passion was in supreme command. Crowded together around the entrances, many were trampled down by their companions; others, stumbling on the smoldering and smoked-filled ruins of the porticoes, died as miserably as the defeated. As they drew closer to the Temple, they pretended not even to hear Caesar's orders, but urged the men in front to throw in more firebrands. The rebels were powerless to help; carnage and flight spread throughout.

Most of the slain were peaceful citizens, weak and unarmed, and they were butchered where they were caught. The heap of corpses mounted higher and higher about the altar; a stream of blood flowed down the Temple's steps, and the bodies of those slain at the top slipped to the bottom.

When Caesar failed to restrain the fury of his frenzied soldiers, and the fire could not be checked, he entered the building with his generals and looked at the holy place of the sanctuary and all its furnishings, which exceeded by far the accounts current in foreign lands and fully justified their splendid repute in our own.

As the flames had not yet penetrated to the inner sanctum, but were consuming the chambers that surrounded the sanctuary, Titus assumed correctly that there was still time to save the structure; he ran out and by personal appeals he endeavored to persuade his men to put out the fire, instructing Liberalius, a centurion of his bodyguard of lancers, to club any of the men who disobeyed his orders. But their respect for Caesar and their fear of the centurion's staff who was trying to check them were overpowered by their rage, their detestation of the Jews, and an utterly uncontrolled lust for battle.

Most of them were spurred on, moreover, by the expectation of loot, convinced that the interior was full of money and dazzled by observing that everything around them was made of gold. But they were forestalled by one of those who had entered into the building, and who, when Caesar dashed out to restrain the troops, pushed a firebrand, in the darkness, into the hinges of the gate. Then, when the flames suddenly shot up from the interior, Caesar and his generals withdrew, and no one was left to prevent those outside from kindling the blaze. Thus, in defiance of Caesar's wishes, the Temple was set on fire.

While the Temple was ablaze, the attackers plundered it, and countless people who were caught by them were slaughtered. There was no pity for age and no regard was accorded rank; children and old men, laymen and priests, alike were butchered; every class was pursued and crushed in the grip of war, whether they cried out for mercy or offered resistance.

Through the roar of the flames streaming far and wide, the groans of the falling victims were heard; such was the height of the hill and the magnitude of the blazing pile that the entire city seemed to be ablaze; and the noise—nothing more deafening and frightening could be imagined.

There were the war cries of the Roman legions as they swept onwards en masse, the yells of the rebels encircled by fire and sword, the panic of the people who, cut off above, fled into the arms of the enemy, and their shrieks as they met their fate. The cries on the hill blended with those of the multitudes in the city below; and now many people who were exhausted and tongue-tied as a result of hunger, when they beheld the Temple on fire, found strength once more to lament and wail. Peraea and the surrounding hills, added their echoes to the deafening din. But more horrifying than the din were the sufferings.

The Temple Mount, everywhere enveloped in flames, seemed to be boiling over from its base; yet the blood seemed more abundant than the flames and the numbers of the slain greater than those of the slayers. The soldiers climbed over heaps of bodies as they chased the fugitives.[2]

The voice continued:

"Josephus stated that 1.1 million Jews were killed during the war. His claim that Titus sought to prevent the destruction of the Temple is most likely fictitious. Josephus and Titus were at the time brothers, as Vespasian had adopted Josephus a short time before. Josephus had every reason to make his brother—who would become emperor—look good. In truth, the Temple was ransacked and looted by the Romans. Fire was the easiest way to liquefy and steal the gold.

"It is believed that the famous Roman Colosseum was funded with the gold stolen from the Temple."

Another article or blog appeared...

> As you enter the Colosseum from the main entrance on the west side a large inscription is chiseled into the archway above. Archeologists have been examining this archway inscription, scrutinizing the embedded holes that once held a raised text. Many argue the marks in the archway inscription says, "The Emperor Titus Caesar Vespasian Augustus ordered the new amphitheater to be made from the (proceeds from the sale of the) booty."
>
> The mention of the word booty (MANVBIS in Latin) was what gave scholars the clue on who helped finance the amphitheater. Sitting just outside the Colosseum is the Arch of Titus showing the spoils or "booty" from Titus' sack of Jerusalem.[3]

The voice stated, "The Arch does not depict a brokenhearted Titus who grieves over the destruction of the Temple; rather, it depicts victory and glorious looting. A special coin was made—the Judea Capta coin—to mark the crushing of the Jewish Revolt."

The south panel depicts the spoils taken from the Temple in Jerusalem. The Golden Candelabrum or Menorah the main focus and is carved in deep relief. Other sacred objects being carried in the triumphal procession are the Gold Trumpets and the Table of Shewbread. These spoils were likely originally colored gold, with the background in blue. In 2012 the Arch of Titus Digital Restoration Project discovered remains of yellow ochre paint on the menorah relief.[4]

"Domitian, Titus' brother who succeeded him as emperor, had the Arch built to honor the military victories of his brother."

Vespasian faced a serious deficit when he became emperor, but the spoils of war from Judea—the riches of the Temple treasury, the golden vessels from the Temple, the seized personal treasures of Jewish citizens and the sale of the Jewish captives themselves—provided enormous wealth for the emperor and the plundering army commanded by his son Titus. Thus did the conquest of Judea fund the most recognizable structure of imperial Rome.[5]

A picture appeared of this Arch. I was very familiar with this picture. For some reason I always thought it was from Israel, when it fact it was Rome. Not only did Rome steal the identity of the Jewish Messiah, but they also literally stole the identity of the Jewish soul by looting the Temple. Ah! Now I remembered the angel's word about the Coliseum having a heavenly connection. The items from the Temple, which he said was based on a heavenly design, were now in Rome. They didn't merely rob the Jewish people, but God Himself! Vespasian thought he was the Jewish Messiah—as his adopted son Josephus told him—so why not have his son return to Rome with what was *rightfully his*, the treasure from the Temple! The voice continued, somehow knowing I needed a second to collect my thoughts.

> The sheer proximity of the Arch of Titus and date when building began led many archeologists and scholars to believe the gold and sacred Temple treasures from Jerusalem were brought to Rome, then sold, and the proceeds from the sale of those artifacts helped fund the Coliseum that is still standing today.[6]

CHAPTER XVIII

And just like that I was brought back to Nathan as he continued to recount the history, having no clue what I was experiencing.

"Rabbi Yochanan ben Zakkai, having secured the favor of Vespasian, now at Yavne, formed a new Sanhedrin, the ruling Jewish Council."

I wondered if that was the same Yavne that is about 15 miles south of Tel Aviv. Omri Caspi, the first Israeli to play in the NBA, grew up there. Not that Nathan cared about the NBA...I smiled as he continued.

"The rabbi worked tirelessly to create a new Judaism. He was concerned that with the crushing of Jerusalem, the Pharisee movement would not survive without a new theology for a post-Temple Israel."

After I got past my grief for the Jews in this era, Nathan's story was becoming really fascinating. Of course I could not let Nathan understand that I was hearing all this for the first time. He was convinced I lived through it with him and was merely dispassionately writing as he dictated. This was killing me, because I had so many questions. But the angel knew best. He would fill in the blanks at the right time.

"With the Temple destroyed, they were in a bind. Instead of falling on their faces and asking God, "*Why?* Why did You allow the Temple to be destroyed?" they went into *spin* mode and spun a most unbiblical story that replaced blood sacrifice with human works. The entire Torah centers on the idea that there must be blood sacrifice for sins to be forgiven because no one can earn salvation or redemption on his own. They turned Judaism into the exact opposite of what it was.

"After the first Temple was destroyed, the Jews longed for it be rebuilt. They lamented her destruction." Nathan looked to me and said, "Write down the words of Psalm 137 here." I didn't know Psalm 137 and I knew if I asked him, my ruse would be exposed. However, as I put the pen on paper I simply wrote!

> *By the rivers of Babylon we sat and wept when we remembered Zion. There on the poplars we hung our harps, for there our captors asked us for songs, our tormentors demanded songs of joy; they said, "Sing us one of the songs of Zion!" How can we sing the songs of the Lord while in a foreign land? If I forget you, Jerusalem, may my right hand forget its skill. May my tongue cling to the roof of my mouth if I do not remember you, if I do not consider Jerusalem my highest joy* (Psalm 137:1-6).

"Now from Lamentations," he exhorted. I documented the Scripture:

> *The roads to Zion mourn, for no one comes to her appointed festivals. All her gateways are desolate, her priests groan, her young women grieve, and she is in bitter anguish. Her foes have become her masters; her enemies are at ease. The Lord has brought her grief because of her many sins. Her children have gone into exile, captive before the foe. All the splendor has departed from Daughter Zion. Her princes are like deer that find no pasture; in weakness they have fled before the pursuer. ...The enemy laid hands on all her treasures; she saw pagan nations enter her sanctuary—those you had forbidden to enter your assembly* (Lamentations 1:4-6,10).

"This brokenness was nowhere to be found at Yavne. Instead, all energy was put into seeing Judaism survive—post Temple.

"They knew that we Messianics taught that the Temple was destroyed because, in light of the death of Yeshua, it was no longer needed. Not to mention that Yeshua prophesied this judgment during His lifetime." (See Matthew 24; Luke 21:20-21.) "Gentiles all over Europe and Asia were no longer converting to Judaism in large numbers, but they were attracted to the Way."

Nathan finally paused to give me time to refill my inkwell and rest my hand. I thought it was a perfect time to offer a comment. "Such jealousy from our leaders in Judaism," I said.

Nathan gave me a piercing stare. "They were no longer our leaders, and they knew it."

I nodded in agreement, picked up my quill, and dipped it in the inkwell.

"Under the New Covenant, we preached eternal life and forgiveness of sins—we taught that you could be made new, regenerated by the Holy Spirit. Through immersion, you left your old life and sinful ways in the water and came out brand-new in the Messiah. Just as the Israelites left slavery in Egypt and came through the Red Sea as free men."

I cringed. I was foolish to challenge Paul's analogy that water immersion could be seen in the crossing of the Red Sea.

"The Jewish brothers who rejected the faith but continued to seek a righteousness based on their own works, apart from grace, had little to offer. The very focal point of their religion—blood sacrifice at the Temple—lay in ruins.

"Ben Zakkai could not rebuild the Temple, and a Temple-less Judaism was confusing apart from the idea that Yeshua was the last sacrifice. In fact, it is well known that the forty years after Yeshua's resurrection until the Temple's destruction, God rejected the Yom Kippur sacrifices year after year."

"How do you know—eh." *Whoops.* "I mean, eh, yeah, continue. You're doing great, Nathan."

He looked at me a little confused and then continued. "Every year on Yom Kippur the *cohen*" (Jewish priest) "would lay his hands on the scapegoat, imparting the sins of the nation. That goat would be released into the wilderness." (See Leviticus 16:10.) "We would wait in expectation to see if God received the sacrifice and forgave our sins. There were several signs that would take place to confirm this.

"First, the *cohen* would place his hands in an urn and pull out two lots, one in each hand. One said, 'For the Lord' and the other said, 'For Azazel' (scapegoat). If the lot marked 'For the Lord' landed in the right hand of the priest it was considered a sign of God's favor. However, every year from the death and resurrection of Yeshua until the Temple's destruction the lot 'For the Lord' was found in the left hand, symbolizing God's rejection of the offering.

"This was no accident. One of our teachers did the math and concluded that the chances of this to happening forty times in a row would be more than one in one trillion! Clearly God was sending a message that judgment was coming and that there was no more need for sacrifice."

"Incredible," I mumbled. Statistics would be useful in the twenty-first century, for sure. It seemed the people in my generation respected knowledge that could be proven. Perhaps that's why Ariel asked me to take this dictation. I silently prayed that God would help me to remember all that I learned under Nathan's tutelage.

"Second, a scarlet cord would be tied to the door of the Temple as the scapegoat was released. If God received the sacrifice, the scarlet cord on the door of the Temple would turn from crimson to white. It stopped turning white the year Yeshua died!" he said with emotion.

"Third, the western most light on the Temple candelabra would not burn. It is believed that this light was used to light all the other lights of the candelabra.[1]

"And the last sign was that the Temple doors would open by themselves. This terrified the rabbis, as they interpreted this as an omen of judgment to come.[2]

"Despite this clear warning and the fact that judgment did come, ben Zakkai and his followers did not turn to Yeshua. Some did, of course, but not in high numbers. Instead, ben Zakkai created a new *bloodless* Judaism. He convinced the new Sanhedrin to agree with him that sacrifice was not needed for atonement, but prayer would suffice. He based this on Hosea's prophecy, *'I desire mercy, not sacrifice'* (Hosea 6:6).

"Of course, the prophet was not calling for an end to sacrifice. The prophet Haggai prophesied more than two hundred years later that the glory of the second Temple would be greater than the first—referring to the fact that the once-for-all sin sacrifice, Yeshua, would visit that Temple. In other words, they based their *new Judaism,* a Temple-less Judaism, on the out-of-context words of a Jewish prophet when another Jewish prophet two hundred or so years later prophesied about the Temple being rebuilt—and that God is not confused. Beyond that, the entire Torah is built on the concept of blood sacrifice."

"Maybe you could add something about what the prophet really meant?" I suggested, hoping to get some insight myself.

"Well, you know of course, Levi, that God was not saying sacrifice has no value, but if people were not coming to God with the proper humility and dedication, or if they were sacrificing one day and taking advantage of their neighbor the next, God was not pleased. He would not receive the sacrifice. A sacrifice has no value to someone who does not have a humble, contrite heart. Look at the rest of the verse: *'and acknowledgment of God rather than burnt offerings.'* These were people who were not serving God, but just carrying out a religious act. Offerings have no power apart from faith and repentance, just as Yeshua's sacrifice only gives power to those who believe *and* repent." (See Acts 2:38.)

"But make no mistake, Leviticus is clear, *'For the life of a creature is in the blood, and I have given it to you to make atonement for yourselves on the altar; it is the blood that makes atonement for one's life'* (Lev. 17:11). Without the shedding of blood, there can be no forgiveness of sins!" (See Hebrews 9:22.)

"You are writing this all down, aren't you?"

"Every word!" To be honest, ever since iPhones and iPads came into being, I rarely used a pen. When I did, it was illegible. If I had to write for more than a few minutes my hand would cramp up. However, just like languages had been provided, I had a supernatural ability to write everything down in some sort of Hebrew shorthand.

"Maybe we should take a short break. Let's walk for a bit," suggested Nathan. I agreed and stood up and headed for the door. He didn't move. "Are you going to help me?"

Goodness, he is blind! I hadn't noticed. No wonder I'm writing.

"Of course, let me just make sure the materials are safe." I took his hand and helped him to his feet. Arm and arm we walked out into the courtyard. The Sea of Galilee was spectacular. Fishing boats were bringing in their catch. The sun shone high overhead. It must have been around noon. Clearly it was spring. The weather was perfect. The grass was deep green and thick and the flowers were in bloom.

I guided my old friend, whom I barely knew, as we walked around the courtyard. Though I had been with him less than an hour, there was a beautiful intimacy between us. I genuinely felt that he was my longtime companion.

We walked for about fifteen minutes, the wind of the salty sea upon our faces and the sound of the seagulls overhead. Nathan updated me on his family for a bit, and then spoke of his love for Yeshua and sang an ancient Hebrew hymn into the wind. It was here that I ceased collecting facts and felt the heartbeat of the Messianic Jews of the first century. Nathan's faith was real. His love for Yeshua was real.

"Oh, for the days when I could see the beautiful Sea of Galilee," reminisced Nathan. He lifted his face to the sky, eyes closed. "Maybe we could write out here for a while. I want to enjoy the sun's heat on this old body." I led him to a comfortable chair where he seated himself.

"I'll be right back. I am just going to get my writing materials." As I walked into the room a beautiful warmth, a peace, came over me, even more inviting than the sunlight outside.

"Hello, David." I turned to see a kind, gentle man, and he knew my *real* name.

"And who are you?" Obviously some silly trick of Ariel. Or maybe he is some biblical figure I had not yet met. If not John the Baptist, maybe Pedro the Presbyterian or Larry the Lutheran?

"David, I have been sent to rescue you from this trap."

"Trap?"

"David, you're a good person. You give to charity; you're kind to people. Your rabbi who guided you through your Bar Mitzvah and other milestones of life was correct. You don't need someone to die for you—*blood, ech!*" He made a disgusted face. But yet he was so likeable. "David, if you pray/*tefilla*, repent/*lahzur b'tshuva*, give/*tsadaka,* and keep the commandments/*mitzvot*, God will be pleased with you.

"Take my hand and I can relieve you of this nightmare. Look how your wife thinks of you now. You can be sure that at this very moment she is making plans to leave you. She thinks you are crazy. If you continue, you will return to an empty home. Sadly, Lisa will convince a judge that you are crazy—with your talk of angels and demons—and a danger to your daughters. You will be lucky to get supervised visitation rights. Imagine that, David—not only will you not be able to raise your precious little girls, but this nonsense will lead to them looking at their father like someone who needs to be institutionalized—and there is a good chance you will be!"

My daughters. I was filled with fear. What had I done? I couldn't focus on anything other than Lisa's angry and confused face from the last time I saw her at the diner—but she wasn't leaving the diner, she was leaving our home donned with a look of utter betrayal, my precious girls behind her, scared of me. The scene flooded my mind.

"Are you going to tell more people in the Jewish community? They will throw you out. There is still time to turn things around—to get things back to normal."

"But my dad! He believes too! People will listen to him."

"I am sorry, David, but you father is dead."

"No! I saw him—I talked to him."

"Another trick of that demon, Ariel. I hate to tell you this, but when you wake up from this nightmare, you will be burying your father."

A wave of nausea came over me. I was dizzy. Visions of my dad's cold, bloodless body filled my mind. *No, this can't be. I still need my father.*

"Take my hand, David," he said with that warm inviting voice. "Let's get your life back."

CHAPTER XIX

And then it hit me. This was a demon—that same lying demon from a week ago. He was trying again, using that warm, gentle, almost drug-like persuasion. Anger rose up within me. The nausea left quickly. Power began to erupt in my *kishkas*—my inner being. I looked at him with eyes of determination.

"I know who you are. You're a liar. Now get out!"

Within seconds he transformed into a giant demonic being and as he grew in stature, so did the anger in his voice as he screamed at me. *"I will kill you! I will kill your father and your family! We will not give up."* At that, I saw at least ten more join him, five on each side. *"You are as good as dead."*

His words, so bold and confident, terrified me. I felt a shiver go down my spine. What was I doing? But the boldness was also still there. There was an inner war taking place inside of me over which emotion would I give in to—fear or boldness? I chose boldness!

"*Get out* I said. God will take care of me. Now, leave!"

They screamed in anger.

"Get out I said!"

They continued unabated.

Finally, something welled up within me and I yelled back, "In the name of Yeshua the Messiah...*get out, now!*"

They screamed again, even louder, but this time *in agony*. In a matter of seconds, something like a vacuum cleaner just sucked them up like dirt from a rug; they were gone. I stood there alone, sweating and shaking. The heavenly power that was in me slowly dissipated and my soul returned to the peaceful serenity of the Sea of Galilee. *Nathan!* He was still out there. Surely he heard the commotion.

I grabbed a rag and dried off my brow. I took a deep breath and then even smiled, realizing the power that is in the name of Yeshua. *That* just happened! I smiled at the thought. *Oh, how my life has changed in one week!*

Nathan was sitting there peacefully, obviously oblivious to what I had just encountered. I now better understood the nature of the enemy. *This war is real. But in the name of Yeshua, I have power to overcome. This could be a movie!* I smiled again.

"Ah, you're back." He heard me coming. "Shall we continue?"

"I'm ready when you are." I looked at my hand. It was still shaking, but as soon as I grasped the pen my whole body calmed down and I could write.

"Okay, where were we? Yes, we were speaking about the need for sacrifice. When the Lord spoke angrily against sacrifice, it was not to condemn the very institution that He founded in the Torah, but to express His displeasure at those who would circumcise their flesh and not their hearts. It is like Yom Kippur. If you read the passages in Leviticus 23 and, more importantly, chapter 16, the focus is not on fasting—it is hardly mentioned—but on the scapegoat, the sacrifice. Fasting can't remove sin any more than good deeds, giving, prayer, or repentance. Fasting on Yom Kippur was never meant to remove sin—that would indicate that our own deeds are enough to achieve atonement. Instead, fasting was meant to express our humility before God as we brought the sacrifice. But the sacrifice was central. Without it, fasting was and is useless."

"It would be like—uh..." *Careful David, your anecdotes can't include cars or iphones!* "Eh, like going before a judge, hoping for mercy for a crime you committed. You would want to handle yourself in way that communicates contrition. You're guilty—your contrition can't change that, but it can change the heart of the judge."

"Excellent example, David. Fasting is communicating to God that humility. Even as believers, repentance alone cannot work salvation for us—only in conjunction with the blood of Yeshua.

"With no Temple, there would be no more sacrifice and Judaism was pointless. Instead of turning to God's Lamb and finding the true Hebraic expression, ben Zakkai created a new Judaism. Fasting became the focus on Yom Kippur instead of the sacrifice. The daily prayer times replaced the daily sacrifices. But all the prayers in the world cannot cleanse a guilty soul, only the substitutionary sacrifice of an innocent Lamb.

"About a decade after the devastation of Jerusalem, ben Zakkai was succeeded by Gamaliel II, the grandson of the rabbi who persuaded the Sanhedrin to let Peter, John, and the other disciples go free. What is interesting is that his argument, *which they received*, was that if Yeshua was not the Messiah, then his following would soon disappear, and if He was the Messiah, there was nothing they could do to stop Him. And here we are, a half century later!"

The blind man smiled and I remembered well how Ariel allowed me to see the scene played out before the Sanhedrin.

"Gamaliel II will be remembered for one primary act. Many Jewish believers still attended traditional synagogue. The Messianic Jews had returned from Pella to a cold reception from the rest of the Jewish community that had survived the Great Revolt. The Zealots had been utterly defeated. Their last stand was on Masada—the Dead Sea mountaintop fortress built by Herod the Great one hundred years earlier in case he ever needed to escape. It was a big enough to be a small town. It had everything he would need to survive, including storehouses and large cisterns filled with rainwater. Herod never had need for it—and in fact, never even visited."

Lisa and I had hiked up the Snake Path at Masada. We saw all those things—the cisterns, the storehouses, and an amazing view of the Dead Sea.

"At the outbreak of the revolt" (66 CE), "some of the Jewish rebels took the fortress from the Roman garrison that had guarded it. After the fall of Jerusalem, hundreds of Zealots fled and joined them there. They survived for several years until the Romans decided it was time to conquer the Zealots once and for all. They withstood the Romans for many months by throwing down rocks. However, when the Romans started using Jewish slaves to build their infamous catapult, the Zealots stopped the stoning, not wanting to kill any more Jews. Of course, in Jerusalem before the defeat they had no trouble killing their kinsmen, but maybe seeing their outer defeat—that God had not led them in their revolt—they had a change of heart.[1]

"Two survivors related to Josephus what happened next. The fighters had two choices—slavery or death. They knew what the ruthless Romans would do to their women. They would be raped over and over again and the men would be made slaves. Their leader Eleazer ben Yair made an impassioned speech, saying it would better to die by suicide than to fall into the hands of the Romans."

> Since we long ago resolved never to be servants to the Romans, nor to any other than to God Himself, Who alone is the true and just Lord of mankind, the time is now come that obliges us to make that resolution true in practice. ...We were the very first that revolted, and we are the last to fight against them; and I cannot but esteem it as a favor that God has granted us, that it is still in our power to die bravely, and in a state of freedom.[2]

"According to the two surviving women, the 960 Jews on Masada killed each other. Ten men were chosen by lot to kill the others. Here is a quote by Josephus."

> Nor, indeed, when they came to the work itself, did their courage fail them, as one might imagine it would have done, but they then held fast the same resolution, without wavering, which they had upon the hearing of Eleazar's speech, while yet every one of them still retained the natural passion of love to themselves and their families, because the reasoning they went upon appeared to them to be very just, even with regard to those that were dearest to them; for the husbands tenderly embraced their wives, and took their children into their arms, and gave the longest parting kisses to them, with tears in their eyes.
>
> They then chose ten men by lot out of them, to slay all the rest; every one of whom laid himself down by his wife and children on the ground, and threw his arms about them, and they offered their necks to the stroke of those who by lot executed that melancholy office; and when these ten had, without fear, slain them all, they made the same rule for

casting lots for themselves, that he whose lot it was should first kill the other nine, and after all, should kill himself. Accordingly, all these had courage sufficient to be no way behind one another in doing or suffering; so, for a conclusion, the nine offered their necks to the executioner, and he who was the last of all took a view of all the other bodies, lest perchance some or other among so many that were slain should want his assistance to be quite dispatched; and when he perceived that they were all slain, he set fire to the palace, and with the great force of his hands ran his sword entirely through himself, and fell down dead near to his own relations. So these people died with this intention, which they would leave not so much as one soul among them all alive to be subject to the Romans.[3]

"Families lay down together and awaited their death. Then the ten men choose lots to see who would kill the other nine. The final man killed himself.

"The Romans arrived expecting a battle, but found the fortress on fire and everyone dead, save two old women and three small children. Josephus writes, 'When the Romans saw the mass of slain, they were unable to take pleasure in the sight, even though the people were their enemies.'"[4]

Of course, I knew the story of Masada, but never told from this point of view.

"When news of the defeat of the Zealots reached Pella, we knew we could go home. We were sure when we fled that the next time we would be in Jerusalem, would be with the Messiah, as He sets up His kingdom. Clearly we were warned to flee, but His return must still be in the future. The chilly reception was expected from the survivors, but we continued to attend the synagogue."

Wow! I thought. Jewish believers in Jesus were still part of synagogue life and attending Shabbat meetings after the Great Revolt. This is so different from what we are taught. We are force-fed a lie that Jesus started a new religion—He left Judaism and started Christianity for the Gentiles. However, here we are over forty years later and these Jews—Nazarenes, as Nathan calls them...us—are still identifying as Jews.

As I was thinking, I had not even noticed that the scene had changed around me. I was in a room—a familiar room. But it was different.

CHAPTER XX

I peered out a window onto a street of ancient Jerusalem below, and then I knew exactly where I was. Yes, it was the room where Yeshua ate His last meal—a Passover Seder. It was also the place where He appeared to His disciples after He rose from the dead. I looked around. The low table was in the center with a few scattered stools and a tall wooden table that held a wash basin.

Nathan was gone. *What am I doing here?*

"I thought I would give old Nate a break."

I turned, expecting to see my angel, but it was someone else. A man in his fifties stood by the soft light coming in the other street window. Salt and pepper hair and short beard. Filled out, but in shape. A round, confident face. And he was dressed like I might dress—like I might dress at home, in Philadelphia. I was hoping this wasn't another outfit worn by an angel of light.

"Are you ready to continue, Levi? Or should I call you David?"

"Who are you?"

"Well, Ariel thought you might have some questions, so he sent me."

"Who are you?" I asked again. "Where are you from?"

"I am Simeon Ben Clopos, also known as Simeon of Jerusalem, but my favorite is, wait for it...*Saint Simeooooon.*" He waved his hands as if he had been introduced. "It's got a ring to it, don't you think?" He joked. "I replaced my cousin Yaakov, the brother of our Master, as the apostolic leader of the Jerusalem community of Messianic Jews, or Nazarenes as we called ourselves back then. My father, Clopos, was the brother of Yeshua's *stepfather,* Joseph."

"Buuuuut...you're wearing Levis, a black t-shirt, and hiking boots?"

"Well yes, I should explain. One of the great benefits of being dead, or better yet, being in heaven, is that I am not governed by the same rules of time and matter as you are. Would you prefer this?" He snapped his fingers and was dressed like one might expect from a first-century rabbi. "Or maybe this." Now he looked like an Orthodox Jew from Poland or somewhere in Eastern Europe. His beard was instantly longer. "Heck, I can even wear a dress—your culture might not accept it, but some very manly cultures did." He snapped again and he was dressed in a Scottish kilt. He snapped again and he was dressed as Roman centurion with that little *sorta-skirt* they had. "But I prefer this." Snap, and back to Levis. He pulled out one of the taller stools and motioned for me to sit down with him.

I shook my head. "That was quite a fashion show."

Simeon threw back his head and laughed heartily. "Glad you liked it, my man. Glad you liked it."

I grinned. "I guess clothes really don't 'make the man,' as they say in America."

"Let's hope not—especially not the clothes other people picked out for me." Simeon picked up two stools and carried them over to the window. "Sit, sit. It's nice to feel the sun on your face, no?"

I nodded. Indeed, fake sunshine, heavenly sunshine, or earthly sunshine—I liked it all. I sat down across from Simeon. It felt like he was giving me a tour all dressed in his Levis and black t-shirt.

"David, my wardrobe has become a bit of a joke among me and my friends here. After seeing some of my paintings—or, I should say, paintings of me on earth—I decided to upgrade my wardrobe. Look at this one." He flicked a picture on the wall behind the table. "Just look at that. This guy has me at about nine feet tall with a halo. And just so you know, we didn't wear crosses. That is like wearing an electric chair around your neck. Kinda creepy."

That was a subject I wanted to know about. "When did people start wearing crosses?"

"Well you see, that is why I am here. Ariel felt you needed to be able to ask a few questions. Your time with Nathan is great, but you're too afraid to ask him anything."

"But he thinks I lived with him through this."

"Point taken. But this is for your learning, so we want you to ask questions, okay?"

"Okay," I replied.

"By the way, it was in the fourth century."

"What was in the fourth century?"

"You asked about crosses. Constantine was the first Roman emperor to embrace Christianity—at least his weird version—and publically promote the use of crosses in worship. Crosses were already used in pagan worship, and some Christians began to use it for the obvious reason that Yeshua died on a cross. Constantine promoted its use in Christianity to make it easier for pagans to embrace the religion. He claimed to have had a vision where he saw a cross and accompanied by the words *en touto nika*."

"Eh...I don't speak Latin or Greek or whatever that was."

"Greek, of course," he laughed. "In Latin it would be *In hoc signo vinces*. It means, 'In this sign, you will conquer.'"

"God told him to conquer in the name of the cross?" I asked.

"No! The great commission is to preach the message of Yeshua—His death and resurrection, forgiveness of sins through His sacrifice, His unconditional love and desire to show mercy to all who ask—not to conquer other nations and force a religion upon them. So Constantine either, number one, made it up," Simeon said as he held up one finger, "or number two, was deceived by Satan, or number three, it was real, but he misinterpreted. Maybe the meaning was not to conquer peoples, but *sin*."

"You don't know which it was? But you're in heaven." Well, I think I was still in heaven. I was in the upper room where the last Passover meal was eaten.

"Well, right now I am actually with you in Jerusalem. But yes, I do know, but we have ground rules. In your training we can only reveal what is known—what you can prove. If you go back to Philadelphia and tell people about a man who can change clothes quickly from nineteen hundred years ago, who is that going to help? The Word of God is all you need. Beyond that, we teach you history—history you can prove. Which is why we are in this building specifically."

"But the angel allowed me to see my grandfather, to hear his story, and when I shared it with my wife I had no proof. She thought I was nuts...seeing a movie of my dead grandfather when he was a teen at the end of the Holocaust."

"Well, that just proves my point. Who does that help when you proclaim the unprovable? But as for your grandfather and what Ariel showed, you must know that he only does what he is told. Maybe the Father yet has a plan and you just need to be patient?"

I could do that. In fact, I needed to not be so defensive. It was starting to sink in. Simeon was here to lighten things up. He was definitely good at that! And I was taking my scribe job far too seriously. So I attempted to flow with Simeon and switch gears here. I did need to dig deeper about the crosses. "One more thing, Simeon. Does that mean that crosses are pagan?"

"No," he paused. "The hyper-religious love to label things demonic or pagan, but there is no such thing as an inherently pagan symbol. Pagans don't get to copyright their symbols in heaven's registry. A symbol only has meaning when the user gives it meaning. In your world, the homosexual movement—"

"I think they like to go by LGBT community..."

Simeon raised one of his bushy black eyebrows. "You'd like me to be politically correct?"

I shrugged. "Just saying."

"Okay, the LGBT community adopted the rainbow for their symbol. Of course God created the rainbow as a sign that He would never flood the world again. So the fact that they use it doesn't mean they are promoting God's covenant—quite the contrary. It does present a spiritual battle over the symbol. Of course, the rainbow is different from stars and crosses in that it was created with a specific meaning.

"Symbols are pagan to pagans. Stars, crosses, etc.—they are just symbols. You choose to give them meaning.

"I will add this. If the pagans were using a cross as a demonic symbol, then it would have been confusing for Christians to also use it. Someone, believer or unbeliever, could assume you were pagan. For instance, if you were the leader of a pro-life movement and your logo reassembled the swastika—something that has been associated with death—you would confuse people. Is the swastika demonic? Not inherently. It has been used in Hinduism and Buddhism for centuries in a quite favorable manner. Not that I am advocating for false religions—I am merely saying that it was not used to murder people in those contexts. When you see a black swastika surrounded by a white circle on a red flag, what do you feel?"

"Nazis. Death. Six million. My grandfather."

"Exactly, because that was the meaning that Hitler gave to it. But someone from China might see the same symbol, not knowing the history of the Holocaust, and have a completely different reaction.

"It is like Paul said to the Corinthians. Idols have no power."

We know that "An idol is nothing at all in the world" and that "There is no God but one" (1 Corinthians 8:4).

"But he adds that we should not eat meat sacrificed to idols because those former pagans who are used to it being connected to idol worship would stumble to see a believer eating such meats." (See First Corinthians 8:7–10.) "For them it would be sin, because they are still under the impression that an idol has power."

Simeon was on a roll, so I sat back and listened.

"There are those today who claim that the six-pointed star is demonic or pagan. Where is that written in God's Word? In fact, if you look at the carvings in the ancient synagogue in Capernaum—the Master's headquarters in the Galilee," he snapped his fingers and we were standing in what appeared to be the ruins of an ancient city. To the left was clearly the Sea of Galilee. "We find five- and six-pointed stars, along with palm trees. They were just decoration with no symbolic meaning." He snapped his fingers and we returned to Jerusalem.

"What if pagans and occultists just start grabbing up all the symbols—whether they are crosses, stars, dots, or even question marks—and give them meaning? Does that mean that no one else can ever use those symbols for something good? Getting back to stars, the Star of David was the adopted symbol of the First Zionist Congress in 1897. Theodore Herzl, the father of modern Israel, wrote in his diary after the conference, 'Today I created the State of Israel. In five years, perhaps, and certainly in fifty, everyone will see it.' Exactly fifty years later, the UN voted for Israel to become an independent nation.

"Which is amazing when you consider that they embraced the *demonic* six-pointed star," he added in jest. "Dalet (ד) is the first and last letter in the name of David (דוד). And in ancient Hebrew the letter was closer to a triangle. David's name in Hebrew, then, can be represented symbolically as two interconnected triangles—a hexagram. Some claim that the Star of David came from this insignia. It was common for kings to put their sign on the shields of their soldiers. David's could have easily have been two Dalets, one inverted, forming a six-pointed star.

"And yet others claim that the hexagram is a very ancient symbol that has *inherent* spiritual power. Because it is used in black magic, witchcraft, occultism, and zodiacal horoscopes by astrologers, it must be demonic— they reason. God created the stars in the sky, and just because someone thinks they are speaking to them doesn't mean we should stop marveling over the beauty of God's creation any more than we should stop marveling over a rainbow after a thunderstorm because the homose—I mean the LGBT folks use the rainbow.

"Do you think that pagans or occultists never used shofars? Of course they did and still do. Go to Africa today and you will see it in all kinds of tribal religions. Shofars and trumpets were the email/telephone system of the ancient world. Yet God tells the Israelites to use the trumpets symbolically on Feasts of Trumpets, every new moon and before they would go out to war."

> *When you go into battle in your own land against an enemy who is oppressing you, sound a blast on the trumpets. Then you will be remembered by the Lord your God and rescued from your enemies. Also at your times of rejoicing—your appointed festivals and New Moon feasts—you are to sound the trumpets over your burnt offerings and fellowship offerings, and they will be a memorial for you before your God. I am the Lord your God* (Numbers 10:9-10).

"Oh, and I am sure we can find someone to claim the moon is from Satan, and yet God tells the people of Israel to use it as their calendar. Come on, David. I am not going to let Satan steal God's symbols!"

"What you're saying is true," I answered. "But about David's star being two Dalets?"

"Ground rules, David, ground rules. If you can't prove it, I can't tell you—which, again, is why we are here. Now stop getting me sidetracked," he said in mock frustration, then grinned at me. For the first time I noticed his front two teeth had a gap between them, even here in heaven. It seemed to fit his face, though.

"I will tell you this, David, our brother Paul wrote to his son in the faith, Titus, about such things. He said, '*To the pure all things are pure, but to those who are defiled and unbelieving nothing is pure; but even their mind and conscience are defiled*'" (Titus 1:15 NKJV). "And I think that statement applies here. Does that make sense?"

I nodded. "It does. Okay, then please tell me, why are we here?"

"Nathan was telling you about Gamaliel II, right?"

"Yes, the grandson of the great rabbi Gamaliel."

"By the time that Gamaliel II replaced ben Zakkai, it was clear that he wanted us—the Nazarenes—out; so he cleverly added a nineteenth benediction called the *birkat haminim*, a prayer against heretics, to the *Amidah*. Interestingly, the other name for the *Amidah* is—"

"The *Shmoneh Esre*," I jumped in, "the Eighteen Benedictions."

"Yes, but it should be called the *Cha Esre*—the Nineteen Benedictions—for the one that was added. It was intended to weed out Messianic Jews, who were being considered heretics more and more by the new ben Zakkai Judaism. Jews recite the *Amidah* thrice daily."

"Yes, we pray through it in our *minyans*.[1] Recently I have been attending the *mincha* afternoon prayer service at my synagogue."

"Yes, but here is what you don't know. When you pray through the Amidah *now*—now that you are a believer in Yeshua—you are unwittingly forced to pray a curse upon yourself. One of the prayers, the one that Gamaliel II added, is directly aimed at Jewish believers, Nazarenes."

On the wall behind the Passover table there was a niche—a recess in the wall. A screen dropped down. Why wasn't I surprised? Words appeared and Simeon read them aloud.

For the apostates let there be no hope. And let the arrogant government be speedily uprooted in our days. Let the *Notsrim* and the *minim* be destroyed in a moment. And let them be blotted out of the Book of Life and not be inscribed together with the righteous. Blessed art thou, O Lord, who humblest the arrogant.[2]

"The word *Notsrim* is Hebrew for Nazarenes."

"What does the word *minim* mean?" I asked.

"A *min* is a heretic. *Minim* is plural."

"So I have been unwittingly praying a curse on myself the past several months."

"Well, not exactly. You didn't know what you were saying, as you don't speak Hebrew, and second, over the centuries the prayer was changed. Non-Jewish Christians began to assume that the synagogue was praying a curse upon them. In as early as the first centuries we find church fathers voicing the claim that the Jews curse the Christians in their prayers. These accusations caused the Jewish community to change the language over time. Without exception, the word *Notsrim* was expunged from all Jewish prayer rites. Some Reform prayer books omit this benediction entirely.[3]

"In the middle of the second century Justin Martyr accuses Jews of cursing all believers."

"Ariel taught me about him. He had a fictional debate with Jew named...eh, Try or Trophy...?"

"Close, Trypho," he helped me. "Listen what he says here in the same book."

For you curse in your synagogues all those who are called from Him Christians; and other nations effectively carry out the curse, putting to death those who simply confess themselves to be Christians.[4]

"He wasn't completely wrong. He was referring of course to the *birkat haminim*, the benediction against heretics. He assumed that *Notsrim* meant all believers, when in fact the synagogue cared little about what other nations worship—well, except for one thing, which I'll mention in a few minutes. Their goal was simple: With no Temple they were creating a new Judaism based on the Oral Law, traditions, and the local synagogue. Anyone with a different opinion must be weeded out.

"It was not just the Nazarenes they wanted out, but all who didn't line up with the new rabbinic Judaism—Sadducees and Essenes as well. And despite its defects, Pharisaical Judaism, now called Rabbinic Judaism, was a system that God used to keep Israel as an identifiable people for two thousand years without a geographical homeland. There is no other testimony in antiquity of a nation being separated from her homeland for more than a generation or two and surviving. It was indeed one of the great miracles in world history—but rabbinic Judaism played a role. Despite their rejection of the Messiah, the very system that they built to replace Him ended up saving them as a people! Oh, the mysteries of God!"

Simeon seemed overcome by the story he shared until he was no longer talking to me, but to God.

"Oh, God, Your mysteries are great! Your wisdom and foresight are beyond man's knowing. Your plans are perfect and You rule the nations."

Simeon continued to worship for a couple of minutes, tears flowing down his face, falling on his beard, to his t-shirt and Levis. I still didn't know how to worship, but I too was overcome with emotion. And then he looked over at me and smiled. "The Lord is good," he said, "and His mercy endures forever."

He regained his composure and continued. I remained dumbfounded, however, still experiencing deep emotions that I never felt, or maybe it was the presence of God or an angel. What I did know was that it was still all so new to me, and yet so wonderful.

Simeon sighed deeply. "While *Notsrim* or Nazarenes meant Messianic Jews back in my day, many Christians like Martyr assumed they were its intended target. Today the word *Notsrim* has completely lost its Jewish context. In modern Hebrew it refers to orthodox Christians—such as Greek or Russian Orthodox or Catholic. And, well, we certainly could not pray a curse upon ourselves that declared us to be apostates and heretics. This had its intended consequences, as the majority of Nazarenes left the traditional synagogues and we had our own meetings—not just our regular Motzei Shabbat[5] (Saturday evening) meetings. We built our own synagogue for weekly Torah study and Shabbat morning meetings."

"Really? There was an actual Messianic Jewish *Bet Knesset*—synagogue—in the first century? Where was it?"

He pointed to the screen as the lights grew dim.

A movie started with Nathan—the younger Nathan, but older than the first version I met—who called out, "Simeon has called for a gathering at the home where the last Passover was held. Come!"

"With the blessing of the apostles," began a carbon copy of my friend in Levis, but clearly in clothes more suitable to his day, "I humbly accepted before the war the charge to take up where our dear brother Yaakov left off. He led the community, along with the apostles, for nearly thirty years.

"When we returned from Pella we planned to rebuild our lives here. By God's grace, we have rebuilt here—in our city—the City of David, where our Messiah, my cousin after the flesh, was tortured and crucified because of our sin. It was He who said that this testimony must go forth from Jerusalem to the ends of the earth." (See Acts 1:8.) "When the Temple stood we met gladly in her courts. However, now that it is gone and given the fact that we are being forced out of the local synagogues, we will establish our own synagogue right here, where He had His last meal."

Simeon looked around the room, memories lighting up his face. "Here, where He ate the Passover supper with His beloved disciples. And where He appeared to them eight days later, proving that death could not hold Him captive. We will rebuild here and continue in the mandate of our Messiah—to reach our people and the world."

The lights came on and the screen returned. "You built a synagogue here? And given the ground rules, I guess you can prove it—or at least I will be able to prove it back home."

"Good, you are paying attention. But don't take my word for it. Listen to this modern-day professor give his take."

We turned to the screen where a man, possibly at a university, was lecturing. He was thin and wiry, I'll guess in his late forties, with reading glasses far enough down his nose that you could see his eyes. He spoke at a podium before a room full of young people—clearly students.

> One of the most amazing sites in Jerusalem is also one that is overlooked by more than 99.9 percent of tourists, and sadly, even educated tour guides don't realize its significance. Millions of tourists pass through this site every year. In fact, I would guess that less than 1 percent of 1 percent realize that when they are in the Upper Room, they are actually standing in a building that became the first *Messianic* synagogue.
>
> The very first Jewish believers did not see a need for a synagogue of their own. They all continued to go to the traditional synagogue—the only place to hear the Scriptures read on a weekly basis—and then, they met together on the first day of the week (believed to be Saturday evening, not Sunday—a work day in Israel). These meetings were held in homes, and they also met daily in the Temple Courts as well (see Acts 2:46).
>
> However, persecution grew intense in sixties. It is believed that Yaakov (James), despite being one of the most respected Jews in Jerusalem, was martyred through a conspiracy led by the Pharisees in 62 CE. The Book of Hebrews encourages the Jewish believers to stand strong in the face of persecution (see Heb. 12:1–4).[6]

"Here he talks about the history that you already know, but it's quick, so we will listen," instructed Simeon.

> Then in the late sixties—no, not that sixties—the Zealots, a Jewish sect seeking independence from Rome, rebelled. The Roman armies surrounded Jerusalem and prepared to raze it to the ground. The Messianic Jews were warned by angel to escape according to the historian Eusebius.[7] They remembered the words of Yeshua.

> *When you see Jerusalem being surrounded by armies, you will know that its desolation is near. Then let those who are in Judea flee to the mountains, let those in the city get out, and let those in the country not enter the city* (Luke 21:20-21).

> *The Second Coming was just around the corner* they assumed. They fled across the Jordan River. After Jerusalem was destroyed and the Zealots were thoroughly defeated, the Messianic community returned to Jerusalem.[8]

"Yes, I remember that well. We were expecting His appearance was just around the corner," quipped the apostle with a bit of nostalgia.

> Now, this is where our story gets interesting.

> In 1948, during Israel's War of Independence, a shell exploded near the traditional site of King David's tomb (we now know that is not his tomb) and the site of the Upper Room. In 1951, an Israeli archeologist, Jacob Pinkerfeld, was tasked with repairing the damage. In doing so he discovered the original floor of the building and an alcove. Bargil Pixner, the renowned Benedictine monk, biblical scholar, and archaeologist, writes, "Similar niches at similar heights above floor level have been found in ancient synagogues and were presumably used to house an ark for Torah scrolls."[9,10]

Without interrupting, Simeon smiled and aggressively pointed at the screen. No, not at the screen, at the recess behind the screen. He whispered, "That's the niche where we kept our Torah scrolls."

In other words, this room, the Upper Room, was actually an ancient synagogue. The question is, *was it always a synagogue,* and if not, *when did it become a synagogue?* Some claim that the Roman General Titus spared the area during his conquest in 70 CE. However it is more likely—since we know that the entire city was destroyed—that it was rebuilt into a synagogue after the 70 CE war. We know that in the time of Yeshua, forty years prior, it was not a synagogue, but merely a room.

Pinkerfeld concurred that this was indeed a synagogue; unlike churches that faced the east, the building was oriented toward the Temple or where the Temple once stood. Pinkerfeld was correct; it was a synagogue, but his conclusion that it could not be a church, or for our purposes a gathering of Yeshua believers, because it did not face east is erroneous. Churches didn't begin to face east until the second half of the fourth century according to Bixler.

Bixler claims he erred also in his assumption that the building was facing the Temple. It was an obvious assumption, but when actually measured, the niche or the alcove that was discovered is slightly off. Instead of facing the Temple, it faces a most interesting place.

Just think for a minute. You have returned to Jerusalem. The city is in ruins. The year is 72 CE or 73 CE. The Temple is gone! Please understand the significance of this. The Temple was the center of Jewish life and religion. Even in the lives of first-century Messianic Jews the Temple was very significant. The believers met there for worship and teaching, as well as for outreach (Acts 3-4; 5:25). This must have been a huge blow. In addition, the Second Temple was the most amazing structure of its time. It was a marvel and a wonder. And now it was in ruins.

The writer of Hebrews warned of this when he said that that which *"is obsolete and outdated will soon disappear"* (Heb. 8:13). Scholars have wrongly assumed he was speaking of the entire Old Covenant, when in fact he was referring to the sacrificial system—as six years later the Temple would be burned to the ground.

So, without a Temple, the Messianic Jews return to the other highly significant place—the Upper Room—as their headquarters. Facing rejection from traditional Jews, they rebuild it into their own synagogue. In just a few years, the Pharisees, under Gamaliel II, will add a "blessing" to the *Amidah*—prayed three times a day—that calls all Messianic Jews heretics and curses them. In fact, while we know the Messianic Jews returned in 72-73 CE, it is possible that they did not build their synagogue until this self-imposed curse became a part of *Amidah* and forced them out of the synagogue.

But when it came time to orient the niche, they conclude not to point it in the direction of where the Temple once stood, but rather in the direction of its replacement.

In fact, the synagogue's orientation is toward what is presently the Church of the Holy Sepulchre. Of course, there was no church there at the time—that came centuries later. And I can tell you from firsthand experience that that church is one of the strangest places I have ever been. It is a house of tradition and superstition and hardly represents New Covenant faith. However, at the time the synagogue was built, that place was and still is believed to be the *site of Yeshua's tomb and His crucifixion* at Golgotha.[11]

How powerful is that! Without a Temple, the source of sacrifice and forgiveness, they rightly discerned that the new source of everlasting forgiveness and redemption was Golgotha. But should it point toward the place where He was crucified and uttered the words, "It is finished," or toward the place of His resurrection, where the proof of redemption lie? How about both? He was buried where He was crucified.

At the place where Jesus was crucified, there was a garden, and in the garden a new tomb, in which no one had ever been laid (John 19:41).

If we needed any more proof that this building was the first Jewish synagogue erected for the exclusive use of Messianic Jews, we have it in the form of suppressed graffiti that Pinkerfeld found under the later floors (he removed several floors to get to the original). The graffiti was only later published and claims that the building was erected in the first century.

"One graffito has the initials of the Greek words, which may be translated as 'Conquer, Savior, mercy.' Another graffito has letters, which can be translated as 'O Jesus, that I may live, O Lord of the autocrat.'"[12]

The fact that the words are in Greek is evidence that it was later used by Gentile Christians after all Jews were barred from the city in 135 CE. This was in response to the last Jewish rebellion. The Roman Emperor Hadrian expelled all the Jews and turned Jerusalem into a pagan city. He even built a Temple to Venus on the place where Yeshua was crucified.

But how did these Gentiles know for sure that this was the place of the Upper Room and the first Messianic synagogue?

"Though Hadrian banned all Jews from Jerusalem in 135 CE, Christians not of Jewish ancestry could and did live in Jerusalem from Hadrian's time on. Eusebius even preserves a list of the Gentile bishops of Jerusalem."[13]

The clear evidence supports the idea that the Messianic Jews returning from a self-imposed exile after the Roman conquest of Jerusalem, built the first Messianic synagogue in the former Upper Room and oriented it to face Golgotha—the place of Yeshua's execution and resurrection.[14]

"That's amazing," I said. "But wait a minute. As the professor said, churches didn't orient themselves to the east until much later. This was built in the first century. So how do you know that it wasn't a church, but a Messianic synagogue?"

"Other than the fact that I built it, you mean?"

"Ground rules," I shot back.

"Touché again, my young friend. You are pretty quick. First of all, let's deal with the word *church*. It is not in the Bible."

"Yes, Ariel taught me about that. The word in Greek is ek... ek-something."

"*Ecclesia*, and it means simply an *assembly* or *called out ones*."

"Called out for what?"

"If we look at Acts 19:32, 39, and 41, we see something quite interesting. The word *ecclesia* is used, but it's *not* referring to a gathering of believers. It is referring to a city council that was actually quite hostile to believers. So in a secular sense, it means those who are called out for a meeting—a gathering. In the biblical sense it means those Jews and Gentiles called out from the world to the Messiah.

"*Ecclesia* is the equivalent of the Hebrew word *kahal*, assembly, where we get the word *kehila*, community. In Israel today, a Messianic congregation would be called a kehila. Hebrews 2:12 quotes Psalm 22:22 where is says '*I will declare your name to my people; in the assembly* [or *kahal*] *I will praise you.*" The Greek word that the writer of Hebrews used for *kahal* (assembly) was not the one for church—*kyriakon*—but *ecclesia*.

"*Kyriakon* means 'belonging to the lord.' We only find it in the New Covenant twice and never referring to an assembly. Once when it refers to the Lord's Supper, and then again in Revelation, referring to the lord's day."

"Yes, and the lord's day referred to Caesar, not Yeshua."[15]

"Good memory David. *Kyriakon* was not specific to Yeshua, as the word predates the New Covenant. It could refer to a pagan temple when referring to a building. *Kyriakon* often referred to a holy place or temple—specifically the building, *not* the inhabitants. The word wasn't used specifically for houses of New Testament worship until the time of our good friend Emperor Constantine. He had large buildings erected, such as St. Paul's Cathedral and St. Peter's Cathedral."

"Yes, I have seen them both."

"Well, that was three hundred years after our Master. One of the first English translations of the Bible was the Tyndale Bible in 1526, and they never used the word *church*. They always translated *ecclesia* correctly as *congregation*. One reason was probably because they were familiar with Hebrew and Greek—many earlier English translations were not from the original Hebrew and Greek, but from the Latin Vulgate, such as Wycliffe's Bible. Most others translations from that era also used *congregation*, not *church*.[16] Not so with the King James Version of the Bible. King James demanded fifteen rules be followed by the translators, one of which was strangely that *ecclesia* must translated as *church* and not *assembly* or *congregation*.

"In truth, David, our first-century structure could not have been a church because there were no churches! The earliest known New Testament building specifically for worship dates back to 229 CE, in an ancient city called Dura-Europus in what is now Syria. This was two hundred years after the resurrection and nearly a hundred and fifty years after we built our synagogue.

"From the beginning we met either house to house or in the Temple courts. Even in Europe and Asia, they met mostly in homes and sometimes gathered all the believers in a city together. Often it was at the homes of those with larger structures that the believers gathered. We have evidence that in Rome, the first believers met in other non-religious building like warehouses or apartment buildings."[17]

"Why didn't they build buildings?"

"Good question, and it makes sense if you were talking about Philadelphia in the twenty-first century. In fact, today there are whole movements dedicated to the idea that buildings are evil. *True houses of worship must be in homes,* they assume. This obsession is based on noble desires—to increase fellowship, provide a more intimate setting where people can open up, hold each other accountable, pray for one another, support one another in difficult times, and see each member move in the gifts of the Spirit. These are things that are hard to do in a large gathering. And it is one of the reasons that we met in homes. But this assumption is also based on a false premise—that believers from the Empire chose to meet only in homes.

"The reason believers did not build buildings was because being a believer in Yeshua in the Roman Empire was against the law—an offense punishable by death, as both our dear brothers Paul and Peter can attest. Any first-, second-, or third-century believer would tell you plainly they were in hiding. It would be akin to North Korea today or the USSR in its heyday. Being a believer was *illegal.*

"We have this testimony from the first-century senator and historian Tacitus."

> [Emperor] Nero punished a race of men who were hated for
> their evil practices. These men were called Christians. He got
> a number of people to confess. On their evidence a number
> of Christians were convicted and put to death with dread-
> ful cruelty. Some were covered with the skins of wild beasts

and left to be eaten by dogs. Others were nailed to the cross. Many were burned alive and set on fire to serve as torches at night.[18]

"Remember the Coliseum? It was originally called the Flavian Amphitheatre, the family name of Vespasian, Titus, and Domitian, the evilest of them all. It was common during the midday session, before the gladiators would fight, to entertain the crowd by feeding criminals, slaves, and, yes, believers in Yeshua to wild beasts such as lions. It is no wonder they met secretly. Remember the quote from Justin Martyr."

"Yes, he claimed that the Jews cursed Christians in the synagogue."

"In the second part, he says, 'and other nations effectively carry out the curse, putting to death those who simply confess themselves to be Christians.' There was some truth to this. By the time Justin Martyr wrote this there was intense competition between the synagogue and the growing body of believers, and the feelings between them were fierce. You will learn more of this later, but Rome did indeed carry out the wishes of the *birkat haminim*. Not that they could blot out a believer, Jew or Gentile, from God's book—as the *birkat haminim* calls for, but Rome destroyed the lives of countless believers.

"And then in 313 CE everything changed. Emperor Constantine became a Christian—the first emperor to embrace Christianity. He made it legal to believe in Yeshua. For three hundred years believers had suffered torture, starvation, and death, but now they were allowed to openly worship. Very soon buildings, called churches, were built—in Rome as well as throughout the empire."[19]

"But your building was dedicated in the first century. Weren't you concerned about Rome?"

"Rome allowed the nations it conquered to continue in their religions with one caveat: They had to also worship Roman gods. The religion of Rome was simple. Worship the Roman gods and prosperity would continue. Rome didn't care if these other nations worshiped their own gods as well. But faith in Yeshua was a problem. Believers believed in only one God, and as part of their creed they could not include the worship-ing of the Roman gods. Beyond this it was political. Not every Roman leader believed in these gods, but it was the glue that kept the empire together politically."

"That would be a problem for Jews, wouldn't it?"

"Read this," requested Simeon, and I looked to the screen and there was an article with part of it highlighted. I read it out loud.

> In 63 [BCE], the Romans conquered Judea, the land of the Jews. Rome immediately recognized it had a problem because the Jews refused to pay homage to Roman gods. Rome gave in and exempted Jews from this requirement. Rome did this in part because the Jews had helped Roman general Julius Caesar win an important battle several years earlier. Soon Rome recognized Judaism as a legal religion, allowing Jews to worship freely.[20]

> Rome had good reasons to tolerate the Jewish religion. First, it was a well-established religion with a long history. Most important, Rome wanted to keep the people of Judea from revolting. Neither of these reasons applied to Christianity. This new offshoot of the Jewish religion had little support at first among the people of Judea. In fact, many Jews would have been pleased if Rome had suppressed it.[21]

"Let me interrupt here, just to say, and I know you have already learned this, Jewish acceptance of Yeshua was far more widespread than history has recorded. While this author is correct that many Jews would have loved for the Messianic faith to disappear, he is incorrect in saying that it 'had little support at first among the people of Judea.' Josephus records that just before the Great Revolt in 66 CE, there were only about six thousand Pharisees in Jerusalem. Compare that with the 'tens of thou-sands' of Messianic Jews who were in Jerusalem to celebrate Shavuot[22] in 49 CE."

When they heard this, they praised God. Then they said to Paul: "You see, brother, how many thousands of Jews have believed, and all of them are zealous for the law" (Acts 21:20).

"Just wanted to make sure we are clear on that. Let's continue."

Yet when Rome first became aware of Christianity around [30 CE], it did nothing to stop it. Thinking this sect might weaken the always bothersome Jewish religion, Emperor Tiberius asked the Senate to legalize the Christian faith and declare Christ a Roman god. But the Senate refused. Instead, it pronounced Christianity to be an "illegal superstition," a crime under Roman law.

Although Christianity was now officially illegal, Tiberius still hoped this new religious sect would further his goal of pacifying the empire. As a result, he ordered Roman officials not to interfere with the new religion, a policy that lasted about 30 years until the time of Nero.[23]

On the night of July 18, [64 CE], a fire began in the area of the Circus Maximus, the great arena in Rome for chariot races and games. The fire spread quickly and for six days consumed much of the city, including Emperor Nero's palace.

Immediately, the rumor spread that Nero himself had caused the great fire to clear space for a new palace. He was also accused of playing the lyre (a stringed instrument like a small harp) while watching the spectacular conflagration. Although he probably did play the lyre at some point while watching the fire, he was almost certainly not responsible for it. Nevertheless, the suffering people of Rome believed him guilty.

Fearful that Roman mobs would turn on him, Nero cast about for a scapegoat to blame for the fire. He pointed to an unpopular small religious minority, the Christians.

Christians made an easy target for scapegoating. The common people of Rome believed rumors about Christians. Some thought Christians practiced cannibalism because the sacrament of the Eucharist called for believers to symbolically eat the flesh and blood of Christ. Others believed that Christians practiced incest because they preached loving their brothers and sisters. Many believed Christians hated humanity because they kept secrets and withdrew from normal social life. Many pagans feared that the gods would become angry and punish the Roman people since Christians refused to participate in the old religious rituals. These fears and rumors helped Nero shift public opinion to blaming the Christians rather than him for the great fire.

Since the Christian religion was still illegal, it was easy to order mass arrests, trials, and executions. The Christian martyrs suffered horrible deaths. Roman historian Tacitus described Nero's methods of execution:

Dressed in wild animal skins, they were torn to pieces by dogs, or crucified, or made into torches to be ignited after dark as substitutes for daylight. Nero provided his Gardens for the spectacle, and exhibited displays in the Circus, at which he mingled with the crowd—or stood in a chariot dressed as a charioteer.[24]

"Over the centuries, until Constantine, persecution came in waves. There were times when it was much safer to be a believer than others, but never could one be too sure. Domitian was one of the most violent and believed himself to be a god."

"Right, he tried to kill John by boiling him in oil, but he survived," I added, feeling glad not be completely clueless.

"And in 250 CE, Emperor Decius sought to usher in a pagan revival and had many believers killed."

> For almost 40 years, the legalized Christian Church flourished in the Roman Empire. Then, in 297, Emperor Diocletian initiated one last terrible Christian persecution.
>
> Diocletian had come to power at a time of crisis. Prices of goods were climbing rapidly, German tribes threatened the western part of the empire, and the Persian Empire was attacking in the east.
>
> Diocletian moved boldly. He set price controls. He doubled the size of the army. To govern the empire more easily, he broke it into two parts—the Greek-speaking east and the Latin-speaking west.
>
> Suspicious of the loyalty of Christians to the Roman state, Diocletian started persecuting them. He demanded that all Christian soldiers resign from the Roman army. He forbade gatherings for Christian worship and ordered the destruction of churches and sacred writings. Christian members of the government were tortured and executed.
>
> Other edicts followed when Christian uprisings took place in the eastern parts of the empire where Christianity was strongest. Bishops and priests were arrested, tortured, and martyred. In 304, Rome decreed that all Christians sacrifice to the pagan gods or face death.
>
> Following Diocletian's retirement in 305, a civil war broke out to determine his successor. It raged on for almost a decade. Even so, the persecution of Christians continued. Galerius, Diocletian's handpicked successor, hated

Christians and organized a war of extermination against them in the eastern empire. Christians were mutilated, burned alive, and crucified. Hundreds of Christian men, women, and children were forced to labor in government mines. Crowds in Roman arenas shouted, "Let there be no Christians!"

Galerius grew disheartened when he saw that his efforts had failed to stamp out the Christian religion. Dying of cancer that was literally rotting his body, Galerius suspended the persecution in 311. He then pleaded for Christians to pray for his health. But he died, and the oppression resumed.

Constantine, who was fighting for control of the western empire, had a vision that he would win an important battle if he fought under the sign of the cross. He quickly had artisans mark his soldiers shields with crosses and sent them into battle. When they won, Constantine became a strong supporter of Christianity.

Constantine emerged from the civil war as the new emperor. In 313, he proclaimed that every person was free "to follow the religion which he chooses." Under Constantine, Christianity rapidly became the dominant religion.[25]

"Now before you get too fond of our friend Constantine, he will later become extreme in his desire to separate the New Testament from its Jewish roots. In fact, he would become just plain ruthless. While he embraced 'Christianity,' he did not embrace Christian values and was full of pride, a wicked and blinding sin. He set the stage for the Church to become the most oppressive force in Europe. Christianity, from Constantine until hundreds of years into the future, killed more fellow Christians than the pagans had. Doctrine became legally binding and enforced by government.

"Constantine had his own sons put to death and suffocated his wife. He also oversaw the death of a nephew and his father. He was a killer.

"In 325 he called for the Nicea Council. There were three hundred and eighteen bishops in attendance, and none of them came from a Jewish background. The bishops could not do enough to espouse their love and devotion to Emperor Constantine."

> Some bishops, blinded by the splendor of the court, even went so far as to laud the emperor as an angel of God, as a sacred being, and to prophesy that he would, like the Son of God, reign in heaven.[26]

"Constantine the Great would have no opposition to implement his changes from this gang. And his goal was to do away with Passover. In his own words."

On the screen a quote appeared:

> And truly, in the first place, it seems to everyone a most unworthy thing that we should follow the customs of the Jews in the celebration of this most holy solemnity, who, polluted wretches, having stained their hands with a nefarious crime are justly blinded in their minds. It is fit, therefore, that rejecting the practice of this people, we should perpetuate to all future ages the celebration of this rite, in a more legitimate order, which we have kept from the first day of our "Lord's" passion even to the present times. Let us then have nothing in common with the most hostile rabble of the Jews.[27]

"He was rabid with hostility toward the Jews, but still it is true— until he became emperor it was illegal for Christians to even build their own buildings, even when the persecution was not active.

"But, as noted, Judaism was legal. Rome had no fear that a faith based in Jerusalem would destabilize the empire, but the Gospel, which came out of Jerusalem, was spreading fast. It was a real threat. Hence the persecution. Christians were considered atheists. They didn't embrace the Roman gods and thus they were also accused of being traitors. Neither did they honor Caesar as a god, disrespecting the empire. In the early 80s the Nazarenes were still seen as a sect of Judaism—not part of the persecuted Christians.

"So, that was a long answer to a short question, but it simply could not have been a Christian church because that was not legal in the Roman Empire after Nero in the 60s until Constantine in the early 300s."

"Why did you call yourselves Nazarenes?"

"Yes, right on time."

"I'm sorry?"

"Your question is right on time. It was a pleasure talking to you, David. And by the way, I think I can tell you this. He made it up."

"Who made what up?"

"Constantine—he didn't see a vision. He was just using Christianity as a means of gaining political power."

And then he was gone.

CHAPTER XXI

I was still there in the Upper Room/synagogue—alone. *What do I do? Is Ariel coming to get me? Can I go home now?* I thought of my father—alive somewhere in all of this. I was homesick. I couldn't wait to go home. I wanted to see my father again and could only hope he would wake up and convince Lisa that I wasn't crazy. My heart ached with love for my wife. Oh, that she would know the truth and together we could embrace this challenge. *As a family* we would embark on this journey!

"So I hear you are asking questions about the Nazarenes?"

I turned around, startled. A man stood before me. Medium height. A hard, leathering face—yet full of empathy. A thick grayish beard and mustache. His blue eyes caught the sunlight and I saw more than kindness—I saw a man alive in Spirit.

Dressed in clothes from the first century, a dark brown tunic covered him. He was strong and clearly had been through his share of battles.

"Mati."

"I'm sorry?"

"You want to know who I am, yes?"

"As a matter of fact, yes."

"I am Mati, otherwise known as Matiyahu—the gift of God," he smiled.

Not exactly modest, is this fellow.

"No," reading my thoughts, "that is what my name means. *Matat* means 'gift,' and *Yahu* is short for 'Yahweh.' In English they call me Matthew. And my other name is not uncommon to you, Levi."

Yes, my first-century time-traveling name.

"Nice to meet you...eh..."

"Call me Mati. Come, take a seat. Let's get to it."

Mati chose the soft cushions on the floor around the Passover table. I was relieved to take a new position and get off those hard stools for a while. *I guess I'll have to wait a little longer to see my family.* I knew when I returned to earth I would long to be here again. Yet when I was here, I longed for earth. I shook it off. Ariel sent Mati here because there was more to be learned, and I was determined not to miss a thing.

"So, about the Nazarene name," I started.

"Yes, the Nazarenes," Mati said. He stroked his coarse gray beard thoughtfully. "Most people assume that that the followers of Yeshua were called *Notsrim* or Nazarenes because he came from *Natzeret* or Nazareth. They are only partly right. Just as you would call someone from Yerushalayim a Yerushalayimi or someone from Tel Aviv a *Tel Avivi*, someone from Natzeret would be a *Notsri*. However, there is more to this story.

"In my account of the life of Yeshua, I stated something that has confused scholars to this day, but was clear to my readers in the first century."

> [Joseph] *went and lived in a town called Nazareth. So was fulfilled what was said through the prophets, that* [Yeshua] *would be called a Nazarene* (Matthew 2:23).

"Anti-Messianics have sought to use this verse to confuse young Jewish believers by claiming that the New Testament is false. After all, there is no prophecy from the Hebrew Scriptures that claims that Yeshua would be called a Nazarene. Or is there?

"First of all, what is a Nazarene? In the context of the claim it would be someone who lives in Nazareth. However, one must look deeper to see the wordplay—something that was very common in Hebrew literature.

"The word for Nazarene that is used in the Hebrew New Testament is *natsri* (נִצְרִי). The root of this word is *natsar* (נָצַר). From this root we get the Hebrew word *netser* (נֵצֶר). And a *netser* is a *branch*.

"With this information, let's see if there is anything regarding a branch and the Messiah in the Hebrew prophets."

Mati was a skilled teacher. Several passages appeared on the screen in front of the niche.

> *In that day the **Branch** of the Lord will be beautiful and glorious, and the fruit of the land will be the pride and glory of the survivors in Israel* (Isaiah 4:2).

> *"The days are coming," declares the Lord, "when I will raise up for David a righteous **Branch**, a King who will reign wisely and do what is just and right in the land"* (Jeremiah 23:5).

> *In those days and at that time I will make a righteous **Branch** sprout from David's line; he will do what is just and right in the land* (Jeremiah 33:15).

> *Listen, High Priest Joshua, you and your associates seated before you, who are men symbolic of things to come: I am going to bring my servant, the **Branch*** (Zechariah 3:8).

> *Tell him this is what the Lord Almighty says: "Here is the man whose name is the **Branch**, and he will **branch** out from his place and build the temple of the Lord"* (Zechariah 6:12).

"Okay, problem solved, right?" I asked.

Mati smiled and stroked his beard again. "Well, not exactly, Levi. You see, in all these verses the Hebrew word for *branch* is *tsemach* (צֶמַח), not *netser*. In Modern Hebrew, *tsemach* means plant, but in ancient Hebrew it also could mean branch. Hence every major English translation translates *tsemech* in the verses as *branch*. So despite being two different words with the same meaning, it could still be a clever wordplay between the name of the city and the Messianic prophecies:

■ Yeshua is from Nazareth,

- so He is a Nazarene (*Notsri*),

- which is the same as *netser* (branch),

- and the prophets spoke of a *tsemach* (branch) coming forth to be the Messiah and King.

"Well, that is proof enough for most believers to see that I was referring to these prophetic passages when I said that Yeshua would be called a Nazarene—a *Notsri* according to the prophets—but probably not good enough for those who oppose Yeshua. Those you will need to stand up to, like Rabbi Goodman."

"You know my rabbi?"

"I know of him. And don't lose hope. He may come around sooner than you think."

I was still wounded from the way Rabbi Goodman attacked me when I came to confide in him about my interest in Yeshua a few months ago. He wouldn't even hear me out, he just spoke over me. Heck, he practically shouted. I didn't like being talked to like I was a wayward child. I wasn't. I just sought the truth. If he would just—

"'*Forgive us what we have done wrong, as we too have forgiven those who have wronged us*' (Matt. 6:12 CJB). Just a little quote from my book you might want to remember. I was reciting the Master. David, there is no greater sin than not to forgive. Yeshua died in order that *all* your sins would be forgiven—past, present, and future. For you to hold one tiny, slight sin against someone mocks the blood of the Messiah."

I suddenly remembered seeing Yeshua stumble to the ground with His stake falling upon Him. The Roman soldier made me carry it. I remember as I bent His gaze arrested me. I have never felt so unclean in my life—so guilty of sin. And yet I also knew by the time the encounter ended that He would forgive me.

"Are you so special that you should be forgiven—you who's had the privilege of a divine visitation—whereas Rabbi Goodman, as wrong as he is, has never seen an angel, a prophet, or come face to face with Messiah as you have?"

He was right. In light of what Yeshua did for me, bitterness and unforgiveness could no longer be options.

"Yeshua told us a story about a man who had a large debt. He was forgiven the debt, one hundred percent. But then he demanded payment from some poor fellow who owed him a small amount."

"Yes, I see the hypocrisy," I managed to say.

"After He taught us to daily forgive, He said:

> For if you forgive others their offenses, your heavenly Father will also forgive you; but if you do not forgive others their offenses, your heavenly Father will not forgive yours (Matthew 6:14-15 CJB).

"It is impossible to enjoy God's forgiveness and freedom when you are holding others in prison."

I didn't like being lectured—by Rabbi Goodman or by this man. But Mati was right.

"David, I know you think I am being tough, but you are offended by one encounter with a rabbi. Did he strike you? Did he slander you? Did he threaten your family? No. But the time will come where you might have to endure such threats and physical harm for the sake of the kingdom, and you must have a pure heart. You have to love those people. Our dear brother Paul was one of them."

"Yes, he put believers in prison and was in authority when Stephen was martyred."

"And how did he turn out? The Lord opened his eyes. He became the most influential tool God has ever had. And what were Stephen's last words before he succumbed to his wounds? 'Lord, do not hold this sin against them' (Acts 7:60).

"Do you know how powerful that final act of intercession was—pleading for the souls of his killers? Those seven words saved Sha'ul. Those seven words held back God's hand of judgment."

I foolishly added, "I think it was eight words."

"Hebrew, not English, and this is serious, David. I wrote down the words of our Rabbi, and it may one day be a reality in your life."

> *Be on your guard; you will be handed over to the local councils and be flogged in the synagogues. On my account you will be brought before governors and kings as witnesses to them and to the Gentiles. But when they arrest you, do not worry about what to say or how to say it. At that time you will be given what to say, for it will not be you speaking, but the Spirit of your Father speaking through you.*
>
> *Brother will betray brother to death, and a father his child; children will rebel against their parents and have them put to death. You will be hated by everyone because of me, but the one who stands firm to the end will be saved. When you are persecuted in one place, flee to another. Truly I tell you, you will not finish going through the towns of Israel before the Son of Man comes* (Matthew 10:17-23).

"I died as a martyr, as did my fellow apostles—save John, whom they tried unsuccessfully to kill and eventually exiled. David, the calling on your life is big. So don't get bogged down by insults and personal attacks. If you continue on this path, there will be many more to come. To quote Jeremiah:

> *If you have run with the footmen, and they have wearied you, then how can you contend with horses? And if in the land of peace, in which you trusted, they wearied you, then how will you do in the floodplain of the Jordan?* (Jeremiah 12:5 NKJV)

"These are mere tests to prepare you for the real thing!"

Whew. He was right, but I was glad he was finally ready to let it go.

"Let's move on."

I nodded, afraid to say anything else and accidentally incriminate myself.

"So we looked at several verses where *tsemach* refers to the Messiah and concluded that that would be enough proof to warrant calling the Messiah a *Notsri*, but not enough proof for an anti-Messianic apologist. So we must ask, is there even one verse that uses the same word *netser* for branch and refers to the Messiah? Yes! One of the most famous Messianic prophesies of all is in Isaiah 11:

> *A shoot will come up from the stump of Jesse; from his roots a* **Branch** [netser/נֵצֶר] *will bear fruit* (Isaiah 11:1).

"So if you had any doubts about my usage of the word *natsri* meaning *branch*, they should definitely be put to rest. And most scholars believe—and rightly so, I might add," he winked at me in jest, "—that I had the deepest knowledge of the Old Covenant prophecies of all the gospel writers. Not to toot my own horn, but *Baker's Evangelical Dictionary of Biblical Theology* states," he changed to a fake voice, to be clear he was not impressed with himself, "'Matthew has a special fondness for the Messianic prophecies in Isaiah and other prophets.'[1] It is noteworthy that they point out Isaiah from all the prophets—the book where we find the branch/*netser* verse.

"I was writing to the Jews. The other guys were writing to the world. I used prophecy from the Old Covenant sixty-two times because I knew I had to make the case from the *Tanakh*—the Hebrew Scriptures—that Yeshua is the Messiah. It makes no sense that I would risk my credibility by adding the verse about the Nazarene if it wasn't clear to my Jewish readers what I meant—that it was a wordplay based on Isaiah 11:1. If I was seeking to hoodwink my readers, I had no need with sixty-one other prophecies. It would only cut at my believability.

"An interesting footnote is that the same root is used in the verb *l'natser* (רצנל) which means *to guard, keep, or maintain*. Yeshua was the only human who was able to *l'natser* the Law of Moses completely. I quoted Yeshua as saying that He came not to destroy the Law of Moses, but fulfill it." (See Matthew 5:17.) "Wordplays were very common in the writing style of my era. The Lord gave me tremendous grace to use the writing tools and style of my day to convey Yeshua, the Branch— the *Notsri*."

I shifted on my floor cushion and took a drink from the goblet that appeared in front of me. Sweet water. "I experienced that grace here as I filled in as a scribe for Nathan. You know, I'm a writer by trade. I'd like to experience the kind of grace you are talking about so that my writing conveys Yeshua, the Branch—the *Notsri*."

Mati smiled at that, and I couldn't help but notice that his moustache practically covered his teeth. "Yes, you always know when you are writing above your own capability. It is quite a beautiful gift from God. But regarding the Nazarenes, let me add a second footnote. The historian Epiphanius who lived in the fourth century recorded that at one time, 'all Christians were called Nazarenes in the same way.'[2] But he goes on to claim that they were called another name as well.

"They were called *Iessaioi*. That would be Greek; in Hebrew it is *Yishai'im*. And in English *Jessians*."

"What does it mean?"

"It is a further confirmation of the *Branch/Netser* prophecy. Jesse was the father of David and thus the father of the Messiah. The Isaiah prophecy doesn't merely refer to a branch, but to the 'Branch of Jesse.' The fact that believers called themselves Jessians is proof they saw Yeshua as the fulfillment of Isaiah 11:1, and it helps us understand that the name *Nazarene* was not merely referring to Yeshua's hometown, but to the branch prophecy.

"David, we're rooting for you," he stuck out his massive hand and shook mine. Firm grip. A real man, this Mati.

"And it was my pleasure, my *honor* to meet you. I will not forget your words—not about the Netser, that too of course, but about forgiveness and persecution."

"I know you won't." He was gone and my hand was still sticking out in front of me, grasping the air.

CHAPTER XXII

Like when an act of a play ends and a new one begins, everything went dark. When the curtain arose, I was back with Nathan sitting together on first-century "patio furniture" beside the Sea of Galilee. The sun was still high in the sky, and my pen and scroll were before me.

"Again, the Jews of Jerusalem rebelled against Rome, seeking freedom," he shared, having no idea that I had been gone. "This time the believers stayed and fought. I was already old, but the younger ones were ready and willing to die—until..."

"Until what!?" I suddenly forgot I was writing down the story of a dying man. "I mean, please continue. Like you said, there isn't much time."

"Levi, you know the story; why are acting like there is any suspense?"

"Well, there is power in a story well told!" That answer seemed to satisfy him.

He smiled and continued. "At that time, Rabbi Akiva was the leading rabbi. The military general was named Simon bar Kokhba. He was an amazing military strategist. But he was also ruthless. He gained our independence for a short time, but then Rabbi Akiva did the unthinkable—he claimed that bar Kokhba was the Messiah!

"Oh, what a mistake. In Rabbi Akiva's theology, the Messianic age would only last one generation, the span of a man's life. He believed bar Kokhba to be that man. The believers fighting with him fled. They could not give their allegiance to a false Messiah. Bar Kokhba ordered the execution of many. Others escaped. After the war, it was clear that the Nazarenes were no longer considered part of the Jewish community."

Nathan was paused. On the wall, like an old projecter was playing a film, I saw a man teaching. Tall, thin, around sixty I would guess, with glasses and thick mustache. He shared in his clearly New York accent,

"Amazingly, Rabbi Akiva is up there with Moses in Jewish thought. Listen to the words from a Jewish website:

> Among the many great figures in Jewish history, Rabbi Akiva arguably represents a combination of everything that is heroic about the Jewish people more than anyone else. At the least, he is one of the most beloved figures in Jewish history, a person whose influence and stature is a source of inspiration throughout all of the ages. Whatever one says about Rabbi Akiva one can never say enough. The Talmud (Menachos 29a) compares him favorably to Moses, which is the ultimate compliment in the Jewish lexicon. He is the national hero of the Jewish people for all time.[1]

Imagine if Moses declared a false Messiah, I thought to myself. Jewish leaders condemned the followers of Yeshua, who I believe is the real Messiah, but place Rabbi Akiva in the company of Moses, when he declared a false Messiah, which led to the complete destruction of Jerusalem and the banishment of every Jew from Jerusalem.

The film disappeared and Nathan was "un-paused." "We face hostility from both our people after the flesh *and* Christians from other nations. The Pharisee sect within Judaism[2] appears to have won out over the others, which rejects Yeshua as the Messiah, and the churches in Asia and Europe are becoming increasingly hostile toward the idea of Yeshua as a Jew. In their mind, He was the last of the Jews and His human ancestry is at best inconsequential and at worst an embarrassment.

"There is increasing hostility between the *Ecclesia* (Church) and the synagogue. And neither group wants to tolerate Jews who embrace Yeshua but continue to be Jews. The *Ecclesia* sees itself as the new Israel, replacing old Israel. They claim God is finished with the Jews and compel us to cut ties. Many have because of persecution. Some of us Nazarenes hang on, knowing, as Rabbi Saul wrote, eventually, '*all Israel will be saved*'" (Rom. 11:26).

There was both fear and sadness in Nathan's eyes. Though I had only known him these past few hours, I felt like he was my friend. He obviously thought I was his longtime companion. I put my hand on his shoulder as tears welled up in his blinded eyes.

And *swoosh!* I was back with Ariel. Paul was no longer there, but there was that angel with a mischievous smile, standing at the "scroll table" in front of the big white screen. I looked at my desk. Yep, the espresso was still there.

"You could give me some warning!" I was slightly annoyed by the fact that he was enjoying dropping me into places with no preparation and sometimes, as just now with Nathan—to whom I genuinely would have liked to say *good-bye*—it felt like an emotional roller coaster. But still, what a way to learn!

"It's too much fun this way. And honestly, it is a much better story like this."

"Who's going to believe me? My wife thinks I'm nuts. And if you didn't kidnap my dad, which I am grateful for, mind you, he would not have believed me."

Ariel pointed to my desk chair and I took his cue and took a sip of the coffee. *Still hot.*

Ariel smiled and walked over to Dad's desk and sat on the corner of it again. "More importantly, was your question answered?"

"Indeed it was. But what happened to the Nazarene Jews after the 135 revolt?"

"After the rebellion was crushed by Hadrian, the Roman empire took drastic measures to ensure this would never happen again. He almost lost the war to the Jewish freedom fighters. He exiled all Jews from Jerusalem, circumcision was outlawed, and he changed the name to Aelia Capitolina, meaning that the city was now dedicated to Jupiter—the false god, not the planet," Ariel added with a wink.

"The penalty for a Jew who entered Jerusalem was death. As Nathan told you, all the leaders of the Jerusalem congregation were Jewish, from

Jacob the brother of Yeshua until the expulsion in 135 CE, numbering fifteen in all.[3] That ceased. After 135 CE, all the bishops of Jerusalem were Greek—that is, until Messianic Jews began to establish communities in Israel after 1948.

"In addition, the name of Judea was changed to—want to take a guess?"

I thought for a minute before surrendering. "I don't have a clue."

"Would you believe Palestine?"

"But I thought *Palestine* came from the Arabs?"

"You and most of the world think so, but before 1948 there was no such thing as an Arab Palestinian nationality. It was invented by Yasser Arafat. Before '48, a Palestinian was anyone who lived in the *region* of Palestine—Jew, Arab, or whatever—it had no religious or national connection. Try and guess what the name was of the Jewish-owned newspaper in Jerusalem that is now known as the *Jerusalem Post* before Israel declared independence."

"No!" I said incredulously. "*The Palestine Post?*"

"Bingo!" said the angel.

"But you just said it goes back to the Romans," I shared, confused.

"The Romans borrowed the name from the ancient Philistines who were then nonexistent as a people group. The name stuck throughout the centuries and more than a dozen different rulers from the Romans to the British.

"But back to your question—after 135 we find continued contact and dialogue between the Nazarenes and the rabbinic Jewish community. This is not surprising, because the Nazarene Jews lived in the same geographical areas with predominantly Jewish communities. However, as the distrust grew, the separation and isolation from the Jewish community were increased. Different steps along the way affected this separation— the flight to Pella, the *birkat haminim*, the refusal of the Nazarenes to recognize and support bar Kokhba. By the middle of the second century, the rift was complete.[4]

"The Nazarene community continued to be an identifiable Jewish believing community for several centuries, but eroded over time. The Mohammedans destroyed the last of the Nazarene communities.[5]

"Interestingly, Dr. Ray Pritz of Jerusalem, who is considered a leading expert of *your* day on the ancient Nazarene community, uncovered that in the fourth century there was a group of people who called themselves Nazarenes. Here are some of their characteristics and beliefs. The citations next to them are from the source—the *Panarion* authored by Epiphanius—a fourth-century heresy hunter." On the screen appeared a list.

- They use both Old and New Testaments (7,2).
- They have a good knowledge of Hebrew and read the Old Testament and at least one gospel (most likely Matthew) in that language (7,4; 9,4).
- They believe in the resurrection of the dead (7,3).
- They believe that God is the creator of all things (7,3).
- They believe in one God and His son Jesus the Messiah (7,3).
- They observe the Law of Moses (7,5; 5,4; 8,1).
- Earlier they were called Iessaioi (or Jessians) (5,1-4).
- They had their origin from the Jerusalem congregation which fled to Pella before 70 (7,8).
- Geographical location in Pella, Kokaba, and Coele Syria (7,7).
- They are hated and cursed by the Jews (9,2-3).[6]

"The being 'cursed by the Jews' must have been referring to the Nineteenth Benediction," I stated and asked at the same time.

"Right, and not only were they rejected by Judaism, but also by the Church, which was overwhelmingly Gentile, because these Jewish believers continued to live as Jews. They adhered to circumcision, the Feasts, and everything. The Church assumed that they were Judaizers—meaning that they continued to embrace these God-ordained rituals as a condition of salvation. They could not understand why anyone would want any connection to the 'wretchedness of Judaism.' Constantine and the bishops of Nicea had already outlawed using Passover as a means to honor the resurrection. The Church had become an enemy to the Jewish people."

"He outlawed Passover?" I was confused.

"As a holiday used to honor Yeshua's resurrection. The first believers, Jews and Gentiles, for quite some time used Passover as a means for celebrating the resurrection. It is clear that believers understood the symbolism between the Passover lamb and Yeshua, the Lamb of God, from Paul's writing to the Corinthians." The screen lit up with a passage.

> *Your boasting is not good. Don't you know that a little yeast leavens the whole batch of dough? Get rid of the old yeast, so that you may be a new unleavened batch—as you really are. For Messiah, our Passover lamb, has been sacrificed. Therefore let us keep the Festival, not with the old bread leavened with malice and wickedness, but with the unleavened bread of sincerity and truth* (1 Corinthians 5:6-8).

"Now, what is interesting about this passage is that Paul speaks to the primarily Gentile congregation in Corinth using terms that would only be familiar to someone who understood the Passover tradition. Second, while the passage is about purging out sin—a little leaven—he encourages them to keep the Passover feast. There was no Easter at this time, and Passover was the logical vehicle to celebrate the resurrection of the Lamb of God—the Messiah."

"Okay, so what about the Messianic Jews?" I asked.

"The Messianics were caught in between. Judaism would not claim them and in fact cursed them, while the larger Church—*Ecclesia*—world thought them to be heretics simply because they continued to live as Jews. And the feelings were mutual. The Nazarenes refused to accept the authority established by the Pharisaic camp after the destruction of Jerusalem—from Yochanan ben Zakkai—and in so refusing they adjudicated their own isolation from the converging flow of what we call Judaism. Just as they rejected the Church's setting aside of the Law of Moses, so also they refused the rabbis' expansive interpretations of it.[7]

"In fact, Messianic Jews today, the spiritual descendants of the Nazarenes, are the most hated, despised people group on earth. First, they are a subgroup of the two most persecuted groups in earth—Christians and Jews. And yet they are rejected and often persecuted by the Jews and the Christians. Hitler would have gladly killed them for being Jewish. And radical Islamists would kill them for believing in Yeshua as the Messiah."

I stared into my coffee cup, and held it closer to my face, taking in its soothing aroma. Frankly, I didn't like the sound of this. It's like signing up to play for the losing team, knowing you'll not only lose the war but be bloodied in the battles. I thought they called this message "Good News"! Ariel kept teaching, seemingly unaware of my thoughts at this point.

"The Nazarenes never gave up hope that their brothers after the flesh would find the Messiah. We have this quote from their commentary on Isaiah: 'O Sons of Israel, who deny the Son of God with such hurtful resolution, return to him and to his apostles.'[8] They agreed with Paul who wrote, *'Brothers and sisters, my heart's desire and prayer to God for the Israelites is that they may be saved'*" (Rom. 10:1).

"And they will. Ezekiel said that not only would they come back to the land of their forefathers, but once there they would find spiritual life." I read from the screen.

> *For I will take you out of the nations; I will gather you from*
> *all the countries and bring you back into your own land. I*
> *will sprinkle clean water on you, and you will be clean; I will*
> *cleanse you from all your impurities and from all your idols.*

I will give you a new heart and put a new spirit in you; I will remove from you your heart of stone and give you a heart of flesh. And I will put my Spirit in you and move you to follow my decrees and be careful to keep my laws. Then you will live in the land I gave your ancestors; you will be my people, and I will be your God (Ezekiel 36:24-28).

"See, they will come back," Ariel insisted. "In fact, they are already coming back! Grab my hand, David."

CHAPTER XXIII

I took Ariel's hand and braced myself. Sure enough, the angel and I were flying through space, through light, faster and faster. And then, as if someone pressed a hyper-speed button, within two or three seconds we sped through space and just as quickly landed back where we started, in the snow-white light before we entered the teaching room.

"Dad!" Relief washed over me. I grabbed him before the time warp thing separated us again.

"David!"

Our bear hug was interrupted by Ariel's hands on our shoulders.

Oh, no.

"Okay men, it's time to go home."

"Now? Both of us?"

"Both of you."

I was ecstatic! I was not guaranteed my father's well-being on earth until now. "Ariel, why didn't you tell me before that Dad would wake up and be healed? Why wait all this time?"

Ariel look from me to my dad and back to me again. "It is Father's desire that you return to your work with the daily support of your dad. I didn't know that until now. But I think Father knew that your heart should be willing to obey Him with or without the healing and support of your earthly dad."

I shrugged. "I guess that makes sense." I turned to my dad, grinning. "You're coming baaaaaack!"

Harvey threw his head back and laughed. "And as your advocate, not your enemy."

I asked, "Ariel, how is this going to work? Will Dad awaken when we arrive?"

"That would too easy. Let's use this to our advantage, David. Your father will still be unconscious."

I looked from Dad to the angel. "How is that to our advantage?"

"David, I want you to gather your family together at the hospital. When you return it will still be the same day, but late. You are to sleep at the hospital. However, the next morning, Saturday, morning, everyone will be there."

"Do it at 9:00 AM. Tell them the truth—the truth about everything. They won't believe you, of course. Flying through space with your father, meeting Bible characters, fighting demons, and reliving history will certainly be too much for them—and with Harvey still out... *nah*, they're definitely not going to believe you," Ariel laughed.

I frowned. "That may be funny for you, but my wife already thinks I am losing it. Now you want me to go public in front of my whole family."

"No, David, your whole family *and Rabbi Goodman*!"

A wave of fear and nervousness swept all over me. I remembered the words of Mati. I had to forgive Rabbi Goodman. But still, the way he attacked me left me a bit uneasy around him and intimidated.

"Even Rabbi Goodman? Won't he be at the synagogue?"

"Oh thanks, I'll write that down. Maybe we should reschedule." He smiled and paused. Ariel was obviously being facetious. "David, a lot has been put into this. Father knows exactly what He is doing.

"This is all part of your preparation as an apologist—an evangelist. One thing you will need to do is learn to overcome the spirit of fear and intimidation." He knew my thoughts. "You will stand before people in high places. When you give in to fear, it cuts into the anointing, the power of God to move through your words. You must speak boldly, confidently, no matter who is listening. Jeremiah was told:

> *"Do not say, 'I am a youth,' For you shall go to all to whom I*
> *send you, And whatever I command you, you shall speak. Do*

not be afraid of their faces, for I am with you to deliver you,"
says the Lord (Jeremiah 1:7-8 NKJV).

"Don't be afraid of their faces?" I repeated.

"Yes, when you speak for the Lord you cannot focus on their anger, but God's purpose. You must trust Him to use you. He will give you not only the power, but the words as well. Did you catch this part when Matthew was sharing with you?"

> *At that time you will be given what to say, for it will not be you speaking, but the Spirit of your Father speaking through you* (Matthew 10:19-20).

"Intimidation is a spiritual power—a demonic one. It is one of many ways the enemy seeks to manipulate God's people. Remember Elijah?"

I looked at Dad.

"Sure, we studied Elijah," Dad answered.

"He is most famous for what happened in First Kings 18—he called down fire from heaven and birthed a revival in Israel. They put to death the false prophets who were leading Israel into idol worship. He stood up to the king and to his false prophets.

"However, First Kings 19 reveals the sad end to the story. The very next day Elijah received a message from Queen Jezebel. She threatened him and in fact promised him that very soon he would be just as dead as those false prophets. We would expect the man of God, the prophet who has just called down fire from heaven, to call down fire on her. But instead he runs away and wallows in self-pity. Let me read to you."

> *Elijah was afraid and ran for his life. When he came to Beersheba in Judah, he left his servant there, while he himself went a day's journey into the wilderness. He came to a broom bush, sat down under it and prayed that he might die. "I have had enough, Lord," he said. "Take my life; I am no better than my ancestors"* (1 Kings 19:3-4).

"He stood up to nearly a thousand false prophets and to the king of Israel, but he runs from one woman?"

"It doesn't make sense," I added.

Dad chuckled. "He wouldn't be the first man to run from a woman."

I rolled my eyes at Dad's dry sense of humor. "Too funny, Dad."

Ariel grinned. "The story went like this. Except for the fact that there was a spirit—a demon of intimidation—in her that was so strong that even God's prophet fell prey. We see this type of demon alive today in radical Islam. They are terrorizing the world, and instead of standing against this terror, governments pass laws against speaking out against Islam. If Winston Churchill were to write today what he wrote over a hundred years ago, he might be labeled an Islamophobe."

> How dreadful are the curses which Mohammedanism lays on its votaries! Besides the fanatical frenzy, which is as dangerous in a man as hydrophobia in a dog, there is this fearful fatalistic apathy. The effects are apparent in many countries, improvident habits, slovenly systems of agriculture, sluggish methods of commerce, and insecurity of property exist wherever the followers of the Prophet rule or live.[1]

"Islamists are committing mass murder all over the world, and there are politicians in England who want to make criticizing them illegal. Like Elijah's response to Jezebel, it doesn't make sense; but then again, the spirit of intimidation isn't designed to make sense. It is active and there is no doubt that people will seek to silence you through intimidation.

"And now, your first test. You are to gather your family. As Paul once wrote, '*Jews demand signs*'" (1 Cor. 1:22), "and we are going to give them one for the ages!

"Tell them that your father will rise up on the next day at the same time, completely healed—in fact, a new man." We both looked at my father. "Of course, Harvey, you will be able to verify everything David says after you are raised out of the coma."

Harvey grinned and put his hand on David's shoulder. "I can't wait to do it. Son, I am so proud of you. I don't know what is ahead of us—if they'll think we're crazy. But we know what we have seen and heard. We can't both be crazy. As a lawyer, I never backed down from a fight. And what was I fighting for? Wealth? Fame? Self-importance? Yes, *and* sometimes my client. If I was willing to put that type of energy into something that is fading, I sure as heck won't back down when we are proving something eternal. You go back. I'll be there soon. Right angel?"

"Right, Harv. Just don't doubt, David. Everything's going to work out. In fact, we've got a nice little surprise for you."

"Surprise?"

"You will see. Something good I promised regarding your grandfather." Before I could even process all this or say good-bye to my father, Ariel took my hand and we were flying. "Before I send you back, I just wanted to show you something."

We floated before a massive timeline, like in an IMAX theater.

"Once Christianity became the religion of Rome, things changed quickly. Buildings were erected, not only in Rome but also in Jerusalem—all over the world. The buildings became the focus instead of the people. The New Covenant mentions nothing about the importance of buildings, but a whole lot about loving people, sacrificing for people, and reaching people. Massive amounts of money were raised to erect the most magnificent edifices. In the same way, Judaism focused on tradition and ritual over relationship; so did the Church."

I saw the Sistine Chapel, adorned with the paintings of Michelangelo—*The Creation of Adam* and the incredible ceiling.

"Amazing, aren't they?"

"Yes," I said, mesmerized.

"But it's death, David. It is religion without God built with funds that the Church raised through lying to people about false doctrines such as purgatory."

"Yes, you explained before. They told all the people that they could get out of purgatory sooner if they helped fund the buildings."

"And not only did the Roman Church become focused on outward customs and sacraments, they perfected a theology whose seeds began to sprout as far back as 49 CE in Rome."

"That is when the Jews were expelled from Rome, like you and Paul taught me. They believed that God was judging the Jews and that is why they had to leave."

"And as you know, Paul corrected this false theology and pleaded with future generations for Christians to bless Israel and provoke them to jealousy." (See Romans 11:11, 25-26.) "But they did not listen. After the destruction of Jerusalem in 135 CE, the Church began to refer to itself as the new Israel. She had replaced Israel as God's people.

"Not just that, but many of them taught that God hated the Jews and that Christians should hate the Jews. John Chrysostom was the Bishop of Constantinople. He is one of the most revered early Church leaders. So immense were his oratory skills that he was called the *golden-mouthed*. However, he was an enemy to the Jewish people.

"In his eight sermons against the Jews...well, listen for yourself."

The man appeared in the giant IMAX and spoke with great boldness.

And so it is that we must hate both them [the Jews] and their synagogue. This is why I hate the Jews. Although they possess the Law, they put it to outrageous use. They are become worse than the wild beasts, and for no reason at all, with their own hands [the Jews] murder their own offspring, to worship the avenging devils who are the foes of our life. The synagogues of the Jews are the homes of idolatry and devils, even though they have no images in them. The very idea of going from a church to a synagogue is blasphemous; and to attend the Jewish Passover is to insult Christ. To be with the Jews on the very day they murdered Jesus is to ensure that on the Day of Judgment He will say "Depart from Me: for you have had intercourse with my murderers." The Jews do not worship God but devils, so that all their feasts are unclean. God hates them, and indeed has always hated them. But since their murder of Jesus He allows them no time for repentance. It was of set purpose that He concentrated all their worship in Jerusalem that He might more easily destroy it. [The destruction of Jerusalem] was not by their own power that the Caesars did what they did to you: it was done by the wrath of God, and His absolute rejection of you. When it is clear that God hates them, it is the duty of Christians to hate them too.[2]

"Man, that dude has some serious issues," I said as he disappeared from the screen. "Hitler would have loved him!"

"Augustine, the most respected theologian of the church fathers, taught horrible things as well against the Jews." Another man appeared on the screen and said, "Jews deserved death but were destined to wander the earth to witness the victory of the Church over the synagogue."[3]

I cringed. This was the kind of rhetoric that causes Jews to fear Gentiles.

"My point is that most of the Church leaders completely ignored Romans 11, which speaks of God's future revival amongst the Jewish people and how the Church is to play a loving role in this. They developed a theology that makes the Jews the eternal enemy of their Father. Many call this replacement theology, and under this banner Jews have suffered the most horrible felonies at the hands of those who claim to love the greatest Jew in history—Yeshua.

"This is just an appetizer. On your next journey—"

"Oh! We are not done?"

"We are done for today, but I will see you again. I and the many others you have met have been equipped by the Father to share the message of Yeshua in its original Jewish context. You know the prophecies and the history of the first Jewish believers. Next, I and some more special guests will equip you to defeat the dastardly doctrine called replacement theology.

"From the Scriptures you will show that God has not rejected Israel or revival in His future plans. You will be used to open the eyes of Jewish people to Yeshua and open the eyes of many Christians to God's heart for Israel. Yeshua is waiting to return. But He will not return to a Church that has rejected His physical brothers. You will not only call them to repentance, but call them to pray and intercede for Israel.

"Look! I want you to see two more people before I send you on your way."

On the screen appeared an old woman. She seemed to be praying—I guess at the Temple.

"This is Anna. She is a prophetess. She was widowed at a young age. Instead of seeking remarriage, she devoted herself to prayer and fasting. She worships here in the Temple day and night. She prays for Israel's redemption. She is eighty-four here, which means she has been praying like this for more than sixty years."

An old wiry fellow entered the screen. He had a baby in his arms, and the man was crying profusely.

"This is Simeon. Like Anna, he is a prophet and has been praying many years for the Messiah to come."

"Why is he crying? And holding a baby?" I inquired.

"God made him a promise that he would not die before he would see the Messiah."

"Is that who I think it is?"

"Yes, it is Yeshua. His parents brought Him to the Temple to be dedicated."

The old man began to speak:

> Sovereign Lord, as you have promised, you may now dismiss
> your servant in peace. For my eyes have seen your salvation,

which you have prepared in the sight of all nations: a light for revelation to the Gentiles, and the glory of your people Israel (Luke 2:29-32).

I was deeply moved by his words and felt tears begin to well up. *And I always thought that Christmas was a Gentile holiday.*

"God used Simeon and Anna and thousands of others like them to birth the first congregation that took the message of Yeshua to the nations. What happened on Shavuot when the Holy Spirit fell on the Jews in Jerusalem started many years before in the prayers of God's people. In the same way that a baby is hidden in the womb for nine months, much of what the Father does begins in secret, in the prayers of His children."

The screen faded to darkness and slowly illuminated a silhouette of a "womb." Light shone within and showed people in prayer. Some with hands raised, some on their knees, and others with heads bowed. I barely knew how to pray to Yeshua, yet I knew what Ariel said was true.

"We are all part of the generations before us who have lived and prayed and believed. A seed planted in the ground grows roots long before the farmer sees anything break through the earth. Prayer is like that. Each prayer has power, and they build upon each other long before you see the answer."

Ariel nodded, then he took my hand and we began to float again.

"Even as God used them to pray for the Messiah to come, He will use the believers from all over the world to pray for the Jews to return to their Messiah, even has Hosea said, *'Afterward the Israelites will return and seek the Lord their God and David their king. They will come trembling to the Lord and to his blessings in the last days'*" (Hos. 3:5).

"But David is dead?"

"It speaks not of David, but his seed—the Messiah Yeshua. The Father is going to use you to help raise up that *womb of prayer* all across the world that will awaken Israel. And just as Paul said, when the Jews

turn to Yeshua, it will mean *'greater riches'* and even *'life from the dead'!"*
(Rom. 11:12,15).

"Good-bye for now, David," said Ariel as he let go of my hand and
floated away from me.

I traveled slowly, not really flying but floating my way through a tun-
nel of time, escorted by angels on either side. As we glided, the angels
sang praises to Yeshua—the Lamb of God.

> *Worthy is the Lamb, who was slain, to receive power and
> wealth and wisdom and strength and honor and glory and
> praise!* (Revelation 5:12)

I felt their words in my heart—even in my skin, which jumped in
spasms as glory coursed through my veins. Everything in me pulsated
electrically with praise, and I joined creatures I heard distantly in heaven,
and perhaps even those on earth and under the earth and on the sea.
Together we proclaimed:

> *To him who sits on the throne and to the Lamb be praise and
> honor and glory and power, for ever and ever!* (Revelation
> 5:13)

My descent reminded me of the day that I kissed my bride at the altar
and together we walked from the front to the back of the room, man and
wife. Just as our friends and family watched us leave the altar that day,
angels watched me now as I left heaven. One group after another stood
"in the pews" on either side, and as I passed they turned their heads,
smiled, and sang, "Glory to God!" I was filled so completely with God,
glory, and heaven's thoughts that all fear left me.

I don't know how long this lasted—maybe five minutes. But then
things sped up quickly, so fast that all the angels were just like beams of
light on each side. Suddenly, I was sucked back into this world. Everything was dark.

I quickly discerned that was because my eyes were closed. The smell. I was back at St. Luke's. I lifted up my head and saw that I had been asleep on my father's stomach. I wiped the drool from my mouth and looked up. It was 1:00 AM—presumably Saturday morning. The lights were out, but there were enough machines with lights in the room so that I could see. The door was closed.

I looked at my father. He was shriveled and appeared lifeless. Tubes in his mouth, in his nose. Not much had changed on earth since I was last here. I leaned over and kissed his cheek. "See you in the morning, Dad."

I got up and walked into the hallway. The lights were dimmed. I was desperately thirsty and searched for a water fountain. On my way back I noticed Theresa, the friendly nurse, sitting by the desk at the nurses' station. I wasn't ready for human interaction, so I tried to get back to the room undetected.

Too late. "David, you're still here."

"Yeah, I fell asleep in my dad's room," I answered, which was technically true. I assume my body was here resting in my father's room. "I think I will just sleep on the chair in his room. I am too tired to drive home." *Plus I don't think my wife is talking to me,* I thought.

"You are not sleeping on no chair in my hospital. Come here, child." I loved how she talked me. "The room next to your father's is empty and they just put a clean set of sheets on the bed. Let's get you situated in there."

"You're amazing, Theresa. Thank you so much."

"That's what I do, that's why I am here."

We entered the room and she pointed to the bed.

"There you are, David. Good night."

"Theresa?"

She turned to me. Her white uniform and her beaming countenance reminded me very much of the angels who just lined my "road" back to earth. I had to ask her.

"Do you believe in Jesus?"

"You bet I do."

"When did you start to believe?"

She was eager to share. "I grew up in church, but didn't take it seriously for a long time. It was part of my culture, but I didn't have a real connection with God. When I was eighteen my father died. I was angry. Some people come closer to God in tragedies—not me. I loved my daddy and I was furious at God—if there was a God. I left the church.

"But my roommate in nursing school, Sheila Davis, she was persistent. And she was the real deal. She lived like Jesus in front of me—every day. I was jealous. I wanted what she had, but I was not ready to forgive God for taking my daddy. After about a year I was even more lost. I was not a happy person. I was not at peace. I knew I could hang on to this bitterness for the rest of my life or I could have what Sheila had.

"We prayed together. I asked Jesus into my life and He changed me. Sheila and I cried for hours together that night. I know my daddy is with Him, and while I miss him I know I will see him again."

"But David, you're Jewish. Why are you asking me about Jesus?"

"What do you think of Jews believing in Jesus?"

She started trembling. I started to freak out wishing I never brought it up. Tears began to well up in her eyes. Soon she was shaking and sobbing and I didn't know what to do. Had I offended her? Scared her? I didn't know. I helped her sit down. She calmed down and wiped the tears off her face.

"David," she looked up, "do you believe in Jesus—Yeshua?"

She knew His Hebrew name?

"I do now. Since Sunday morning actually. Just before all this happened with my dad."

She started sobbing again.

It is one thing for my fellow Jews to be mad at me for believing in Yeshua—now Gentiles are mad too?

This time she was *really* sobbing. I was scared she was going to wake people up. I got her some tissues and she tried to compose herself.

"Two weeks ago—" She still couldn't talk. "Two weeks ago I had a dream. In the dream I saw Yeshua standing over the Western Wall in Jerusalem. He was more than a hundred feet tall. The people inside were oblivious to His presence. I could see people worshiping at the wall, some putting little notes in its cracks. I saw a young man—barely a teen—reading from a Torah scroll surrounded by a group of people."

"It was his Bar Mitzvah," I explained.

"Tour buses lined the streets, and religious Jews were seeking donations as people came down the steps from the Jewish Quarter to the Western Wall Square. Only I could see Yeshua.

"He was not weeping, but tears came down His cheeks into His beard. Outside of the city walls were ferocious wild beasts. I knew they were demons. They were the most vicious animals I had ever seen—some were more like massive wolves, three times the size of a normal wolf, drooling with anticipation before the attack, while others were like giant tigers or leopards. Blood dripped from their mouths, but they wanted more.

"They wanted to jump over the walls of the city to attack God's people. But they would never make it over. The walls kept them out, but they were making progress."

"Like the Romans attacking Masada," I whispered.

"Jesus's heart was broken for His people, and then He looked right at me and said these words:

> I have posted watchmen on your walls, Jerusalem; they will never be silent day or night. You who call on the Lord, give yourselves no rest, and give him no rest till he establishes Jerusalem and makes her the praise of the earth.[4]

"I knew I had heard the words before—from the Bible, but I was not sure of the reference. I thought that it was more of a question, 'I have posted watchmen?' I knew for sure that he was asking me to be a watchman on the walls of Jerusalem. Then He turned away and looked at the people and said:

Jerusalem, Jerusalem, you who kill the prophets and stone those sent to you, how often I have longed to gather your children together, as a hen gathers her chicks under her wings, and you were not willing. Look, your house is left to you desolate. For I tell you, you will not see me again until you say, 'Blessed is he who comes in the name of the Lord.'[5]

Theresa sniffed and blew her nose again. "I memorized those verses by heart after I woke up. See, Yeshua was broken over the state of the Jewish people. I could literally feel His heart. It was the heaviest burden I had ever felt. Again He looked at me and said, '*I looked for someone among them who would build up the wall and stand before me in the gap*'" (Ezek. 22:30).

"He was asking me to pray—to intercede for His people. But seeing the demonic forces seeking to bridge the gap and jump over the wall, I was scared. I was torn between the burden I was feeling for the Jewish people and the fear of tangling with these wild beasts." She looked at me just then, searched my face for a moment. Then quietly she whispered, "Then all of a sudden I felt this surge of love go through me—the compassion of God toward the people. I knew that even if it cost me my life, I would fight—I would stand in the gap.

"And then I woke up. It was just after 4 AM, but I could not go back to bed. I was consumed with this burden. For many years I have had a deep love for Israel and the Jewish people. But it was nothing like this. It was superficial. This was life and death.

"I attend a Messianic congregation sometimes in addition to my home church, Resurrection Chapel on North Seventeenth. But the burden I had that morning was not some cute infatuation with Jewish customs or blowing a shofar—not that that is wrong. It was just that this was so deep. I knew that someone's life or salvation was hanging in the balance.

"I spent from just after 4 AM until noon praying, groaning, pleading with God for Israel's salvation. And I memorized those scriptures He spoke in the dream. I didn't have a shift until 2 PM. But even at work I just wanted to weep for Israel—for the Jewish people. For the next several days all I could do was pray. I started saying, 'Lord, give me one Jewish family, one Jewish family.' Over and over for days. At work, tears of love for Israel would not stop falling down my face. I would be working and weeping. Unless I was doing something that required focus, I was praying."

I was getting goose bumps. It was becoming clear that she was praying for me—for my family. I wiped back a tear.

"My daddy loved Israel and so does my mom. But not everyone in the church I grew up in felt that way. I can't repeat some of the things I heard about Jewish people out of the mouths of people who say they love Jesus—the Jew!

"If only they could see the empathy and love He had for His people as He stood over them crying.

"David, this burden was on me day and night for about ten days. And then boom, just like that, sometime Sunday morning, maybe ten minutes before your father arrived, it just lifted off of me. I don't mean that I stopped caring or even stopped praying—I just suddenly had peace. Like a mother who has just gone through nine months of pregnancy, and then twelve hours of agony, suddenly getting to hold her baby. I knew without a doubt that a Jewish person somewhere—maybe a whole family—came to Yeshua.

"The rest of the day I was filled with an inexplicable joy."

She looked up at me with her big swollen eyes, wide open and said, "It was you. It was you, David!" and then burst back into tears. She looked at me again and said, "I wasn't even supposed to be here tonight. I got off at 10 PM, but they asked me to stay an extra four hours to cover for another nurse whose son was sick."

We both just sat there in awe for moment.

"Theresa, we're not done. I know why you are here tonight. I am going to share something with you that will be very hard to believe."

I spent the next hour sharing with her most of the story—particularly my encounter with Yeshua and the war over my soul. She listened in a state of awe in between intermittent weeping. When I was done, I told her what would happen over the next day. It was clear that she had a part to play—to pray. She was carefully placed into this story for a strategic purpose. I remembered well those demons I encountered—from both journeys. They would not back down to yelling or screaming or reasoning—only to prayer, real God-ordained prayer. When I used the name of Yeshua against them, when I spoke of His blood, they screamed in agony. Clearly prayer is a powerful weapon.

"Theresa, God has placed you here to pray. In just a few hours I am going to tell my family that my father will rise up in exactly twenty-four hours—that is what the angel told me. I will share with them that Yeshua is the Messiah, and I don't expect them to react well. And the angel told me that the rabbi will be here. How? I don't know, as it is Shabbat, Saturday morning, and in addition to the fact that they have services at Beth El, he doesn't drive on Shabbat. Well, I will leave that up to the angel to work out."

Theresa sat there and shook her head. "Lord, have mercy. Lord, have mercy. Lord, I give You praise. I give You praise."

I waited until she blew her nose again, then added, "One more thing. Remember earlier tonight when I made that crack about sleeping on my couch?"

She nodded.

"Well, I was only half kidding. I told Lisa last night at the restaurant about my experience. It really scared her. She thinks I'm crazy and I can't blame her. I thought I had some proof. In one of my visions or journeys—one day I need to figure out a vocabulary for everything I went through—anyway, I saw my grandfather as a young man. Like I said, he survived the Holocaust. But in the vision he had a young brother, Chaim. No one in my family has ever heard of him. He was shot by a Nazi guard when they arrived at Auschwitz.

"I foolishly told Lisa I could prove that my visions were real by proving that Chaim was real. However, she quickly rebuffed me—claiming it is impossible. My grandfather is dead and his one surviving sister is not completely all there at eighty-five. Theresa, I need your prayers."

It was past 2 AM and Theresa was off the clock. And I needed to get some sleep before my big meeting in the morning.

"David, I am going to go home, but I don't expect to sleep much. I feel that same burden coming back on me. I will be in prayer at least until your meeting is over. Then I will come back tomorrow night and check on you. Eventually I will need to get a few hours' rest. Let's pray. Yeshua said, 'If two of you on earth agree about anything they ask for, it will be done for them by my Father in heaven. For where two or three gather in my name, there am I with them'" (Matt. 18:19-20).

Before I knew it, she grabbed my hands and started praying quietly but fervently, with passion and not a few tears. I had never prayed with anyone before. Yes, I had prayed at the synagogue through siddur,[6] both during the week and during Shabbat services, but those are set prayers written by someone else. This was different. She was talking to God as if He were in the room. Well, that is what she said, 'there I am with them.' This was awesome. Two people can agree in prayer and Yeshua will answer!

"Amen," said Theresa.

"Amen," I repeated. I felt like a kid with a new toy—prayer.

She wiped the tears away and we both stood up. She looked at me and said, "David, what in the world are we wrapped up in?" Smiling she embraced me tightly, like a mom sending her son off to war. After a half minute she asked for my phone.

She typed in her number and pressed send and then cancel. "Now you have my number. Keep me posted."

"I absolutely will. You're my partner in this." I hugged her again.

She picked up her bag and headed for the door. She turned and smiled at me saying, "Well, *my* life just got more exciting."

She left the room and I climbed into my hospital bed. I could still get about six hours of sleep. I lay for some time in the bed, too wired to sleep, going over in my head all that had happened and all that was about to happen in the morning.

CHAPTER XXIV

I opened my eyes and looked around. It took a moment to remember that I was on the hospital bed next door to my dad's room. The large round clock on the wall said 8:30 AM. I only had a half hour. I jumped up and went to the sink. I washed my face and brushed my teeth with my finger and a travel-size tube of toothpaste that the hospital put in the rooms. I dried off my face and then stared at myself in the mirror. *Okay, here goes nothing!*

No. I stopped myself. I was not taking a chance. God had planned this day out. I had nothing to fear. I needed to be bold and confident—like the angel said, quoting from Jeremiah. "Don't be afraid of their faces. For I am with you to deliver you!"

Showtime.

I exited the room, turned left, and then left again. I entered a room called the "family room" and it was full of people. My mom, my sister, her husband Mark, and Lisa.

"David, where have you been?" My mother said in a voice that expressed both concern and anger. "We've been looking everywhere for you."

"I was here. I feel asleep in the room last night and Theresa the nurse said I could use the room next door. What's going on?"

"They called us early this morning," said my sister Hope. "Daddy had a heart attack in the middle of the night. It was mild enough, but given that he had already suffered a major stroke, it caused a lot of damage."

"David," my mother burst into tears and Lisa grabbed her. "He's brain-dead, David," she said as she sobbed.

I sure hope Theresa is praying, I thought.

"The doctors say there is nothing they can do," my brother-in-law Mark gently shared. "They want to take him off life support."

"No! He's not dead." I looked at the clock. I still had twenty minutes before I was to proclaim his resurrection.

No one responded. They just assumed I was in denial. Lisa came over and took my hand. That was a good sign. She hadn't packed her bags just yet. *We'll see how she reacts in fifteen minutes.*

"I need to talk to you...to all of you," I said as Lisa squeezed my hand. Was it support, or was it, *keep your crazy, loony mouth shut about angels, demons, and the Holocaust?*

"Let's go into the lounge." Everyone exited and after four minutes— bathroom, coffee—we reconvened in the longue.

8:49 AM.

"How do I begin? Dad is alive." Before anyone could protest, I said, "Just give me a few minutes to explain. Please don't interrupt." I refused to make eye contact with Lisa. *How can I be afraid of a face if I didn't look at it?* I reasoned.

"Something happened to me last Sunday morning."

I didn't reveal every detail, but enough to make it clear that I had been visited by an angel, I witnessed Yeshua's death, that the New Testament was written by Jews, that in the first century tens of thousands of Jews believed He was the Messiah—and that I was now one of them. It was now 8:59 AM.

"David, why are you bringing this up know? At a time like this?" my mother said, clearly exasperated.

"You are right—it does seem inappropriate. But it is connected to Dad. And I can prove it. I can prove it all."

"How?" asked Hope.

9:00 AM.

"Because at this time tomorrow, Dad will get up out of bed. He will be completely healed and will confirm everything I have shared. In fact, he was with me."

"He was with you?" asked Mark.

"He, too, was with the angel." I knew I sounded crazy to them. I just had to see it through.

"David, you're not making sense," my mother said franticly. "He is brain-dead. He can't recover. Don't you understand?"

I ignored her and said, "Any minute Rabbi Goodman is going to walk into this lounge." It turned out to be a desperate but lucky guess on the timing of the rabbi, because just then he opened the door. Or maybe someone was truly in control.

Everyone was stunned.

"Well, I called him this morning before we left," shared my mother.

"Did I know that? No. None of you could even find me because I was sound asleep in this hospital!"

"What's this all about?" said Rabbi Goodman.

"David claims that Harvey is going to wake up tomorrow, alive and well," explained my mother.

"But the doctor says he's brain-dead," added Hope.

"David," the rabbi turned to me, "I know these things are hard to accept."

"No, Rabbi, I'm not in denial—in fact I have never been more sure of anything in my life! Come on, don't we believe in miracles?" Faith surged through me, and I looked from one face to the next as I spoke. "Did God not part the Red Sea? Didn't David slay the giant? Did God not rescue the three Hebrew young men from the fiery furnace and Daniel from the lion's den? Did not an angel appear to Abraham and stop him from killing Isaac? Did Elijah call down fire from heaven or not?"

I turned to the rabbi, face to face. "Is the God of Abraham, Isaac, and Jacob alive or is it just a myth you've been peddling for all these years?"

"David!" my mother scolded me. "Don't speak to Rabbi Goodman that way."

"I am sorry, Mom. Rabbi, I am not trying to offend you or be rude, I am just asking, 'Is it real or isn't it?' Why can't God do today what He has done in the past? Forget about my faith in Yeshua for a moment—do you believe in God?"

He looked at me, stunned. That was the first that he had heard that I was now a believer. He looked at me with confusion. I could hear his thoughts, *How could you do this to your family—particularly at this time?*

And then there was my question still hanging in the air, "Do you believe in God?" He didn't know how to answer. Of course he believed in God, but if he agreed then he would have to also agree that miracles can happen. If he claimed he didn't believe in God, well then, he might as well go sell insurance, because his days as a rabbi would be over.

"You don't need to answer that, Rabbi—just give me twenty-four hours. At the very worst, we are in the same position tomorrow and we can take him off life support and bury him and you guys can commit me. And at best, I am not crazy and we will be enjoying the presence of Harvey Lebowitz for many years to come."

My mother gasped. I saw Lisa take her hand and squeeze it tight.

I was not only not intimidated, I was enjoying myself. Not in a prideful way, but there was an awesome energy that came over me as I took my stand in boldness. What did Ariel call it...the *anointing*. I liked that, the anointing!

"It can't hurt," said Hope. She looked up at her husband, Mark, and then back at Mom.

"So we are agreed—twenty-four hours." I didn't give anyone time to object—and who would? There was nothing to lose. Even the insurance company wouldn't pressure us to take him off life support so soon.

I sipped the awful hospital coffee and said, "Listen, I love you all, and I love Dad. Everything will make sense tomorrow. Don't be afraid."

I left them to themselves and headed back to my father's room. I would not be leaving for at least twenty-four hours. I sent a quick text to Theresa, "So far so good. Keep praying!"

CHAPTER XXV

Lisa walked in about a minute later and closed the door. *Here we go.* She was the one person I loved most in the world, and I could not bear for her to think I was crazy. Everyone else—I would survive, but not Lisa. Even just for twenty-four hours, it was killing me that she might think she had lost me or that I had lost it.

"Lisa, please," I said, "let's just wait twenty-four hours, then we can talk."

She ignored my plea and walked over and sat down next to me. She put her hand gently on my leg and looked at me with tears in her eyes. I knew she wouldn't leave me, not yet. Plus she is so close with my family that even if she divorced me, she could never divorce them. But she looked upset; clearly a speech to come to my senses was about to be delivered.

"I want to show you something, David," she said softly. "Last night I stayed with your mom. I woke up around 2 AM wide awake. I went to your father's office to use his computer. But the Internet wasn't working. So I searched for the modem to reboot it. It was in the basement. Afterward, I noticed a box full of smaller boxes in the corner, all marked *Zayde*. I thought about our conversation earlier in that evening and started searching through boxes.

"I found a book. It looked like a diary or memoir. Each entry was dated. It was all written in Yiddish so I couldn't read it, but the dates were in numbers."

Yiddish means *Jewish German*, as in the German of the Jews. It was developed by the Ashkenazi Jews of Germany and used by Jews all over Eastern Europe. In the thirteenth century they began to use the Hebrew alphabet, and by that time their German included many words and phrases from Hebrew. Yiddish became its own distinct language. This was the language of my grandfather and most of the Jews who died in the Holocaust.

"The entries start in 1946 and last for about seven years. He stopped writing in it in 1953.

"Even though I could not read it, I found this inside." And she handed me a photo. It was a family. A mother, a father, and *four* children. Under each person was a name in Yiddish. However, because they used the Hebrew alphabet I could pronounce the names—and so could Lisa.

"Tuvia," I said. "That is my grandfather, Zayde."

"Yes."

And next to him a younger boy with the name חיים written underneath him.

"Chaim," I almost shouted.

"He had a brother. You were right."

We both burst into tears and embraced tightly.

"I love you!" I said as I squeezed her.

"I love you too—and I am sorry I doubted you."

"It is understandable. If the roles were reversed I don't know that I would have believed you.

"Wait, you said this happened at 2 AM?"

"Maybe a little after. But yeah."

"That was right after I prayed with Theresa! She said if we agreed in prayer in Yeshua's name, He would answer us. And you woke up and found the photo at possibly the exact same time!"

"Theresa the nurse?"

"Yes, she's on the team! Last night when I came back from, well, from the angel with my instructions, I ran into her in the hallway. It turns out that God has been preparing her for this moment. Two weeks ago she had a crazy dream."

I related all the information to Lisa, including how Theresa's burden lifted off of her the same morning that I began to believe.

Lisa still didn't know what to make of it all, but she had seen enough to at least stand with me until the next morning. Without the benefit of the angel and so many other guests, her whole life was being turned upside down. All her life, like me, she'd been told *Jesus is for the Gentiles—we have Judaism.* The man Jesus was utterly not Jewish to us and certainly not the Messiah. Any Jew who embraced Him was probably a self-hating Jew, ashamed of his people—and most definitely a traitor. In a span of twelve hours Lisa's world had been shaken to the core. Twelve hours ago I dropped the bomb, and she was quite certain that I was out of my mind; now here we were, less than twenty-four hours before *t-minus zero,* sitting together hand in hand, with my comatose father in front of us. Unlike me, she had no time to digest or consider—just *boom!*

And somehow, what I expected to be a horribly long and tense day between us turned out to be one of the most beautiful days I can remember. My sister took my mother home, and Rabbi Goodman, who only drove on Shabbat because of our family emergency, returned to the synagogue.

The sun was bright and it was unusually warm for early March. I spent the rest of the day sharing with Lisa all that I'd seen and learned. This time, instead of thinking I was crazy, we actually took out the Bible, thanks to the Gideons, to confirm the things that I had learned.

"John the Baptist was Jewish?"

"I know, right? Who knew?"

And it was like that all day. My brain-dead dad lay in front us, but we ignored him and studied the Word of God. I did wonder if Dad could hear us. If so, he was applauding! It was simply wonderful.

Around 8 PM Theresa showed up. When she saw Lisa in the room, she tensed up, remembering what I had told her the night before.

"It's okay, Theresa. We had a breakthrough. Hand me the picture, Lisa." I showed her my granduncle Chaim and explained how Lisa found the photo just after we prayed. Theresa teared up and began to spontaneously worship. Her way of worship was so different from the rote prayers we repeated in the synagogue. I don't know if I had ever been as happy and fulfilled as I was that day. And the next day I would see my father again.

At 9 PM I sent Lisa home to be with the girls. I wasn't leaving my dad's side until tomorrow morning. Theresa stayed with me until about 11 PM. We spent most of that time praying. I was loving my new "toy." Theresa quickly taught me that prayer was pleasure, but it was also a weapon. More important, it was sincere communication, and I could just talk to God from my heart at any time. At midnight I fell asleep in the chair at my father's bedside.

CHAPTER XXVI

I woke up at 6:30 AM. I got some coffee and waited. Six and half hours is normally enough sleep for me, but I was sluggish. Still, I wasn't going back to bed. I needed to get ready, only I had no idea what I needed to do to get ready. I grabbed the Bible that Lisa and I read from the day before. We bookmarked the story of Yeshua raising a young boy from the dead at his funeral.

I read that story, but I wanted more. I decided to Google on my phone "passages, Jesus, healing." *Hmmm, "Googling," a verb. I wonder what Nathan and Simeon would think of Googling.* I smiled thinking about my amazing adventure back to the first and second centuries. The world had changed so much. I wondered if I would ever see Nathan and Simeon again in this life. I longed to tell Nathan who I really was and how God used him to teach me.

Several stories came up. I tapped until I found the story about Yeshua healing the servant of a Roman soldier. He told him that He did not even need to come to his home, but Yeshua just needed speak the word and his servant would be healed—and he was! Next I read about a synagogue leader who came to Yeshua and begged Him to heal his daughter. *A synagogue leader!* More evidence that Jews believed in Yeshua.

Yeshua agreed to go with him, and on the way a woman approached Him. She had been bleeding for twelve years. *Wait, I know this woman. It's Chaya from the movie.* She was the first Jewish believer I met, or at least witnessed, when this journey began one week ago today. Yeshua healed her, and she went from being an unclean outcast to a happily married mother. I remembered her last words. She said that several years after her healing, Simon Peter preached to Gentiles, and to her shock they were immersing Gentiles in water. Ha! That would hardly be controversial today. A Jew being baptized today may stir the waters. What was normal in the first century was taboo today.

I continued to read and was fascinated by His story. And then the Passover—I remembered it. It was in the room that Simeon and his congregation converted into a synagogue. I knew what would come next. At the end of Mark 14, He was arrested. I didn't know if I could read about His crucifixion. Unlike most people, I witnessed it—I was there; I *virtually* carried His cross. I decided to skip to His resurrection—I wasn't ready to relive that. At the end of Mark 16, He shared some powerful words with His disciples.

> *And these signs will accompany those who believe: In my name they will drive out demons; they will speak in new tongues; they will pick up snakes with their hands; and when they drink deadly poison, it will not hurt them at all; they will place their hands on sick people, and they will get well* (Mark 16:17-18).

I can do miracles? I can heal the sick? I am a believer, so I should be able to do these things. Faith was rising up in me. I never dreamed that reading the Bible could be so invigorating. All my life I viewed the Bible as history at best and boring at worst. And I viewed the New Covenant books as strictly forbidden—off-limits!

I looked at the clock; it was already 8:15 AM. I had been reading for an hour and a half. It seemed like ten minutes. Just then, Lisa arrived. With *real* coffee, but I didn't need it. We embraced. I knew she wasn't where I was, faith-wise, but I also knew she was much closer than anyone else in my family.

"Well, this is it," I tried to be reassuring. She took out the picture of my grandfather's family and put it against her heart. That was her one shred of evidence that her husband might not be crazy, and she was holding on to it, rooting for me to be right.

"Yes, I guess so. This is it."

Theresa came in next, dressed in her nursing uniform. "I wasn't supposed to work this morning, but I switched with one of the other girls. Everyone's happy to get a Sunday off, and I wasn't going to miss this. In fact, I am missing my own meeting at my church."

Theresa gave Lisa one of her patented mama hugs and then me.

"I called Pastor Jackson last night, and he'll have the whole congregation praying with us in the early service. I didn't tell him everything. To be honest, even though he is a man of faith, I wasn't sure if he would completely believe me," she chuckled.

By 8:30 AM my mother and sister arrived, along with Hope's husband Mark. It was extremely uncomfortable. After knowing these people nearly my whole life, I felt like a stranger—a circus act. That would all change in a half hour—hopefully.

At a quarter to nine, Rabbi Goodman arrived. More awkwardness. In their minds the straightjacket was already being fitted for me. They're thinking that by 9:05 I should be comfortably getting used to my rubber room.

Nervous small talk...

8:55 AM.

It was t-minus five minutes, and the tension was palpable. Suddenly doubt started to creep in. *What if I'm wrong? What if is he doesn't get up?* I began to panic inwardly.

One minute to go!

I tried to think about all the passages I had read, but nothing—no faith, just fear.

9 AM.

I looked at my father. He was lifeless, like a vegetable. As I looked him, faith seeped out of me. Maybe even some of them expected something to happen, so strong was my insistence that he would rise at 9 AM—now they would feel betrayed, given false hope only to be let down. I was faltering. As the clock hit 9:01, Harvey was still just lying in his bed, brain-dead and shriveled up.

9:02.

Still nothing.

Hope started crying, realizing that her father was gone. Mark took her out of the room. My mother gazed at me in anger. Rabbi Goodman was expressionless. Sure, he could have called me out, but he was of man of wisdom and grace. Now was not the time. Lisa looked at me sad at the fact that I had been wrong, and sadder yet that her de facto father was gone.

Theresa looked puzzled, but determined. Like someone who just fixed a car according to the manual, but it still wasn't starting. She didn't say a word—of course this was not her family—but she was communicating to me, *This ain't over!*

9:05 AM.

Still nothing. The man had tubes going in and out of him, holding on to life by a machine. I was experiencing a mixture of embarrassment and anger. I wasn't angry at the angel, I was angry at the thought that I must have done something wrong, and yet I was out of options.

A 9:10 AM I said, "Could everyone please leave the room. I need a few minutes by myself." They assumed that I had realized my absurdity and needed some time to say good-bye to my father.

Without a word everyone left.

"Theresa, can you stay?" Everyone, save Lisa, was puzzled why I would ask the black nurse, old enough to be my mother, to stay. But it wasn't time for confrontations.

The door closed.

"I don't understand! I did what he asked me."

"I don't understand either, but I know beyond a shadow of a doubt that God has led me to you and I believe your story. Let's pray."

Theresa started praying fervently. In fact, she wasn't even speaking English anymore. It sounded like she was just making up words, but she seemed to be fluent in this made-up language. *Just go with it. Is this any stranger than anything else you have experienced in the last week?* I thought.

We held hands and kept praying. About twenty minutes later she looked up at me and said, "This ain't over! I don't understand, but we are not done." I wish I could say that I felt the same faith, but I was out of gas. My toy was not so shiny anymore. It was time to admit defeat.

At 9:45 Rabbi Goodman gently opened the door. "David, we need to chat."

I looked at Theresa as if to say, *It's okay.*

"I'll be prayin' in the next room."

"You can leave the door open," said the rabbi, possibly fearing for his life as he was about to reason with a crazy man.

"David, your family wants to make a decision," he sat down next to me. "I don't think it is fair to keep them waiting. You can only imagine how they are now, after this buildup."

I felt horrible.

"I don't blame you—oftentimes we do and hear the strangest things when our loved ones' lives are on the line. I once had a congregant lock herself in a room for two days unwilling to admit that her husband had been killed in a car accident. She wasn't crazy—just overwhelmed with grief and stress."

I wanted to explain to him that this was not the case here. I had no doubts about my journeys and what I had discovered. My encounter with Yeshua as blood dripped down His brow, mixed with sweat and dirt, was seared into my memory. It was real. But trying to convince him would be fruitless—especially after this embarrassment. Instead I did something else that had to be done.

"Rabbi," I looked up at him, "I forgive you."

"Ah, you forgive me—for what?"

"Not long ago—of course you remember—I came to you and opened up about my search. When I mentioned that I was intrigued by Yeshua— by Jesus—you attacked me. You used guilt and manipulation to make me feel ashamed. 'How could I, a Jew, even consider Jesus, after all they have done to us?' Despite all the history of what so-called Christians have done to Jews, it doesn't reflect on the man Jesus—who lived hundreds of years before their actions."

He was silent.

"There is no command in the New Testament that instructs Christians to kill or ever hate Jews. In fact, the New Testament actually teaches the Gentile believers in Yeshua to love Israel—the Jewish people. His entire ministry was in Israel *to Jews;* how could He instruct Gentiles to hurt the Jewish people? He didn't even teach Gentiles!

"The things that have been done against Jews in the name of Jesus are reprehensible—forced baptisms, expulsion, pogroms—but these were perpetrated by misguided zealots, imposters with a *political* agenda, not *religious.*

"I understand what my grandfather suffered—in fact, I understand far better than you can ever imagine." I didn't elaborate about meeting my sixteen-year-old grandfather. "But these people were not Christians.

"Rabbi, if I told you I was black, what would you say?"

"Excuse me, David?"

"Honestly, what would you say? How would you respond?"

"I would say that you are mistaken."

"Based on what?"

"Eh...you're not black, you're white."

"Exactly; now what if that nurse, Theresa, comes in and says she is actually a brain surgeon? Would you believe her? Despite the fact that she has a nurse's uniform, and you have witnessed her doing the work of a nurse—not a surgeon—would you believe she's a doctor?"

"I suppose not."

"Exactly; so if someone says he is a Christian and expresses his *faith* by killing Jews—the physical, blood brothers of Yeshua, a Jew Himself, people He loved and wept over—then that person is a liar—a fraud. Just because someone calls themselves a Christian doesn't mean it is so. As Yeshua hung on the tree crucified, He didn't demand revenge, He didn't call out for a holy war against the Jews—no, He said, *'Father, forgive them, for they do not know what they are doing'"* (Luke 23:34).

My phone made the sound of getting a text. I ignored it. I was actually, in the midst of this crazy day, once again finally feeling the presence of God as I shared with the rabbi.

"David, I don't think this is the time for a theological discussion. We can do that later."

"You're right." My phone alerted me again, but I really didn't care who was texting me; I needed to finished with the rabbi. "But you attacked me for simply searching for truth. You accused me of being a traitor to my family and my people. Should we not be able to search for ourselves? Can we only rely on the interpretations of rabbis and sages from the past? We are a rebellious people—we are outspoken. We are not easily intimidated. 'Ten Jews, eleven opinions?'

"Was it not Prime Minister Golda Meir who told Nixon, 'You are the president of one hundred fifty million Americans; I am the prime minister of six million prime ministers.' We are lawyers and doctors and politicians and businesspeople; we created Facebook, Google, instant messaging, and Waze, but when it comes to the subject of Jesus, we are told we are idiots, incapable of thinking for ourselves.

"Who was it who excommunicated Eliezer Ben-Yehuda when he wanted to see Hebrew restored as the language of the future Jewish nation? It was the orthodox rabbis. Yet Hebrew is the language of Israel today. And when Theodore Herzl wanted to see Israel restored as a nation, who resisted him? It wasn't the socialists or the atheists, but the rabbis of Europe. They railed against Herzl until he had to move the First Zionist Congress from Munich to Basil. They claimed that the idea of a Jewish state contradicted the Messianic promises. Yet, in 1948 Israel was established.

"I am not trying to belittle them...or you for that matter. I am merely suggesting that if our sages missed it on the two most critical issues in modern Judaism, could it be that they missed it all on an ancient one as well—namely Yeshua?"

I was on a roll, but I didn't want to push too hard. Still, there was the issue of my father. That had to be my focus. *What went wrong? Is it too late?*

"Okay, I'm getting off my soapbox. I wanted you to know that you hurt me very deeply when you attacked me, but more importantly I also wanted you to know that I forgive you completely and I understand why you did it. Your intentions were good—you were seeking to protect me. Thank you. But I cannot accept the dogma that says I can't think for myself. Particularly when this reasoning is based *not* on what is written in the Tanakh or New Testament, but rather on what some toothless, illiterate Crusader did a thousand years ago against the innocent Jews. I refuse to give him that kind of power over me."

Rabbi Goodman's phone chimed. Seeking to get out of this conversation he checked his phone. It was now 9:57.

"David, do you know someone named Ariel?"

"What?"

"He just sent me a text asking you to check your phone."

It was Ariel who was texting me! I grabbed my phone to check the text.

> "Good morning, David. Just to be clear DST doesn't start in
> Israel for three more weeks. Did I say at the same time tomor-
> row? Or did I say 24 hours?"

The clocks! It didn't even register with me. This week had been so crazy that I hadn't even noticed.

"Rabbi, did they move up the clocks last night?"

"Spring forward, fall backward."

"So Daylight Savings Time began sometime last night." I said out loud. "No wonder I was so tired this morning—I lost an hour of sleep. There's an extra hour! Rabbi, we are not done yet!"

He had an "Oh *great!*" look on his face.

I looked up at the clock.

9:59 AM.

Suddenly, a warm, yellow light began to fill the room. The presence of angels was obvious, and I wasn't the only one who could see it. Rabbi Goodman began to freak out. He nearly hit the ground as he backed up out of his chair. He reached behind for the door, but it slammed shut. He turned around to open it, but it was *angelically* locked!

"Yes, yes, yes," I shouted. "Hallelujah—it's happening!" The room was filled with heavenly noise; the singing of angels was like a mighty waterfall. I looked at him and shouted, "It just got real, rabbi!" He looked positively terrified.

10:00 AM.

This is it, I thought. I looked at my father and expected him to jump up. But he didn't. He just lay there the same. It was now 10:02 AM and the angels were still there. The room was still filled with their singing, but my dad was still brain-dead! *What do I do?*

As I looked his body, I could feel the faith seeping out of me. I was so sure a second ago. But seeing him shriveled up like that...

Don't be afraid of their faces...

Yes, from Jeremiah. I needed to not focus on the state of my father's body, but on the power of God to heal him. Faith was rising again.

And then that verse I had read that morning came back to me:

> *And these signs will accompany those who believe: In my name they will drive out demons; they will speak in new tongues; they will pick up snakes with their hands; and when they drink deadly poison, it will not hurt them at all; they will place their hands on sick people, and they will get well* (Mark 16:17-18).

Suddenly, I shouted in a language I didn't know—just like Theresa earlier. It poured out of me like a rushing river of life—like mighty thunder I shouted. After about two minutes of praying, groaning, and shouting—and completely freaking out the kidnapped rabbi—I slammed my hands down on my father's chest and cried out in Hebrew—though I don't know Hebrew—"*Bshem Yeshua Hamashiach m'netsaret, ani m'tsaveh otchah lakum v'lichiot v'lihira'pe!*"

Then in English, "In the name of Yeshua the Messiah from Nazareth, I command you to rise up and live and be healed."

As the words came out of my mouth, a shaft of pure white light, made up of strands like wires, from every color on earth, burst through the ceiling like a laser beam into my father's heart. It sent me flying backward, falling into the chair where I had slept. Rabbi Goodman was still clinging to the doorknob, resigned to the fact that he was not going anywhere. In fact, I think by now he would have chosen to stay!

The laser moved from his heart to his head.

Suddenly, all the tubes and wires began to pop out of their machines and from my father as well. The machines were completely fried. I heard people banging on the door, as presumably my family was trying to get in. *They probably think I've gone crazy and kidnapped the rabbi. It will all be clear soon.*

And then *boom*, my father shot up out of his bed like a rocket as life filled up his body! And then he came crashing down on the mattress. Like a blow-up toy, his shriveled body received life, and the strong, energetic Harvey Lebowitz who raised me was back. He was breathing heavily, and the rabbi was in complete shock. They didn't teach him this in rabbinical school, or pastors and priests in most seminaries for that matter.

The singing subsided and the normal color returned to the room. "You're back!" I proclaimed.

"Right on time, from what I have been told," said my father. "*That* was intense." He got out of bed completely healed. We embraced hard.

I held his shoulders and looked him in the eyes. "We've got work to do, Harvey," I said, calling him by his first name as I did from time to time as a term of endearment.

"Yes we do, son, yes we do." One more hug and—

"Harv...?" said the rabbi in stunned disbelief as the door swung open, pushing the rabbi forward. First my mother ran to him and threw her arms around him. Then my sister. All the women were weeping with joy. Though I had little to do with it, I felt a little bit like a hero.

Lastly he embraced Lisa who whispered to him, "I know your little secret." She looked into his eyes through her tears. "Guess your son's not so crazy after all."

In the corner was a plump, middle-aged nurse, tears quietly flowing down her face. "Dad, there is someone you need to meet."

"Theresa, I presume?"

Everyone was a little shocked. He'd been in a coma since she entered into his life.

"Are you kidding? Your songs of praise in this room were ever with me—from the time I was shipped in here from the ambulance and even during my little journey, I could hear your prayers and songs of worship. Always in the distance, but always there."

He gave her a big embrace. And then he looked down at his scanty hospital gown and said, "Somebody get me some clothes! And how 'bout some food?"

Dad was ready to leave, but the doctors came in and demanded that he let them check him out. Dad just wanted to leave, but I said, "Hey, let them check you. That way we'll have documented medical proof of what just happened here."

Mom handed him his morning coffee. "You've got five minutes, Doc, and then I'm out of here."

They were dumbfounded. Just over twenty-four hours ago they were declaring him brain-dead and encouraging my family to pull the plug. Now we were laughing and joking with the brain-*alive* Harvey.

"Mr. Lebowitz, we can't just let you leave," said the cardiologist. "You've just suffered a heart attack, not to mention a stroke."

"And to be clear, you can and will let me out of here or the next time you see me will be in a court of law, where I will sue you, your hospital, and your staff for unlawful imprisonment. And believe me, my case and my lawyer will be good," referencing his Jeopardy commercials—not that they didn't know who he was. In truth he would not have sued and probably wouldn't have had a case, but that is one of the great things about being a lawyer—you can throw around a bunch of legal jargon to get your way.

After an x-ray and a few tubes of blood, Harvey was marching his clan out of St. Luke's. Theresa had to stay at work, but she promised to come by as soon as her shift ended. Mark pulled up his Range Rover and we all piled in. I was the last, but before I did, a hand grabbed my arm. It was Rabbi Goodman. He still was somewhat in shock. The others knew Harvey was healed. They knew it was supernatural and dramatic. But Rabbi Goodman saw everything—he experienced everything.

"David, I am sorry."

"For what?"

"For everything. For jumping on you like I did. For not believing you last night or this morning. And for judging you. I don't know what to make of everything I saw today, but I was there—I can't deny what I witnessed. I don't understand it, but it happened. No matter where I end up on this, I am so happy for your father. You're a good man, David."

"Those words mean a lot to me, Rabbi. Thank you." To have my rabbi's affirmation regarding everything that happened lifted my spirit. We gave each other a warm, manly embrace, including a couple pats on the back.

"You are welcome to join us, Rabbi," I said, pointing to my seat in the car.

"Come on, Aaron, join us," my father yelled out through the passenger seat window, calling him by his first name. Dad had wanted to drive, but we vetoed that. He wasn't going to sue *us!*

He walked to the window and bent down. "You know what, Harvey? You guys go and enjoy your reunion. To be honest, I've got a lot to think about. My future and my faith—my career! I think you understand."

"More than you know, Aaron," replied my father. "We all have to rethink a few things."

Within twenty-five minutes we were seated in Herschel's East Side Deli. Dad was dying—bad choice of words—*longing* for a Reuben. We sat down and ordered. *Oh how my life has changed from one Sunday to the next,* I thought.

The waitress brought dad a massive Rueben dripping sauerkraut and dressings.

"Harvey, maybe you should take it easy. You just had a heart attack for goodness' sakes," chided my mother.

Dad looked to Mom and smiled. "Barbara, you've been nagging me for forty years, and I love your nagging. You nag because you love. And you can nag tomorrow all you want, and I will love you for it then as well. But not today. Today I eat what I want! And I want a big, fat Rueben!"

With that he took a bite and chewed. Suddenly he got very serious, stopped chewing and grasped his chest. My heart skipped a beat. Mom's eyes widened. Harvey smiled. "What? Too soon for heart attack jokes?"

I looked at Lisa who was watching me, eyes twinkling as she smiled.

I winked at her. "Harvey's back. And wait 'til you hear what we'll all be doing the next few years."

ENDNOTES

Chapter III

1. Yiddish for grandfather.
2. *Tsurus* is Yiddish for trouble.

Chapter V

1. See Second Peter 3:8.
2. Lubavitch is one of the largest Chasidic sects in Judaism.
3. Another name for Lubavitch.
4. "With the help of God."
5. You can read Josh McDowell's article, "Liar, Lord or Lunatic," at http://www.josh.org/liar-lunatic-or-lord-2.

Chapter VII

1. Virtually every Scripture used in the New Covenant to prove that Jewish believers are no longer required to keep kosher has been taken out of context. Mark 7 and Matthew 15 have nothing to do with kosher laws, but traditions of washing one's hands ritually before eating. We have just addressed Acts 10. Paul's allowing the eating of meat sacrificed to idols also has nothing to do with kosher laws, but the fact that there is no power in idols. However, to be clear, while I see keeping kosher as part of our calling as Jewish believers and pleasing to God, it is not a prerequisite of our salvation. No one will be in hell because they ate shrimp, and no one will get into heaven because they didn't.

Chapter IX

1. No one knows exactly how the congregation in Rome was birthed. Romans Catholics teach that Peter, whom they believe was the Bishop of Rome (the first Pope), planted it. We cover this extensively in the first book—why Peter could not have been the Bishop of Rome. The most

logical conclusion is that Paul sent disciples to Rome. If not, Paul would not have felt an apostolic obligation to write to them. It is clear that Paul writes as someone with authority regarding doctrine and deep love for them. Another valid theory is that Roman Messianic Jews who had received Yeshua during the first Shavuot outpouring returned to Rome to birth the Roman Messianic Community. However, if this were true then Jacob (James), not Paul, would have felt the apostolic responsibility for them.

2. There are different views regarding the exact date, but we know that the early church historian Orosius gives the 49 CE date.

3. David Pawson's *A Commentary on Romans* helped me greatly here and I highly recommend it.

Chapter X

1. Acts 13:14–16, for example.

2. Jason J. Barker, "Be Transformed: An Interactive Study of the Epistle to the Romans," Antiochian Orthodox Christian Archdiocese of North America, 2005, http://www.orthodoxyouth.org/romans/html/introreasons.htm.

3. Suetonius explains the expulsion came about because of the "disturbances and riots among the Jews at the instigation of Chrestus." Most church historians today agree that this refers to Christ. Christians were also frequently referred to as "Chrestianoi." Apparently, there was an internal dispute among the Jewish residents of Rome over the Messianic claims of Jesus, as had happened in Jerusalem (Acts 8:1), Antioch (Acts 15:50), Iconium (Act 14:1–7), Thessalonica and Berea (Acts 17), and elsewhere. But Claudius had little tolerance for their debate and expelled all the Jews. Dr. Buehler, "Why Paul Wrote Romans," International Christian Embassy Jerusalem, May 2010, http://int.icej.org/news/commentary/why-paul-wrote-romans.

4. *Tanakh* is an acronym in Hebrew taking the first letter of *Torah, Prophets, and Writing*. In Hebrew that would be T, N, and Kh, for Torah, Nivi'im and K'tuvim.

Chapter XII

1. "Modern Israeli Inventions," Free Republic, accessed December 18, 2015, http://www.freerepublic.com/focus/fnews/1600302/posts.

2. Thomas S. McCall, "What Is the Olive Tree?" Zola Levitt Ministries, March 2001, http://www.levitt.com/essays/olivetree.

3. Some maintain that *continuing in His kindness* refers to continuing the faith, not continuing in kindness to Israel. First, it is important to know that the word *His* is not there. It should be "continuing in kindness," and in context Paul is warning them against haughtiness toward the Jewish unbeliever. For more on this, see my blog post: http://roncan.net/continuekindness.

Chapter XIII

1. "Catechism of the Catholic Church," Vatican, The Final Purification, or Purgatory, accessed December 19, 2015, http://www.vatican.va/archive/ccc_css/archive/catechism/p123a12.htm.

2. *Tefillin* are a set of small black leather boxes containing scrolls of parchment inscribed with verses from the Torah, which are worn by observant Jews during weekday morning prayers. It is taken from the admonition in Deuteronomy 6:8: *"Tie them as symbols on your hands and bind them on your foreheads."*

3. Bava Metzia, 59. This video fully explains the issue: http://realmessiah.com/index.php/en/talmud and choose the one on Bava Metzia 59.

Chapter XIV

1. *"In my vision at night I looked, and there before me was one like a son of man, coming with the clouds of heaven. He approached the Ancient of Days and was led into his presence. He was given authority, glory and sovereign power; all nations and peoples of every language worshiped him. His dominion is an everlasting dominion that will not pass away, and his kingdom is one that will never be destroyed"* (Dan. 7:13-14). *"Then the Lord will go out and fight against those nations, as he fights on a day of battle. On that day his feet will stand on the Mount of Olives, east of Jerusalem"* (Zech. 14:3-4).

2. Reshit Hakatzir, or Firstfruits, comes on the first Sunday after the first Shabbat after Passover. This was the day Yeshua rose from the dead. For more, see my blog on this: http://roncan.net/firstfruits1.

Chapter XV

1. The last two paragraphs are actually a quote from William Krewson, "The Roots of Replacement Theology," Messianic Association, Misinterpreting Scripture, accessed December 22, 2015, http://www .messianicassociation.org/ezine10-replacement.htm.

2. From a lecture from Dr. Gary Burge of Wheaton College given at the Christ at the Check Point conference in Bethlehem.

3. Steven L. Anderson, "Israel Moments 1-10 Christians Are Citizens of Israel," Faithful Word Baptist Church, August 2014, Israel Moment #1, http://www.faithfulwordbaptist.org/israel_moments_1_10.html.

4. Justin Martyr, "Dialogue with Trypho," Early Christian Writings, Chapter XI, Chapter CXXXV, accessed December 22, 2015, http://www .earlychristianwritings.com/text/justinmartyr-dialoguetrypho.html.

5. Paul F. Pavao, "Death of James, Jesus' Brother," Christian History for Everyman, James the Just Arouses the Wrath of the Rulers, accessed December 22, 2015, http://www.christian-history.org/death-of-james .html.

6. Ibid.

7. *Hosanna* is actually two words—*hoshia na*—and means *save please.* However, by the time of Yeshua this biblical phrase had become a "cry of hope and exultation," according to John Piper. This makes sense, as we would not say "Please save to the son of David." That makes no sense. However, *Salvation to the Son of David* is clear. For more on this go to: www.desiringgod.org/sermons/hosanna.

8. Pavao, "Death of James," The Death of James the Just.

9. From Jerome, quoting Hegesippus, a Jewish believer and historian. Also from the *The Panarion of Epiphanius of Salamis.*

10. According to Josephus, there were about 6,000 Pharisees in Jerusalem in the days prior to the Temple's demise. And in 49 CE we know from Acts 21:20 there were tens of thousands of Jewish believers.

11. Acts 15:5 shows that one of the delegations at the Jerusalem Council were Pharisees who were believers in Yeshua.

12. Ray Pritz is a respected scholar in Israel and has written one of the finest scholarly works on the first Jewish Community, *Nazarene Jewish Christianity*. He relies on Eusebius, Josephus, Justin Martyr, and a second century historian, Hegesippus, who was most likely a Jewish believer, amongst others. He wrote an article on the subject here: http://caspari .com/new/images/stories/archives/Mishkan/mishkan13.pdf.

Chapter XVI

1. *Kehila* means "community" in Hebrew. It comes from the Greek word *ecclesia*. The word *church* is the word that is most commonly used from *ecclesia*, but it is a wrong translation. *Church* comes from a Greek word that refers to a building where people meet. *Ecclesia* refers to the people who meet. You can even see the same root of KHL in both *ecclesia* and *kehila*.

2. From the Historian Eusebius: "For when the city was about to be captured and sacked by the Romans, all the disciples were warned beforehand by an angel to remove from the city, doomed as it was to utter destruction. On migrating from it they settled at Pella, the town already indicated, across the Jordan. It is said to belong to Decapolis" (Epiphanius, *De Mensuris et Ponderibus*, 15).

3. We will explore this word more later. The first mention of the fact that the Jewish believers were called Nazarenes is in Acts 24:5 where the lawyer Tertullus calls Paul "a ringleader of the Nazarene sect."

4. "Some information comes from a tenth-century Patriarch of Alexandria named Euthychius (896-940 A.D.), who wrote a history of the church based on all the ancient sources that were available to him. According to Euthychius, the Judéo-Christians who fled to Pella to escape the Roman destruction of Jerusalem in 70 A.D., 'returned to Jerusalem in the fourth year of the emperor Vespasian, and built there their church.'" Bargil Pixner, "Church of the Apostles on Mt. Zion," *Mishkan*, no. 13 (1990).

5. Joseph Telushkin, *Jewish Literacy* (New York: William Morrow, 1991), https://www.jewishvirtuallibrary.org/jsource/Judaism/revolt.html.

6. Ibid.

7. Josephus, *The Wars of the Jews*, Book 2, Chapter 14, Section 5, http://sacred-texts.com/jud/josephus/war-2.htm.

Chapter XVII

1. Josephus, *The Wars of the Jews*.
2. Josephus, qtd. in "The Romans Destroy the Temple at Jerusalem, 70 AD," EyeWitness to History, 2005, http://www.eyewitnesstohistory.com/jewishtemple.htm.
3. Chris Katulka, "Who Helped Finance the Roman Colosseum?" The Friends of Israel, February 18, 2013, http://www.foi.org/blog/who-helped-finance-roman-colosseum.
4. "Arch of Titus," Wikipedia, Description, accessed December 23, 2015, http://en.wikipedia.org/wiki/Arch_of_Titus.
5. Biblical Archaeology Society Staff, "Jewish Captives in the Imperial City," Bible History Daily, May 11, 2015, http://www.biblicalarchaeology.org/daily/biblical-sites-places/temple-at-jerusalem/jewish-captives-in-the-imperial-city/.
6 Katulka, "Who Helped Finance the Roman Colosseum?"

Chapter XVIII

1. Mitch Glaser and Zhava Glaser, *The Fall Feasts of Israel* (Chicago: Moody Press, 1987).
2. This is not merely a myth, but confirmed by Jewish history and recorded in the Talmud. Although they do not tie it to Yeshua's death, we know that He died in 30 CE; the year that, according to the Talmud, God stopped receiving the Yom Kippur sacrifices. A record of these events can be found in the book of Yoma 39a, b.

Chapter XIX

1. In Israel, Masada is a symbol of heroism. But we fail to remember that those on Masada had become enemies of their own people. Furthermore, Josephus identifies them as Sicarii, either a separate group from the Zealots or a splinter group. Some scholars claim they were driven out of

Jerusalem by their Jewish brethren because of their ruthless ways. Once at Masada they committed murderous acts against other Jews in nearby En Gedi. For a scholarly examination of Masada, I recommend this article: http://www.bibleinterp.com/articles/masada.shtml.

2. Josephus, *The Wars of the Jews*, Book VII, Chapter 8, Section 6, http://sacred-texts.com/jud/josephus/war-7.htm.

3. Josephus, *The Wars of the Jews*, Book VII, Chapter 9, Section 1, http://sacred-texts.com/jud/josephus/war-7.htm.

4. Ibid., Section 2.

Chapter XX

1. A *minyan* is a quorum of 10 Jewish men that is required for a prayer service.

2. The Gale Group, "Encyclopedia Judaica: Birkat Ha-Minim," Jewish Virtual Library, accessed December 24, 2015, https://www.jewishvirtuallibrary.org/jsource/judaica/ejud_0002_0003_0_02999.html.

3. Ibid.

4. "Ante-Nicene Fathers, Vol I: Justin Martyr," St-Takla.org, accessed December 24, 2015, http://st-takla.org/books/en/ecf/001/0010557.html.

5. Refer to the first book in this series, *Identity Theft,* to see why we believe that the "first day of the week," when the believers met, was Saturday night, not Sunday morning.

6. This is taken from an article I wrote and published on my website, Messiah's Mandate: Ron Cantor, "The Most Powerful Site in Jerusalem that Almost No One Sees," April 11, 2015, http://messiahsmandate.org/the-most-powerful-site-in-jerusalem-that-almost-no-one-sees.

7. *Early Christian History, Ecclesiastical History of Eusebius Pamphilus* (c. 265–339) Bishop of Cesarea, in Palestine, written in A.D. 325, Book III, 5:4.

8. Cantor, "The Most Powerful Site in Jerusalem."

9. Ibid.

10. Bargil Pixner, "Church of the Apostles Found on Mt. Zion," CenturyOne Foundation, May 1990, A Mortar Shell and a Dig, http://www.centuryone.org/apostles.html.

11. Keith W. Stump, "Where Was Golgotha?" Grace Communion International, Golgotha Outside City Walls, accessed December 24, 2015, https://www.gci.org/Jesus/golgotha.

12. Pixner, "Church of the Apostles," A Peculiar Orientation and Revealing Graffiti.

13. Bellarmino Bagatti, *The Church from the Circumcision* (Jerusalem: Franciscan Printing Press, 1971), 121.

14. Cantor, "The Most Powerful Site in Jerusalem."

15. You will need to read *Identity Theft* to understand this. Or check out this blog I wrote http://roncan.net/caesarworship or this video I made http://roncan.net/lordsday.

16. The Coverdale Bible (1535) used *congregation*; the Matthew Bible (1537) used *congregation*; The Great Bible (1539) used *congregation*; the Geneva Bible (1560) used *church*; the Bishop's Bible (1568) used *congregation*.

17. Everett Ferguson, "Why and When Did Christians Start Constructing Special Buildings for Worship?" ChristianHistory.net, December 11, 2008, http://www.christianitytoday.com/ch/asktheexpert/ask_churchbuildings.html.

18. Tacitus, *The Annals*, 109 CE.

19. C.N. Trueman, "Rome and Christianity," History Learning Site, March 16, 2015, http://www.historylearningsite.co.uk/rome_and_christianity.htm.

20. "Religious Tolerance and Persecution in the Roman Empire," Constitutional Rights Foundation, 1997, Rome's Treatment of the Jews, http://www.crf-usa.org/bill-of-rights-in-action/bria-13-4-b-religious-tolerance-and-persecution-in-the-roman-empire.

21. Ibid., Initial Attitude Toward Christianity.

22. *Pentecost* is the Greek way of saying the Hebrew *Shavuot*. Many Christians are unaware that Pentecost is not a Christian, but a Jewish holiday—one of God's appointed times from Leviticus.

23. "Religious Tolerance and Persecution in the Roman Empire," Initial Attitude Toward Christianity.

24. Ibid., Nero's Persecution.

25. Ibid., Christian Bloodbath.

26. Charles George Herbermann, *The Catholic Encyclopedia*, vol. 4 (New York: Robert Appleton, 1907), 300.

27. Isaac Boyle and Eusebius, *Historical View of the Council of Nice: With a Translation of Documents* (Boston: James B).

Chapter XXI

1. Walter A. Elwell, "The Old Testament in the New Testament," Bible Study Tools, accessed January 19, 2016, http://www.biblestudytools.com/dictionaries/bakers-evangelical-dictionary/the-old-testament-in-the-new-testament.html.

2. Epiphanius, *The Panarion of Epiphanius of Salamis*, 29 "Against Nazoraeans," 1.3.

Chapter XXII

1. Berel Wein and Yaakov Astor, "Rabbi Akiva," Jewish History, 2011, http://www.jewishhistory.org/rabbi-akiva-2.

2. The precursor to modern-day Orthodox Judaism.

3. From the historian Eusebius.

4. Ray Pritz, *Nazarene Jewish Christianity* (Jerusalem: Magnes Press, Hebrew University, 1988), Kindle locations 4691–4695.

5. Daniel C. Juster, *Jewishness and Jesus* (Downers Grove, IL: Inter Varsity Press, 1977), 21. Bagatti, the Roman Catholic author who wrote *The Church from the Circumcision*, documented Muslim towns with forgotten symbols that were Jewish Christian in his view, and he surmised that some elements of Jewish Christianity continued to exist until Mohammed.

6. Pritz, *Nazarene Jewish Christianity* (Kindle Locations 1365–1370, 1349–1359).

7. Ibid., Kindle Locations 4701–4703.

8. Ibid., (Kindle Locations 4710-4711).

Chapter XXIII

1. Winston Churchill and F. Rhodes, *The River War: An Historical Account of the Reconquest of the Soudan* (London: Green and Longmans, 1899).

2. These are series of quotes taken from Chrysostom's *Eight Sermons Against the Jews*. For full text, see Chrysostom, *Against the Jews,* accessed December 27, 2015, http://www.tertullian.org/fathers/index.htm #Chrysostom_Against_the_Jews.

3. David R. Reagan, "Anti-Semitism," Lamb Lion Ministries, The Origin of Replacement Theology, accessed December 27, 2015, http://christinprophecy.org/articles/anti-semitism.

4. Isaiah 62:6-7.

5. Matthew 23:37–39; Luke 13:34-35.

6. A *siddur* is the Jewish prayer book containing the set order of daily prayers and for Erev Shabbat, Shabbat services, and other minor holidays. The word *siddur* comes from a Hebrew root meaning *order.*

ABOUT RON CANTOR

Messianic Jewish communicator Ron Cantor embraced Yeshua as an eighteen-year-old, drug-using agnostic. Today he serves as the Congregational leader of Tiferet Yeshua, a Hebrew-speaking, Spirit-filled fellowship in Tel Aviv.

Ron served as a Messianic rabbi at Beth Messiah Congregation in Rockville, Maryland before heading overseas to Ukraine and Hungary where he and his wife Elana trained nationals for Jewish ministry. Ron then served on the faculty of the Brownsville Revival school of Ministry teaching and mentoring young leaders.

Ron travels throughout the U.S. and abroad sharing passionately on the Jewish roots of the New Testament and God's broken heart for His ancient people Israel. Ron has been privileged to bring the Jewish-roots message to Brazil, Ukraine, Switzerland, France, Russia, Hungary, Israel, Germany, Cyprus, Italy, Canada, Argentina, Uganda, and Nigeria.

In June 2003, Ron and Elana returned with their three children to the Land of Israel where they now live and minister. During this time, Ron has served as the associate leader of King of Kings Community in Jerusalem, as well as the interim senior leader. Ron heads the Isaiah 2 Initiative, an Israeli-based vision to see the Good News go forth from Zion to other nations. In their trips to Nigeria and Ukraine they have seen tens of thousands of people profess faith in Yeshua.

You can find Ron's teaching videos on his YouTube channel: http://roncan.net/ron-youtube.

Ron is married to Elana, a native-born Israeli. They have three daughters, Sharon, Yael, and Danielle.

Below are the links to social network sites related to *Identity Theft*:

- *Identity Theft* on Twitter: #IDTheftbook or #JerusalemSecret.

- Follow Ron Cantor on Twitter: www.twitter.com/ RonSCantor.

- Ron's blog, website and ministry in Israel: www.MessiahsMandate.org.

- Leave a review of the Jerusalem Secret for others on Amazon.com: http://roncan.net/js-amazon.

Inviting Ron to Speak

If you would like Ron Cantor to come and speak to your conference or congregation, please send an email to roncan@me.com. Ron makes several trips to the U.S. each year from Israel and would love to minister at your conference, congregation, or event.

Free Book!

When you subscribe to our email list, I will send you my eBook free: *The 15 Most Important Facts about the Israeli/Palestinian Conflict.* Just go to: www.roncan.net/15Facts (make sure the F is capitalized).

I would also like to send you my monthly newsletter free of charge so you can:

- Stay informed concerning what is happening in Israel.

- Know how to pray for Israel.

- Continue to grow in your understanding of the Jewish roots for the faith.

Just send you address to roncan@me.com asking to subscribe.